Contents

Prelude 1		**003**
①	Nevertheless, **Hachiman Hikigaya**'s life goes on.	007
Prelude 2		**033**
②	Eventually, he'll **become used to this relationship**, too.	037
Prelude 3		**055**
③	Surely, he will **remember that season** every time he smells that scent.	059
Prelude 4		**105**
④	And then **Yukino Yukinoshita** quietly waves.	111
Interlude		167
⑤	Gallantly, **Shizuka Hiratsuka** walks ahead.	169
⑥	Just like that time before, **Yui Yuigahama** implores.	203
Interlude		225
Interlude		227
⑦	The **heat touching him** is the only feeling that does clearly get across.	237
⑧	**That door** is opened once more.	265
Interlude		311
⑨	Even if it's faded by the passing months, that green **remains green**.	319
⑩	That's why **Hachiman Hikigaya** said…	337
Translation Notes		353

MY YOUTH R♥MANTIC C☻MEDY iS WRØNG, AS I EXPECTED

Wataru Watari
Illustration Ponkan⑧

VOLUME
14

NEW YORK

MY YOUTH ROMANTIC COMEDY IS WRONG, AS I EXPECTED Vol. 14
WATARU WATARI
Illustration by Ponkan⑧

Translation by Jennifer Ward
Cover art by Ponkan⑧

This book is a work of fiction. Names, characters, places, and incidents are the product of the author's imagination or are used fictitiously. Any resemblance to actual events, locales, or persons, living or dead, is coincidental.

YAHARI ORE NO SEISHUN LOVE COME WA MACHIGATTEIRU.
Vol. 14 by Wataru WATARI
© 2011 Wataru WATARI
Illustration by PONKAN⑧
All rights reserved.
Original Japanese edition published by SHOGAKUKAN.
English translation rights in the United States of America, Canada, the United Kingdom, Ireland, Australia and New Zealand arranged with SHOGAKUKAN through Tuttle-Mori Agency, Inc.

English translation © 2022 by Yen Press, LLC

Yen Press, LLC supports the right to free expression and the value of copyright. The purpose of copyright is to encourage writers and artists to produce the creative works that enrich our culture.

The scanning, uploading, and distribution of this book without permission is a theft of the author's intellectual property. If you would like permission to use material from the book (other than for review purposes), please contact the publisher. Thank you for your support of the author's rights.

Yen On
150 West 30th Street, 19th Floor
New York, NY 10001

Visit us at yenpress.com
facebook.com/yenpress
twitter.com/yenpress
yenpress.tumblr.com
instagram.com/yenpress

First Yen On Edition: June 2022
Edited by Carly Smith & Yen On Editorial: Anna Powers
Designed by Yen Press Design: Wendy Chan

Yen On is an imprint of Yen Press, LLC.
The Yen On name and logo are trademarks of Yen Press, LLC.

The publisher is not responsible for websites (or their content) that are not owned by the publisher.

Library of Congress Cataloging-in-Publication Data
Names: Watari, Wataru, author. | Ponkan 8, illustrator.
Title: My youth romantic comedy is wrong, as I expected / Wataru Watari ; illustration by Ponkan 8.
Other titles: Yahari ore no seishun love come wa machigatteiru. English
Description: New York : Yen On, 2016–
Identifiers: LCCN 2016005816 | ISBN 9780316312295 (v. 1 : pbk.) | ISBN 9780316396011 (v. 2 : pbk.) |
    ISBN 9780316318068 (v. 3 : pbk.) | ISBN 9780316318075 (v. 4 : pbk.) | ISBN 9780316318082 (v. 5 : pbk.) |
    ISBN 9780316411868 (v. 6 : pbk.) | ISBN 9781975384166 (v. 6.5 : pbk.) | ISBN 9781975384128 (v. 7 : pbk.) |
    ISBN 9781975384159 (v. 7.5 : pbk.) | ISBN 9781975384135 (v. 8 : pbk.) | ISBN 9781975384142 (v. 9 : pbk.) |
    ISBN 9781975384111 (v. 10 : pbk.) | ISBN 9781975384173 (v. 10.5 : pbk.) | ISBN 9781975324988 (v. 11 : pbk.) |
    ISBN 9781975324995 (v. 12 : pbk.) | ISBN 9781975325008 (v. 13 : pbk.) | ISBN 9781975325015 (v. 14 : pbk.)
Subjects: | CYAC: Optimism—Fiction. | School—Fiction.
Classification: LCC PZ7.1.W396 My 2016 | DDC [Fic]—dc23
LC record available at http://lccn.loc.gov/2016005816

ISBNs: 978-1-9753-2501-5 (paperback)
       978-1-9753-3366-9 (ebook)

10 9 8 7 6 5 4 3 2 1

LSC-C

Printed in the United States of America

Cast of Characters

Hachiman Hikigaya........... The main character. High school second-year. Twisted personality.

Yukino Yukinoshita........... Captain of the Service Club. Perfectionist.

Yui Yuigahama................. Hachiman's classmate. Tends to worry about what other people think.

Saika Totsuka................... In tennis club. Very cute. A boy, though.

Saki Kawasaki................. Hachiman's classmate. Sort of a delinquent type.

Hayato Hayama................. Hachiman's classmate. Popular. In the soccer club.

Yumiko Miura.................. Hachiman's classmate. Reigns over the girls in class as queen bee.

Hina Ebina...................... Hachiman's classmate. Part of Miura's clique, but a slash fangirl.

Iroha Isshiki..................... Manager of the soccer club. First-year student who was elected student council president.

Yoshiteru Zaimokuza.......... Nerd. Dreams of becoming a light-novel author.

Kaori Orimoto.................... Went to Hachiman's middle school. Student at Kaihin Makuhari High School.

Shizuka Hiratsuka............. Japanese teacher. Guidance counselor.

Haruno Yukinoshita........... Yukino's older sister. In university.

Komachi Hikigaya.............. Hachiman's little sister. In her third year in middle school.

Prelude 1...

Just one thing.

I was going to tell her *one* thing, but it wound up taking so long.

As I was hesitating amid the crowds at the station, the sun that had once warmed me fell into the distant ocean, leaving my exposed fingers completely numb to the cold.

If I was to believe the clock display on the cell phone in my hands, it had been one hour and fifteen minutes since I had left the school. I'd been watching the screen the whole time, but I hadn't even noticed the numbers ticking by. A weak sigh slipped out of me when the time finally registered.

The streetlamps and business lights had all turned on, and the stream of students in uniforms was gone now, replaced by an increasing trickle of people in suits.

Slowly moving my stiff fingers, I typed one character after another into the still-unfamiliar messaging app, rereading my words closely. When I was done, I brushed the paper-airplane icon with my finger so lightly I wasn't even sure I'd touched it. I wished it would get lost on the way.

But the text I'd composed was displayed immediately inside a bubble.

Can we meet now?

That was all I'd written.

It was just a few words—no deeper meaning at all—but she was sure to pick up on something anyway.

I stared at the message I'd finally sent.

I checked the clock display, thinking a minute or two had to have passed, but the number hadn't changed. It was frozen.

I remembered that I'd been told you could erase sent messages, and my finger moved on its own, but it didn't reach the screen. If I recalled correctly, the recipient would get a notification that you had erased the message. I suspected she would contact me anyway in that case, so I would end up hearing from her regardless.

As I was lost in thought, suddenly the *Read* notification popped up.

And then after just a second's pause, her reply came: *I'm coming now.* She didn't ask for the reason or where I was or anything. The energy of it was very like her, and it made me smile.

So I told her my location and put away my phone. Her apartment wasn't far away. She would head over soon.

As I waited, I quietly shut my eyes and listened closely.

The wind, the rustling leaves of the treetops. The departure bell of a train. The engine sounds of vehicles. The barkers from an *izakaya*. The background music playing out of the shopping mall. The voices of people passing by, talking. The tune of "Tooryanse" coming from the pedestrian walk signal.

The shaking breaths that occasionally mingled with that array of sounds.

And then I heard her footsteps. They were airy and loud like a polka, then turned quiet like a waltz before eventually coming to a stop.

So then, where shall I begin? How much should I say? Slowly opening my eyes, I looked at her as she stood in front of me.

Her casual outfit—a thick trench coat, an off-the-shoulder sweater, and cuffed jeans—fit her vivacious nature perfectly, while the scarf loosely wrapped around her neck added a hint of girlish softness.

I think she truly is a cute, charming person.

"Good evening," I called out to her, and she smiled brightly, her pale-pink hair gathered in a bun that swayed as she nodded.

She must have run all this way. She was still panting, and I thought I heard an *uh-huh*, but it was more of a sound than a word. She fanned her face a bit with her hands before pulling off her scarf.

Seeing her, I knew this season would come to an end.

Nevertheless, **Hachiman Hikigaya**'s life goes on.

The droplet that trailed down my cheek vanished into the water's surface, sending little ripples outward through the bathroom sink. In the tense silence of the morning air, the only sound was of dripping water.

I opened my still-wet eyelids a crack, and my hazy vision caught the first light of dawn shining through the window and sparkling on the water in the sink. The pool below me reflected my sleepy eyes and ever-so-familiar morose expression. When I pulled the plug, that image slowly disappeared along with the dirty, milky-white liquid.

Grabbing a towel, I scrubbed my face and let out a deep sigh. When I inhaled again, I got a whiff of the menthol from my face wash. The mirror presented me with the same old sour expression, but I looked refreshed enough to seem somewhat crisper than usual. At least, I think I looked better than the day before.

Maybe endings aren't as hard as people make them out to be.

The day before, the Service Club competition that had gone on for nearly a year had concluded with my loss.

The slight sigh into the towel over my mouth didn't feel resigned—more like relieved.

It was over now.

Only one thing remained: I had to grant the wish that had been entrusted to me—no, I just had to fulfill the contract that had been left to me.

Yukino Yukinoshita's wish was to grant Yui Yuigahama's wish.

That was the one thing I could do.

I slopped on some Nivea face cream to get myself energized, and I briskly washed my hands. As the months had progressed, the water was no longer so frigid that it tortured me to wash my face first thing in the morning.

My fingers were still left cold, though. I made sure to wipe them on a towel to warm them up.

The residents of this small house were all otherwise soundlessly sleeping. I padded slowly along the hallway to avoid breaking the silence. There was nobody in the living room, where the ticking of the wall clock could be heard clearly.

I'd usually be fast asleep around this time, too.

My parents must have still been asleep—or had they already gone to work, since this was a busy season? I wasn't quite sure, but whichever it was, it wouldn't cause me trouble.

Circling into the kitchen, I turned on the electric kettle. I was giving the instant-coffee jar a couple of shakes into a mug while waiting for the water to boil when the living room door opened with a loud bang, making my shoulders twitch.

"Whoa… That startled me…," I muttered in an attempt to calm my racing heart.

Looking over with great trepidation, I saw the family cat, Kamakura, yawning in front of the door as he stretched in that smug way of his. At some point, our kitty had learned the power move of leaping up to a doorknob and hanging off it to open the door. It freaks the hell out of me when he does it in the middle of the night.

When I looked back at the counter before me again, the instant-coffee powder was in a heap in my mug. It must have spilled out when I'd been startled.

"Come in slowly, okay…? If you do that during a job interview, they'll throw out your application then and there," I said, but of course the cat wasn't going to listen, and Kamakura was washing his face.

As I was giving the cat a sour look, Komachi, in her pajamas, stepped out from behind him. When she noticed me, she rubbed her eyes and yawned. "Oh, morning, Bro."

"Hey, morning," I replied, and she nodded back before ambling over to the fridge to pull out the milk. I got a mug from the overhead cupboard and silently held it out.

Komachi accepted the mug, mumbling gratitude under her breath, "Uh-huh, thankee, thankee." She still seemed half in a dream as she wandered over to the *kotatsu*. Meanwhile, Kamakura followed after her whining, *Hnaa, hnaa*, and pestering her for milk by rubbing his head against her, but Komachi prodded him with her foot to casually ward him off. She poured milk into her cup, then tossed it back all in one go.

She gulped the whole thing down and let out a *pwaa!*, and that seemed to wake her up properly. Her eyes flared wide, and she did a double-take back toward me. "Huh?! It's so early! Why are you up?!"

"Come on… You're the one who's late… Late to notice…"

Her eyes were wide and round, and her mouth hung open, a milk mustache still above her lips. "What's up? Do you have something to do today?"

"No, not really. I just kinda woke up…" I took out another mug so I could reduce the instant-coffee pile to something reasonable, then poured in hot water from the kettle.

Beyond the fragrant rising steam, some very black, highly bitter, and only partially dissolved stuff lurked in the mugs. Even split into two cups, it was still pretty strong, but, well, that just meant it needed a lot of milk and sugar. Mugs in hand, I headed for the *kotatsu*.

Once Komachi was snuggled into the *kotatsu*, she scooped up the loudly meowing Kamakura and put him in her lap, eyeing me intently with her milk mustache still on her face. "Hmm…"

I couldn't tell whether she was probing me for information or feeling appreciative, so I sidestepped the matter by handing her a few tissues from the nearby tissue box. "Mustache."

"Oh, whoops." Komachi dabbed around her mouth while I reached for the milk on top of the *kotatsu* and sloshed some into my mug. Once I had made two servings of café au lait, I slid one over to her.

She watched this blankly at first, but then she smiled and accepted the mug, raising it up in gratitude. "Thanks."

I answered with a nod, clasping my mug to warm my fingers. I blew weakly at it to cool it down and took a sip.

Komachi did the same, holding the mug in both hands. She glanced over at me, and once our eyes met, she nodded. "…Uh-huh. Looks like you got *some* sleep… Though your eyes always look rotten, so it's hard to tell," she added jokingly.

Apparently, it was so rare for me to wake up early, she'd been worried there might be something wrong. *Aw geez, that little Komachi is so nice…* To show my own sort of appreciation for her consideration, I put on a cocky grin and chuckled. Look, I show her attitude because I'm shy! You can't have gratitude without attitude!

"Don't be dumb. I slept so hard. I'd even say this is my best morning in the history of Hachiman. Look at these sharp eyes." My eyes flared wide for her, flashing like I was about to fire off a Starburst Stream—hm, maybe I wouldn't call that flared eyes. Sharp eyes. Sharp nail eyes.

Komachi's eyes, meanwhile, narrowed into suspicious slits. She put her hand to her chin, then she tilted her head quizzically. "…Sharp, huh…?"

That was a weird reaction. I started feeling kind of unsure. Why was she looking at me like that…?

Komachi's lips formed silent, unintelligible words before suddenly breaking into a smile. "Well, if you're feeling good, that's enough for me."

"I'm fine. It wasn't long, but I did sleep well." I really did feel awake. Maybe I'd calmed down now that I was over that big busy spell, or maybe I'd been tired from all the kerfuffle. The night before, I'd fallen asleep like a battery on its last few percent.

I'd slept deeply enough that I hadn't dreamed. It had just taken a long time to get there.

That was because the moment I'd gotten home, I'd gone to bed to toss and turn as I stared at my cell phone, obsessively wondering whether I should let Yuigahama know about what had happened. I'd tried writing her messages, but they kept being too long or too short. I'd written and erased and written and erased them over and over. In the end, I'd realized that messaging her late at night would be a bad idea, and as I was agonizing about how to talk about this stuff directly with her another day, my eyelids had fallen, and I'd drifted off.

Judging by the time I could last remember seeing on my phone, I'd slept about three hours.

One theory says human sleep is composed of approximately ninety-minute cycles that are made up of REM sleep, in which your brain activity increases, and non-REM sleep, in which your eye movement and heart rate slow. In order to feel good upon waking up, it's best to match your waking to the shallow sleep after REM, rather than during the deep-sleep stage of REM.

If you master this sleep technique, then even once it's time to go into the workforce, you're guaranteed to become a wonderful slave, fulfilling the three vital requisites of safety, security, and sale prices. You sleep in one-and-a-half-hour chunks, and after that, you can continue to work forever! Waaah… I'll die, though…

Well, even if I was going to die, that was further down the road. In fact, I think I had somewhat more life in me compared with my usual.

Komachi saw that clearly, and as someone who lived with me, she'd know best. She brought her slightly bitter coffee to her lips and muttered, "Hmm… Well, fair enough. You kinda seem like you're refreshed. Or relieved, at least."

"My work is done now." I put my hand on one shoulder and rolled my neck around, and a pleasant cracking sound rang out.

Komachi tilted her head at my words, asking me with just her gaze, *Work?*

"I talked to you about the prom, right? That was— Well, they can do it now."

"Ahhh, you did mention that. Oh, yeah, yeah, you're having a prom. I'm really looking forward to it!" Komachi said with a toasty-warm smile.

If this prom became a regular event, Komachi would be able to attend it in the future, now that she would be going to Soubu High School. Maybe since I'd told her about it, she'd been looking forward to her own high school graduation. Thinking about that made me smile.

"Well, let's not get ahead of ourselves...," I said. "Your entrance ceremony comes first. Oh, wait, I guess your middle school graduation ceremony comes first."

"Yeah, next week," Komachi answered nonchalantly.

"For real? That's soon! Huh, what time? Where? Can parents and guardians apply to go?"

"No, no, no! It's weird you want to come. You weren't invited, and you have school anyway," Komachi shot back quickly, waving her hands around. She was being serious.

I didn't know what to say. Instead, an *unghh* sort of grunt came out of me.

This goes without saying, but you can't come when you're not invited.

For example, at a class party, alumni party, or even just a casual hangout among friends, if someone who wasn't invited shamelessly barges in, it guarantees the vibe will get really awkward. It might even ruin it entirely. And then on top of that, not only on social media but in IRL conversations afterward, they'll launch into a competition for the funniest digs, like, *Um, so now I'm gonna ask* "Why did he come?" *and you all give me your best answers. Oh! That was fast, Tsubura.*

Well, if an outsider shows up when people are having fun with their friends, a little bit of criticism is to be expected. It really sucks when something suddenly shows up without an invitation—like deadlines. They can never tell when they're unwanted. They'll be like, *Hello, I'm a deadline... I'm right behind you...* Then you turn around, and there it is! It's totally like psychological horror—the occult, even. They've got something in common with ghosts and *youkai*... Wait, does that mean deadlines aren't real?

So I began to think, but based on my experience, things like deadlines and submission dates clearly do exist. Deadlines dooo exist! What doesn't exist is the possibility that I can attend Komachi's graduation ceremony.

With a moan, I glanced at Komachi. Her arms were folded as she let out a dissatisfied huff. Judging from the deep line between her eyes, it didn't seem like this time I could just insist, *It's okay! Big Bro is uninvited basically everywhere all the time anyway, so I'll be fine! People can scowl at me, and I won't be bothered at all! I'm used to that!*

After some more groaning, I said, "…I know, I won't go. It was a joke."

Komachi let out a short sigh of exasperation. She closed her eyes and nodded as if to say, *Mm-hmm, so you finally understand?*

"As long as you get it… Well, Komachi'll probably cry, and I don't want people seeing me like that," she added quietly, sneaking her eyes away.

As her brother, I'm used to her tears. I wouldn't think anything of it, but Komachi's at the age where she gets shy about that. No, wait. Now that I think about it properly, it's not that I don't think *anything* of it. I think it's supercute! Even when she's not crying, Komachi is always, constantly, and forever adorable.

Even now, the way she was deliberately clearing her throat in an attempt to change the subject was cute, and so was the way she smiled brightly to hide her shyness. And how she opened her mouth to talk was cute!

"So," Komachi continued, "a graduation celebration from you will be a separate item!"

"Yeah…I guess there's lots of stuff we've got to celebrate. We still haven't had your birthday party," I said. I gave her a crooked smile of apology. With everything being so busy lately, I had put off all sorts of things. I most regretted not celebrating Komachi's birthday properly.

She gently shook her head. "It's okay. You don't have to be unreasonable about it. It's totally fine to do it when you can. Besides, everyone's still busy, right? You've got the prom."

I was sure Komachi meant that innocently, but for an instant, my words caught in my throat. "...Yeah. Well, that's...right... Oh, I do have tons of spare time. Sure, I have lots of things to do, but it's not like they're the kind of stuff you schedule," I added quickly to cover my pause, throwing in a casual shrug to make it seem like a joke.

But that kind of desperate clowning would never work on Komachi. Being siblings and having lived together for fifteen years, she knew everything about my habits and personality. Most likely, even if I hadn't paused, even if I hadn't rattled off those excuses, she would have picked up on something.

She eyed me suspiciously. "Listen..." But she stopped suddenly, like it was hard for her to keep going. She brought her cup to her mouth. Sipping at her coffee to moisten her lips, she seemed to be weighing whether to continue.

Even if she didn't expressly voice it, I'd basically figured out what she wanted to say. I decided to wait for her, sipping at my cooling coffee as well.

Once I silently prompted her to go on, she set down her mug. "Did something happen, Bro?" It was a probing question to figure out how I was feeling.

She'd asked me a similar question in the past. It was sometime between late fall and early winter, soon after the school field trip. Back then, she'd said it like a joke, but this time was a little different. She must have hesitated to ask because she knew how that had turned into a rare fight between us.

But Komachi had to ask anyway. This wasn't out of mere curiosity or because it was somewhat entertaining—she'd chosen to take this step forward for my sake, with the knowledge that it was bound to lead to a quarrel. That consideration and kindness made a smile tug at my lips.

The words popped out of my mouth. "...Yeah. Something did."

My response must have been a surprise, because her mouth dropped open. She blinked her big eyes two, three times. "Something happened?"

She sounded so silly that I couldn't keep that smile from growing.

"Yeah… Really, a lot of stuff happened." It came out softer than I'd meant it, as if I was nostalgic for a time that wouldn't return.

It finally hit me that those days had truly come to an end.

"Lots of stuff?" she asked.

"Yeah," I answered, in a far firmer tone than I'd even expected myself. There was no hesitation or pause, and I looked straight into Komachi's eyes.

"I see. Hmmm," she said innocently, then fell silent. She was staring at my face thoughtfully.

Unable to take her silent stare, I opened my mouth in spite of myself. "Huh, what?"

Komachi didn't even bat an eye. "Oh, I was thinking it was creepy how you answered so honestly."

"Whaaat…? But you're the one who asked," I said, slumping weakly.

Komachi huffed. "I mean, normally I wouldn't expect an answer."

"Oh, I see… Well, yeah. True." Despite my complaints, that did make sense. Komachi nodded in an exaggerated fashion.

I couldn't deny it.

I could have just babbled off some nonsense as a cover story. It would have been fine to snap back at her and not talk about it, like I had before. This time I hadn't tried to play it off at all. I'd smiled and let my words fall out of my mouth.

That must have looked suspicious to Komachi—now she was uneasy. "…Can I ask what happened?" Choosing her words carefully, she examined me with a flick of her upturned eyes.

I rubbed my chin as I looked over at the wall clock, and Komachi's head followed for a moment until she turned back to me, pressing her lips together as she waited for a response.

It would be a little while before it was time to go to school, but it still didn't seem like enough time to get into it. Besides, I shouldn't have brought it up first thing in the morning. Most of all, I still had something left to do. No matter what I said, it would only be half the story, because the story wasn't over. There were important things to come.

I couldn't say a lot here. For now, I said the only thing that seemed clear to me. "I'll talk about it properly once everything is over." Once we were at an appropriate conclusion, I would eventually tell Komachi everything, without lies or deception.

But not now. That would be far, far in the future. I didn't know when that would be.

Komachi paused before replying. Eventually, she nodded. "...Okay, I understand."

I knew that she was trying to be kind by not asking further. I felt like I was taking advantage of her, so I added as an excuse, "...Sorry. With things as they are, it might be kinda hard to get everyone together to celebrate."

On Komachi's recent birthday, she'd made a small request of me, but I probably wouldn't be able to make that happen for her. I wanted to say something to let her know that. I was fully aware this was for my own satisfaction, yet it'd be insincere to say nothing.

It was a vague way to put it, such an irresponsible thing to say, and there was no way she would understand. But Komachi's eyes were studying me with an exasperated sort of kindness. "Oh... Hmm, well, it is what it is," she answered in a lighthearted manner. Though her tone was cheery, some loneliness showed in her smile.

In an instant, it was gone. With a *Good grief* sort of sigh, Komachi jabbed a finger at me, then spun it around as if catching a dragonfly. "I told you, didn't I? Worst case, I'm fine with just you."

"O-oh..." Overwhelmed by her energy, I flinched away slightly, and Komachi thrust her finger out even farther, shoving it into my cheek.

"In fact, in Komachi terms, I was going to surprise you with something to say thanks during the celebration, so this is actually convenient! I'd just be embarrassed if other people saw!" She squealed—or made some kind of screechy noise—and covered her cheeks as she made a show of shyness.

"Whoa... What a hell of a surprise... Even knowing about it beforehand, I'm still moved...," I said, matching her lighthearted manner.

Komachi puffed out her chest with a smug chuckle. "Right? That was worth a lot of points, in Komachi terms!"

"Yeah…in Hachiman terms, that's a high bar, though… Am I gonna be surprised enough…?"

Komachi ignored my anxieties, putting on a particularly over-serious, subdued expression before she muttered with humorous solemnity, "Well, let's have a quiet event with just the family this time."

"Why're you saying it like that? Is this a private funeral? It's totally got that vibe…," I grumbled.

Komachi broke into a smile. "All right, then… Let's have breakfast." She stood up, humming, and she headed for the kitchen.

Then Kamakura popped out from under the *kotatsu* to follow after her. It seemed it was time for his breakfast, too. He must have been hungry indeed, as the claws he usually tucked away were flashing and clicking on the floor.

Hey, stop that—you'll scratch up the place, I thought like a head of household as I heard the clicks, and then I looked upon him like a pet papa as I thought, *We've got to get his claws trimmed soon*.

Suddenly, the sounds stopped. Kamakura had turned back to me and was making a quiet *hnaa* like he wanted something.

Noticing his meowing, Komachi stretched up a bit to poke her face out from behind the kitchen island. "Oh, Bro, feed Kaa his Churu treats."

"Roger." I heaved myself up. Kamakura continued to shove his face against my legs, purring all the while. It seemed the cat had figured out that Komachi was busy, so he was bothering me instead. *Oh dear, our boy is so smart…*

Glancing over to check the time, I saw it was somewhat earlier than when I normally had breakfast.

Well, I've woken up early for once. It's been a while, so today, I'll lavish this cat with love and attention.

× × ×

In class that afternoon, I was staring at my own fingers.

The sky had been clear and blue since morning, with the

temperature rising along with the sun. Though the wind was blowing hard, it was bringing in warm, wet air from the south.

And with the heat on in the classroom, it was even a few notches more comfortably warm. I hadn't slept enough, so slumber had lured me in countless times since I got to school. I'd been alternating between nodding off and lying facedown on my desk all day.

I'd just woken up from a pleasant noon nap. However, the tips of my fingers felt strangely cold, probably because I'd fallen asleep with my arm as a pillow and cut off my circulation.

That day and the day before had been blessed by bright sunlight, but it'd be chilly over the next day or two. This cycle of hot and cold would repeat every two or three days to slowly bring in the spring.

The rows of cherry blossom trees along the river on the way to school were still a long way from budding, still bearing the same wintry-looking boughs. Give it another month, and they would be in full and brilliant bloom. They didn't call it the Hanami River for nothing.

Komachi will be going down that way to school by then, I thought, envisioning my "Concept Sketch of the Future II" as I unassumingly yawned.

I checked the clock through my slightly watering eyes and saw it would be a bit longer until class was over. It was sixth period, so maybe that was why just about everyone's focus was wandering—mine especially—and a relaxed air was flowing through the classroom.

That went double for this class—math. Those like me who had settled on private liberal arts for university would have no math classes in third year. If you didn't plan to take the subject on your entrance exams, you weren't going to put effort into it.

I killed time by watching my classmates. Some nodded off, some were on their phones under their desks, and some stared out the window. Everyone was dealing with their boredom in their own ways.

Meanwhile, others were ignoring the class to endeavor in their own studies, perhaps because the end-of-term test was close. This is what's commonly known as "stealth work." If you make a token effort to hide your textbook with a different one, the teachers will let it slide. But there are also some dauntless daredevils who'll have a stack of reference books on their desk with red check sheets sticking out as if to say, *Am I doing something wrong? I'm studying, though?* I won't name names, but I mean people like Minami Sagami.

Though in her case, it seemed less that she was serious about her future and looking ahead to entrance exams, but more as if she was doing it to make a show of how hard she was working. If not, then she wouldn't be inserting nonchalant humblebragging at break times, like "Oh nooo, there's no universities I can go to at aaall. I've gotten Cs in all my recent mock exams! There's just nooo way!" to extort remarks like "Oh no, that's not true!" from her friends. At this time of year, if your mock tests get Cs, you'll generally get in. In fact, I want to say, *Set your sights a little higher.*

Is she like that even at home...? Her baby brother must be having such a rough time of it... Oh yes, don't the Kawa-somethings also have a little boy? I thought with the affection of a neighborhood housewife as I glanced over to the seats by the window at the front of the class.

There hung a bluish-black ponytail over a slightly hunched back, and it seemed she was poking at some task in her hands with a needle—some actual stealth work there... The air around Kawa-something seemed to be from last century...

Of course, some kids were actually paying attention. Actually, most were. Of them, the one in gym clothes sitting slightly to the rear of me had an extremely cute studious manner.

And this student was—I shall not hide it—my friend Saika Totsuka... Maybe I'll say it again. My friend, Saika Totsuka.

Totsuka was looking intently at the blackboard, nodding as he scribbled away with his mechanical pencil. His hand stopped pensively to smoosh his pencil against his lips.

Then he noticed me and waved the pencil at me. His silken hair glistened under the sunlight streaming in from the window, and even his smile seemed to be sparkling. *Aw man, this is so cute. Is this the secretive moonlight lighting up the night sky? He's too star twinkle...*

But I got embarrassed when he noticed me staring, so I nodded casually back to him and then turned to face front again.

The class was almost over, so I opened my abandoned notebook and copied down a token amount of content from the blackboard. If I kept looking around any more than this, everyone would think I was a weirdo after all. Though they did already think that.

As I was scratching along with my mechanical pencil, the bell rang and class ended. Homeroom was just for a few brief announcements, and then the school day was officially over.

I just had one thing planned after school.

It was to tell Yuigahama about the day before, about everything that had happened, and to ask what her wish was.

As I listened to the chatter and bustle that filled the classroom, I sluggishly began packing my stuff to go. I didn't have much, though. Once I put my arms through my coat sleeves and wrapped my scarf around my neck, I was basically done.

So next… I made some contemplative gestures, opening and closing the empty bag as I sneaked a glance to the rear of the classroom to see how Yuigahama was doing.

As our classmates were leaving the classroom in twos and threes, the usual faces remained in the sunny spot at the back corner by the window.

It was the same old familiar scene: Yumiko Miura in the middle, sitting in her own seat with her long, beautiful legs folded; Yuigahama there in her coat; and Ebina, borrowing a nearby chair to sit in as they talked about this and that. Hayato Hayama was watching them with a mature, almost parental smile while making the odd comment, and from there, the discussion spread to the three stooges, Tobe, Ooka, and Yamato.

As usual, their clique just seemed a bit too special for most to approach. And on top of that, they seemed really into their current conversation.

This made it even harder to go talk to Yuigahama.

The other day had been a similar sort of situation, and I'd managed to talk to her then, but then she'd gone off about how I should "talk to her normally." "Normally" is the hardest part, you know.

So this called for a fresh idea. If I made use of the wisdom of humanity, I could avoid going to talk to her. Even Murasaki Shikibu once said that when something is hard to say, you can communicate it through a letter!

I quietly pulled out my phone and tapped the e-mail icon. That brought up the compose window for an unfinished e-mail. The subject and text were both completely blank, with the address alone filled out.

Even after working on it into the previous night, I hadn't been able to figure out what to put. In the end, I'd never sent it, but the blank draft had remained.

In the empty text box, I wrote, *Do you have time today?* and pressed the Send button.

The results were instant as Yuigahama reached into her blazer pocket. Her eyes darted down to the phone, but she never broke the flow of conversation with Miura and Ebina.

Then she glanced at me. When I nodded back at her, she let out a bit of a tired sigh. "Ah, I got a thing." With a bright smile on her face, and without saying for what, she informed her friends that she was leaving and ambled over to me.

But with each step she took forward, her expression become more and more disgruntled. By the time she'd reached my seat, her cheeks were puffed up. "I told you to just talk to me normally!" she said quietly, taking care not to let others hear, but I still felt lectured.

"...Uh, this was the most reasonable option, though," I said.

"It's weird to message me when you're this close!"

"The nice thing about e-mail is that distance is irrelevant." No matter how shy you are, you can say all the nasty stuff you want through the Internet. ☆ I hear even the cool kids will cut loose online these days…

Yuigahama narrowed her eyes at my nonsense, looking down on me with a dull expression. I cleared my throat evasively.

So, well, let's start over and ask normally this time. "…Do you have time today?"

"Today…?" she parroted back at me, freezing for a minute. Her right hand reached for her bun and fidgeted with it, probably unconsciously. She seemed put on the spot. *Guessing that's a no.* "Hmm…" She paused before glancing over at Miura and Ebina. Then she smiled like she was a little at a loss. "I might? I might be hanging out with Yumiko and Ebina, though."

You might…? Saying it twice, isn't that too uncertain? Might, might, you might only hear all that might from My Hero Academia *fans.*

But I firmly kept all that drivel to myself.

Yuigahama hadn't actually decided on her plans for the day. Depending on how her chat with her friends went, they could be going somewhere to hang out after school, and I didn't want to get in their way.

My business didn't have to be that day. As long as I was sure we'd talk about it eventually, that was fine. Even if today didn't work, we could decide on a future time for it.

The calendar displayed on my phone showed nothing but rows of empty days. Since I was the one with a flexible schedule, I should adjust my own for her convenience. "Well, it doesn't have to be today. It could be tomorrow or the day after, or the day after that, or after that."

"That's too many options! You've really got nothing going on, huh, Hikki…?" Yuigahama said, half surprised and half disheartened.

It was my duty to inform her of her slightly mistaken perception. I straightened up and corrected her. "No, it's not like I'm doing nothing. I do have lots of things to do." For example, like watching the anime I'd just recorded, or reading the books I'd bought but hadn't read yet, or *Builders*, which I'd abandoned after developing the first island. Or the weight training that I hadn't continued with for more than three days despite excitedly buying that protein powder, or streaming a solo marathon *Aikatsu!* watch party. Anyway, I had a lot on my plate. I couldn't do it all, even if I spent my whole life on it. I mean, I could watch *Aikatsu!* over and over for the rest of my life. Ahhh, if I only had five lives! Then I could watch *Aikatsu!* five times.

I was thinking about saying something like that, but before I could, Yuigahama made a little impressed sound, and I missed my moment. "Huh. What're you doing?" She cocked her head, watching me with her big eyes. Her gaze was overflowing with curiosity, and it seemed like she was just asking because she wanted to know. But if she was going to be so sincere and straightforward, I wanted to keep that crap from before to myself.

"...W-well, lots of stuff. Uh, there's, like, super a lot of stuff? But... Well, that's stuff I can do any time," I muttered under my breath as I sneaked my gaze away, ending the conversation there. I cleared my throat while I was at it, fully regaining my composure to turn back to Yuigahama again. "So I'll go with whatever day you pick. Let me know soon when's good for you," I said.

Yuigahama folded her arms and started to think for a bit. I sensed she had some misgivings. To my surprise, though, she smiled and finally nodded. "Mmm, then today's fine."

"Are you sure?" I gestured with my eyes in Miura's direction, meaning, *Your promise with them isn't a problem?*

Yuigahama smiled lightly at me. "Uh-huh. It's not like we'd actually decided anything, so it's fine."

"Oh. Sorry," I said with a shallow bow.

Yuigahama gave a little shake of her head as if to say, *Don't worry about it.* "Then I'm gonna go get my stuff," she said, trotting over to her friends. She'd have to gather her things, say good-bye, et cetera.

I decided to go out to the hallway first. It was really embarrassing to be seen leaving the classroom with Yuigahama. The classroom door was closed, probably because the heat was on. It rattled as I slid the door open and then closed behind me.

The moment my fingers left the handle, the chill startled me.

The cold had lingered this whole time in my fingers, like thorns that couldn't be removed. I thrust my hands into my coat pockets and leaned against the wall.

The hallway windows were firmly closed, and the warmth from the heater leaking out from the classrooms made it far cozier than I'd expected.

But my fingers—
The fingers that had last touched that door were still cold.

× × ×

The pleasant sounds of metal bats, calls yelling for the ball, the tones of the brass band…

Even though the after-school sounds grew farther away as I walked, I felt like they could be heard just that much clearer.

When we reached the school gates, most people were already long gone. Fewer students could be seen coming and going. There was no one on the roads weaving through the residential districts or in the park next to us, either. The wind rustled the branches and leaves. It would turn chilly this evening.

Pushing my bicycle along the sparsely trafficked road, I walked slower than usual to match Yuigahama's pace. "Sorry for taking up your time."

"No, it's totally fine," she said with a casual shake of her head, and I nodded back at her in thanks. She walked beside me in a bright manner.

Even if the delivery of my invitation sucked, I was finally going to talk to Yuigahama.

But where was I supposed to begin?

Explaining everything that had happened would probably take a while. For things like this, maybe someplace calm and quiet would be best. If it was too loud or had a lot of people going by, worrying about others overhearing would make it hard to have a serious discussion.

So then Saize or a café or something wouldn't be quite right… Hmm…

When I couldn't think of anything, Yuigahama apparently remembered something. "Ah! Oh yeah, I heard from Yukinon yesterday. That we can have the prom."

Hearing that out of the blue startled me. It just about froze my feet in place, but I somehow pushed myself forward and found the words to fill the silence. "O-oh… So you heard?"

"Yeah, in the evening. She sent me a message, and then we met for a bit to talk." Her gaze lowered just slightly, but she was still smiling.

"Oh…" I grinned sheepishly. Considering their relationship, it wasn't strange for Yukinoshita to have told her that much. Yuigahama had always been just as worried about whether the prom would happen, and it was normal for Yukinoshita to keep her informed via text.

It was just… The way Yukinoshita had acted so quickly on it reminded me so vividly of the old Yukino Yukinoshita. Put kindly, someone who was swift and decisive. Put less kindly, someone who jumped to her own conclusions without consideration for the situations or intentions of others. A person who charged right in.

It made me a little emotional.

Thinking back, even I wasn't different from before. I was still waffling around, as usual. I mean, when something came up, I'd taken my sweet time finding a reason, following which I'd been unable to even send an e-mail. It had taken all my effort to start this conversation and get to this point.

But thanks to that, I'd reached a decision.

Coming to a halt, I pointed to the park and asked, "Can we stop there for a bit?"

Yuigahama knit her eyebrows for a moment, but eventually, she nodded. "…Sure."

I had to have a proper talk with her now, or I'd put it off forever.

I bought a cold can of coffee and a warm black tea at a nearby vending machine, then headed into the park. After stopping my bicycle at the bench under a streetlamp, I sat down and prompted Yuigahama to do the same with a glance. She squeezed the shoulder strap of the backpack over her shoulder. Her expression looked kind of stiff, but by the time she took a brisk step forward, her cheeks had relaxed into a slight smile.

As soon as she was by my side, she set her backpack down on the bench. "Ohhh, I think it's been a long time since I've come to a park." Though it was the kind of park you'd find anywhere, Yuigahama was looking all around as if she was unfamiliar with it.

Then her gaze locked on one point. She was staring at some swings. They were very much the typical, ordinary playground equipment, and it wasn't like there was anything unique about them.

But Yuigahama pattered over to them with light footsteps.

"Ah, hey, wait up!" I cried, calling to her to stop, but she started rattling the chains of one of the swings. Now that she'd killed my first attempt to broach the subject, I followed after her.

"Wow, these swings are so small. Were they always like this?" She took a seat on one timidly. She slowly started to pump with her legs, and the chains started creaking along with it. "Whoa, whoa! It's been so long since I last did this! It's kinda scary! Way more than I expected!" She slammed her feet on the ground in a panic. "Phew!"

I offered her the plastic bottle of tea. "You don't worry about the danger when you're a kid. I jumped off the swings all the time, and every time, I'd fall and scrape my knees."

Yuigahama accepted the tea with a quiet thanks and took a sip. "Ahhh, I think I used to do that, too… Wow, I'm surprised you did stuff like that." She wrapped her arms around the chains, rocking slowly back and forth with her feet on the ground as she looked up at me. For an instant, her teasing gaze flicked to the swing beside her.

But I wasn't going to accept that invitation. I took a seat on the fence around the swings instead.

After popping open the tab of my coffee with one hand, I took a sip. "Yuigahama." I swallowed the lingering bitterness at the back of my tongue and continued. "Tell me your wish."

I supposed she didn't know what I was getting at, because she pressed her lips together as if pausing to think, then smiled awkwardly. "What's that supposed to mean?"

"Sorry, I shouldn't have put it like that. I mean, like, something you want me to do or a wish you want me to fulfill," I said.

"Huhhh?" Yuigahama sandwiched her clasped hands between her thighs, swaying side to side as she started to think. It only took her a moment to come up with something, though. "There's lots of stuff. Like, I want you to be more natural when you're coming to talk to me.

And I want you to not make little glances at me—oh, and I want you to reply to e-mails faster and to not be so picky with your food. Oh yeah, and—" Yuigahama started counting down on her fingers, criticizing me for one thing after another.

It seemed like this list would go on forever at this rate, so I cut her off emphatically. "I get it, I get it! Sorry! I'm sorry for being born, okay? Hearing you say that out loud, I'm pretty awful, huh? That blows…," I muttered. The self-loathing was closing in. If she went any further, I'd get depressed for real.

Yuigahama tilted her head with an expression of utter seriousness. "Did you only realize that stuff now…?"

"It hits different when someone else says it to you. And, like, that was a lot. It was a long list, and it was all criticism. Geez, that hurts… Well, I will try to work on my faults where I can, though."

"I know that's never happening, so it's fine…" Yuigahama sighed wearily, shoulders slumping.

Oh no, she gave up on me… Everything she'd listed was a flaw I was aware of, though, so I wanted to do my best to fix them…but I was also aware that wasn't easy, so all I could do was grimace.

As I was covering these thoughts with an internal *na-ha-ha!*, Yuigahama let out a dissatisfied huff, but she was quickly struck by something else. "Oh, but I kinda want you to not suddenly make plans at the last minute, like today. It's fine when I'm not doing anything, but there are times when I, like, wanna be prepared."

It was true that lately I kept springing plans on Yuigahama. I remembered that Yuigahama had been talking with her friends about doing something today, and I had butted in. The guilt started to eat at me. "Ah, yeah. I'm sorry about that, honestly."

Yuigahama nodded. "And…"

"There's more? There's a lot, isn't there? Sorry for everything!" I said, and she giggled. That made me smile in spite of myself.

Just how easy would it have been if we could have talked like this forever—without saying any of the important things, pretending it was the same as always, deliberately never getting to the point?

But allowing myself to do that would be betraying myself.

I tossed back the can of coffee in one go and squeezed it as if doing that could somehow warm my cold fingers. I easily dented the flimsy aluminum. I tried rolling it in my hands to fix the dent, but that just warped it even more.

I knew the can wouldn't go back to its original shape, but I couldn't stop toying with it. It made a silly-sounding popping noise every time, until my sudden sigh joined its sounds. "…That's not the sort of thing I'm asking about." It came out far softer than I'd meant—gentle, even. I looked up from the can to Yuigahama.

She was still sitting on the swing. She got a bit of momentum going, then watched her toes thrust forward as she lazily swayed back and forth. "So then what was it?"

"I meant about the competition. The one where whoever wins gets the others to do what they say."

"…The competition isn't over yet, though." She sounded kind of sulky, her tone more innocent than usual, making the corners of my mouth quirk up. Sometimes Yuigahama's expression would turn startlingly mature, but right at that moment, she looked awfully childish. It was kind of funny to me.

"Well, true… But I acknowledged my loss. So that means…the competition is over."

"Says you."

Beyond where she sat, the sky in the west was starting to grow dim. The ratio of deep red and azure gradually shifted as the hasty first star twinkled.

"No, I lost. I lost so completely, it even felt good," I said, craning my neck to look upward.

That defeat did actually feel refreshing.

The issue of the prom had unexpectedly wound up becoming our final competition. Yukinoshita had immediately realized my prom plan was a fake that wouldn't affect her victory, so she had accepted my offer to compete. When it came down to it, I'd lost at reading Yukino Yukinoshita—not her plans or her thoughts, but just how determined she was.

I heaved a great sigh to release the tension in my body. My breath dissipated into nothing.

Even if there was no winner, a competition between two was over when a loser was decided.

"So let me grant your wish." I finally finished saying the words that had been stuck in my chest the whole time. It had taken me a hell of a long time to utter this one thing.

It wasn't just right now. I'd thought somewhere in the depths of my heart throughout the past year, ever since back when the competition had begun, that I would eventually say those words.

Yuigahama dug in her feet and brought the swing to a stop. The chain creaked, and she pressed her lips together, waiting for the sound to fade. "I'm greedy," she muttered eventually, "so I can't decide on one thing… Is that okay? Can I get everything I want?" Lifting her falling chin up again, she smiled mischievously.

I shrugged at her. "That's pretty normal for people who are making wishes… Well, I'll manage somehow, as long as it's within my ability."

"I think you should stop that." Yuigahama's eyes slid down, but she spoke clearly. Her profile looked sad, and it made my voice catch. "You're always like that. Saying you'll do what you can even though you can't, and then somehow you manage it in the end. All you do is give yourself stress." She flapped her legs, and the action made the swing slowly set into motion again. "So maybe I'll just ask for simple stuff. I don't really get what you mean by 'my wish,' but there are things I want to do."

"Huh. Like what?" I dutifully followed the swing with my eyes as its arcs gradually lengthened.

"First…I want to help Yukinon. I want to see this prom all the way through."

"Uh-huh."

"And an after party. With the UG Club? And Special Snowflake and Yumiko and Ebina…"

"Ahhh…"

"And I want a party for Komachi-chan, too."

"Yep."

"Also, I'd like to go somewhere to hang out."

"Okay."

She swung close, then away, then close again, tossing out a request each time, and I offered noncommittal remarks to each one to let her know I was listening.

These wishes were nothing surprising. I'd figured she'd bring up helping with the prom, and I seemed to remember she'd said something before about an after-party, too. And as for Komachi, all I could say was that I was thankful. I frankly didn't get her wanting to hang out, but if she was fine with it, I would accompany her anytime.

Gradually, the swing lost momentum, and Yuigahama's voice grew softer. "And…"

Loud chattering voices passed on a nearby path on the other side of the hedge. I saw a group of boys and girls in uniforms like ours.

I didn't spot any faces I knew, but Yuigahama was silent until they went by. The swing was still during that time as well, and the lonely creak of the chain was all that followed.

I didn't say anything, just looked over at Yuigahama and waited for her to speak.

She seemed to notice. She smiled at me with the sunset at her back. "And maybe…I want to grant your wish, Hikki."

In the growing ultramarine of the darkness, the fleeting afterglow of the sunset and the streetlights mingled to beautifully light her slender face.

I couldn't make a noncommittal noise this time.

In the first place, I was doing this to grant Yukino Yukinoshita's wish.

Yukinoshita's wish was for me to grant Yuigahama's wish, but now Yuigahama was saying she would grant *my* wish. Bouncing from one to the next like this, we'd go around in circles forever.

"My wish, huh? That's hard…" I didn't know how to respond.

"Right? So think it over while you're granting my wish. And I'll think about it, too," Yuigahama said, getting momentum with a *hup!* onto her feet. The swing wavered slightly back and forth, chains jangling. She spun around to face me, with the warm glow of the setting sun still at her back. "…And then I'll tell you the rest… So actually tell me what you want, Hikki."

The burning red sun stung my eyes, and I narrowed them automatically. My vision blurry from the bright light behind her, I nodded back.

She watched me, her smile shining beautifully.

Prelude 2...

A tremble ran through my hand and went straight to my heart.

I'd been thinking that there had to be something going on, so I wasn't surprised. My heart quivered with a feeling of resignation, like, *So it's finally happened.*

The teacher called him out that day after school, and as I watched him go, I was pretty certain he wouldn't come back to the classroom.

I really couldn't bring myself to want to go out for fun.

After getting home, I immediately collapsed onto the living room sofa still in my uniform and blankly stared at the ceiling. Mom kept nagging me that it would wrinkle my skirt and blazer, so I lugged myself off to get changed, but in the end, I slumped onto my bed. Once I was buried in my fluffy futon, my whole body wouldn't move at all. I was stuck.

My phone vibrated a single time.

Was it from him—or from her?

I didn't know, but it was probably nothing good.

Wishing it was from someone else entirely, I dragged my arm over to bring my phone in front of my face.

At the very top of the screen was a message from her.

I didn't have to even bother opening the app to see the entirety of the message displayed in the push notification, so I read it without letting the sender know I had.

Can we meet now?

That was all it said. It didn't actually tell me anything. I could tell that something had happened, though.

I wish I could have pretended I hadn't noticed it.

Sneaky thoughts rose in my mind, like what if I *did* just pretend I hadn't seen it? What if I waited a while before replying? Then wouldn't we be able to go on a little longer like this?

But even more than that, I was so glad that she wanted to talk to me about this. My eyes even stung a little with tears. My feelings were all over the place.

I think I'd probably always been waiting for her to approach me because I was scared to say it myself.

That's why all I sent her was *I'm coming now*, then I put on the coat I'd tossed away. Her reply came while I was at the door, shoving my feet into the sneakers with their heels crushed, and I checked my phone to see where she was waiting.

There was a place that we had to go.

Not far from here—it was close by. I'd be over soon.

Though I really hadn't planned to run, once I was outside, my feet went faster and faster.

The street by the station was full of people, but immediately I found her sitting on the bench under the light of the streetlamps. Her back was perfectly straight, hands laid over her skirt with her eyes closed. She was as still as a statue. It was a really cold night, and even though she was wearing a coat, it didn't seem like the chilly air bothered her.

She slowly opened her eyes at the sound of my footsteps. She smiled, and it was beautifully clear like the winter night sky. "Good evening."

Her smile was so captivating, I couldn't talk. This has to be what they mean when they say "breathtaking."

I pretended I was out of breath from running and nodded without saying anything. Pulling my scarf off right away, I sat down beside her—'cause it seemed like I'd be entranced forever if I didn't.

I'd never seen a girl so beautiful. I think I've seen lots of cute and pretty girls, but this was the first who'd ever been so beautiful I forgot how to breathe.

Instead, I let out a long sigh as I asked her, "What's up?"

"I wanted to talk a little," she began, but then paused a moment. Then slowly, choosing her words carefully, she continued. "...We can have the prom now."

Hearing that finally gave me peace of mind. "Oh, that's great news." I'd been worried for a while now. For just an instant, that grumpy face crossed my mind, and I let out a sigh of relief. It was a pretty big sigh, so maybe that's why she giggled.

"It's thanks to you," she said.

I didn't do anything.

I hadn't. I couldn't.

Instead of saying that, I gave a little shake of my head.

She watched me, but then her eyes suddenly shifted away to something in the distance as she murmured, "...And...thanks to him."

Her words made a shudder run through my body. I couldn't look her straight in the eye, and my gaze fell to the ground. "...That's not true. It's 'cause you worked hard," I said, trying to comfort her.

But now she was the one shaking her head. "It's fine. I understand. I relied on him again..." Her tone was light, and there was something childlike about it, totally different from her usual mature manner of speech. It startled me a little. I finally looked back up at her and saw her smiling bashfully—I couldn't tell if she really was just being shy or if it was to cover something else.

"I knew he was going to do that, but I couldn't refuse him." She raised her eyes just a bit, gazing far away. I turned in the same direction, but there were only skyscrapers over there. "But now that's over, too."

You'd think the city would be filled with nighttime hustle and bustle, but I could hear her soft, fragile voice clearly. It was just like the lights of the buildings shining in the distance.

Her voice reminded me of a pale glow, like red lights in the darkness coming and going, fading gently into a delicate blur.

Her voice mingled with the sound of the fiercely blowing wind. "I told him the truth. I told him everything." Her long hair fluttered in the wind, hiding her face like a veil. When it settled, she combed it back with her fingers to tuck it behind her ears.

And then she smiled again.

It was fresh and new, as if the breeze of the spring night had washed away so many things.

I'd probably always loved that beautiful smile, and I still did.

Seeing that, I realized this relationship would come to an end.

Eventually, he'll **become used to this relationship**, too.

Bright was the noon sun shining its halcyon rays over my lunch break during my time for munching, in the same spot as always.

With the calls of the tennis club's noon practice forming a chorus in the background, I was zoning out while eating my lunch. The temperature had cooled somewhat since the day before, but it wasn't awful to be outside. Though it was chilly in the morning and evening, the middle of the day wasn't cold enough to wear a coat anymore. It felt really nice to bathe in the sunlight with few clouds in the sky. The seasons had changed drastically over the past few days, and the city was starting to feel like the beginning of spring.

I carelessly shoved the leftover pastry I'd bought from the school store into my mouth and washed it down with some tea. A satisfied *phew* left me of its own accord as I leaned my cheek on my hand and closed my eyes in the warm sunlight.

As I was listening to the *ponk, ponk* sounds of balls ringing out from the tennis court and the voice of the tennis club captain, Totsuka, the crunch of shoes on sand joined the noise. I reflexively turned around to see a pale-pinkish bun bobbing there. Yuigahama also saw me and raised a hand up to chest height to wave.

"Hey, what's up?" I greeted.

"Just came by while I was buying a drink. Here." She held out the can of MAX Coffee, pressing down the back of her skirt to sit down beside me.

While I accepted the still-warm Max can, I didn't know what to do with it, so I tossed it up and down. "Huh. What's with this? Is it for me? How much was it?"

"It's fine. You treated me the other day."

"Oh, okay. Then I'll take it."

"Mm."

Oh my gosh, did she come here just to return the present...? What a dutiful girl...

I opened the tab with a *pshht* and slurped at the warm, sweet Max can. *Mm-hmm, mm-hmm, this is what it's all about.* I was nodding to myself at the gradually spreading warmth, when I suddenly felt eyes on me.

Next to me, Yuigahama was holding her knees in front of her, watching me with her head cocked. Her gaze reminded me of a sunspot. It was really warm, and it made me a bit restless.

I avoided her eyes to hide my agitation. Instead, I read the list of ingredients on the Max can in my hands. *Is this stuff okay? Like, I'm suddenly feeling this weird high—wait, is Max can the kind of thing you shouldn't abuse? Isn't there...lots of dangerous white powder in it...?* I wondered, and yes, there was! The dangerous white powder that gives you a high! A sugar high!

I spent a while indulging those vapid thoughts, and once I'd settled down, Yuigahama started talking to me. "What'll we do for the after-party? When should we have it?"

"Ah..." was all I initially said to fill the silence. I was still thinking over what to say. Yuigahama had mentioned stuff about an after-party the previous night, so she was probably focusing on it as one of her wishes.

She wanted an after-party to show appreciation to the people who had helped us with the recent dummy prom: Zaimokuza, the UG Club guys, Miura, and Ebina, but...with that lineup, there was no way Zaimokuza and the guys would be happy about the idea...

However, Yuigahama was enthusiastic, so I couldn't say no.

In the end, I couldn't argue against it, and Yuigahama must have taken that as agreement, as she started tapping away on her phone to check something. "Yumiko and Hina said they're free today, and I'm free, too, so I was thinking today could work."

"You haven't asked if I have any plans, though," I said.

Yuigahama pouted. "Hikki, you already said you're free. Tomorrow and the day after and the day after that."

"True…" Since she'd gotten commitment out of me in an unexpected way, there was nothing to do but to shrug. You've got to watch what you say! And on top of that, it was true that I was free, so I couldn't deny it.

"So then, that just leaves Special Snowflake and the guys…" Yuigahama was implying, *Check what their plans are for me.*

"Today's fine," I answered immediately.

"Huh? You sure?" Yuigahama tilted her head with a blank look.

I nodded firmly. "It'll work out. I'm positive those guys have the time. I know all about it."

"You sound really sure about that…"

The UG Club is a mysterious group with unclear activities, and Zaimokuza went without saying—there was no way those guys would have plans. I'm also a member of a strange club and have a similar sort of lifestyle, so I can tell. I know all about it.

But Yuigahama was the kind of person who was generally expected to have real plans, so she doubted me. She pressed her lips together huffily and glared at me. "…If they don't come, you'll be the only boy there."

"Whoa, brutal…" The only ones who can enjoy what society calls a harem are kings. When you're actually the only boy in an all-girls space, you'll just about puke and be dripping all over like an iced tea in summer, armpits sweating nonstop. The best-case scenario is that they leave you alone. Some try to be nice to you and say stuff like, *You've been sweating for a while—are you okay? Are you hot?* Never mind sweat from your armpits—it's a Niagara Falls from your mouth.

When we were in the familiar clubroom, I was more or less used to it, so I could trick myself with some theoretical armor beefed up with excuses. But in an unknown environment, I'd be as timid as a kitten and sure to spend the whole time frozen like a Jizo statue.

But if you added Zaimokuza and the UG Club duo in, then oh my, how strange! Now you'd have four Jizo statues!

Well, there is the saying that even barren trees enliven a mountain. They would be better than nothing. Whatever Miura and Ebina thought aside, it would at least help me emotionally.

"I've kinda got to think about how to put it...," I said. "If you invited them in the usual way, they'd definitely refuse."

"Really?" Yuigahama tilted her head, not quite convinced.

I nodded firmly at her. "Really. If they're told someone like Miura is there, they'll never come. Going to an after-party with cool kids you've never met before is basically torture. You wind up stuck staring at the clock for two hours straight while desperately ordering refills for your drink. You'll even spend more time going to the bathroom than sitting in your seat. I know all about it."

"You know too much about it! This is totally your actual lived experience!"

Nodding as I ignored Yuigahama's anguished cry, I stroked my chin. "The problem is that they aren't directly acquainted with Miura and Ebina."

That must have convinced her. "Ahhh... Well, yeah..."

I do believe Miura is a good person, but still, if that high-pressure attitude of hers hits them the first time they meet, they really would wilt. I was still wilted after all!

But apparently, people who are used to that see it as a trivial issue. Yuigahama suddenly clapped her hands and turned back to me, waving a finger as she started trying to persuade me. "Oh, but Snowflake knows both Yumiko and Hina, right? If he could help..."

"The problem is that they aren't directly acquainted with Miura and Ebina..."

"You're repeating yourself!"

"Don't be dumb. I'm not even sure I'm acquainted with her. Zaimokuza will see her as less than a stranger. And besides, there's no way he could help anyone in a social situation."

"Well, so then…you do your best, Hikki." Yuigahama pumped her fists in front of her chest like, *You can do it!*

All I could do was force a grin at that innocent smile of hers. *She can tell me to do my best, but it's just impossible…*

Why was she trying so hard to place creatures of different habitats in the same place together? *Putting a Miurlion and a Slavemokuza in one building—is this a coliseum or what? Didn't you learn in world history that these things are basically blood sports?*

But being another of the slaves, I had no choice but to follow Empress Gahama's orders. "…Well, I'll try inviting them. Where are we gonna have this after-party?"

"I figure, like…," Yuigahama said, looking up at the sky thoughtfully, "…we go to some karaoke place," and then looked back at me again.

Her questioning gaze made me hesitate for a moment. "Hmm, okay… Then that could maybe work out somehow." *All right, so then what sort of rationale will I use to make them come?* I was calculating as I continued, "I'll talk to them after school."

"Mm-hmm, okay." Yuigahama nodded, then wrapped her arms around her knees again and shifted in her seat. Now a few inches closer than before, she gently held back her soft hair as it fluttered in the chilly wind, tucking it behind one ear.

I watched from the corner of my eye as my cold fingers squeezed around the lingering warmth of the can. The sickly-sweet coffee touched my lips.

I'd thought that would be it for this discussion about the after-party, but it didn't look like Yuigahama was getting up.

…Well, the weather is nice, and it's not like this spot belongs to me. I totally don't mind if she relaxes here for a while.

I checked the tennis court to distract myself from my restlessness. The *ponk, ponk* of the tennis balls had stopped, and the tennis club was heading out.

Since they were just done practicing, the boorish tennis club guys looked quite filthy, but I found one of the group who stood out particularly. He was just like the goddess of the moon in Greek myth, the pretty and curey-curey tennis club captain, Saika Totsuka. Twincool! ☆

As Totsuka wiped off his sweat and lightly adjusted his tennis bag on his shoulder, I gave him a wave. When he noticed me, he raised his hand for a tiny wave in front of his chest.

It's the best feeling in the world when you feel like you're exchanging wordless little signals others can't see… To make a comparison, it's almost like the feeling of going to a voice actress's live show, and while everyone else is waving penlights everywhere and desperately doing fan chants, he's one step back standing like M. Bison with a boyfriendly expression and just nodding along slightly. Wait, doesn't this mean they're basically dating? No, he's a stranger…

Seeing Yuigahama and me, Totsuka let the club member next to him know he was going, then daintily trotted up to us.

Yuigahama gave him a wide wave in return. "Ohhh, Sai-chan, yahallo!"

"Yeah, yahallo." Panting a little, Totsuka returned the gesture and greeting, smiling brightly at me as well.

Mmm, what a wonderful greeting… I found myself trembling at the beauty of the Japanese language… *Is that Japanese? What language is yahallo, actually…?*

As I was lending some serious thought to this deep question, Yuigahama was ignoring me. "Your club? Wow, it looks like it could really help you lose weight." She sounded impressed.

"L-lose weight… Hmm, y-you think? I don't really know if I have." There was more than a little confusion in Totsuka's smile.

But Yuigahama waved her hands, her expression serious. "No, no, Sai-chan, you're so skinny. Put on some weight. It's not fair."

"Unfair…?" Totsuka asked, conflict seeping into his expression. Yuigahama started prodding his side. "Ah, hey, stop…"

"See! You're so thin! Hikki, he's so thin!"

Totsuka squirmed around, trying to avoid her pokes, but Yuigahama ignored him and beckoned to me.

Ohhh? May this humble servant also touch upon his honored personage? I thought, and I started reaching out.

I *started* reaching out, but…

"Hachiman…stop her…" Totsuka was looking at me for help with teary eyes. The moment I saw that, I couldn't make another move. Now that I had that arrow to the heart…

And so I'll change the subject instead! "Totsuka, are you free tonight?"

He tilted his head in surprise. Yuigahama stopped her poking as well, cocking her head in the same way.

"We were talking about going to karaoke," I said. "Before, right, we talked to you about the prom and stuff. Since that all worked out, this is, like, kind of a celebration…"

We'd consulted Totsuka about the dummy prom, too. You could even say Totsuka's presence there was what had made me feel like I could open up about the whole situation. I still hadn't thanked him properly for that, so I really wanted him to be at the after-party.

"Yeah, yeah! You should come, Sai-chan!" Yuigahama excitedly clapped her hands.

Totsuka struggled to find how to reply. "Ummm… If it's after my club," he said bashfully, and I nodded in return.

Eventually, the bell rang to let us know lunch was over.

"Let's go back to class," Yuigahama said, rising to her feet, and she swept off the sand stuck to her skirt.

I stood up after her, finishing off what little remained of my coffee. I threw out the pastry wrapper and the can on the way to the school building and stuck my cold fingers in my pockets.

Now, the plans for the day were set. When Yuigahama had brought up an after-party, I honestly hadn't felt great about it, but I was starting to look forward to it a little.

× × ×

The spring sun, just starting to set, filled the aerial walkway.

Two pairs of footsteps ticked out a rhythm in the quiet, peaceful space.

Yuigahama was accompanying me for some reason; she'd rushed a little to come up beside me. *Whyever is she coming...?* I wondered, but I didn't say it out loud.

"Is Snowflake in the clubroom, too?" she asked.

"Probably," I answered briefly. The UG Club guys and Zaimokuza were likely still maintaining the dummy prom website and social media. Since I was going to inform them of our completed mission status, it would be very convenient to use that opportunity to invite them to the after-party.

As we approached the special-use building, the after-school bustle grew distant, and eventually, we arrived at a dead-silent corner: the UG Club room.

I opened the door without hesitation. Zaimokuza noticed us immediately and thumped his way over to welcome us in. "Herm, Hachiman. So you have come. Yahallo!" He fluttered his trench coat as he greeted me with a sonorous voice. Behind him, Sagami's little brother popped his head out, adjusting his glasses, and Hatano also pushed his glasses up with a bow.

"Oh, yahallo, then."

"Hey, yahallo."

Mm-hmm, what a wonderful greeting! I thought, feeling quite satisfied with myself, but from behind, I heard an incredibly aggrieved sigh.

I glanced behind me. *Waaah, Miss Gahama is looking at me so scaaary...* With her eyes cold and half-lidded and her cheeks puffed up like balloons, she seemed very much in a mood indeed.

"Hikki...make them stop that," Yuigahama said in a super-low voice, tugging at my sleeve.

You didn't mind it when Totsuka said it, though... Well, of course! Because Totsuka's cute! And these guys aren't.

I pacified her with a *Now, now* gesture as I offered her a chair. She sat down reluctantly, and I pulled up a nearby chair as well and took a seat with a thud.

"Well, so, um. There was something I wanted to talk about today…," I began, and the UG Club and Zaimokuza both turned to me. "With your help, we're now in a position where we can hold, so I came to let you know. It wasn't for long, but thanks for your work. You really helped us out. We're grateful." I bowed my head deeply, and Yuigahama did the same. "So the dummy prom management is now concluded."

They must not have expected us to actually bow, as Sagami and Hatano seemed momentarily startled. But they immediately let out short sighs with grins.

"Oh, really?"

"Great."

"Aye, and so that chapter comes to a close! So thought Yoshiteru…," Zaimokuza declared as he got this faraway look in his eyes, but I whisked right by that, clearing my throat with a *gfem, gfem* and adopted a sharp expression.

"Therefore, as of now, this committee is disbanded. And I forbid the greeting *yahallo* moving forward," I said, and a momentary silence was born.

After that hushed tranquility, Sagami's and Hatano's glasses both slid down.

"Whaaa…?"

"N-no way…"

"Why're you upset about this…?" Yuigahama sighed in exasperation. She shot the UG Club members a dull stare.

Since the ban on *yahallo* had nicely killed any excitement, I decided to hit them while they were down. The best time to deceive someone is when they're rattled or weakened! If you see them in low spirits, that's your chance!

"So we're going to karaoke," I said about as casually as a scam artist saying, *Oh, Mom? Hey, hey, it's me* over the phone.

The UG Club pair looked at me with leaden eyes.

"…With who?"

"With friends?"

Only Zaimokuza was full of beans, maintaining his usual level of energy as he unnecessarily added, "But Hachiman has no friends."

"I don't wanna hear that from you…," I shot back right away.

But Zaimokuza laughed fearlessly. "Moha-ha-ha-ha, indeed!"

"So you weren't friends with those guys, Snowflake…?" From Yuigahama's words alone, you'd think she was surprised, but the incredibly apathetic *uh-huhhhh* sound she made afterward was oozing with clear disinterest.

That sent the pair into shock.

"Huh?"

"Huuuh…?"

Whatever are they so surprised about…? Are they so shocked to hear they're not friends with Zaimokuza? Isn't that something to be glad about?

But then Sagami and Hatano muttered, "Those…guys…" one word each, shoulders slumping. It seemed the blow was from Yuigahama failing to remember their names, and their glasses slid down in despair.

Hmm, I get that. Gahama has been like the princess of this crew lately, so I'd had a real sense that they'd kinda made friends… However, the theory that she might not even remember my name because she calls me Hikki and has never called me by my full name is awaiting verification.

"Whatever, let's just go to karaoke later today." I rushed them so that I could fire the finishing blow while they couldn't process the implications.

But Sagami and Hatano both scowled. They clearly had a problem with this. Hatano adjusted his glasses from where they'd slid down and down to wind up like Kawabata from Chemistry. "Huh, later today? Inviting us so randomly, this guy is too much…"

Sagami also seemed to recover from his shock, pushing up his bangs while shoving his glasses up so high on his face it was like, are they Ray-Bans? Was he trying to look down his nose at us? "This guy's got to be a little crazy…"

"Mayhap enough to say so?" Even Zaimokuza joined in as the trio began a whispered attack on my character…

It seemed Yuigahama couldn't just stand by and watch, as she came in to back me up. "Ummm, it's kinda like a celebration for wrapping things up. Do you guys have any plans? I heard everyone's okay with today..." She shot me a cold glance. That look was hard-core saying, *See, I knew it wouldn't work...* And then on top of that, she was secretly jabbing me with her knee under the table. *What do we do?*

Man, I wish I could shrink away...like a northern white-faced owl in front of its natural enemy...

While thinking, *Now, how do I trick them into this?* I glanced over to see Sagami and Hatano cleaning their glasses lenses.

"Well...if it's already been decided, I suppose I must go along with it."

"Agh. Well, it's not like I can't open up my schedule."

Turning their gradually reddening cheeks away, they put their glasses on again in an indifferent manner. They were both being kinda curt, like a pubescent listener trying to act smart when he's on a live phone call with a voice actress on a radio show.

"Really? Great!" Yuigahama smiled brightly, and Sagami and Hatano cleared their throats repeatedly, mumbling stuff like *yeah, well, okay, uh-huh* under their breaths.

I thought about complaining to them like, *Hey! Boys! Aren't you, like, acting differently with Yui?* But it wasn't hard to imagine that I'd probably do the same in their position. That realization made me want to groan and writhe in agony.

"Karaoke, hmm? 'Tis unavoidable. So then we ought to have some light provisions." Zaimokuza's tone had some weight to it, and the two glasses guys gave big nods.

But Yuigahama alone answered a beat late. "Light provisions...? Oh...like sushi."

"No."

Why are you so convinced? It's weird to respond to him like Oh, I see, *okay?* Waving around fish like *aji* or *kohada* would totally be a nuisance—what kind of celebration is that? The management would cart you off. You'd get kicked out on the spot.

Of course, I didn't even have to clarify, as Sagami and Hatano understood. "I didn't bring my pen today."

"I guess I'll go buy some Liumu at Daiso."

As the two of them conversed, Yuigahama's head finally tilted. You really have to be careful when you use English terms around this girl! "Your pen? Liumu?"

"They mean penlights and Cyalume glow sticks," I explained.

By the way, with glow sticks, for some reason there's a trend for voice actress *otaku* to abbreviate the brand name as Liumu, while idol *otaku* shorten it to Sai (personally researched).

There might be a tendency to think, *Who would go to the trouble of getting lights for karaoke...?* but you occasionally hear about these types. I also hear big groups of them will get together to rent a party room and create concert-level hype.

Otaku do in fact have an affinity for karaoke, so it's not strange at all. I mean, when you look up the play history on a karaoke remote, it's all Showa-era ballads and anime songs, so it's fair to say at this point, karaoke is a hobby for the elderly and *otaku*.

If you're going to have a good time with some trusted friends, karaoke is the optimal choice.

The issue was that for the lineup today, never mind trusted friends, they didn't even know one another's names...

But with the three of them getting all excited and badgering each other about how they wanted to do this and that and more and more, I really couldn't tell them that... I mean, since if I did, then they wouldn't come.

Let's end this quick, before they catch on. Giving Yuigahama an eye signal to say, *Let's get going*, I stood from my seat. "I'll go ahead and book the room. Once we've got a place, I'll message you."

"See you guys soon!" Yuigahama rose to her feet as well, and we both tried to leave the clubroom.

That was when one half of the glasses pair stopped us. "Oh, hold on a second. Should we delete this website now, then?"

I turned back to see Sagami turning the laptop in his hands toward us. Displayed there was the website for the dummy prom.

It had been set up as a fake throwaway, just to make Yukinoshita's prom happen, so the website had done its job. There was no need to maintain it any longer. In fact, if you considered how it might invite unnecessary confusion, it should be deleted.

What had been written there, and what hadn't been written there, was all over anyway.

So then it was fine for them to delete everything. No—they should delete it as soon as possible.

But what came out of my mouth was "…Yeah. Well, there's no rush, so whenever you have time is fine."

Even if they didn't delete it now, it would eventually be lost in the digital ocean without anyone witnessing its passing. But forcing its suicide would erase any trace of those sharp, stinging days, and that made me hesitate.

It was a sentimental thing to say, if I do say so myself, and it brought a wry smile out of me. My twisted lips pulled up a tick, and an almost self-mocking sigh spilled out.

However they took that sigh, Sagami and Hatano looked at each other, then responded with short nods. I thanked them with a nod of my own, then turned away from them.

And away from that picture of the girls standing in front of the sunset sea.

× × ×

I slowly walked through the deserted hallway after school. All the students who had been there during the day had already gone to their clubs or home, and the school building was deserted.

Leaving the UG Club room to head for the front entrance, Yuigahama and I were talking about which karaoke parlor to go to when, eventually, we came to the door of the student council room.

The door opened, and a girl with a short pale bob popped out. It was Iroha Isshiki, the student council president. The student council exited after her.

Yuigahama spotted a head of long, flowing black hair in the group and rushed off to her. "Ah, it's Yukinon."

In the spot Yuigahama waved to and then hurried toward was Yukinoshita. Yuigahama leaped on her and wrapped her arms around her. Yukinoshita seemed discomfited but let it happen.

"So that thing we talked about yesterday," Yuigahama said. "It looks like spring break's all full."

"That's no problem. I can get as much time as necessary during the latter half," Yukinoshita answered, gently and slowly peeling off Yuigahama, who was practically rubbing her cheeks against Yukinoshita's.

From what I overheard, I guessed they were talking about their plans for spring break or something, but still, I felt weird about joining in.

I came to a stop there, and being at loose ends created time for unnecessary thoughts. I wondered how to act natural, but I also understood I shouldn't stop there, so I moved my feet ahead, though slowly.

Then Isshiki, among the group, noticed me, and her face jerked my way. "Oh, you were here, too?"

"Well, yeah. Hey," I said.

I saw Yukinoshita check out of the corner of her eye that I was there, and our eyes met. But she immediately looked away again. The moment she blinked, my gaze slid to the side as well, toward Isshiki, who was standing diagonally across from me, so I asked her instead, "…Things going well?"

Isshiki's expression went blank, and she blinked her big eyes a few times before she quickly answered. "Well, are they? Huh?" With a slight smile, she turned the question to Yukinoshita.

"W-well, I suppose," Yukinoshita whispered under her breath, startled by the sudden question. Swiping her bangs to the side, she closed her eyes thoughtfully. "Though the process of getting started couldn't be described as the best, it's not as if there are any major issues currently."

Awfully vague way of putting it. Yuigahama and I exchanged a moment's glance. *But what does that all meeeean?*

"Well, it's, like, decent enough," Isshiki said with a casual shrug to fill the silence.

I see—that was really ridiculously difficult to understand, but I guess it's basically like, neither good nor bad.

This sort of made sense to me, but it seemed that was not the case for Yuigahama. Still clinging to Yukinoshita, she swung her arm back and forth. "Yukinon, your explanation is a mess! It sucks!"

"I-I'm sorry… Things really aren't going well enough that you could call it going smoothly, so I'm unsure of how to say it…" Yukinoshita was making plaintive noises as she blushed bright red, lowering her head in embarrassment. Her fingers fiddled with her bangs even faster, and we could hardly see her face at all.

"That's way too honest! …But it's very you to be like that, Yukinon." Yuigahama grinned and squeezed the arm she was hugging even tighter.

"You're too close…," Yukinoshita muttered in a vanishingly quiet voice, but she seemed semi-resigned to it, letting Yuigahama do what she wanted.

The two looked the same as ever, just like they'd always been, maybe even closer than before. That was a huge relief.

"…Sounds like things are okay," I said.

But Isshiki's expression turned a bit grim. "It's, like, just barely managing for now. We still don't know for sure." She tilted her head, seeking agreement.

Yukinoshita forced herself to act pleased. "I do intend to ensure we make it in time."

"You heard her," said Isshiki.

"Huh. Well, don't push yourselves," I said.

"Come on, come on, we're, like, already pushing ourselves to the brink here. I mean, it's the only way at this point. Frankly, I'd really like some extra help." Isshiki's eyes flicked over to Yukinoshita, checking with her.

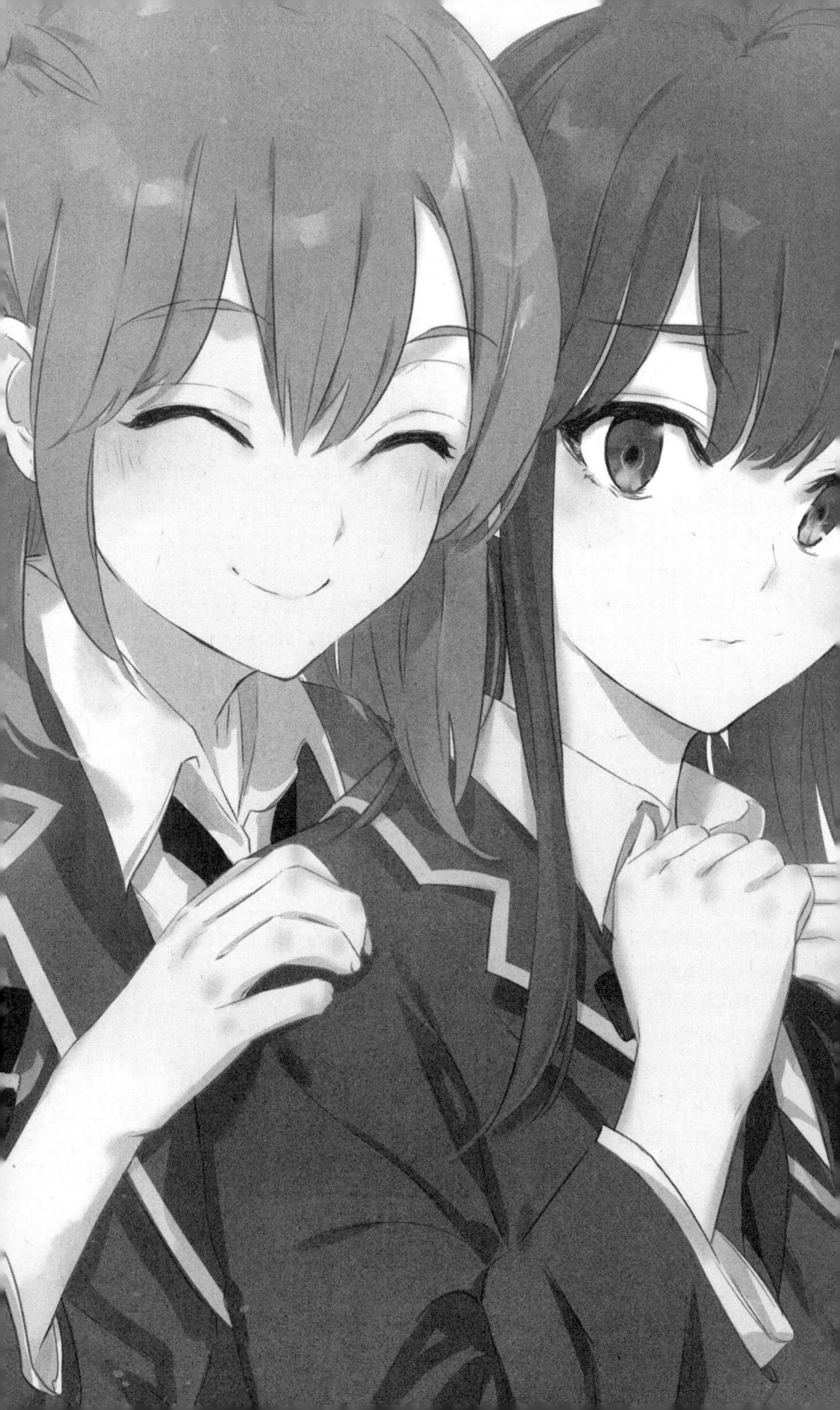

But Yukinoshita didn't reply instantly; instead, she put a hand to her mouth. She thought this over for a while before her torrent of words came. "It's true that today and tomorrow is the turning point for us, so that will mean burdening everyone... But I think we can manage without calling for any additional help thanks to all your hard work, Isshiki." She smiled brightly at the end, and Isshiki blushed, choked silent with an *urk!*

"...Well, today's no good, but I could help tomorrow or something, so let me know," I offered.

"Can you really?!"

"Isshiki," Yukinoshita chided her, "tomorrow is the tech rehearsal, so there won't be any major tasks. It won't be necessary to have a lot of people."

"Oh really...?" Yukinoshita's and my eyes converged on Isshiki. She raised her hand a bit, awkwardly. "Um, I'm, like, not a translator..."

"Sorry, I'm just really bad at Japanese," I said. "I don't feel like I can talk properly with Japanese people."

"It's got nothing to do with language! It's communication skills! Even in another language, you could never manage...," Yuigahama told me sharply.

How rude... I am actually on the better side, when it comes to body language. I'm confident that with strained smiles, profuse sweating, and sighs alone, I can tell people all over the world, *I want to go home now...*

And so, as I was sweating profusely and sighing with a wry smile, Isshiki's shoulders slumped in resignation. "Well, if that's how it is, then there's not much you can do... Yukino's bad at conversation, too, anyway."

Yukinoshita's eyebrows twitched upward. "Isshiki? You're gravely mistaken. Some argue that it's insolent to speak directly with people of higher status than you. Didn't you know?" Swishing the hair off her shoulders with the back of her hand, Yukinoshita smiled a little at Isshiki.

Isshiki was highly disturbed. "Whoa, scary..."

But, well, there is that culture, too, you know! I see. So differences in status live on in the modern world after all. Generally, you can get away with anything if you're distinguished as a member of the upper classes.

I was feeling convinced about this when, a few steps away, the student council clerk timidly addressed us. "Um, we're about to head over to the gym…"

"Oh, I'm sorry," Yukinoshita apologized to the clerk, disentangling her arm from Yuigahama. "Then we're going to go… See you."

"Yeah, see you." Yuigahama waved a hand lightly; Yukinoshita nodded back at her, then prompted Isshiki and the others with a *Let's go* gesture, and they started walking off.

Right before we parted, Isshiki scooted over to me, put a hand on my shoulder, and used it as support to stretch up a bit and whisper in my ear. "…Please help on the day of. Actually, you're totally welcome whenever."

"If I have the time…"

"I know you have nothing better to do, so you should just admit you're gonna help. You're such a hassle."

I bent my back away from her to escape the sweet breath that wafted at my ear, and Isshiki puffed up her cheeks at me. Then, grumbling, she trotted on after Yukinoshita and the others.

I watched them go; then Yuigahama and I turned around and headed for the entrance.

"I'm glad it looks like things'll go well," Yuigahama said brightly.

"Yeah," I replied as I asked myself some questions.

Will it go well? Will I be able to behave better?

As we walked away, the distance between us grew. Already, our places to go were in two different directions.

Our relationship had ultimately been only temporary, established because of a special environment. Since that situation had fallen apart, of course the distance between Yukinoshita and me would grow.

Just as I had grown used to that time and that space.

This relationship would also stop feeling uncomfortable to me. I'm sure.

After getting used to it and getting along, where it gets you in the end is forgetting—and I'm sure I'll get used to that distance, too.

Prelude 3...

When I was done speaking, she sighed.

"Oh...," she murmured, and then she fell silent.

As the night went on, a coldness joined the blowing wind.

Listening to the rustling of the leaves in the treetops, I found myself holding my own arms. Perhaps it wasn't just the wind making me feel chilly, but the silence that had grown in that brief time. I watched her, wondering what she would say, and suddenly, our eyes met.

She smiled, sliding over the bench to get close to me. And then she asked gently, "What did you talk about?" Her big, round eyes twinkled with mischief as she looked at me coyly.

Her gaze was kind, and I could see a glimmer of wisdom lurking beneath her curiosity. Her wide-opened eyes were moist from trying so hard to never show that cleverness. I love that kindness of hers so much.

I didn't feel like I could hide anything from that searching gaze. Just like when I'd told him, I put together the words slowly, with no deception. "I told him about...how it was fun...and how the past year we've had together was full of firsts for me, and unknowns, and that it was very...fun."

I was rambling, but she looked down and closed her eyes, nodding over each thing as she listened. Eventually, she looked up again, with a smile this time, but it seemed bashful and somewhat sad.

"I feel the same way… It's weird. It's like this is the end."

It made my eyebrows sink down, too. "Yes, because it is."

"Huh?" she replied. But there was no surprise in her expression. That was to be expected. We'd always been conscious of the ending, ever since this winter began after all.

"I mean the competition. It's over."

Her expression darkened into gloom, exactly as if the light had been flicked off. "I wish you wouldn't just end it without asking. I don't intend to let it stop…at all…"

"Sorry… I'm sorry. But I want to end it now." I couldn't smooth things over, and my feeble attempt spilled out of me. I should have been able to find a better way to put it, but it was difficult to avoid the truth without lying, so instead, I squeezed her hand. "I want to grant your wish, at least. Because your wish is my wish, too."

"…That's not what I want." She squeezed my hand back. It wasn't very hard, but there was warmth in it. She looked up, long eyelashes trembling as she stared at me firmly. "I want everything. Like this forever—everything."

That was what she'd said to me on that snowy day.

Those words had probably spurred me into action. Ever since I'd heard them, ever since he'd rejected them, always…

I believe that wish was something she, I, and he all shared in common. Something we all dreamed of. Or so I would imagine—those days had been so comfortable. That was also why I understood that it was unlikely her wish could be granted just as it was.

"…I can't make things be completely the same, but I believe they will be similar." *This is the right way to be. This must be the correct conclusion.* "I'm sure he will make everything come true."

She's the one person I can call a friend. Because it's her, I wanted him to grant it for her. But I felt awkward about saying something so terribly selfish and sentimental, so I remained silent as I gazed at her.

"I don't know…" She tilted her head with a strained, helpless smile, smooshing and stroking her bun. "I feel like he'd do it in a really unexpected way, so it's honestly hard to ask…"

I couldn't help but grin. Well, she was completely right. If you considered how things had gone in the past, it wasn't difficult to imagine. He'd always granted people's wishes through methods that never would have occurred to us or in ways we didn't even want.

That reminded of a short story I'd read a long time ago. "…I understand that a little. It's like the monkey's paw."

"A monkey? What?" She tilted her head and blinked.

That was kind of cute; I flashed my teeth in a grin. "It's nothing… I'm talking about how a twisted person won't be honest about his feelings."

"Definitely. He should just do things normally, but, like, he's so weird about everything…" She sighed, which I found amusing.

"Indeed. I wish he would put himself in the position of those forced to go along with it."

"Really."

We were both laughing, but suddenly, a pain ran through my chest.

The realization that we would no longer be dragged into his reckless schemes cut off my laughter.

She must have wondered about that unnatural silence, as her anxious gaze questioned me, but I shook my head in response.

"…Where should we go for spring break?" I brought up something completely unrelated, making an effort to smile at her.

I knew my expression was abnormal, poorly executed, and awkward, but nevertheless, I would have to get better at smiling from the next day onward.

The truth was I didn't know what sort of expression I was supposed to make, and I couldn't figure out whether to meet her eyes. I wasn't sure if I could speak naturally, and I didn't have a single idea of what to say for small talk. I couldn't remember how I had acted before.

But even so…

…I'm sure I will get better and better at it. I'll be able to do it one day.

3

Surely, he will **remember that season** every time he smells that scent.

We had rented a room in the karaoke parlor by the station. Bass was pounding through the wall from the next room over. If you pressed your head to the wall with your face turned to the ceiling, you could hear it even clearer.

Actually, that was the only thing I *could* hear.

How strange, when there's seven people in this room…

Though this was a fairly large room for our group size, nobody was even talking, never mind singing—all that could be heard was coughing, sighing, and the slurping of drinks from the drink bar through straws.

The only other sound was the cold strike of plastic on plastic. I glanced over toward the noise and saw Yumiko Miura leaning on one hand, tapping on her phone with displeasure.

Ebina and Yuigahama sat to either side of her in a line, while I was beside Yuigahama with a little space between us. After me was Zaimokuza, Sagami, and then Hatano, all seated on the gently curved sofa.

Right in the middle where I sat was the borderline that cleanly divided us into boys and girls, and it kinda made me feel like Moses. But thanks to being in the middle, I had a clear view of how things were going on both sides.

There was Miura, annoyed, and Ebina, totally unfazed. Yuigahama was smiling helplessly. Meanwhile, Zaimokuza and the UG Club guys were fidgeting restlessly as their eyes wandered all over.

This was supposed to be the after-party for the dummy prom, but there wasn't a speck of fun to be found anywhere in this room, except perhaps in the fun-ereal atmosphere.

Back in the UG Club room, I could have sworn they'd been excited about this, but now they were so quiet. *You guys are way too chill. Did you take some downers or something? I don't think this is what they mean by "getting down."*

Well, this was the first time the UG Club guys had met Miura's clique, so some discomfort was inevitable. Our species will immediately look down on our brethren, but women will activate our shyness. And when you get to my level, you're more than just shy—you'll take it for granted that you're twice shy, three times shy. I always feel like a newbie. Once a freshman, always a freshman.

As a result, I hadn't opened my mouth even once in front of Ebina and Miura.

Since nobody was singing and the mood was silently declining, Yuigahama tugged at my sleeve and whispered in my ear, "H-Hikki... This is kind of awkward..." A refreshing scent with citrus notes tickled my nose, and her whisper in my ear tingled like a play bite.

"Seriously...," I said with a sigh, twisting around. This may have been the first time I'd ever agreed with anything so earnestly and sincerely. *You're too close... That's embarrassing, okay?! Particularly when you do it when other people are here! Look, Miura and Ebina are staring! But it's not like I hate it, so please do it another time!*

Communicating that to Yuigahama with my eyes, I inched away. Her expression turned momentarily questioning, but once she figured out what I was trying to do, her gaze jerked away shyly. *Now we're good...* I was sighing in relief when she gave my sleeve a slightly weaker tug, sliding toward me to close the distance again. *Why?*

"Hikki, do something..."

"Uh, I can't...," I answered with a forced smile, maintaining my cool as I leaned slightly forward. Gently removing Yuigahama's fingers from my sleeve, I contemplated silently in the Gendo pose.

In this situation, any attempt to create excitement would be as cringeworthy as trying to sing a duet by myself. Knocking out Zaimokuza with the karaoke remote and heading straight out the door even seemed like an option.

"So, like, what did you tell Miura and Ebina?" I asked her.

"Huh? I said it was karaoke with you and the guys…," she said like it was nothing, cocking her head.

"I'm actually impressed they came after that explanation… Is Miura a ridiculously good person or what…?"

"You didn't say anything to Snowflake and the guys, either…"

"'Cause if I did, they wouldn't have come." The Zaimokuza, Sagami, and Hatano trio were in fact glaring at me resentfully right at that moment.

But we couldn't stay like this forever.

So for now, I reached out to prepare myself to whack Zaimokuza with the remote, and that was when a hand smacked my wrist. It was followed by a tug on my sleeve—this time from my other side…

I looked over to see Zaimokuza with moist and wibbling eyes, looking at me like a big abandoned dog. "H-Hachiman…"

"Shut up, Zaimokuza. Shut up. Be quiet."

"I haven't said a thing this whole time, though. This is so awkward." He was whispering, but because his vocals were ridiculously clear, I could hear him perfectly. That may have been why Hatano and Sagami scooted over to me as well.

"…Seriously. If I asked a hundred people, *Is this a wake?*, a hundred and eight of them would answer yes," Hatano piped up.

"You're including tax…?" I groaned.

"I hear it's going up…," said Sagami with a bitter look just like Hatano's. They were both speaking in the tiniest whispers.

See, before you know it, we've got two more, and it's a hundred and ten people. A ten percent tax rate!

But this whispered conversation didn't last long. The heavy air filling the whole room smothered their snickers, too. When cold laughter turned to dreary sighs, all the boys as a group quietly checked out the situation on the other side.

Miura was bouncing her folded leg and spinning her loosely curled hair in her fingers, not at all trying to hide her boredom. The boys were all withered.

Although Miura's attitude was fearsome at first glance, you might call it kind from another angle. She was expressing her dissatisfaction and disgruntlement with her whole body, emitting a *Don't talk to me* aura, which was simpler to deal with. We didn't have to force ourselves to be involved with her, which was less stress for us.

But Yuigahama must have been worried about Miura, as she slid over the sofa to stick up against Miura's side and started tapping at the remote. "Yumiko, what do you wanna sing?" she said, bumping her friend playfully with her shoulder.

"…Hmm…" It seemed Miura couldn't ignore that. Unenthusiastic as she was, she did reluctantly look down at the remote Yuigahama passed to her.

The two of them brought their faces close, and as they were whispering to each other, Miura's mood gradually seemed to improve, and occasionally, she would let out smothered giggles or smack at Yuigahama's thigh. Seen from the outside, it looked like a pair of good friends fooling around together, a very moe-ful scene indeed.

So leaving Miura to Yuigahama… Our problem is this one right here, I thought, stealing a glance at Ebina.

Though she had been wearing a huge grin this whole time, it was born of a politeness that kept you from seeing deep into her eyes. *This is it. This is the real scary one…* When someone deals with you in a mature way, it's hard to know what they're really thinking. How are you supposed to respond?

Is this quite all right? I wondered when Ebina suddenly opened her mouth.

"The UG Club plays games, right?"

"Ah, yes." Hatano twitched in response, answering all in a fluster. Though Sagami didn't say anything, he was nodding at high speed.

Confirming their reactions, Ebina smiled brightly. "Ohhh. What kind of games do you play?"

"Uh, board games and stuff…"

"Ohhh, board games, huh? I play them a lot, too."

"Oh, really?"

"They're really popular right now, huh?"

"Yeah."

"Like Werewolf."

"Yeah…"

"And escape games?"

"…Yeah." Hatano and Sagami took turns replying to Ebina.

All these yeah, yeah, yeah, yeah, yeahs looping over and over into a fadeout. Is this a 90s J-pop song?

Ebina's show of consideration resulted in superficial communication, but it was still akin to conversation. Unfortunately, this did little to relieve the tension.

Tangibly feeling the air slowly but certainly inching into gloom, I breathed a long and anemic sigh. When I happened to look beside me, Zaimokuza's lips were flapping like a goldfish. I get that. It makes you imagine the oxygen has gotten thinner, huh?

Zaimokuza and I caught each other's gaze for just an instant out of the corners of our eyes and nodded just a tick. We whispered to each other in voices so quiet, our vocal cords barely moved.

"This is bad, huh?"

"Indeed it is."

"Should we deepen this conversation?"

"Wouldn't that only deepen the wound?"

"Indeed."

We fell silent again, expelling weak, faint sighs instead of words.

Flat conversation is worse than silence. With silence in particular, Zaimokuza and I are Seagal-level professionals. This miserable conversation was like an insipid dating event. I had to maintain my silence until it was over. I was practically putting myself into a meditative state when suddenly the end came.

"That's nice. Board games are fun. What other stuff do you do?" Ebina asked nonchalantly with the faintest smile. Sagami and Hatano both looked at each other. Their glasses flashed.

Seeing this, Zaimokuza's antenna went up like he sensed something, and he pleaded in an ultra-quiet voice, "N-no, don't!" as his hand reached out very slightly. But it was such a minute gesture, the UG Club guys didn't notice his call for restraint.

Sagami adjusted his glasses. "Well, we're not limited to only major games such as Catan and Scotland Yard… We also play the classics like chess, shogi, and reversi, as well as lateral thinking puzzles that can be played without special pieces."

"Of course, we also go to Game Market to play the newest games. There's also tabletop RPGs, I suppose. Lately, there's *CoC*—ah, that's *Call of Cthulhu*—and such. Well, ultimately our goal is to design one ourselves, so we do intend to try some of everything. We have a variety in the clubroom if you're interested, so we can play anytime." Hatano pushed up his glasses with an arrogant smirk. The two of them had rattled that off so fluently, it was as if their stammering answers until now had never happened.

…Why is it we get talkative when it's our field of specialty? Whenever someone gives us an opportunity and acts interested in our hobbies, we have the bad habit of seizing the chance to establish dominance.

The UG Club guys' nostrils were flared wide as they huffed with satisfaction, but Zaimokuza and I were dying from the secondhand embarrassment. We were dying over here.

Nonetheless, Ebina was as impressive as ever. With her understanding of our species, she showed no particular reaction, nodding and casually ignoring the ranting. "Yeah, huh." A noncommittal and inoffensive remark.

Yuigahama and Miura sitting next to her, however, were slack-jawed. "They were talking crazy-fast…"

"Whoa…"

Though neither of them said much, it was plain and apparent from their words and faces that they were incredibly weirded out. Actually, Miura was physically jerking away. *Don't do that—for their sakes. Please?*

Sagami and Hatano both noticed that, and their previous confidence transformed into grimaces as they tried to cover their discomfort. They hung their heads weakly.

In the end, the suffocating air returned.

Looks like we're screwed now…, I thought, ready to give up, when there was a knock on the door.

I wondered if the food we'd ordered had come. Without waiting for a response, somebody kicked the door open with a loud bang.

"Whoooo!"

"Whoooo!"

Thumping his way in with his nasty, thick voice was Kakeru Tobe, and twincooling his way in with his delightfully pretty voice was Saika Totsuka. Even when he says the same thing, why is it so much cuter when he does it? Totsuka is too Totsucute, isn't he? Twincool! ☆

Then Hayato Hayama popped in from behind the two of them. He was carrying a tray with a bunch of different drinks from the drink bar.

"Sorry for the wait, Hachiman," said Totsuka.

"Ohhh, Totsuka. So you came," I said, shoving Zaimokuza aside, to open up a space there. The plan here was that Totsuka would automatically come to sit next to me! I tremble at my own godlike manipulation, if I may say so myself.

Wait, I invited Totsuka from the beginning, but the other two…? I thought, directing a questioning look over at Hayama and Tobe, who were sitting next to Miura and the girls.

Totsuka picked up on that and sheepishly said, "Oh, we happened to bump into each other on the way back…and when I mentioned karaoke, Tobe…"

"Ohhh, I get it…"

Tobe shrewdly secured the spot next to Ebina, excitedly and blushingly mussing the hair at the back of his head. "Huh? So you guys were here, too? Whoa, I had no idea! Isn't this totally a coincidence?"

He was putting up an absolutely garbage act. But this time, I'd be willing to give him an Oscar that's not from the trash bin.

Hayama and the guys showing up seemed to make Miura a lot more comfortable, and the seats on the other side turned peaceful... Well, the UG Club guys were not having a great time, but this was somewhat preferable compared with the icy malaise before.

Conversation grew all around the room, and once things had shifted into something more befitting an after-party, Yuigahama tapped on my shoulder. "Should we have a toast?"

"...Should we?" I said, twisting my lips upward as hard as I could.

"You really seem like you don't want to...," Totsuka said beside me with a strained smile.

"Someone who's cut out for that sort of thing should do it," I said, glancing over at the perfect candidate. He must have heard us talking, because Hayama glanced over at us and shrugged. Then he returned to his conversation with Miura. I figured Hayama really wasn't very nice after all...

Still, I was the one who'd come up with the dummy prom plan, which was the reason we were having this after-party. If there were going to be thank-yous, it would make sense for me to be doing the toast or remarks.

"...Well, I guess I'll just say a few words," I said, which pleased Yuigahama, and Totsuka did a little wave in front of his chest.

With their kind reactions prodding me onward, I cleared my throat in a slightly dramatic manner and stood with my glass in hand. "If I could be so bold as to say a few words..."

Yuigahama and Totsuka clapped like, *Hear, hear!* The others were confused, but the desire to go along with things made them clap as well.

I wasn't used to this, so it felt a little difficult to get through, but I gave my opening remark. "...Um, while we're at the height of festivities..."

"That's what you say when an event is over," Hayama said with exasperation as I was taking a breath.

Giving him a *Shut up, shut up, I'm talking now, I'm talking now!* sort of gesture, I continued my brief statement. "Thanks for the other day. Everything went well because of you guys. Thank you. And so, a toast." It was a simple pronouncement, but once I said it, everyone repeated it in chorus, clinking their glasses with those nearby.

This was finally looking something like an after-party, somehow. With a sigh of relief, as if to say, *Please enjoy*, I sank into the sofa.

× × ×

I suppose this was the moment when you'd say the festivities were at their Hakonesia Peak. Right now, everyone looked like they were having the most fun.

Though at first there had been some discord between the UG Club and Miura and Ebina, Hayama had smoothly mediated between the two groups, and thanks to him, a sprinkle of conversation had begun on both sides. When Tobe took the lead to start singing, Totsuka shyly followed. That momentum grew until everyone took turns singing.

So then, of course, it came Zaimokuza and the UG Club's turn to sing, but…Hayama helped out there, too. He smoothly input anime songs from bands known for being from Chiba, gave a comment like "Do you know this one?" sang a bar of the first hook, and nonchalantly handed over the microphone. Zaimokuza timidly accepted it, and when the UG pair followed, everyone felt like they could have a shot.

It was a high-level technique, bringing up the idea in such a way that Zaimokuza and the guys could have fun while also indirectly showing them that Hayama's clique also knew songs like this.

As usual, Hayama was sharp. Let him handle superficial socializing like this; he's a genius at it…

As I was watching Hayama, half awestruck and half ultra-freaked out, someone else's eyes were on him, too.

"Hayama is such a good guy…"

"I feel like this is the first time I've met an older kid worth looking up to…"

Hatano and Sagami were practically entranced, eyes filled with tears as they stared at Hayama. Then they regarded me and Zaimokuza with disdainful, mocking scoffs.

But I fully understood that Hayama was of a different class, so I wasn't going to get mad about the comparison now. *Listen, though, should you really be having it show on your faces that blatantly? I don't think that's very nice. Perhaps I should make a naggingly snide comment right now as your elder. As your elder! Because that's what elders do!*

So I clapped a hand on Sagami's shoulder, since he just happened to be the closer one. "Huh, so you like Hayama, huh? You have the same taste as your sister. You're a lot like her."

"Tsk!" Sagami clicked his tongue with extra aggression and scowled.

That's it—that's the expression that turns you into her spitting image. Heh-heh, that's exactly what I wanted to see...

As I was snickering with my dark joy, Zaimokuza shrugged, letting out an exasperated sigh. "Hachiman, that's exactly why they said that."

Even Zaimokuza's sniping at me for this... And hey, they don't respect you, either.

But I'd basically launched a surprise attack on some younger students to take them to an after-party, then been nasty to them on top of that, so I probably deserved it. Of course they'd disparage me.

As I was thinking about how I'd make up for it, Totsuka suddenly patted my thigh. His touch was so soft; desperately swallowing the weird noise threatening to escape me, I asked with my eyes, *What is it?*

"I'm gonna go get a drink." Totsuka tilted his head and waved his empty glass. He had to mean I should let him through so he could go to the drink bar.

That gave me a light-bulb moment. "Oh, I'll go. I'll get refills for everyone else, too, while I'm at it."

"Are you sure?"

That question implied hesitation. Apparently, Totsuka was offering to come with me, so I shot a wink at him like *ba-ding!* ☆ Basically, *Leave it to me.*

"Well, since I'm already up."

I hopped to my feet to keep him from protesting, retrieved the glasses from atop the table, and scooted out of the room.

With the glasses on the tray, I heaved myself to the drink bar.

Then, in front of the espresso machine, I discovered Miura, spinning her loose sausage curls around her fingers as she pondered over something—what to drink, I'm assuming.

She noticed me but didn't say anything. Well, it's not like I'm gonna talk to her, so that makes two of us!

I stood in front of the dispenser beside her and started to pour some cold drinks. Miura was standing about half a step farther back than me as she reached out to press the cappuccino button. From the espresso machine came a groan, followed by steam and the sound of coffee pouring in. I peeked out of the corner of my eye, right when white foam was rising to the brim atop the black espresso.

Opening her mouth, Miura muttered, "Hey..."

I wasn't sure who that was directed at, but it was a little loud to be talking to herself. I turned my head toward her, thinking she was addressing me, but her eyes were focused on the cup on the machine.

White foam slowly spread over the surface of the drink, until a couple of bubbles popped.

"What're you thinking?" she said.

"About what?" I finally managed an answer, now certain she was talking to me, but her question was too vague, and it didn't quite make sense. My hands never stopped, taking out one glass to replace it with another beneath the machine.

The karaoke parlor's advertisements, the singing seeping out from nearby rooms, the low humming of the dispenser, the clink of glasses—there were so many noises all around, but it felt weirdly quiet.

Eventually, a faint sigh joined the silence. "About Yui...," she said.

A surprise attack! I stopped my busy hands—no, they stopped on their own.

"...Ah." I offered her a meaningless reply to fill the silence, but I regretted it. I should have pretended I didn't know what she was talking about. Or maybe I should have fully committed to ignoring her.

I couldn't do that, because there was something still bothering me. So she'd caught me unawares, and I'd replied without thinking.

Miura's breath caught softly, and it seemed like she was patiently waiting for me to continue.

But I had nothing to say. My desire to be sincere kept any words from coming out.

I understood that it was cowardly to say nothing here, but so was exhausting all my words in an attempt to gain Miura's understanding.

When I said nothing, Miura snatched up her cup impatiently. It clinked as she set it on her tray, and she sighed in irritation. "It's not like we're friends or anything, and I don't care about you, so it's like whatever," she said, starting out more roughly, but then she exhaled quietly. Her tone turned gentle and hoarse. "…But it's different with Yui." There was a quality to her voice that made me think she'd been crying, so I felt compelled to make eye contact.

There wasn't a single teardrop there—the depths of her eyes actually held a blazing fire. "So if you're gonna do something, could you just commit? That sort of thing pisses me off." Her bold glare made my breath catch. It was fair to say she had overwhelmed me.

Not at all because she was frightening or scary—I think I was overwhelmed by her kindness.

Thinking about it, she'd always been watching out for the people in her life with an earnestness that was borderline arrogant. Of course she was like that with Hayama and Ebina, and she clearly also cared about how Yuigahama was doing, too. And since the Service Club hadn't really been doing anything lately, Miura would have had lots of opportunities to spend time with Yuigahama, so she'd have some things on her mind.

Though her gaze was not truly directed at me, it was still strong enough to pierce through me.

I was sure that if I said something irresponsible just to get out of this, she would catch me instantly.

"…I'll do my best," I said with a nod. There were no lies in that, but no truth, either. But I couldn't think of anything else appropriate to say.

Miura glared at me but eventually swept the hair off her shoulders and snorted like she was bored. "That's all. Bye." And to tell me the conversation was now over, she spun around and left.

Watching her go, I couldn't help but mutter to myself, "She's a good person…"

I hadn't thought I'd said it very loudly, but it was loud enough for Miura. She froze on the spot. Then she turned half back to me. "Huh? What's that supposed to mean? Ew," she sneered, her expression twisting in distaste. She twirled her loose golden curls around a finger as she strode off even more briskly than before.

I caught a glimpse of her pink cheeks behind her swaying hair, and I muttered the same thing to myself as before, but under my breath this time.

× × ×

When I returned to the booth, it was Hayama's turn to sing.

Everyone was swinging and bouncing the glow sticks that Hatano and Sagami must have supplied. They were whooping and yelling their names and doing fan chants and all kinds of stuff, and the flashing disco ball was really adding to the wild party vibe. For some reason, Tobe was swinging around a wet mini-towel. He'd clearly lost his head. Anyway, there was a lot of enthusiasm.

Miura was the one person amid this spectacle who was entranced as she swayed a penlight side to side. *She looks so happy, totally nothing like before… I'm glad the queen is having fun…*

Ignoring the fervor of the room, I set the drinks on the table and plopped onto the sofa.

I can't get into moods like this. I never know where to put myself.

Of course it went without saying for Tobe and Yuigahama and that crowd, but even Zaimokuza and the UG Club guys seemed used to this from *otaku* events, but the most I could do was keep the beat with my knee as I bounced my leg.

It's not like I was trying to be cynical about this. It's just that I get shy—like, it's almost embarrassing to see myself getting all excited and loud. So I put up this whole cool act. But just knowing about it doesn't mean I can fix it!

All I could do was do my best to watch the thigh Totsuka was smacking with a tambourine.

As I was leaning on my arm, sipping my coffee, and staring off into space, Yuigahama noticed me and came to my side. "This is kinda nice, huh?"

"What is?" I asked.

Yuigahama's gaze slowly swept the whole room. She let a sigh of relief slip out and beamed at me. "...Everyone kinda, like, getting along. Having fun."

"Well, I figured they would with the right trigger. Cringe *otaku* and country skids have basically the same mental processes after all," I said, glancing over at the guys to check out Tobe and the UG Club in particular, and Zaimokuza while I was at it.

Yuigahama pouted huffily. "It's not like we're wasting time... And similar how? Aren't we total opposites?"

"The two groups have a lot of things in common. Getting cocky when you're a part of the in-group, liking shiny things, a tendency to wear black clothing..."

"That sounds more like a crow..."

"Nah. Crows are smarter."

"That's so mean!" Yuigahama cried out in mild reproach, but if you looked at Tobe whooping as he swung around a towel or Zaimokuza yelling, "Yeah, tiger!" as he spread light pollution with his ultra-orange glowstick, it wouldn't be hard to come to the same conclusion I did...

Honestly, I do think this theory that cringe *otaku* and country skids have basically the same mind-set isn't necessarily wrong. Besides, those hometown-bound trashy kids will often be into anime and manga and stuff.

I've heard stories that back in the day, when the so-called *otaku* quadrant brought manga to school, you'd have delinquents reading it during class and totally getting into it, and then they'd even borrow more. And if we're talking even older demographics, I hear their introduction to anime was through pachinko or pachinko-slot machines.

Anime and manga are seen as representative of pop culture, and in the modern era, as the discriminatory, disdainful implication has faded from the word *otaku*, the gap between the two groups has shrunk even further.

There are plenty of examples of regular businesses doing collaborations to produce anime merch, and even on TV variety shows, *otaku* culture is more often spoken of in a positive way. It's undeniable that part of that is commercial intent, but still, it's clear that the groundwork has been laid for its broad acceptance.

Seniors aside, if we're talking about the younger demographic, the era when people will criticize you just for liking anime and video games is over. The spread of social media and video upload sites has made trends and popularity more clearly visualized, leading to the sense that *otaku* culture has even been established as a fashion.

We are in an age when trend-hopping high school girls are playing FPSs on their phones, anime- and game-related keywords are trending in rows on social media, and e-sports are on their way to becoming Olympic events. Though *otaku* culture was once a subject for contempt, the urge to shun it has clearly waned. Though it would be a stretch to claim that anime—and what's commonly referred to as moe anime in particular—is generally accepted, though.

But it's certain that anime culture has become familiarized among young people.

This is particularly striking when it comes to music-related things. The rankings on the hit charts go without saying, but you can even see the trend in real-life events. Famous DJs and composers will often make songs for voice actors and anime openings or endings, and you can also see many examples of sampling used as a subcultural sign. There are more anime song events at clubs. I hear that even at large events you'd assume would have no connection to the *otaku* world, some DJs will put on anime songs. People go nuts for it.

When it comes to music in particular, it's not contradictory to combine the nerds and the cool kids.

Actually, I figure since extroverts' and partiers' value systems are based solely on what they consider fun, they wouldn't necessarily hate something just because it's from something nerdy. As long as they have their friends and their crowd there, they can enjoy anything. That's what the extroverted partier "Whoo!" type is all about.

And Tobe does actually really seem to be having fun right now…

As I was pondering these matters, Yuigahama slid her shoulder up to mine. I reflexively drew back and tried to put distance between us, but she tugged on my sleeve, keeping me from moving away.

I still tried to twist around, but she cupped a hand around her mouth. I supposed she wanted to tell me a secret. If she was going to be like that, then I had to listen. Tilting my head slightly, I moved my ear closer.

The room was filled with the booming of the speakers and everyone's shrieks, but her murmur tickled in my chest. I could hear her clearly. "…Wanna come over on Saturday?"

I doubted my ears, and when I gave her a look out of the corner of my eye, Yuigahama was bashfully playing with her bun.

I replied on reflex before I could even think of what she meant. "No, I don't…"

Yuigahama immediately puffed up her cheeks. "You said you were free."

"Yeah, well, I *am* free." *But that doesn't mean I have a reason to go.*

Or so I was about to continue, but Yuigahama started talking first. "Didn't you say you were gonna bake a cake for Komachi-chan's present? So I was thinking, why don't we do that?"

"Ohhh… I get it. Well, if that's what you mean…sure," I answered with a groan. "Thanks."

Right, I had asked Yuigahama before about Komachi's birthday present. That had gotten pushed to the side, what with the "self-restraint" fiasco for the prom and everything, but Yuigahama must have remembered. If she was going to be this considerate, then I couldn't say, *I dunno, it's a little embarrassing, so I can't…*

She nodded firmly and giggled. Was she looking forward to it? "Okay! My mom's gonna be there, so she can teach us lots of stuff."

"That makes this even harder…," I grumbled to myself, shoulders slumping. I don't at all hate Gaha-mama—I like her, actually. This wasn't a personal thing. When someone has the title of "female classmate's mom," I suddenly feel like she's just too much for me to handle. I am, in fact, a rather bashful blushing sweet seventeen.

However, the surrounding cheers overtook my complaints. I looked over right as Hayama finished his song, and I joined in to clap a perfunctory applause along with everyone else. Hayama bowed dramatically—quite princely, just like a curtain call. He was surprisingly good at playing along.

After the outro faded, a relaxed air momentarily hung in the room. The intro for the next song began right away, and Tobe looked around. "Who's next? Who's next?"

"Ah, me, me!" Yuigahama hopped to her feet, stepped over to Miura and Ebina, and took a mike.

Sitting in a line on the sofa, the three girls started to sing a pop tune with a swaying beat. The boys lazily waved glow sticks side to side. I don't know anything about popular songs, but it was cute to see a shy Miura singing and thinking about the boys watching, so I could get behind this!

I've got nothing else to do, so I'd kinda like a glow stick or tambourine, too, I thought, hoping someone would see my *Gimme, gimme* face. Hayama and I made eye contact. There was a quirk of a smile in the corners of his lips as he accepted a glow stick from Sagami and came over beside me. He held it out without a word, and I accepted it without a word. Though I did snap it open, I really couldn't bring myself to swing it around.

…This is awkward. I'm grateful he gave me a glow stick, but why'd he come sit here? If you've done what you came for, then could you go away? Or, like, couldn't he have just thrown a glow stick over to me?

I swayed my glow stick very unobtrusively as I exerted some wordless pressure on him, but whether he noticed or not, he pulled his own drink from the glasses still on the tray and settled in for a long stay. "You're not gonna sing?" Hayama pulled his lips off the straw to ask, his eyes now focused toward Miura and the other girls.

"Well, when you're not getting paid for your performance...," I shot back.

"Funny you'd say that after working all this time for free."

"Free? I've been constantly paying out of my own pocket. I come out in the red every time."

Neither of us looked each other in the eye as we exchanged fairly meaningless banter. It was a pointless conversation, purely for the sake of distracting us from the awkwardness.

But Hayama must have gotten into it, as he leaned slightly forward, turned to me, and smirked nastily. "So you did all that for, what, a man's pride?" he said.

My hand waving the glow stick immediately stopped. Then I covered my face. *Come on.* "...Don't you dare remember that stupid embarrassing stuff cut it out forget it never say that again I'll kill you." I was ready to tear my hair out with regret.

Hayama brought a hand to his mouth, smothering snickers of amusement. *You are such an ass.*

Eventually, his laughter settled, and he gave me a terribly mature look. "You can still come out of the red."

"Doubtful... It doesn't look like I'll get the opportunity for that now." I shrugged and faced forward to escape his eyes. I reached for my glass to indicate the discussion was over now, then took my time drinking my coffee.

Yuigahama and the girls were in front of us, now standing as they sang. The song was coming up to the big hook, and Totsuka, Zaimokuza, and the UG Club guys were getting even more into it than before. Especially Tobe, who was whooping and whacking the tambourine that had been left in the room.

In this deluge of noise, Hayama opened his mouth to murmur, "Hey, so you—," but his voice was drowned out. I couldn't bring myself to ask what he'd said or read his lips. I looked away. He didn't push again, either, just sighed.

"It's so loud..." Those words, not really directed at anyone, were swallowed by the din. Nobody heard my pointless muttering.

All that could be heard was the bright music, loud singing, and upbeat rhythm, but it sounded distant, as if from another room.

That made me remember what that person who'd been drunk—or pretending to be drunk—had said.

That's why I…

I was waiting for the phone ring that would herald the end of these festivities.

× × ×

It was the Saturday after the rowdy after-party. Normally, I would have been spending it how I pleased, lying around at home and having a relaxing time, but things were a little different today.

As per my promise the other day, I was at the Yuigahama residence, fidgeting around. This would make it the second time I'd set foot here. I'd just gone into Yuigahama's room the first time, and Yukinoshita had been with us, too.

But this time, it was just me.

What's more, she'd shown me to the living room, and I was incredibly uncomfortable there. The folded laundry, potted plants I couldn't identify, a box of tissues with a floral-pattern cover over it, dried flowers in a glass cabinet, planters lined up on the veranda, and air freshener with faint woody notes—all of it was so different from my house.

It takes a certain amount of courage for a total stranger to step into a space that has such a lived-in feel, that feels so family-oriented. Oh, no, I'm not at all saying that it doesn't take courage to go into Yuigahama's room. You do, in fact—you really need it. Tons of it.

However, there's a different nuance to the reservation I felt in the living room.

Especially when you can't see any other family members there…

Huh? I was told Gaha-mama would be here… Ever since being shown into the living room, I'd been standing there without anything to do, glancing anxiously all around.

However, there was nobody there besides Yuigahama and me, and it was all quiet. The only sounds that reached my ears were of Yuigahama, rattling around in the cupboards of the kitchen island.

She was dressed pretty casually in an outfit that must have doubled as her at-home wear: an A-line white hoodie dress and fluffy cloth slippers. This was weekend attire, for sure.

I, on the other hand, was in a navy oxford shirt and chinos. This was the safe outfit Komachi had selected for me—specifically, an outfit decent enough that she wouldn't be embarrassed to be seen with me. If I wore a nice jacket over this, I could pass as business casual.

I wasn't specifically trying to dress up; I was going for a clean look, just on the off chance I wound up coming face-to-face with Gaha-papa, so I wouldn't be rude. Or put another way, these clothes meant I was nervous.

Yuigahama, on the other hand, was comfortably humming as she started to pour tea. "I'll bring this over, so sit wherever."

"O-okay..." As told, I pulled out a chair from the dining table and sat down on one of the matched set of four closest to the door. With nothing else to do, I stared at the assorted cookbooks spread out on the table.

I was at the Yuigahama residence that day to bake a cake. The expectation was that hopefully Gaha-mama could teach me, but she was nowhere to be seen. Since it was Saturday, I'd prepared myself for Gaha-papa to possibly be around, but it seemed he wasn't home, either.

...So then...does this mean we're alone at her place?

No, hold on. There's one more member of the Yuigahama family—a fuzzy member, specifically, I thought, looking around for him, when Yuigahama came shuffling over with tea and cookies on a tray. She took a seat beside me and gave me my cup.

"Oh, thanks," I said. "...Where's Sablé, by the way?"

"Mom's walking him. I think they'll be back soon, though."

"Oh..."

She leaned her face on her hand, flipping through a cookbook and occasionally reaching for the cookies. What a homey feeling. *Well, it is her home.*

She was so relaxed here, which told me that she regularly passed her time sitting at this table with tea and cookies in hand.

By contrast, my chair must normally not have been in use. This was the only one of the four chairs that looked like it wasn't ever sat on. Her parents probably used the chairs on the opposite side.

Suddenly, I was curious about said parents, in particular the papa of the household.

"...Just for my information," I began.

"Mm-hmm?" Eyes still on the cookbook in her hands as she bit into her second cookie, Yuigahama cocked her head.

"Might I inquire as to where your father is today?"

"Why're you saying it like that? Ew." Yuigahama cackled at me.

But I couldn't laugh at all. Seeing Gaha-mama wouldn't be so bad—I'd even like to see her—but I had no idea what to do if I were to face Gaha-papa. If I were in his position, I'd most certainly kill me. No matter what kind of relationship it was, once I'd gotten anywhere near his beloved daughter, I was done for—the spirit of "kill the suspicious one."

"Isn't he at work? Not that I know," Yuigahama said quite indifferently, ignoring my concerns.

Phew... I mean, I don't know how I should greet him...

As I was relaxing my shoulders and breathing a sigh of relief, Yuigahama's chair scraped, and she scooched right up to my side. I inched my butt away by that same amount. Then she shoved the cookbook toward me in the slight space that had opened between us, meaning she intended for us to look at it together. "So, like, I considered lots of ideas, but we shouldn't pick anything too hard, right?"

"Totally. Something foolproof would be good." Propping up my face on my hand as well, I leaned my body weight to the opposite side from Yuigahama and flipped through the cookbook with my free hand.

Then whatever shall we make? I wondered with each flip of the page as photos of magnificent sweets caught my eye. Muffins, macarons, tarte tatin, financier, canelé, florentine... Every single one was so fancy and delicious-looking. Komachi would be sure to love any of them.

But whether I could make them was a different question. *Actually, there's no way... First, separate the egg yolks from the white...? Then what? What do you do with the whites, then? Spread it on? Do you spread it on?*

Yuigahama was also groaning as she perused the cookbook, but eventually, she muttered, "...If it's...cookies? Or something? I could do it? Maybe?"

She really doesn't sound sure... She tilted her head a total of five times, then tilted it one last time and flicked her eyes up at me.

With that stare glued to me, I said heavily, with real and sincere emotion, "Okay...then maybe that's something I could do, too."

"What's that supposed to mean?" She smacked me.

It didn't really hurt, but I muttered a quiet "Ow..." as I rubbed my shoulder.

Then a head poked in from behind that shoulder. It was Yuigahama's mother. She must have just returned from her walk. She was wearing a pale spring sweater and a long skirt and was carrying the family dog, Sablé, in her arms. "Hmm? I don't know about that. I think you should pick something that leaves more of an *impression*," Gaha-mama said gently as she stuck her head in between Yuigahama and me to peer at the cookbook.

When she does that, it's kinda too close and warm and soft and kinda smells really good, and I can't handle it! I know this is all coming out at once, but I mean it.

Sablé was super loud in my ear, barking and licking me... "Thank you for having me over...and for helping me today..." I managed to greet her even with Sablé's tongue in my face.

Gaha-mama smiled brightly. "Leave it to me! Mom will do her best!"

"Mom...I'll call for you later, so go away..." Yuigahama stood up with an exasperated sigh and shoved at Gaha-mama's back.

"You're the one who said *Teach me*, thouuuugh!"

"I'll call for you, okay?!" Yuigahama continued to prod at her mother, who kept resisting, and they wound up jostling like potatoes. It's so nice to see a mother and daughter goofing around...

"C-come on… She's gonna be helping us if we have any problems…" It was such a pleasant scene, I could watch it for the rest of my life—and I just might if I didn't do anything. I felt compelled to intervene.

Gaha-mama beamed at me, her ally. "Right! So then Mom should help you pick an idea, riiight?"

Yuigahama let out a dissatisfied huff. "…Okay, fine. What do you think we should make, Mom?" Reluctantly sitting back down, she pointed to the opposite chair.

Gaha-mama giggled at the gesture as she took a seat. "Since you're going to the trouble of the homemade route, I think it would be nice to pick out something thoughtful."

"Something thoughtful…" Yuigahama looked up at the ceiling, mulling this over.

"What do *you* think would be good, Hikki?" Gaha-mama hiked up Sablé higher in her arms, tilting her head so far it took her whole upper body with it. Sablé went along with her, cocking his head to the side as well.

I couldn't help but smile at such a cute sight, but I covered that with a hand. "Something thoughtful… So then something stylish and expensive-looking that gets you likes on Instagram and that you can use to assert dominance among your mommy friends…"

"Watch out how you put it, now." Gaha-mama got a slightly stiff smile, but despite chiding me for my tone, she didn't deny the gist of my remark. *Adult women are scary.*

Yuigahama gave me a pitying look, though. "You're approaching this like a housewife?!"

After considering the options for a while, I suggested, "…Ah, how about macarons?" while staring at Sablé. I was only ever staring at Sablé. I did not look at what was behind the dog and was focused intently on him. Let's call it that. As a result, many other things entered my field of vision, but there's nothing to call that but inevitability.

"*Bzzt, bzzt,*" Gaha-mama said, and I looked up to see her crossing her fingers to make a little X. *What the heck, this woman is so cute…*

Then she cleared her throat and declared in a superserious manner, "Macarons are for receiving, not for making."

"Yeah, I'd be glad to get some, eh-heh-heh." Yuigahama chuckled innocently.

But Gaha-mama put a hand to her cheek and sighed. "The problem is they're difficult to make."

Are they that much trouble? I wondered, looking at the cookbook, and indeed, there was all this stuff there about macaronage that seemed pretty high-level. And they looked fairly expensive, too. So buying or making them would be out of the question.

So then what're we gonna make, eh?

I was wondering that when Gaha-mama cleared her throat. "Mom recommends…fruuuit taaarts!"

"Huh? Aren't those hard?" Yuigahama made a *whoa* kind of face.

I did the same, nodding at Yuigahama's assessment. *Something that sounds so foreign has got to be impossible. I have basically no experience baking, and Yuigahama isn't good at this, either. Any attempt is gonna be a fail tart, you know.* I tried to make Gaha-mama understand with my eyes.

But she smiled brightly and made a sideways peace sign. ☆ Then she winked, too, sticking out her tongue while she was at it. "It's okay, it's okay! You can get store-bought crusts, and the rest is just putting it all in the cup, so no worries! ☆ And besides, once you learn how it's done, you can make them with any fruit you like," she said.

"Then maybe I could manage that, too!" Yuigahama *ooh*ed with sparkling eyes.

True enough, using ready-made products would make it a bit easier. Her explanation won me over as well. "Oh, is that right… Is that right?" With a touch of unease, my eyes slid to the person beside me.

"I—I can do it! I can! …Probably," Yuigahama declared emphatically with a clenched fist as she nodded back at me. But she added a little something unnecessary at the end.

That's what does it, those little additions. That's what makes me uneasy. She's always messing things up with variations and secret spices and "just one little extra!"

But, well, I only had to watch out for that. "All right, let's try it," I said.

"Yeah!" Yuigahama replied.

Gaha-mama saw us nod to each other, and a smile spread on her face. "All right, sooo let's go shopping." She returned our nods, and Sablé barked an enthusiastic reply, too.

Hmm, but maybe Sablé should stay home…

× × ×

It was right before dinnertime, and the Aeon grocery store close to Yuigahama's home was busy and filled with noise.

I was pushing the rattling shopping cart after Yuigahama and Gaha-mama through the bustling store. The basket was piled two levels high with rice, meat, and snacks, and there was a firm weight in the cart handle. They were getting not only baking ingredients, but also the family's groceries while they were at it.

Gaha-mama, walking ahead, glanced back at me with a bright smile. "Sorry for buying so many heavy things, dear!"

"Oh, no, I'm used to this stuff." I accompanied my mom and Komachi sometimes, and I'd shopped with them a lot when I was little. I'd tackled the challenge of how to toss candy into a shopping cart so that your mom wouldn't find out… Yuigahama was doing it in front of me right now!

But this might have been the first time I'd really paid attention to what was around a grocery store. When I went with my mom or Komachi to carry stuff, all I ever did was follow instructions, and when I went shopping on my own, I was usually following instructions to go buy this or that. Then they'd ask me, "Why did you buy this?" and they'd be so grumpy about it. I don't know the difference between silk and cotton; they both taste good…

Since that was the level of shopping skill I possessed, about the only way I could be useful here was by carrying the stuff, so therefore I followed three steps behind Gaha-mama.

"It *really* is different when you have a boy with you. This feels like a new experience!" she said.

With such conversation occasionally interspersed, we circled the grocery store and came to the produce section. There were vegetables, of course, as well as various kinds of fruit, which was what we were after. They had the standard things like bananas, apples, and oranges, as well as a wide range of rare-looking tropical fruit that made me want to specifically check, like, *So then you guys are kiwi-papaya-mango, right?*

"So what sort of fruits will we have?" Standing in front of the produce, Gaha-mama folded her arms and touched her hand to her cheek as she considered with a *hmm*.

Yuigahama's hand shot up energetically. "Peaches!"

"Peaches won't be in season for a while yet. Those come in summer." Gaha-mama spoke gently, but she shot that idea down instantly.

"Oh, really…? I thought peach season was around now…"

"Well, they are kinda springlike." Many of the snacks Yuigahama had been tossing into the shopping cart were actually peach flavored. Well, there is the Peach Festival, so maybe that influences people's impressions. Food manufacturers probably leverage that image for their sales strategies, since March is when they sell seasonal products like white peach-flavored juice, *chuuhai*, and snacks. So it doesn't quite click when you hear there's a different season for peaches.

In the modern era, where we take imports and greenhouse cultivation for granted, I feel like it's gotten hard to grasp what seasons foods come in. This is where a certain manga scenario writer I know of would be saying, *But Japanese food manufacturers are at fault, too.* Who was it that made the white peach flavor?!

As I was pondering such thoughts, Gaha-mama stepped forward. "In season right now are…straaawberrieees!" she said, pointing to the very front of the display, the section that stood out the most, and the packs of strawberries. With the bright vertical banner and a cute pop-up sign, it was just like the Great Star Palace Strawberry Festival.

"Huhhh, that's kind of surprising. Strawberries feel more wintry." Bending at her waist, Yuigahama brought her face close to the strawberries and sniffed at them, her cheeks relaxing as she chuckled. "Smells nice…"

"Then let's do a strawberry tart." I started reaching for them when Gaha-mama gently took my arm and stopped me.

"No, no!" Her whisper brushed my ear, making my upper body jerk backward. That, combined with the sweet scent wafting around the grocery store, made me feel ticklish all over. It just about startled a weird noise out of me, but I gulped that down and gave her a confused glance.

Gaha-mama solemnly stuck up a finger. "Strawberries aren't suited for home baking."

"O-oh, really…?" *How curious… But there are so many sweets out there that use strawberries. How curious. How long is she going to keep holding my arm? How curious. I don't hate it at all.*

As I was wondering this, Yuigahama pulled her mom's hand away and cut between us. "Why not? I feel like there are tons of strawberry sweets."

"That's exactly why. You have plenty of opportunities to eat strawberries, don't you? You've got to make something that will leave a stronger impression," she said.

I looked at Yuigahama beside me like, *What does she mean?* and Yuigahama shook her head like, *I dunno.*

And so Yuigahama and I looked to Gaha-mama like, *So what's the right answer, m'lady?*

Then, instead of an answer, Gaha-mama smiled brightly and asked me something else. "What kind of fruit do you like, Hikki?"

Now that she was expressly asking me, nothing came to mind right away.

As I was pondering this, Yuigahama answered instantly. "Peanuts, right?!"

"Why did you just reply for me? And, remember, fruit. Fruit, okay? We're talking about fruit right now."

"But, Hikki, you love Chiba, so..."

"Hey, you're not thinking you should have the Chibanese eat peanuts, are you?"

Hey, did you know? Peanuts aren't fruit or nuts or donuts. They're legumes. There's a factoid for you. I was just about to display this knowledge with a smug expression, but before I could, Yuigahama pouted at me.

"So then what do you like?" she asked, disgruntled.

"If I have to pick, then pears, I guess. Chiba pears are the best in Japan—no, in the world."

"I knew you'd pick a Chiba thing!"

"Well, Chiba is a part of the reason, but I do just like pears. I especially like Kosui pears—of course there's the flavor, but their crisp texture is great, too. They're so good. My family buys a whole box in the summer."

"You're way more hard-core than I thought! Scary!"

It wasn't like I was going on a particularly intense rant, but Yuigahama's freaking out... How strange... I just answered what she asked me, though...

Gaha-mama, on the other hand, wasn't particularly bothered; she put a hand to her chin as she considered seriously. "Hmm... There aren't any pears at this time of year, either... Well, if it's peaches, there are canned ones."

"Oh, canned peaches are good...," Yuigahama muttered with a pleased-looking grin.

She really does love peaches..., I was thinking with a sidelong glance at her, when Gaha-mama nodded *mm-hmm,* coming to some kind of conclusion.

"Mm, then conversely, that might be good. Canned saves you the trouble of making compote, too."

"Uhhh, conversely...?" As I was tilting my head like, *Conversely to what?* Yuigahama was tilting her head, too.

"Hmm... *compote*..." Yuigahama muttered the English word. "I see... Worry-free and easy..."

"Mm-hmm." Her mother nodded.

That's definitely not the right word—that would be comfort. Whether Gaha-mama noticed her daughter's mistake or not, she was smiling brightly and ignoring it.

I see—so that's the educational policy that gives rise to such a placid and serene attitude. It's not just genes; environment is important, too. I hope she continues to grow up healthy...

Yuigahama must have noticed my warm gaze, as she spun around to face me. "Canned peaches, huh...? What do you want, Hikki?"

"Anything's fine. Komachi isn't really picky. Well, I figure peaches are okay." Pears often appeared in the Hikigaya household in summer, but if we were going off Komachi's preferences, peaches were one of the things she liked. It's not like I particularly dislike peaches, either. In fact, I'd love a pair of big, juicy peaches!

But if we were going to use the canned ones, there was just one thing that concerned me. "If we use canned peaches, then it won't be seasonal anymore," I said with a questioning glance.

Gaha-mama gave me a blank look. But very quickly, a gentle smile came to her face. "Yes, that's true right now... But the season will come again."

Her voice was so gentle, but it came with just a bit of a lonely ring. With her face turned just slightly downward, her profile reminded me of how Yuigahama had looked back then on the swings with the sunset behind her, filled with faint sorrow. I'm sure that's an expression only adults will wear. "Once many years have passed and you're an adult, whenever you have peaches, you'll think, *Oh, I remember back when we did that*, right? That's the wonderful thing about home cooking," she whispered, as if teaching me a secret spell as she closed one eye. It felt like there was a mysterious, magical tinge to her tone. Her words settled into my heart just that heavily.

"Ooh, that sounds nice!" Yuigahama, who seemed to have been listening just as intently as me, said with sparkling eyes.

With our gazes of respect on her, Gaha-mama put a hand over her mouth, giggled, and winked mischievously. "Riiight? This works best on boys!"

"Hey, don't ruin it!" Yuigahama lamented. "Suddenly it feels all calculated…"

A wry smile pulled at my lips. It's true; that will work very well on men.

Every time you smell that fresh, juicy scent, every time you immerse yourself in that enchanting sweetness, you recall that season.

So I'm sure I won't forget today.

Gaha-mama is amazing, as expected—Amazingamama for short. Following the Yuigahama mother and daughter to the canned food section, I watched with a gaze of not just respect, but awe—almost fear.

The two of them looked intimate with linked arms, stepping along lightly as they continued to chat.

"Did you do that sort of thing, too, Mom?"

"I did! You father still talks about the time when—," Gaha-mama began, but Yuigahama cut her off with a sigh.

"Ahhh, yeah. Never mind, actually. It's kinda gross to hear that sort of thing about Dad…"

Poor Gaha-papa…

× × ×

It really is different to stand in someone else's kitchen.

The position of the sink, the way you turn on the tap, the switch for the electric kettle, the way the dishes are stacked, the pattern on the kitchen mat, the smell of the dish detergent—all those differences make it feel fresh and new.

But the freshest feeling thing here was the woman in an apron.

Holding a hairpin in her lips, she loosely retied her long, milk tea–colored hair behind her neck to make a bun. Then she held it with the floral hairpin that had been touching her glossy lips. After putting her arms through the armholes of a frilly pinafore apron, she pulled the apron strings tight behind her.

Seeing Gaha-mama like that, I found my heart unexpectedly pounding.

In the Hikigaya household, it's rare for anyone to bother wearing an apron.

This was completely different from what you'd see in our kitchen. At our house, Komachi will be in her at-home wear of an ultra-boring standard red sweatsuit as she tosses things around in a frying pan, Mom will be in her typical casual wear, dead-eyed as she chucks ingredients in a pot to boil the hell out of some *somen* noodles, and my father (who hardly ever stands in the kitchen) will wear weirdly pretentious pajamas as he excitedly warms up milk in the microwave. And that's not even mentioning that when you get to my level, you'll even be half-naked. And they won't even ask me, *Are you sure that's enough armor?*

When you grow up in a household environment where everything is sloppy, seeing someone wearing a kitschy and cute (i.e. kitchen-cute) apron for food prep can inspire feelings of admiration.

Is this what they mean when they talk about the "careful home lifestyle"…?

Gaha-mama noticed me watching in a daze and smiled brightly. Then she gently took my hand and put a navy-blue server apron in my hands. "I'm sorry—all we have is Dad's apron."

"Ah, no, it's totally okay…" *Actually, I'm totally fine without an apron or anything, so. I'm good naked, I'm good…*, I was about to say, but with her prodding and pushing it at me, I couldn't refuse.

Left with no choice, I wrapped the server apron around my waist. It seemed well used, even comfortable on me. Apparently, in the Yuigahama household, the papa of the family also spent time in the kitchen.

I get the sense that both parents here cook, so how is it the daughter is bad at cooking?

As I was giving Yuigahama a considering look, the girl in question was tying a crisp bow on a rather fluffy, frilly, and girly apron. It was the one she'd bought when she'd gone out with Yukinoshita that one time. It looked like it had been used a little since she'd found it hanging in the store, but I could tell she'd been wearing it with care.

Yuigahama plucked at the frills of the apron skirt and smiled rather proudly. "So? Doesn't it make me look like I'm an actual cook?"

"..."

It actually did look pretty good on her.

The setting sun coming in from the skylight and the indirect lighting along the wall mingled to create a warm brightness, and us being in the kitchen as well made this scene feel as idyllic as something out of a catalog.

It made some pretty stupid fantasies pass through my head.

To shake it off, I blurted out a little too fast, "Yeah, yeah, it looks good—isn't mine pretty good, too?" I smacked the server apron below my waist while I was at it.

Yuigahama's eyebrows came together in a frown. "Hmm... Yeah, it looks good."

"That pause... That pause is concerning."

"Huh, uh, well, it's nice 'cause it makes you look kind of like a café server, but the apron kinda..." Her expression twisted up, and she practically spat out the rest. "...I bet it smells."

"That's mean! To me, obviously, but this is your dad's, right?"

"Yeah. That's why..."

"It's been washed, so it's all right," Gaha-mama giggled. "Let's get started already," she said gently and airily.

"Whoo!" Yuigahama thrust up an energetic fist.

"Wh-whoo..." I was forced to raise a hand as well, about as high as a waving-cat statue. *How embarrassing...*

The ingredients were already lined up on the counter—aside from the stuff that had to be the main ingredients, like the premade tart dough, canned peaches, and whipped cream. She'd even set up all the little details that had to be for decoration, like chocolate sprinkles and other fruits and stuff.

Once we started making them, the fruit tarts Gaha-mama had

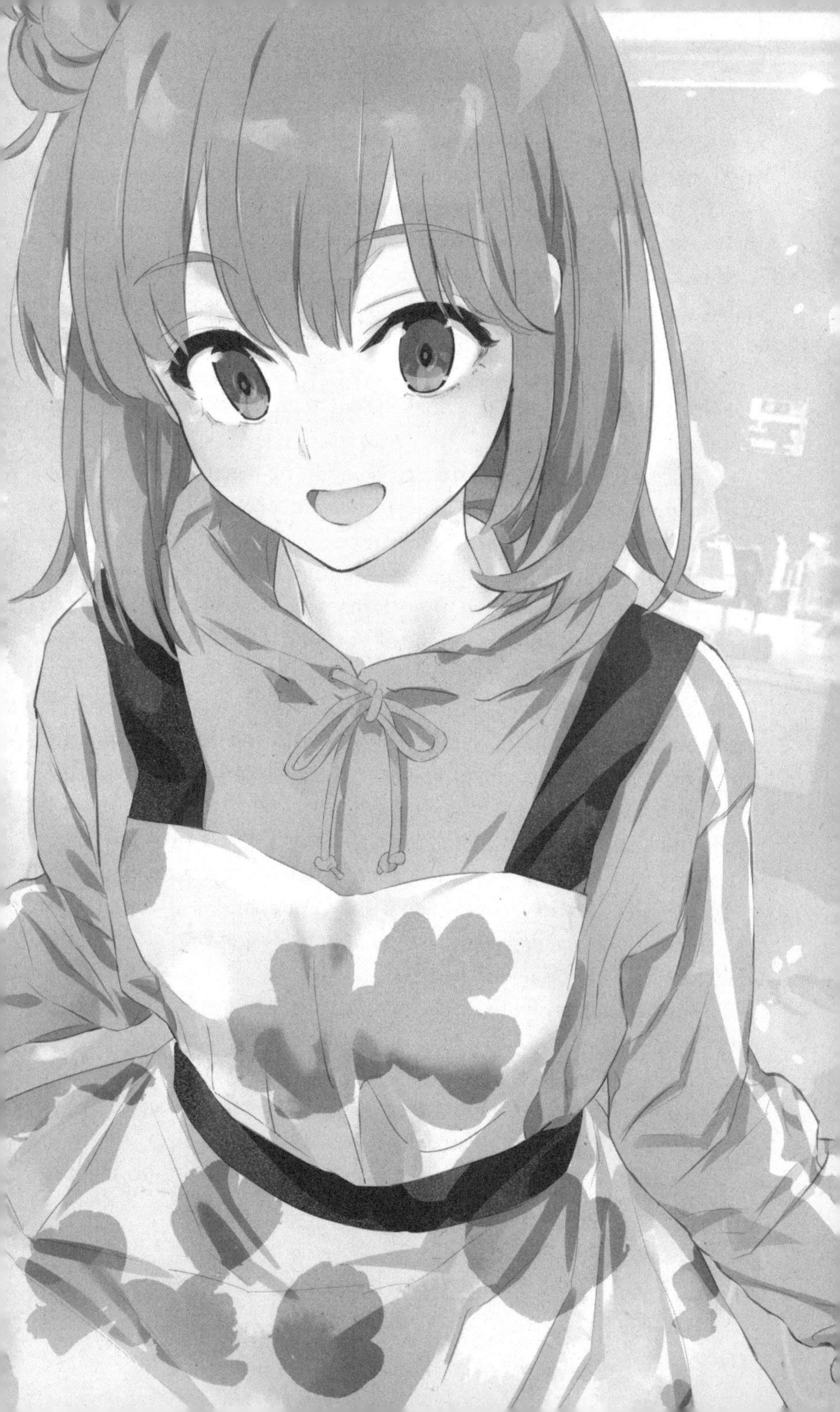

recommended weren't that hard. She'd probably taken into consideration that I was a beginner at baking when choosing the recipe.

We put thin slices of frozen sponge cake on top of the tart dough, then spread whipped cream over it and placed peaches on top. To finish it off, you just had to coat it with this stuff kinda like gelatin lubricant called *nappage* to make it all shiny. Apparently, the peaches change in color once they touch the air, so if you glaze them, they'll stay a nice color longer.

We finished making the first one far more smoothly than I had imagined.

"Since we have the opportunity, it might be nice to make a bunch of different kinds," Gaha-mama recommended, peeking in from behind me, so I decided to try making a few more.

But when something is this easy, it's human nature to want to add some kind of a twist to it—so Yuigahama was immediately struck with an idea. "Oh! I bet it'd taste good if you put chocolate on this." She clapped her hands, celebrating her own idea.

Seeing her snap pieces off bar chocolate was unsettling. Unable to stand by and do nothing, I cut in. "Why would you do something like that? If you just focus on making it normally, you can do it, can't you?"

"Huh…? I thought maybe it'd be…cuter, and taste better," she said as she stuck chunks of chocolate into the mountain of fruit. The jiggling white peach crumbled apart, and there was nothing cute about that ghastly state of affairs. It was such a sad combination, it would make you think, *So it is possible for discord to be visibly manifest*, and it did not seem like it would be a good pairing.

"You should try your ideas once you've managed the basics," I cautioned.

"You're talking like Yukinon…"

That name suddenly coming up made my expression stiffen. "…Yeah. 'Cause it's common sense." I somehow stayed calm.

Regardless, Yuigahama was heedlessly humming as she snapped more pieces off the chocolate bar. "But when she stayed over before, we cooked together? If you combine one thing that tastes good with another thing that tastes good, I think it'll make it better..."

"That's a dangerous assumption..."

"Whaaat? Really?"

Soda and hamburgers both taste good, but if you stew a hamburger in cola, it's clearly going to taste awful... There are rules to this...

When Yuigahama noticed my mouth hanging open in speechless horror, she tossed a piece of chocolate in it and then, with a *Hya*, shoved a peach slice speared on a fork after it.

Since this whole *Say ahhh* song and dance was an accident, I couldn't shyly be like, *N-no, your mom's looking*, and I was forced to munch on the offerings while wiping the sticky syrup from my mouth with my fingers.

"See, isn't it good?" Yuigahama said.

"Listen..." As I griped, I continued to munch, glaring mildly with half-lidded eyes. *I mean, it's not like I'm unhappy about it...but if you could at least give me a heads-up first please then I could like emotionally prepare or think up an excuse for refusing or, like...* So I was about to continue, but the feeling like something was off in my mouth took priority.

The freshness of the peach and the aroma of the chocolate...hmm...do not match...

"...For stuff like this, try it yourself first, okay?" It wasn't like it was inedible, so I swallowed it all, then made that very reserved comment instead of telling her what I thought.

But it seemed the excellence of this expression didn't quite get across, as Yuigahama cocked her head quizzically. "Huh? I thought it'd definitely taste good, though," she said as she tried it herself.

And then after a few seconds, she nodded slightly with an incredibly dubious expression, following which she said nothing at all.

See, they don't go together! Well, Yuigahama's sense of taste is functional, at least. It's just her process that's like that...

So I was thinking when Gaha-mama, watching from the side, put a hand over her mouth and giggled. "If you want to use chocolate, it might be best to do it like this." And then to give us an example, she started working beside us.

After cutting off some extra tart dough of a suitable size, she painted it with chocolate and put fruit on top. In the blink of an eye, a mini-tart was complete.

And then she pinched that in her fingers and brought it to my mouth. "Say *ahhh*."

"Th-thank you. I'm fine." *Blank—clear your mind.* I tried my best to stay calm, sparing no sweat dripping under my armpits and oozing on my scalp. Taking care not to touch her fingers, I accepted it.

"…Boo." Gaha-mama pouted cutely in dissatisfaction, but *ha-ha-ha!* With advance warning, merely suppressing emotions is a simple task for Hachiman Hikigaya—*ha-ha-ha!* But anyway, how cute, *ha-ha-ha.* This cuteness for reasons unknown hit me hard, but I somehow evaded it and focused on the flavor of the tart.

My honest impression slipped out of me. "…It's good. It's great, even."

Before, the flavor balance had been mangled like the Treasure Island murder case, but now the chocolate gently enfolded the crisp texture of the tart and the fruitiness of the peach, and I could hear the sound of the wind…

With a bright grin, Gaha-mama breathed a sigh of relief. "Great! Then, here. You too, Yui. Say *ahhh*!" Gaha-mama brought the tart to Yuigahama's mouth as she was in the middle of her task, and Yuigahama chomped into it with no hesitation.

"Ahhh!"

Do they normally do stuff like this…? I wondered with a lukewarm look at the two of them, and when Yuigahama noticed that, she came to her senses with a gasp, waving her hands wildly with a bright-red face. She was still chewing, so she wasn't saying any words, but I got her meaning: *No that was just you know anyway it's not like that!*

I hastily nodded back at her. *It's okay, it's okay; I get it, I get it. That stuff is nice, too. Sometimes you do that.* This feeding scene was heartwarming.

Whether Yuigahama accepted that or not, she continued to chew, but eventually, her eyes sparkled in surprise. "Oh, this really is good."

"If you're going to put in chocolate, then you spread it on the inside of the tart instead of adding it from the outside. That makes it niiice and crispy," Gaha-mama explained.

"Oh, that makes sense!" Yuigahama immediately started spreading chocolate on the tart dough.

The sight touched my heart. *A man will not act unless you show and tell him... Now I have seen clearly and firsthand what it means to raise someone.*

"Oh... Impressive... You're used to handling things...," I murmured.

Gaha-mama puffed out her chest with a chuckle. "Right? I'm pretty good at cooking."

No, I meant that your handling of your daughter was impressive... But, well, whichever works! Since you look the cutest when you're proud!

"There's no single way to make fruit tarts, so you can just put in what you like. Unexpected combinations can be really good," said Gaha-mama.

"Oh, really?"

"Really," she told me with a gentle smile.

But I still think you should only do that once you have a proper understanding of the basics of cooking and can re-create the taste in your mind...

Even while chatting with Gaha-mama, my attention was on Yuigahama as she cheerfully endeavored in her variations. *Exactly what has this girl been putting in...?*

"How's this, Mom?"

"Mm, that looks good. Now just put in the secret spice, and it's done."

"Secret spice?"

"That's right. This is the ultimate flavoring," Gaha-mama said, cupping one hand around Yuigahama's ear to whisper something.

When Yuigahama heard, her cheeks went pink. "Agh! I did not need to hear that; go away!"

"Ohhh nooo!" Yuigahama grumpily shoved her mother over my way. If her daughter wasn't going to handle her, then of course the new target would be me.

"So then, Hikki, what do you think it is?" Gaha-mama asked me.

"Uhhh, I wonder, ha-ha. Is it an empty stomach or something?" I pretended to be so busy squeezing out the whipped cream that I barely had any attention left for her.

But the grin stayed on Gaha-mama's face, freezing time.

Oh man. This is like that thing in Dragon Quest *where you can't proceed until they get the answer they want!*

I slowly grasped for words. "...Is it like, you know, when you eat a meal someone else is paying for? ...That's good, huh?"

Gaha-mama put a hand to her cheek; she was smiling, but her eyebrows showed worry.

Yuigahama, on the other hand, was completely weirded out. "Hikki, you're kinda getting worse..."

"Though it's true that *does* taste good..."

"You can't let him say that, Mom!"

With her daughter chiding her, Gaha-mama cleared her throat and started over. "Maybe you could try thinking about home cooking."

The ultimate spice that makes food taste great is generally accepted to be hunger, lack of money paid, and munchies when smoking weed (opinions vary). Personally, I think most things are just about guaranteed to be delicious if you put in garlic, back fat, or MSG, but that's definitely the wrong answer for sweets.

So then, it was obvious what answer she wanted.

"Is it heart, then?" I said with a blushing smile, and instead of telling me if I was right or wrong, Gaha-mama grinned back at me.

× × ×

"Well then, let's wait until they've chilled," Gaha-mama said, closing the fridge door.

I forgot if it was called *nappage* or Banagher or what, but apparently, we had to chill the tarts to harden them. Well, most fruits do taste better chilled.

With the whole cooking process about done now, I took off the apron as I headed for the living room. It wasn't a highly difficult recipe, but it was unfamiliar. The mild tiredness only made me feel more fulfilled.

Then I guess I'll just take it easy now, I thought, about to wander my way to the sofa, when there was a tug on the hem of my shirt.

I turned around to see Yuigahama with her dog in one arm and her hand grabbing my hem. "Um, this way…," she muttered quietly, burying her face in Sablé's body to hide her mouth as she kept tugging, trying to take me away somewhere.

"O-okay… Ah, then later." I bobbed my head at Gaha-mama and let Yuigahama pull me out of the living room.

"All right, take it easy," Gaha-mama replied. "I'll call you once it's done." Her laughter reminded me of tinkling bells over my shoulder. I followed after the quickly striding Yuigahama.

She was headed to her room.

I sat down on the offered cushion, while she perched on her bed, Sablé still in her arms.

"Um, what should we do? What do we do?" she asked me, like she was a little lost.

I remembered that she'd asked me something similar before, during the fireworks show. The stupid reply popped out of my mouth by force of habit. "Yeah… What do we do? Go home?"

"We're not going home! And, like, this *is* my home! This is totally my room!" Yuigahama howled, and Sablé followed suit, yipping.

"Uh, I mean there isn't actually anything to do."

"Ahhh, um, well… Oh, wanna look at my graduation album?" Yuigahama reached over to the shelf by her bedside and pulled out a velvet-bound book.

"What's the point of that…? What can you even do with a graduation album besides have a contest to see who gives the best nicknames to ugly girls?"

"We're not gonna do that! Ugh! You really are the worst!" She followed up by repeating quietly, "The worst, really the worst."

It was actually pretty painful to hear her say that over and over, like she really meant it. "I'm just saying that's what it's like—for boys at least. I've heard guys use it as a catalog to get others to introduce them to girls. Like a dating app." When I displayed the superficial knowledge I'd just overheard from Tobe or some guy talking class, Yuigahama cringed.

"That's *the worst*! Did you do stuff like that, too, Hikki? Like getting someone else to introduce you or whatever…?"

"I mean, in my case, I'd have to get someone to introduce me to the person who would introduce a girl to me, first."

"Ahhh, yeah, I see…"

I'm very glad to have gained your understanding.

"Ohhh, but I kinda wanna see what you were like in middle school," I said.

"…Never mind, actually. This is too embarrassing. Nope, nope." Yuigahama released Sablé for the moment and scooted over to tuck the album back into the shelf.

…*Too bad.*

As I was shrugging casually, Sablé tackled me.

"Oh, what's up?" I caught the energetic dog that was woofing and licking at me, and I scrubbed him for a while. Before long, fur was flying. It seemed he was in his shedding season. *Oh, so this is why they didn't let him close when we were cooking…*

Things were making sense to me now, but Yuigahama yelped when she saw how much fur was on me. "Ah! Sorry! Come, Sablé!"

"Uh, I'm used to it from my cat. Just give me a brush."

"O-okay…"

I accepted a brush from Yuigahama and put Sablé on my crossed legs to give him a good grooming. The dog stayed still, making satisfied snuffling noises.

As I brushed him for a while, Yuigahama inched over on her knees, peering at me with deep interest. "Huh. You're a natural."

"Well, that's normal when you have a pet. And then it stops bothering you, even when there's hair floating in your miso soup."

"I dunno about that…" Yuigahama's shoulders slumped in exasperation. Then a thought must have struck her, as she got up, went to the closet, and came back right away.

Then she plopped herself down like a frog with legs splayed to the sides and pulled something out. "Ta-daa. Here," she said.

The object she offered was what they call a roller, a pet cleaner with sticky tape. It's fair to say these are a near-vital item for households that have pets and families that have middle-aged men. Since his hair comes out so readily… And his pillow smells.

Rollers are not only great for regular cleaning, they're also exceptionally convenient for getting hair off your clothes after a pet's been on you.

"Thanks, I'll use it in a bit."

"I'll do it for you." She was already pulling off the cover to roll it all over my shoulders, back, and everything.

"It's fine, it's fine! Cut it out. That tickles." I twisted around and tried to avoid it, but Yuigahama grinned nastily, brandishing the roller even more persistently. The more I tried to run away, the more sadistic it seemed to make her, and she seemed to be truly enjoying herself as she chased me around.

"Gotcha!" she exclaimed.

Feeling the lint roller tickled. It was embarrassing and soft and smelled nice, and I couldn't take it.

Any foolish resistance was bound to cause unforeseen contact to occur, so trying to escape was wearing on my nerves, too. Specifically, my sympathetic nervous system was getting a workout, and I'd been dripping sweat for a while now.

"Hey, stop," I said. "I prefer doing a pat-pat over a roller. Ah! Ah, hey, stop! Seriously sto…"

My IQ points were about to drop by about a trillion, at which point I might start yelping, *N-nuuuu! That's not the roller—that's something else pat-patting meeee!*

Then there was an unexpected knocking on the door.

Yuigahama, who'd been acting gleeful until then, froze immediately and zipped away from me.

"Yui, can I come in?" came the gentle call.

"Yeah."

The playfulness of a moment ago settled, and her expression turned composed. I, on the other hand, was panting hard with Sablé in my arms. I'd been completely exposed as a dangerous furry.

I somehow managed to calm my breathing, and the door opened slightly to allow Gaha-mama to poke her face in. "Hikki, will you be having dinner?"

"No, I'm thinking I'll go before it gets too late..." I really couldn't bother them that much. Absconding when things are good is the act of a sigma male.

"Really?" Gaha-mama looked slightly disappointed at my answer.

But a moment later, she smiled broadly with a chuckle. "But I already made it- ♪," she said, sticking out her tongue with that same wink and a sideways peace sign. ☆

I had thought she was actually quite comforting, unlike Yukinoshita's mother...but this one was a schemer, too!

× × ×

The night wind felt good on my cheeks, and after I'd had dinner and left the Yuigahama residence, the city was sinking into the shades of evening. The baking had gone smoothly, and I carried the fruit tarts in a box.

As I walked cautiously so as not to jostle it, Yuigahama, who'd gone to the trouble of coming out to see me off, examined my face with concern. "Did you eat too much, Hikki? Are you all right?"

"Oh, it wasn't that much. I mean..." Even as I said it, I was feeling overwhelmingly full.

The meal Yuigahama, Gaha-mama, and I had eaten had been

incredibly delicious, but I'd been anxious the whole time, on the edge of my chair wondering when Gaha-papa would come back. So I'd been preoccupied, desperately nodding along at the conversation as I kept on eating the bowls of rice handed to me. They were piled comically high, like something out of *Nihon Mukashibanashi*.

…I mean, eating lots made Gaha-mama happy.

Every time I stuffed my cheeks to scarf down more white rice, she'd give me these looks like, *That's how a boy should be!* which made me feel like *I can do it!* and ask for more.

As a result, I'd eaten way too much. I was so full, just walking down the street made me grimace.

Yuigahama put her hands together apologetically. "Sorry. Mom got carried away. I think it makes her happy when a boy eats a ton."

"Moms can be like that sometimes… When I go visit my grandparents, Grandma does the same. It's basically a Stamina Yarou situation. Dish after dish."

"That much?!" Yuigahama was freaked out, and I nodded at her, totally serious.

Oh, it's not like I dislike that! 'Cause my grandma's cooking and Stamina Yarou are both great! I looove Stamina Yarou! ♡ I love it so much, I would even crush some magnifying glasses under my butt.

While we made trivial conversation, our feet took us to the station, walking side by side. Yuigahama muttered softly, "Thanks for today."

"I'm the one who should be thanking you."

"Yeah, but…I had a blast… Cooking together is kinda nice. It's fun."

"You're more efficient on your own, though." The nasty quip slipped out, and Yuigahama puffed her cheeks at me in annoyance. I gave her a warped smile in return. "But when we actually gave it a shot, it didn't feel like work, you know? It really was fun to make these together."

"Yeah, I think so, too," she said with a peaceful smile.

I nodded back at her, cautiously adjusting my grip on the box in my hands to make sure it was okay as I slowly assembled the words.

"…Maybe Komachi would like that better, too. She really loves house chores and stuff." Experience-type events are all the rage right now, and live entertainment is at its peak. So maybe I should make the experience itself a present for Komachi.

Some things money can't buy—for everything else, there's your parents' money. Master NEET.

As I was thinking such nonsense, Yuigahama sounded impressed. "Oh, I see. It might be nice to bake together, huh?!"

"Yeah, that's why I did this…," I said, holding out the box of fruit tarts. Yuigahama looked at it curiously, cocking her head. "Those cookies were good. So, well, this is thanks for that… Though it's a little early," I added, and I timidly attempted to hand the box over.

Yuigahama chuckled quietly. "They're made of the same ingredients."

"Not at all. I sneaked in a secret spice…" It was true that all I'd had to put into the tarts was stuff that had already been in her kitchen. But still, in my own way, I'd put in just a hint of a secret spice, just as Gahamama had taught me.

Yuigahama was staring at the box, her gaze flickering at me with upturned eyes, teasing. "Hmm… What did you put in?"

"If I told you, it wouldn't be a secret."

"True." Yuigahama smiled, accepting the box.

"Then this is far enough. See you."

"Yeah, see you at school." I nodded back to Yuigahama, who was doing a small wave in front of her chest, and headed for the station.

After going a ways, I suddenly looked over my shoulder. Yuigahama was still there, waving her whole arm at me. I raised a casual hand in reply and started walking again.

The main road in front of the station wasn't so cold. People were strolling along, enjoying the weekend evening, and it told me that the long winter had come to an end. You could see the season in the cityscape as well. The streetlights, the neon signs, and the pale glow spilling from the high-rises and apartment buildings looked particularly bright.

Maybe this was the life that awaited me in the future.

Something like an answer to Miura's question came to my mind.

If I could go from one day to the next while granting each one of her wishes.

I pictured that impossible situation.

Prelude 4...

We talked about lots of things. About our plans for spring break or places to go hang out—nothing but stuff like that.

I knew this was her weird way of sidestepping the issue, though.

She was really bad at avoiding the subject, and her grin was kind of unnatural. *She really is awkward*, she thought. She can do anything else, but she's so bad at telling lies, and telling the truth, and even avoiding things didn't come naturally to her.

I wish we could've stayed how we were, but the time went by quickly, and it got a bit cold. Fewer people were walking by the station, and we were talking less, too. Eventually, the trains would stop, and then neither of us would be able to go anywhere.

I wanted to pretend not to notice that and just talk about unrelated stuff, only fun things, like we had before.

I honestly thought we could have stayed like this forever. I felt that if my wish could be granted like she said, that would be for the best.

But I couldn't be satisfied with that. I needed more.

"...There's so much stuff I want to do," I muttered softly, looking up at a high-rise with a number of dark windows.

She made a quiet listening noise, then let out a sigh like a smile. "Yes."

"Yeah, I want to do everything. I want everything." And then I came just a bit closer than before, touching her shoulder with mine, and laid my head there, as if I would fall asleep like that. "…'Cause I'm greedy. I'll take everything. I'll take your feelings, too."

I'm greedy.

I love fun things and happy things and delicious things. I'm not good at cooking or baking, but I don't mind. I want to put on all the toppings, and I want to try lots of combinations, and I don't mind if it doesn't work out. I'm okay if the result is unpleasant or bitter.

So just once, I'd ask.

If she didn't say anything, then I wouldn't, either. If she said it, then I'd say it.

I know that's unfair, but that makes the both of us, and him, too. We're all unfair. We're greedy people who want that wish granted so badly, even though we understand we can't do it and know it won't happen.

But I'm probably the greediest of all.

Sweet things, bitter things, painful things, difficult things… wounds and pain… I want all of it.

I lifted my head and looked straight at her. I gazed into her eyes. We were close enough you'd think our faces might stick together. "…Tell me how you feel, Yukinon."

The moment I said that, she breathed a sigh that was hesitant or confused, her large eyes wavering with uncertainty. With her soft-looking lips open slightly, her long eyelashes trembled slightly, and she looked like she was about to cry.

I couldn't avert my eyes anymore.

All this time, I'd been trying not to look, pretending I hadn't noticed, but I couldn't do that anymore. I just patiently watched her— her beautiful hair, her moist eyes, and her white cheeks.

She finally closed her mouth—I think she was biting her lip—but in the end, she surveyed the area.

There was hardly anyone else there at the station, and there didn't seem to be anyone in earshot, but she still drew her shoulder close to mine as if she was worried about other people overhearing. The way she seemed so hesitant about touching me reminded me of a kitten.

Then she cupped a hand around her mouth and whispered one thing.

I think they were the words I didn't want to hear, but once I'd heard them, I found myself grinning anyway. My cheeks and mouth, and probably my eyes, too, were relaxing so much I couldn't even do anything about it.

There was an uneasy expression on her face as she jerked away, like she was scared, but her cheeks were red enough I could even see it in the dark.

Seeing that look on her face, I sincerely felt lost.

I wish I could have hated her.

× × ×

I said it.

I didn't want to.

I had never intended to.

Because I knew once I said it out loud, once I acknowledged it, I wouldn't be able to take it back. Like water overflowing from a bowl, or stroking a swelled balloon with a pin, what had always been covered by a thin film would pop.

That was why I had pressed my lips together. I knew I should just swallow those words, but her eyes wouldn't allow that.

It was probably the first time I'd ever told someone something like this, and it would surely be the last. In a trembling whisper, I confessed to her and only her.

When I timidly looked at her to see what sort of expression she would have, what she would say, her expression was brimming with warmth. She didn't say anything, just gave me a little nod.

This had to be the first time I'd said those words aloud, but I suspect she'd noticed a long time ago. She'd been waiting for me to say it.

"Then I'll say it, too." And then she peacefully closed her eyes, put a hand on my shoulder, cupped her mouth with her other hand, and slowly brought her face close.

The gel nails on her slim fingers, her pink cheeks colored with pale blush, her full and glossy lips, her gently curled eyelashes. Everything cute and stylish and pretty about her was moving slowly closer.

Just like giving me a kiss.

That thought embarrassed me, and I nearly bent backward, but I kept myself from doing that and turned my face away.

Eventually, she whispered in my ear, like a play bite from a puppy.

The words I had wished to hear.

I let out a sigh of relief and quietly drew back my chin to swallow the words that had just about popped out of my mouth.

She released my shoulder and inched slightly away. When her eyes met mine, she smiled shyly and squished her bun. "Bet we have the same wish, huh?"

"...Yes."

I think that's the one thing that's certain.

However, I believed we couldn't both get what we wanted, so I'd chosen the closest thing to it—believing that if I could one day do better, it would come true.

When I nodded, almost ready to pray, she shook her head slightly in return. I didn't know what she was denying. I raised an eyebrow, and then she said something I wasn't expecting.

"Hikki's probably the same, too."

That name made me stiffen. She gently laid her hand over mine to ease my tension. "I think maybe he doesn't want you to give up on something that matters to you." Her tone was nonchalant, but the remark was like a knife in my heart. My shoulders had been slumping, but when I turned to look up at her again, her gaze was already far away, focused on a sky full of stagnant stars.

"'Cause the distance between us isn't physical," she said. "Even if we go far away or don't see each other anymore...I feel like the distance of our feelings can't be changed."

"...Is that how it is?"

"Yeah, I think...once your feelings change, then no matter how close you are, it's really far."

I was closer than anyone as I listened to those words.

Her hand had just been lying on top of mine, but now they were a little more connected. Our little fingers gently tangled as if doing a pinkie swear. The overlap between our hands was not at all big, and they were not that warm, and the air was not very cold.

But I could still feel the heat.

"If our wishes are the same, then will you accept all my feelings, too?" *If we do that, then surely we can avoid change*, she said in not so many words.

"Yes. I'm sure I will," I told her.

Just how wonderful would it be if we truly could never change. I closed my eyes, grateful for her words and warmth.

I would never forget them.

Nor would I be able to forget how cold my hand felt when it pulled away.

4 And then **Yukino Yukinoshita** quietly waves.

The light of early spring was streaming in through the windows. A solemn air hung around us while we heard sniffling and choked sobs.

Before me were rows of black uniforms.

Turning to look around a little, I was surrounded by people in formal attire; if this hadn't been a school gym, it might have looked like a funeral.

But the banner hung up high over the stage reading Convocation Ceremony and the blazers with fake flower corsages at the front added some slight color to the event, communicating that this was a special day.

The girls leaning against the friends in line beside them, or holding hands, or letting out smothered sighs, were the exact kind of thing you imagine when you think of good-byes. All reluctant to leave behind those three years of high school, that era of youth.

But only those who were a part of it could share in the pomp and circumstance; for a total outsider like me, it was really just someone else's tragedy being shoved in your face. I'd hardly interacted with anyone in the year above me, so I just spent the time stuck on a folding chair for a few hours, nodding off.

I didn't really have any sentimental feelings for all the boys and girls setting out for their new lives on this fine day—all this event was to me was an appreciation of their release from a long period of educational intervention.

However, I wasn't completely unmoved—there was a twinge of sympathy within me.

Once they had left this school building, the title of high school student and the status of child would be stripped from them. Whether they'd been bad kids since they were very young or had started getting called delinquents in their teens, or whether they'd been sharp like knives and hurt anyone that touched them—no matter what emotions and dreams they were leaving in these chairs and desks, they had to graduate from this control. The boys and girls in those graduation photos would be washed away in the crowds, and they would inevitably change.

Most of the students here would probably go to university after this; they'd be able to placate themselves with a few years' moratorium. But there's still a general societal difference in the way you're treated as a university student. They just got a suspended sentence. In the end, they'd still be expelled from the protection and care given to younger generations.

If I thought about it like that, the array of standard uniforms was ominous—as if they'd been stamped out and were waiting to be shipped off.

I seemed to recall I'd been thinking something similar the year before. When you can't be on your phone, there aren't many ways to distract yourself from your idleness. All I can do is think about random stuff. The year before, I'd played rock-paper-scissors with myself. *Now then, however will I kill the time next year…?* I wondered. Then I realized next year would be my own graduation ceremony.

Oh. I'd been wondering why the school would bother making the younger grades attend the graduation ceremony, but now it finally made sense.

It was to make it clear to us that we had limited time.

Up on the stage, some very important person was making some very important speech.

I had no need to listen, so I checked around me.

Definitely, probably, most likely…once I'd graduated, I would never see most of the people before me again.

Of those who sat here in rows, divided cleanly by gender and class and then ordered by name, how many would I see after graduation?

I'm sure it could happen if I contacted them, but with my personality, I would probably never bother. The more you get used to a new environment, the less you look back on the past. I wasn't sure if I'd ever acclimate to new environments, but most of the people around me would.

So let's take someone who happened to be in view: Saika Totsuka, for example. I'd probably have some kind of interaction with him, and I'd try to maintain that connection. *I mean, since we have enough of a connection now! I'm looking right at him!*

I also wound up noticing Tobe, since he was sitting beside Totsuka, but Tobe, well—I was never gonna contact him. I didn't even know his number.

Next to him, sitting to my left, was Hayato Hayama. Although he had my contact info, he probably wouldn't bother trying to reconnect. And even if he did, I would inevitably have a pubertal reaction like *If I reply right away, he'll think I'm jumping on his message…*, which would lead to me not replying at all, and that would be that.

I didn't even want Hayato Hayama knowing my contact info in the first place. I'd told him my number to get through that kerfuffle back when I ran into Kaori Orimoto again. I still didn't know his.

The result was that Hayama had quite foolishly told Haruno my number without asking me, which had left me with unnecessary stress.

I felt a little sick as I remembered this, and I glared at Hayama out of the corner of my eye. He noticed, shooting me a *what?* look. It seemed I'd stared too hard.

With a shake of my head, I directed my attention elsewhere far away.

Since Zaimokuza was so big, I could see him sitting in the line of Class C, ahead of me. *With him, well, I have the feeling I'll see him after graduation, too.*

So then, what about the rest?

The thought made me strangely restless, and my gaze started wandering this way and that.

A swaying bluish-black ponytail, dubiously flashing glasses, and a restless red-brown short bob caught my eye. Kawasaki's, Ebina's, and Minami Sagami's attendance numbers were apparently all in a row. I'd never think about something like that outside of school functions like this, so it kinda felt like a new revelation. Although there were only two more weeks left in this class, so it was unnecessary information. Sagami's got nothing to do with me. She never really did and never would, not just after this graduation ceremony but next year, too, so it really didn't matter at all.

I could run into Kawasaki at prep school, but we'd probably just acknowledge each other with something between a bow and a nod and keep things like that. And I probably wouldn't see Ebina, either, so long as there was no intermediary. The thin thread that connected the two of us was, ultimately, Yuigahama. Without her presence, I probably wouldn't see Ebina.

Of course, that was true not just of her, but of most of the people I could call acquaintances now.

Pretending I was trying to loosen up my stiff shoulders and back, I stretched out my neck a bit.

A swaying pinkish-brown bun just happened to catch my eye, and beside that, loose, golden, fluffy waves. Yui Yuigahama and Yumiko Miura were sitting side by side. Though I couldn't see clearly from a distance, it looked like they were just slightly holding hands.

Miura was sniffling and wiping her eyes with her sleeve. Maybe she had been affected by the graduation ceremony, or she'd realized her own looming move to the next year and the class change that came with it.

Yuigahama got a crooked smile and handed her a tissue. As she did, it looked as if they whispered something to each other. Then gradually, Yuigahama started pressing the corners of her own eyes, too.

As I watched Yuigahama quietly wipe her eyes, a thought struck me.

Would I see her after graduation?

Though it was just a year in the future, I really couldn't imagine it. Our connection was only maintained right now because there were still opportunities to see each other, like in our club and in class, but once those were done, would we be able to continue the same sort of relationship?

I was about to turn my head even farther…

…and stopped.

I obviously couldn't look at the classes behind me—and I definitely wouldn't be able to see someone who'd be sitting at the end, if you're going in order. I wouldn't be able to see that pure-black hair or what kind of expression was on that narrow, white face.

With a little sigh, I dutifully faced front.

Then there was a slight lean in from my left and a secretive whisper in my ear. The voice was charming and sweet, but also somewhat detached. "You're so restless…"

"…I'm bored. When you're not friends with the people sitting next to you, you have nothing to do for events like these."

"You're talking like you have friends at all," Hayama said sarcastically.

I casually shrugged instead of replying. And then, without turning to look beside me, I straightened up in my seat and stared ahead instead of answering. I meant to show that I wasn't going to talk to him, but that didn't stop him.

"You looking?"

I had just about turned back, so it felt like he'd read my mind. "…At what?" I snapped. I gave him a sidelong glare while I was at it.

Hayama indicated diagonally ahead with a jerk of his chin.

There were no students where he was looking. There were just adults sitting in formal clothing—the visitors' seats. There, I found Yukinoshita's mother. Even from a distance, her black traditional clothing and general appearance quickly caught my eye.

"…Why's she here?" I asked.

"It's not unusual for regional Diet members to come to ceremonies like these, but they often have conflicting plans. She must be here as her husband's representative."

"Huh…" I was apathetic about the whole thing, but Hayama's explanation made sense to me.

It had seemed like the one making a speech onstage had been some big-shot legislator. Thinking back even further, I also seemed to recall the teacher officiating the ceremony had said something about *we're honored to receive messages from somebody or other somewhere, blah, blah*, and after some *if I may presume to read it out loud in their place*, there was a *we have received so many, the following will be abridged*.

"Yeah, I think I remember that from even back in middle school," I happened to say to myself (my special skill).

Hayama's response was an anemic sigh. "I'm sure that's really common with public schools. They show off whenever they can—both at entrance ceremonies and graduation ceremonies."

We were both still facing forward, neither of us looking at each other's expressions as we continued talking to pass the time.

"Huh. I doubt any of the students or parents are listening, though… Well, I guess they keep doing it just because they always have," I said.

Hayama sighed again, sounding fed up. "That's a mean way to put it… You should call it tradition. Besides, there is a point to it. Teachers and parents like it after all."

"What you said is even worse…" I breathed a fed-up sigh of my own, which was followed by a smug-sounding sigh from beside me. I was sure he was wearing that slightly twisted version of his charming smile, an expression he hardly ever showed other people. The fact that I could very clearly envision it irritated me even more.

And there was one more thing that was making me fed up.

I flicked my eyes over to the visitors' seats again, and next to Mrs. Yukinoshita was one other woman with very similar features. Haruno Yukinoshita was wearing a well-tailored black suit, her hands on the bag set in her lap, eyes lowered in a quiet manner.

"…So why's she here, too?" I asked.

"Who knows? Just showing up or going to pay her respects… Something like that, I assume."

"Hmm…" I replied with a meaningless huff, but I was getting a really bad feeling about this.

Would Haruno be showing up to the prom after this, too? Though that was none of my business now, the words she'd left behind lingered in my chest like sediment.

Before I could say as much, Hayama let out a dry chuckle. "That explanation isn't enough for you?"

"No, I guess it makes sense. I dunno." I hadn't even realized how rattled I was. I answered before he'd even completely finished his sentence.

From the corner of my eye, I saw a faint smile on Hayama's face. "Don't say things you don't mean."

I scowled. "Right back at you."

That didn't bother Hayama, who casually ignored me as he looked to the visitors' seats. "…She probably came to see things for herself."

"Huh, I see," I answered to end the conversation, drawing back my jaw.

You can end most conversations by saying "I see." It's a sign that you don't care about what they're saying and you want to hurry and wrap things up.

But Hayama didn't back off, just lowered his voice and continued, "You're not asking *what* this time." He spoke quietly, but there was a clear challenge in his words. When Hayato Hayama teased like this— or Haruno Yukinoshita, the one he got this tactic from—there was no point in keeping your mouth shut. Both of them would draw words from you with their demeanor and presence.

Hayama and Haruno were very similar in only the ways I hated. I'd hardly ever seen the two of them talking alone together, but I was sure they had very fun, thrilling chats.

But I'd recently gotten used to this way of talking. Based on my experience, this is where you throw up a smoke screen to end it.

"I mean, I get it already. That woman shows up for most things her sister does. Doesn't she have anything better to do with her time…?" I said wearily.

Unable to restrain himself, Hayama burst out laughing. "True. She actually tends to go out of her way to make time for it. She's just that obsessed."

"Whoa…scary… She's about as obsessed with her little sister as I am with mine…" Does she have as much free time on her hands as I do? I'd go so far as to say I'm leaving my schedule open all the time for Komachi. *Well, not so much lately, though. If I shower her with too much attention, she'll hate me! Are you listening there, Miss Yukinoshita's sister? If you shower her with too much attention, she'll hate you for it! Also, please listen to that one closely once again, Miss Hikigaya's brother!*

A flat chuckle slipped out of me, drawing a laugh out of Hayama, too. I tried to end it with a joke.

But Hayama wasn't laughing anymore. "It's not just for her sister. I'm sure she's come to see your decision, too."

"…" This time, I couldn't get myself to give him some careless answer. I knew he was right.

When I failed to respond, he jabbed me with his elbow, checking that I was listening. The jolt earned him a click of my tongue and a snappish reply. "You're so restless. It'll get written up on your report card."

"I don't have anything to do. When you're not friends with the people sitting beside you, you've got nothing to do during events like this," Hayama replied sarcastically.

I frowned.

But wait, then wouldn't that mean Tobe's not friends with him, either?

As I was thinking that, said not-friend Tobe's head popped forward from beyond Hayama. "What was that about the guys sitting beside you?"

Hayama smiled brightly, but he said flatly, "It's nothing. You're too loud, Tobe. Be quiet."

Tobe muttered "Whoa…" or something as he dejectedly returned to his original position.

Now that it was finally quiet, I looked up at the podium again.

The very important speech from the very important person had come to an end, and the MC was informing us about the next ceremony on the program. "Next we have the farewell address from our student representative."

At that call, a sweet candy voice answered, "That's me!"

That deliberate-sounding, deceptively cute response… I saw Iroha Isshiki going up to the podium. *Oh yeah, she said something about doing the farewell address… And that she'd been talking with Ms. Hiratsuka about it, and she'd slipped out of the job and was running around avoiding it or something…*

All right, so let's see the fruit of Irohasu's and Ms. Hiratsuka's efforts— mainly the latter, I thought, sitting up in my chair as I watched Isshiki bow in front of the microphone.

Isshiki spread open a piece of paper that had been folded up like an accordion and began reading her address in the calm tones of a model student. "The harsh winter has come to an end, and now is the season when the scents of spring waft faintly in the gentle sunlight." Her ordinary devil-may-care attitude was concealed beneath the student-council-president image that teachers and parents wanted.

Isshiki smoothly read out the farewell address, narrating her memories of the older students and some mildly flattering episodes in club activities or with the student council. Suddenly, her voice caught. "Looking back, they were always supporting me…"

That little performance of occasional sniffles was very Machiavellirohasu…

For other events like this, I'd more often been in the stage wings watching like a producer, but that day, I was sitting in the audience. When you're observing from a different position, it also changes the way you see it. When in arena seating, the correct way to conduct yourself is obviously standing like M. Bison and acting like you're the boyfriend.

But suddenly standing up here would be insane, so this time around, the correct thing to do was to watch her like, *So you found the place you want to be. You shine so much more brightly now.* Like you're in the staff section, mentally putting on Masayoshi Yamazaki in the BGM while observing the proceedings with the look of an old-fashioned man. That's crazy, huh?

But no matter what position I was watching this from, it still felt emotional to see her hold back tears as she read out the farewell address. Even knowing the waterworks were just for effect, in Hachiman terms, her noble effort was worth a lot of points.

Mm-hmm, Isshiki did her best. Very cute, very cute. She had Ms. Hiratsuka getting mad at her, she sometimes skipped out, and she sometimes made a bullshit excuse so she could run off, but she still did her best… Is that what doing your best looks like?

As a fraternal (or even paternal) feeling rose within me, my eyes suddenly started watering. So that Hayama wouldn't notice, I stuck out my chin a bit and looked up at the ceiling.

If Isshiki was going to be student council president the following year as well, then she would be giving the farewell address for my graduation, too. This scene would probably be the same then.

Oh…then once I graduate, I won't see Isshiki anymore…

As I was feeling very deeply moved, the speech reached its final paragraph.

Isshiki folded up the paper in her hands, pausing for a beat.

Her gaze slid ahead, and she wiped the tears beading in the corners of her eyes with the pads of her fingers and smiled. "And so, I, Iroha Isshiki, as a representative of the current students, have been honored to have the opportunity to give the farewell address, with best wishes for the health and future success of our seniors." Saying her name one last time, she bowed. When she came down from the podium, she didn't show that she was crying, leaving primly with her back straight.

Seeing Iroha Isshiki finish the farewell address—a major job for a first-year—with such beauty and dignity, I and everyone else present gave her an unstinting, thunderous applause.

The waves of applause gradually settled, and as far as I was concerned, the event had passed its peak here, too.

After this, I'd be stuck seeing some loudmouths deliberately misunderstanding when their names were called for the certificate handout, giving dumb responses like "Yes, I'm doing good!" and no one would find it funny.

Truly, there's nothing more boring in the world than a graduation ceremony for people you don't care about.

× × ×

...So I had once thought, for a time.

"Next, the reply address from the representative of the graduates," came the announcement, and Meguri Shiromeguri, the previous student council president, responded with energy and walked up to the podium. She bowed in the center, then swept her gaze over the whole audience below. Her eyes moved slowly, as if making eye contact with each and every student. I even got the feeling she looked right at me.

And then she smiled brightly. It was that same fluffy-gentle smile that she'd made at me before.

Her calm tone relaxed the solemn air of the graduation ceremony, too. "Today, on a day graced by warm sunshine..."

But her smile only held for the very beginning, and as she got further in the address, her voice caught, and she bit her lips and hiccupped. Her throat trembled. I imagined she was telling herself, *Don't cry, don't cry.*

How emotional, watching her struggle so valiantly. I just about automatically muttered, *Eeeeemo...* under my breath.

Unfortunately, we *otaku* have the power of the emo-emo fruit, so being emo is kind of our specialty. We cry at concerts, and then on the way back after a show, we'll cry and write a poem about it to post online, and once the Blu-rays of the concert come out, we'll cry some more. The smallest thing will set us off.

That's just how much we love the emo stuff. We are native emo-lovers living in the *tsundere* region, the type who call into a voice actress's radio show or go to events where they hand out merch and act like we know *so* much better than everyone else.

I had to think about stupid things like this, or I kinda really would start to cry.

"And then to bring up more irreplaceable high school experiences, there was also the student council. We had so many events in which all the various classes, clubs, and volunteers all supported each other. I'll never forget the cultural festival and sports festival… They really were tough!" After holding it back all this time, she beamed like a flower bursting into bloom.

That smile caused a sharp numbness deep in my sinuses, and my field of vision started to blur. *Now that I think of it, this really was a heck of a year*, I thought, getting teary-eyed as events rose and fell over and over in my mind, like my life flashing before my eyes. *Wait, am I gonna die?*

The girl standing up at the podium was the one person I could truly call my senior. She wiped her eyes, voice trembling.

Sniffling as I listened, I suddenly felt a *tap, tap* on my shoulder.

I turned around with an aggrieved look. *What?! Shut up, I'm getting into this!* Hayama appeared even more aggrieved. He wordlessly jabbed his thumb to his other side, telling me to look over there.

I glanced that way, and Totsuka was cheerily pulling tissues from his pocket. "Are you all right, Hachiman?" Totsuka whispered with concern as he diligently delivered his tissues down the row like some kinda bucket relay.

Tobe also looked concerned as he passed them along. "D'you have allergies, Hikitani? Is it allergies? Those get nasty, man."

No! Shut up! I'm not allergic to pollen. I get itchy eyes and nose between early spring and early summer, but that's just all in my head. If I acknowledge it, I lose. Instead of saying so in words, I moaned a quiet *uuurgh*.

However he took that, Tobe added some more tissues. "Give these to Hikitani, too. Dude, I have allergies, too, y'know? It always sucks at the start of spring."

"Shhh, Tobe...," Hayama chided him, and Tobe replied with something like a voiceless *Dude...*

How can he be that loud even when he's whispering? He really is so obnoxious. He's a good guy, but an obnoxious one. I guess that's just what you'd expect from someone with allergies. Guys who carry tissues score high, in Hachiman terms. In fact, I score low Hachiman points for not carrying any.

By the time the chain went through Hayama, there were even more tissues. Hayama drew some from his breast pocket and shoved the whole packet at me.

I accepted them and honked. "Bangk yew...," I said in a teary voice as I shoved the packet back at him.

Hayama looked weirded out as he took it. "...You're crying too much."

"No, no, no, this is, like, you know. When you get older, your eyes tear up easy... Lately, I'll cry just from PreCure starting up..."

"So you cry every Sunday morning..."

"Don't forget the reruns. I cry on weekdays, too."

"I—I see..." Hayama was even more weirded out.

My tear ducts were trained on anime for little girls like PreCure and *Aikatsu!*, so they can start up in basically zero frames. I generally wind up crying twice a week, on Saturdays and Sundays, and now there are reruns on MC and Chiba TV, so I can cry a total of four times. Ever since they started airing multiple episodes back-to-back, I wind up crying tears by the gallon just from the OP.

And as I was crying, Meguri's reply address continued. "From this point forward, each of us will be taking one step after another, on our own two feet, toward our own futures. Even when we encounter major life obstacles down the road, we will be encouraged by the memories, the things we have learned, and the pride we acquired here at Soubu High School to live with strength. And so I sincerely thank you very much."

Eventually, she approached the finishing remarks. In terms of a live concert, it's about as exciting as when they say, "Next is our last song..." Here I was worked up like, *Come on, but I just got here!*

But even if the audience wanted it to keep going, just as any concert comes to a close, Meguri's farewell address would also reach its finale.

"As the representative for the graduates, I, Meguri Shiromeguri, feel so blessed that I've had the opportunity to read the reply address so I could offer my thanks to everyone I've been involved with over this time," Meguri finished off, then bowed her head deeply.

A long, long moment passed as her head was neatly lowered. During that moment of silence, all that could be heard were the sobs and the sorrowful sighs of the audience.

Eventually, Meguri lifted her head, and there was her Megurin ☆ Megurin smile. "Thank you so much, guys! I had so much fun! It was the best! Thank you very much!"

Then right before leaving, she squeezed the mike hard and yelled out loud, "Are you all getting cultural?!"

The whole audience stirred. The parents seemed confused, but the students immediately realized what came next and responded with raucous yells of "YEAHHH!"

Meguri grinned wide and sucked in a big breath. "Chiba is famous for...?"

"FESTIVALS AND DANCING!"

"If you're an idiot like me!"

"You've got to dance!"

"SING A SONG!"

For the bizarre call-and-response—essentially a chorus—all graduating and current students shouted back like idiots. The reminder of that moment from the cultural festival elicited smiles from us all. I thought the speech had been meant to make us cry until that point, but it all changed in an instant—in a good way, of course.

That was exactly the kind of mood Meguri had generated as student council president. I'm so disconnected from the older year, it'd be fair to say I don't know them at all, and neither am I interested in knowing them. Still, it seemed like a nice graduation ceremony.

Just having been able to see Meguri's smile made it worth coming to this.

Ahhh, this is actually the greatest, isn't it?

Once I get back, I need to tweet about how the event went in poem format!

× × ×

After the graduation ceremony and a brief homeroom, it was time to go home.

People were loath to say good-bye that day—not just the graduating students, but everyone else, too. Those who were members of clubs, or anyone who'd been involved with the graduates in some capacity, all quickly left the classrooms, presumably to say farewell to the departing students.

Hayama and his sidekicks, the three stooges, always lingered in the classroom a long time, but they were already gone, and tennis club captain Totsuka had also ambled his way out with some large bags in hand.

So as for myself, having had no involvement with the older students, all I had to do was go straight home.

I was in the emptying classroom and briskly getting ready to go when Yuigahama stepped over to my desk. "You're not going to the student council room? Meguri's supposed to be there."

"Oh... Well, I'd like to say a few words to her, but..." This would surely be the last time I saw Meguri. She had helped me with lots of stuff, so it would be polite to say good-bye to her.

But it was a little embarrassing to face her, right after having bawled like a baby. *Will I be okay? My eyes aren't puffy or anything, right? Oh no, I can't see Meguri like this... I've got to, like, lean back against a fridge and sink to the ground, touching a chilled spoon to my eyelids as I mutter,* Don't give in... *Like something out of a face cream commercial targeted at women three years into a dead-end job.*

As I was hesitating, Yuigahama must have felt skeptical about my pause, as she tilted her head quizzically. "But?"

"No, it's fine. It's nothing. Let's go." Trying to explain how my girlishly maiden heart was right about to experience a short in the maiden circuit would be the worst way to add shame on top of shame. Briskly ending the conversation, I stood up with my coat, bag, and the rest of my stuff in my arms.

Yuigahama's head was still cocked questioningly, but when I started walking off, she ambled on after me.

She must have realized the reason for my hesitation by the time we left the classroom because she came up a few steps ahead of me, turned her head back, and stared into my eyes. "…Ohhh. You were crying, huh? That's so funny. Are you shy about it?" She refrained from snickering, but not from teasing.

Her rather big-sisterly look made my voice momentarily catch in embarrassment and shame. "No, I'm not," I said a bit curtly in an attempt to cover it.

But that set off her giggling again. "Yumiko was crying, too, and she was so shy after. She's so cute…" Yuigahama had a warm smile on her face, and she really seemed pleased.

Ohhh, so that's why Miura left right away, hmm. So she was embarrassed, hmm. How adorable…

But it's not like I don't get the desire to cry. I'm kinda like that, too, after all…, I thought, and I found myself trying to justify it. "Well, it's normal to cry over stuff like that… Isshiki's address made me think, *Oh, wow. That no-good girl did her best to come up with a heartwarming speech*, and, like—Meguri! She went up there to do her best with a smile, but then she cried, and she ended her speech with another smile once she was done reading it out. And that chorus at the end was definitely ad-libbed. That was just, wow."

"I don't need a speech about it! Eugh, geez…weird… Don't be a weirdo…"

Well, her reaction was no surprise. *Otaku* will go right to calling stuff ad-libbed and then get emo about it. They'll even call it ad-libbed when there's a script—pro wrestling fans in the making, really. There's a high affinity between *otaku* culture and pro wrestling, which is why Bushiroad is so amazing. Just what's so amazing about them? Their efforts to keep doing it until they succeed, that's what. It's fair to say that's the quality most needed for IP holders these days.

I could have made some suspicious excuse-like counterarguments, but there was a more effective comeback here. "…Hey, you were crying, too." I shot her a dull look.

Yuigahama muttered under her breath. "I mean…that's 'cause Yumiko was crying… We'll be starting a new year with new classes, and then graduation's right around the corner, so…it kinda got me emotional, too." She giggled to hide her embarrassment but then immediately jerked her face away, pink-cheeked and pouting. Then she said under her breath, "…But I kinda wish you didn't see that stuff."

"Same goes to you…" As we jabbed at each other, we descended the stairs, and then suddenly there were more people around.

The third-year classrooms are on the first and second floors of the main school building, so maybe that was why kids were all over the hall, standing around, talking, and endlessly taking photos.

And then even after they were done leaning close together to take pictures, they wouldn't disperse right away. They'd keep finding more to converse about. I couldn't tell whether they were reluctant to go or just crap at communication and had missed their moment to leave. Whichever it was, they clearly had a hard time departing.

We went down the hallway, stepping out of the way of the graduating students and passing by a group that had fake corsages and their graduation albums pressed dearly to their chests. Were they going to gather autographs to fill up the final empty pages?

When I ceded way to the group, Yuigahama murmured as we passed by, "I'm definitely gonna lose it next year…"

It seemed like she was just talking to herself, so I made a meaningless listening sound like an *ahhh* or *huh*.

I could definitely see her crying at graduation. Huddled up with Ebina and Miura and holding hands as they whispered to each other intimately, they would certainly have a hard time saying good-bye.

Their crying today probably hadn't just been because they'd been affected by the atmosphere of the graduation ceremony. It was more than having projected themselves onto the event, imagining the path they would eventually walk down themselves. I think they had gotten emotional because of the even more imminent and real-feeling farewell that loomed ahead.

There were only a handful more opportunities left for us to pass through the door of the 2-F classroom we'd just left.

Even the ordinary classes, the casual lunchtimes, and the mundane scene of the school building empty after hours would be lost before long. We would enter our third year, and even if we saw similar sights, the faces there would change.

Miura had strong feelings about her current class. Of course, that was because Hayato Hayama was in it, but the relationships she'd built with her friends were hard to come by, too. And since she'd had that one quarrel with Yuigahama in particular, she'd be just that much more attached. The same would go for Yuigahama.

So then, on the other hand, what about me?

It's not like I wasn't thinking, *It's just a class change.* I hadn't felt that strongly about it before. I'd never bothered to contact anyone; I'd never made an effort to get closer once we'd drifted apart; I'd never tried to maintain any relationships. The only old classmate I'd seen since middle school graduation was Kaori Orimoto, and that reunion had been the product of coincidence.

If you don't see each other, you grow distant—that's just how things work. And then you get closer to new people. Every time their environment changes, people quickly get used to it.

You get used to it, get along, and get separated once again. If it goes by like this, it ends in good-bye.

We are always in the middle of saying good-bye.

Class changes and graduation ceremonies are probably practice for saying good-bye. By establishing a time limit beforehand, the good-bye is set up for you whether you like it or not. Regardless of anyone's feelings, it *will* happen. This very considerate design enables even those with the worst communication skills to cleanly say farewell. And you even have the plausible rationale of "because of graduation" or "because of the class change," so it comes with the free bonus excuse that there's nothing you could have done, even if you never see each other again.

Thanks to having experienced mini-farewells countless times, I'm now a pro at saying good-bye. I'm already in master territory when it comes to the technique—I can cleanly and flatly end association. I don't even need words. A natural finish that doesn't even make them aware of the parting—*this* is the work of an artisan. It's so frighteningly quick, you'd miss it, if you weren't me. It's a habit of mine to live without being noticed.

So, well, if you look at it from the opposite angle…

…I've never had a proper farewell.

In my part-time jobs, I have staged memorable farewells by flaking out without a word to anyone, then later sending back the uniform by cash-on-delivery. I'd call it a power move, really.

Whatever shall I talk about with Meguri after this? I was wondering as we arrived at the door of the student council room.

Feeling a bit nervous, I knocked on the door.

"C-come in…" The reply came in a stutter. I couldn't quite tell through the door, but it was probably Isshiki.

Why does she sound so tired? I wondered, and upon opening the door, that question was immediately resolved.

Through the door in the middle of the student council room, Meguri was squeezing Yukinoshita and Isshiki in her arms as she sobbed. "Thank you guys so, so much! I really loved the student council!"

"You're too close…" Yukinoshita was helpless in her grasp, while Isshiki was sneakily turning her face away to sigh.

Mm-hmm, I appreciate her taking care like that so Meguri can't see. What a pleasant sight…, I was thinking when Meguri noticed us.

"Ohhh! Yuigahama and Hikigaya! You came!" And this time, Meguri leaped on Yuigahama.

Yuigahama must have been used to intimacy with other girls, as she hugged back completely naturally. Impressive as always… My heart started pounding. *Eek, eek! What if she hugs me, too?!*

"Thanks so much to you guys, too! This was tough, but I had so much fun!" Meguri began as she took Yuigahama's hands.

"Me too!" Yuigahama replied, and Yukinoshita breathed a sigh of relief upon her release. There was something awfully nostalgic about that, and I couldn't help but smile.

For an instant, our eyes caught.

Yukinoshita immediately jerked her eyes away again, looking over toward the clock. "The vendors are going to be here with deliveries soon," she said to Isshiki, "so I'm going to go."

"I feel like it's still a little early…" Isshiki cocked her head skeptically, then rummaged in her pocket and pulled out a paper that looked like the schedule. "Hmm, it's not quite time, but maybe it'll be better than being late. How about I go with you?"

Yukinoshita shook her head. "I'll just be keeping an eye on them, so no one else needs to be there. Well then, Shiromeguri, I'll see you at the prom."

"Yeah! See you later!" Meguri smiled brightly back at her, and then Yukinoshita bowed and left the student council room. Meguri gave her a big wave, then glanced at her own watch. "There's still prom preparation. I've got to go get changed, too…," she mumbled.

Beside her, Yuigahama's eyes sparkled. "Oh! What kind of dress are you wearing?"

"It's so amazing! It's, like, really wow, you know! Sexy."

"Sexy…" Yuigahama was taken aback at the blunt appraisal.

But Meguri pulled out her phone with a gloating chuckle. Yuigahama peered at the picture there, and the two of them started whispering stuff to each other.

"It's not that revealing, but the silhouette is pretty sexy. Really flattering," Meguri explained.

"Ohhh… Sexy."

As the pair were having a quiet conversation, Isshiki popped her head between them to get a peek. "Going right up to the line of what's allowed, huh? It's a cute style, but it feels fetishy."

"Right? When I saw it in the catalog, I thought, *Yes, this one*, and went to try it on!"

"Huh, so did you go with the other third-years? Dress shopping together sounds fun!" said Yuigahama.

"Yep, yep. And since I'd been contacting lots of people for stuff, we all wound up going together." Meguri touched her phone screen and flicked along with her finger. With each flick, Yuigahama reacted *ahhh* or *ohhh* or *wooow*, a twincool ☆ in her eyes.

Isshiki, on the other hand, was the picture of composure. "Ahhh, I see. Oh, thank you so much for notifying everyone about the guidelines and coordinating things."

"It's nothing at all!" Meguri replied. "It'd been so long since I'd done some kind of event—it was so much fun."

The gaggle of young ladies did truly seem to be having fun looking at their phones, but meanwhile, I was fidgeting and glancing all around thinking, *Can I see?*

Being a boy, I find it kind of hard to join conversations like this. Oh, I know that the correct thing to do with topics like these is to not join in. Even if I had been able to squeak out a *Show meee*, I didn't feel like I could offer any opinions there that wouldn't violate compliance standards. The best I could offer would be something like *Hmm, that's hot*. So then it would be better to say nothing. In fact, it would be way, way better.

As a result, I was frozen like a Jizo statue off to the side as I listened to the girls talk excitedly.

As I was Jizoing so hard that I could expect to get some offerings placed in front of me soon, Meguri put away her phone and smiled at me. It seemed she was trying to be considerate. "We never get the chance to wear things like this, so I'm glad you're putting on the prom. Thanks, Hikigaya."

"Oh, well…I don't have much to do with it…since it's Yukinoshita and the others who are doing it." Put on the spot from having the conversation suddenly turned to me, I got flustered and plastered on a pained grin.

"Oh…" Meguri's expression wilted a bit.

My heart prickled with guilt, causing me to do some bizarre backpedaling. "…Well, I do plan to help out some, so I'll be around for the prom."

"Ohhh, that's great. I was thinking it would be nice to see everyone, since this is the end." Relieved, Meguri wore a lighthearted smile. However, her last remark sounded lonely—maybe she herself was aware of that. "I never thought I would graduate…," she whispered, gazing out over the student council room with affection.

Those words were not for us.

Seeing everyone go quiet, Meguri flailed her hands to cover the silence as she babbled, "Oh, of course I knew! I obviously meant to graduate, and I'm going to university! Not that, but like…" Her fluffy, easy smile trailed off as her words did. Suddenly, her eyes watered. "Like… like, you know?" She chuckled as if in an attempt to cover the droplets beading in the corners of her eyes.

Yuigahama returned her smile with a gentle one of her own. "I kinda get it."

Meguri thanked her quietly, genuinely shy, then turned back to us. "…Let's all do something fun together again sometime. Though…I won't be a student here anymore. But you guys all still have time!"

"Yeah…," Yuigahama said.

"…I'll do what I can," I added.

I didn't think that would happen. But there was no point in saying any of that now.

I think Yuigahama and I probably wore similar expressions—as if we were smothering something or holding back, biting our lips, quietly lowering our eyes.

Meguri didn't say anything more, only looked at us kindly. Then her gaze shifted over to Isshiki. "Isshiki. I'm counting on you to take care of Soubu High School." And then she offered a crisp bow, bending properly at the waist.

Isshiki didn't know what to say. Stunned, she blinked a few times, but she quickly pulled herself together and looked Meguri in the eye. "Yes, I will… I mean, I'm pretty much handling it already," she said, forcing a smile.

"Ah-ha-ha, true," Meguri said nonchalantly. After laughing a bit, she smacked herself in the cheeks to get herself fired up. "All right! Good-byes done!"

Then she took one step forward.

"See you later, then! Let's chat lots at the prom! You'd better!" Waving hard, Meguri left.

Even as she was closing the door, right before it closed, she poked her face through the opening to wave some more. *It makes you look like Jack Nicholson in* The Shining, *so please stop. When you do all that, it makes me feel like I've got to wave back, too…*

Once the slowly, slowly moving door closed completely, I was finally able to lower my arm. A tired sigh came out of me.

Isshiki had patiently been watching us. "Wow, you really like Meguri, huh?" she mumbled.

"Oh, I was thinking that, too," agreed Yuigahama.

"…Huh? Does anyone not like her?" I said.

"Ah, I doubt it. And hey, why do you sound kinda mad…?" Yuigahama gave a breathy laugh.

But whyever is Irohasu silent on that point, hmm? You can't be folding your arms and making that face! It's like you assume she must have enemies! That's the problem with you!

Isshiki noticed my mildly chiding look and lightly cleared her throat. Then she changed the subject and put on a nasty smirk. "All right then, for the sake of your beloved Meguri, let's have you get some work done."

Hmm… There's something about that phrasing that bothers me…

× × ×

Isshiki took us to the gym, where the prom would be held.

The light of the setting sun faintly colored the floor and walls in orange, while the heater at the back was blazing red. They kept it from feeling too cold despite how large the space was.

I swept my gaze around to see that the decorating was proceeding smoothly, too; the gym was dressed up in lively balloon art and flower stands and different types of disco balls. Where it had been solemn from the earlier graduation ceremony, now it looked kind of exciting.

And in this festive space, the area around Yukinoshita felt businesslike, almost chilly. She was off to the side discussing something with a delivery employee in overalls.

I watched them from a distance, but the moment it looked like they were about done, Isshiki left us behind and trotted up to Yukinoshita. "Yukinoooo, it's tiiime!"

When Yukinoshita heard Isshiki's call, she bowed politely to the employee, spun toward us, and hurried over.

And then her feet stopped.

"...Hikigaya."

She squeezed the collar of her blazer, swallowing what she was about to say. The confused tilt of her eyebrows was asking why I was there.

Maybe I should have made some kind of excuse.

Unfortunately, I didn't have enough to convince her, but I also understood that there was no point in offering some careless and forced-sounding logic, either. I just happened to be present because I'd let myself get swept away by events. This was the result of passing the buck to someone who was not me.

Of course I couldn't say anything, so I just nodded with a sort of acknowledging look.

"Working hard, huh, Yukinon?! We came to help." Yuigahama stepped in between Yukinoshita and me as we both remained silent.

Yukinoshita bowed her head apologetically. "I see... I'm sorry."

"It's totally fine! Don't worry about it! I was planning to help from the beginning anyway," Yuigahama babbled excitedly.

Yukinoshita finally smiled. "Thank you."

I opened my mouth, thinking I should say something, but Isshiki tapped my shoulder and cut me off. "Well, you can never have too many people. Glaaad to have you," she said lightly, but behind those words, I very intensely felt the pressure: *I don't want to deal with any more of your back-and-forth*. Then she immediately started handing out the schedule.

"So let's discuss what we're gonna do." Once everyone had a copy of the schedule, Isshiki pulled a pen out from her breast pocket and briskly began leading the meeting. "We're having Yukino handle general management while I do MCing and sound. The vice prez is in charge of lighting, clerk's on catering, and for odd jobs, we have the soccer club lackeys, plus we're pulling personnel from some other clubs."

I mostly ignored what Isshiki said as I swept my gaze over the gym interior. Indeed, it seemed there were some unfamiliar faces who were not from the student council. Hayama, as the leader of the captains' association, must have helped them get some hands for manual labor. This enabled Yukinoshita and the student council to focus their efforts on management.

Ohhh, smart, I was thinking, when Isshiki nonchalantly added, "Oh, and we've got someone scary coming for dealing with costume-related issues."

What the heck? Does she mean Kawasaki? She's talking like it's some criminal organization… But she's such a good person… I was appalled.

Meanwhile, Isshiki was writing something into the schedule. Her face jerked up, and she turned her big round eyes on Yukinoshita. "What are we going to do with these two?" she asked.

Putting a hand to her mouth, Yukinoshita paused. "Hmm… If we're going to have them help, then reception, sound, or lighting would be good places, I suppose."

"I'll take the reception. If Hikki did reception…" Yuigahama had stuck her hand up a bit to instantly accept the job, but the second half of that statement was totally vague.

Isshiki took over after that, nodding. "For sure."

As expected of Miss Gahama and Irohasu, they know me oh so very well. I also know myself very well, so I nodded along with them.

Yukinoshita did not join in with them; instead, she turned to Yuigahama. "It's not as if there will be a large number, but some parents will show up, so please make sure to register them if they do. Also, check student IDs."

"We'll have Tobe and the lackeys stand by the reception, so if there are any disputes, just dump everything on them and call for me or Yukino," Isshiki smoothly supplemented.

"Okeydoke," Yuigahama replied lightly.

Wait, so Tobe's a lackey…? And he's on his feet the whole time…?

"So then, as for you…," Isshiki began, looking back and forth between Yukinoshita and me.

"Yes…," Yukinoshita said, but she didn't continue. She bit the edge of her lip pensively. She gave me no instructions.

Using my own skills of inference based on what they'd said earlier, there were two remaining candidates: sound and lighting. "There's a lot of staging stuff that goes into lighting, right? It seems like it'd be hard if you don't know the whole program." I looked over at Isshiki beside me, and she nodded.

"For sure," she replied. "So then please help out on sound. I did mostly plan to handle it myself, but I won't be able to avoid going back and forth, so it'll be a help to have someone permanently stationed there."

"Roger. Anything I should watch out for?"

"I numbered all the songs on the schedule, so if you just put them on like it says on the playlist, there should basically be no problem. And you'll have cues, so it should be fine."

"Huh, okay." So they'd already made a playlist of songs, and they'd already set up the audio equipment. So then all I had to worry about was the technical aspect. "Can I try it out?" I jabbed a thumb over to the right side of the stage, toward the tech booth that was on the mezzanine. Even if I was there only as an extra set of hands, you never knew what sort of situation might crop up once things actually got going. I decided I should try playing around with the equipment so that I could handle its basic operation.

"Oh, sure. Then let's head over." Isshiki took the lead, prompting me to follow, so we all headed off to the tech booth.

We went up the dark stairs from the stage wings and entered a little room. Then, Yuigahama, who came in after Yukinoshita, examined the place with a curious *ohhh*.

It was true this was someplace you wouldn't normally go. I did remember that, during the cultural festival, part of my work on odd jobs had been to do an overall check of the sound equipment, but it wasn't like I'd actually fiddled with anything.

I was starting to worry whether I could actually do this now. I saw the soundboard, lit with forlorn red lights, placed by the small window on the wall.

As prompted by Isshiki, I sat down on the chair in front of the board. Placed on top of the soundboard was a laminated instruction manual, as well as a playlist with lots of stuff written on it.

The soundboard clearly indicated the maximum level with masking tape so that even students could operate it. The fader I'd be using also had colored tape wrapped around the knob so that you'd notice it at a glance. With these kinds of guides, I probably wouldn't have trouble handling it.

"I'm gonna try putting on a song," I said.

"Go ahead," Isshiki said.

I clicked a button, and thus began the kind of danceable EDM that would make someone like Tobe say *This party's gettin' crazy!*

Comparing the script with the playlist, I checked all the sound material that had been set up, actually playing some songs while also figuring out how to handle the audio player. That wasn't much of a problem, either.

Anything else I should check…? I wondered as I had a staring contest with the schedule and the soundboard.

Then I came to a realization: Putting on music wasn't sound's only job. It was fair to say just about everything audio was in that category. So managing microphones would be my job, too.

"What about the mikes?" I asked. "How many, and where?"

"Huh? Oh, hold on..." Isshiki flipped through the schedule.

Yukinoshita beat her to it. "We have one wired microphone at stage right, and Isshiki has one wireless. I'll be putting an extra wireless one at stage left, just in case," she said as she pulled out some white masking tape from her blazer pocket and ripped off strips to stick under each fader. I snatched up a felt-tip pen that had been left on the table and wrote *Yukinoshita*, *Isshiki*, and *Extra* on the pieces of tape.

Now we've checked the mikes. So then..., I thought, flipping through the schedule to check, and I found some unfamiliar words. "What's this *slideshow...*?" I asked about the English word, tapping on the schedule.

Isshiki peeked over from the side. "Oh, this? We gathered photos of the graduates from a bunch of people to put together some slides. It's not much of a compilation, though."

"'Kay..." It seemed there had been various updates to the prom plan that I hadn't been aware of. These days, you can do basic image editing on your phone. I didn't know about the quality, but it wouldn't take much labor, and if it would make the graduates a little happier and more excited for the event, I'd call it extremely cost-effective content.

I guess they've come up with a lot of good ideas. Impressed, I circled the applicable places of the schedule in red as I checked it over. "So then, the only thing that looks like it'll be a hassle to manage is the slideshow. What about the projection equipment?" I spun around in my chair and stopped with Isshiki right in front of me.

But the answer to my question came back instantly from the person next to her. "It's a line-out from a PC. We already went over lighting coordination during the tech rehearsal. I'll be handling the images, so you just have to worry about sliding the fader up and down," Yukinoshita said, already setting up the computer. It seemed she intended to show me.

I'd clear up all my questions now. "Roger. Do you need a black screen at the beginning for the slideshow? How many seconds?"

"After ten seconds of black, there's a ten-second countdown."

"Can we try just that part?"

"Yes. Isshiki, could you give us the cue?"

"…Huh? Ah, sure!" Isshiki suddenly snapped out of her daze, surprised at having the discussion suddenly turned to her.

Yukinoshita gave her a questioning look. "What is it?"

"Oh, I just kinda thought, *Huh, you're talking a lot…*" Isshiki looked over at Yuigahama for backup.

Yuigahama made an awkward face. "Well, this is the usual kinda stuff…" She smiled like she didn't know what else to do and smooshed her bun, and Yukinoshita and I both closed our mouths. Now it was awkward. It felt like the tech booth would drown in silence.

My reflexes took over, which meant jokes. "Uh, sorry! Bet it's freaking you out to see silent Hachiman talking at this stuff, huh?"

"Yeahhh, well, you're not wrong…," said Isshiki.

…Is that true? Do I freak you out, Irohasu?

Isshiki cleared her throat to avoid my resentment, also using the opportunity to check her throat. Then with an air mike in one hand and a total lack of enthusiasm for the rehearsal, she said, "Right. Well then, next is the slideshow. Wooow, click, click, click."

"…Then Isshiki will exit the stage, and the lights slowly dim to black. Once the lights are all out, the images come up." Yukinoshita explained what came next as she worked the computer. She was such a stage director. She smacked the Enter key in a definitive manner.

A black box with no sound was projected onto the screen that was lowered over the stage. Meanwhile, I slid down the faders on BGM and mikes and stuff, raising only the faders of the PC audio.

When I looked onto the stage through the little window, the image on the projector became a countdown, the numbers decreasing with a rattling-film SFX. Eventually, the count reached zero, and with a moving song I knew well from hearing it on ads, the slideshow began.

Along with a tear-jerking emo-emo song, the memories of the graduates' history were displayed, one by one.

Oh, this is pretty well done, I thought, watching the slideshow in a detached mood, when it suddenly hit me. This had to be the first time I'd ever seen these pictures. *So then what the heck are these feelings welling up…?* I wondered.

But Yuigahama murmured the answer. "I kinda feel like I've seen this before..."

"Well, that's what happens when you use this song...," I said, unable to quite put this sense of déjà vu into words.

Isshiki, who'd apparently been the one to make the slideshow, huffed indignantly. "It's fine—the priority is being straightforward and simple. You're allowed to cry!"

"I have the feeling they'll assume it's a parody and laugh, though..." Yukinoshita chuckled, resigned to her prediction.

Well, it wasn't like I didn't get Isshiki's point.

There was nothing particularly unique about this slideshow, and the production wasn't fancy. It was just a string of photos of graduates, or images that looked like they'd been taken with a phone. But with that tearjerker music, it was guaranteed to affect the people in question, and that emotion couldn't be put into words.

Eventually, the music faded out, and then the message *Congratulations on your graduation* displayed over a fancy background, and the slideshow was done.

"So then, once that's ended, the lights go up slowly. Our MC comes onstage again," Yukinoshita explained.

Nodding, I noted the length of the slideshow on the schedule. "...I more or less get it. If this is how it is, then I feel like I can handle putting on the slideshow, too."

"That would be helpful. During the tech rehearsal, someone who happened to be free was able to do it, but once things actually get started, we'll really need someone."

"Mm, well, I'll basically be stationed here, so I'll handle it. While I'm going over everything, can I mess around with the equipment? I wanna make some noise."

"That's fine as long as it's before the venue opens," Yukinoshita said.

"Roger. So is that all we need to talk about?" I flipped through the schedule once more, wanting to confirm that there was nothing else to check. When I looked up from the pages, I found myself staring into Yukinoshita's eyes.

Though her dewy eyes were smiling, they also seemed somehow distant, and my eyes moved to the side.

"...Yes. Well then, please handle things from here. Isshiki, let's go to lighting," Yukinoshita said to her, and then she turned around and started walking out.

Isshiki hurried after her. "Huh? Oh, roger. Well then, laters."

With a casual raise of my hand instead of a response, I spun around in my chair and faced the soundboard again.

Behind me, the loud pattering of their footsteps grew distant. And then, mingling with that sound was the scrape of a chair drawing back.

I looked over, and Yuigahama was taking a seat in the chair beside me. "Think you're gonna be okay?" she asked me with concern.

I gave her a little shrug. "...Well, it'll probably be fine," I answered.

But she still looked kind of uneasy. "Oh...the stuff you were talking about sounded kinda complicated, so I was just wondering."

"If I can get used to it, it'll work out somehow," I said, smiling at her before I looked down at the equipment.

That's right. It's only a matter of getting used to it.

And so, to speed up that process, I reached out to the Play button on the soundboard. My cold fingers slowly pushed up the fader to put on a song with a name I didn't know. It was some EDM I had never heard before.

It was really modern-sounding music, like something that would play in a club, and I scowled in spite of myself. But if I kept listening, my ears would get used to it.

The handling of the mixing board, the unfamiliar EDM, the sampled airhorn that was so grating, and the bass rumbling from the other side of the speakers...

Eventually, it would all become natural to me, and I would adjust.

× × ×

The setting sun was seeping in through the cracks of the blackout shades that had been put over the windows. Joining that light was the single shining ray of a spotlight and the diffuse reflections of the disco balls. I guessed it was time for the final lighting check.

It wouldn't be long until they opened up the gym.

Being in charge of sound, I was scrambling to finish my various final tasks.

"Test, test...ah, test, test..." I checked the wired mike connection on stage right. "Mike check, one, two." As I spoke, my voice came back at me from the speakers.

I looked up at the small window of the sound room on stage left to see the face of the other person on sound, Isshiki. I made a big circle with my arms at her.

Isshiki grinned and also made a big O with her arms like Hakutsuru Maru as she tilted her whole body slightly. That deceptive cuteness...

"Hikigaya."

Hearing my name, I turned around to see Yukinoshita coming over. She was holding some black headphones with added cords and stuff, what you'd call a microphone headset. "I'll cue you with this."

"Wow, this brings back memories." I closely examined the two she handed to me. I'd used one of these before during the cultural festival and the other events.

"..." Yukinoshita didn't really say anything about that; she just turned away from me. "...Give the other set to Isshiki."

"O-okay."

Nothing resembling conversation happened after that.

Our earlier conversation had been so smooth and free of self-consciousness, but now silence hung in the darkness of the stage wings. *If I had something to do, a little bit of silence wouldn't bother me*, I thought, looking at my idle hands, and I saw I was still holding the wired microphone.

Ah, oh yeah. The thought struck me. "Are you using a stand for your microphone?" I called to Yukinoshita, and she turned back.

She looked a bit confused. "Y-yes...I plan to."

As soon as I heard that, I grabbed the mike stand that had been left at the back of the wings. Yukinoshita brought it forward and set the mike in it.

"How's the height? About here?" I squatted down to adjust it, and above, Yukinoshita sighed like she didn't know what to do with me.

"...That's perfect, but...I can handle this myself," she muttered, eyes on the floor, and my hands stopped.

I'd gone too far again, even if it was just to cover the awkwardness, and the inside of my mouth tasted bitter with self-loathing. "...Yeah. Sorry." I released the mike stand and stood up, taking a couple of steps back.

"No, it's nothing to apologize for..."

"Oh...okay."

In the darkness of the stage wings where the lighting didn't reach, that wordless exhalation was like a solid mass, making me hesitate to even move.

Though it had to have been just a few moments, it felt as if I was frozen there for a very long time. Yukinoshita probably felt uncomfortable, too, as she eventually sighed quietly. She practically forced herself to say: "...Um, if I was being strange, I apologize."

"Huh? Uh, no, I think you were normal..." Surprised by her unexpected remark, I was the totally weird one now.

"I'm not sure how I should talk about it..."

Wow... You wonder what she would say in such a stifling moment, and then she says that...

But, well, it was like her.

Yukinoshita wasn't really the type of person who easily read social situations. I'd even say she couldn't. Or perhaps to be more accurate, she was deliberately not placed in an environment where it would be necessary for her to do so.

But she'd spent this past year with Yuigahama and me, and I felt like she'd been gaining that skill bit by bit. Whether that was a good thing, I had no idea. Excessively reading into social situations and trying to act natural can sometimes lead to weirdly spinning your wheels.

The fact was that I still didn't quite understand how to respond, either.

All the more so if she was going to look at me like she was one step away from crying, either from the discomfort or from her shyness. As she constantly fixed her bangs and combed the long black hair over her shoulders, her gaze darting around, I couldn't even guess as to what kind of words I could come up with in reply.

In the end, after a long hesitation, I wound up giving her a pretty foolish, vague answer. "Oh… You could just be normal…"

"Normal… Yes, yes, of course." She nodded like she was swallowing. I nodded back at her to show I was listening, and if anyone had seen us, we would have looked like a couple of pigeons competing for territory. She must have been trying to calm herself, as she was muttering under her breath, "Normal, normal."

The scene oddly calmed me. The corners of my lips relaxed on their own, and that enabled my words to come out smoothly. "Well, it's busy now, so there's not much time to think about other stuff, right? You'll be able to go on normally soon enough, right? Or, I dunno."

"Y-yes. Once things have settled down, I think I'll be able to do a little better…"

We believed that this had to be normal. That was exactly why we were trying to be normal. We wanted to believe that this relationship wasn't strange.

I'd managed to get out a couple of decent sentences there, so maybe that was why Yukinoshita gradually regained her composure, too. Quietly clearing her throat, she made to start over. "I didn't mean anything bad by that, before… Um, it is a fact that we need help, and I am grateful, so…"

"Mm. Well, I basically get it. It's not like I gave this much thought, either… I just wound up helping because things led in that direction. I really couldn't be totally uninvolved." I half grinned.

Yukinoshita shook her head, trying to dispel any worries about that. "I believe this was unavoidable, since Isshiki is counting on you after all." And then she finally smiled at me. It felt like it had been a long time since she'd last used that half-teasing tone, too.

"Relying on me." That's a rather wonderful rewording, isn't it? Is that the political correctness that's in fashion these days?

"Isshiki has grown a lot lately. I figure I'll be out of a job soon. Then I won't be doing this kind of work anymore."

"I'm not so sure about that. I doubt that girl will let go of you so easily," Yukinoshita said.

"That's a scary way to put it. Yikes…," I answered carelessly as I proceeded with the task. Now that I was getting talking, the tension in my body was relaxing, too.

Then, as I was wrapping the mike wire so it wouldn't get tangled, a faint vibration joined that sound.

"Pardon me," Yukinoshita said, pulling out her phone and looking at the screen. Then she breathed a tired sigh. Her features were lit by the phone backlight, and a line furrowed in her brow. That expression remained on her face as she looked up at the little window of the tech booth. Following her gaze, I saw Isshiki in the window of the booth, pressing her hands together and bowing her head.

"…What is it? Did something happen?" I asked.

"It's nothing serious," Yukinoshita said, then left the wings in a bit of a rush.

Is there some kind of problem? Worried, I followed after her, poking my head out of the wings.

And then, below the stage, I saw Yukinoshita and Ms. Hiratsuka talking about something. Yukinoshita's mother and Haruno were coming in after her.

Why's the teacher here…? Actually, why are Mrs. Yukinoshita and Haruno here…? I was wondering when my eyes met with Ms. Hiratsuka's over Yukinoshita's shoulder.

"Oh, you're here, too, Hikigaya? Sorry to come when you're in the middle of setting things up," Ms. Hiratsuka said.

"Oh, it's fine…"

Behind the waving Ms. Hiratsuka, Yukinoshita's mother saw me and smiled. She waved at me just like Ms. Hiratsuka had. "Hikigaya, we meet again."

"Ha-ha… Hi…" I would have liked to leave after just casual greetings, if possible.

However, Mrs. Yukinoshita seemed fully intent on continuing the conversation, beckoning me with little hand gestures. Haruno was staring right at me, and I could tell I wasn't getting off that easy.

I dragged my heavy legs a few steps closer. Mrs. Yukinoshita sounded pleased as she said to me, "So you're participating in the prom. I'm looking forward to seeing that dance you're so good at."

"Ha-ha-ha…," I replied with a flat laugh, and Haruno gave me a skeptical look.

"Dancing? Is that a talent of yours?" she said with a half smile.

"Oh yes, he is. He's quite good. So good, he even had me dancing in the palm of his hand," Mrs. Yukinoshita joked, looking surprisingly innocent as she laughed like tinkling bells.

"Huh…" Though Haruno's tone sounded impressed, her eyes were cold.

As I was caught in her meaningful gaze, Yukinoshita cut between us. "You came to check on things, didn't you? I have other business to deal with. Could we wrap this up quickly?"

"Oh, of course." With her daughter sighing in impatience, Mrs. Yukinoshita restrained a grin, then slowly swept her gaze over the gym.

From what I could tell, Yukinoshita's mother had come to make sure the prom venue was appropriate for high school students. Isshiki must have contacted Yukinoshita to deal with her. Well, since Yukinoshita was in charge of managing the event, it was an appropriate choice of personnel.

"You've prepared things well in such a short time. This was worth going to the trouble of putting up a fake to buy time." Mrs. Yukinoshita's gaze circled around everything from walls to ceiling, and then she nodded. Her eyes slid over and, when they saw me, froze. "And besides, after having seen such a wild proposal, I don't have the urge to complain about this. This should satisfy the nitpickers, too… It's a rather well-arranged plan."

"Uh, it's not like I did all that. It was all…" I just about to say *thanks to your daughter* when, behind Mrs. Yukinoshita, Haruno's eyes narrowed. She never said anything, but her gaze seemed to be testing me.

I didn't run my mouth any further.

I shouldn't butt in on this. I could loudly insist that the credit wasn't mine, but there was no point. It would only have the opposite effect.

Mrs. Yukinoshita tilted her head at me, waiting for me to continue.

I couldn't reply, though. I turned toward Yukinoshita.

Even if this was just a trivial exchange of words, it shouldn't have been me facing her mother, but Yukinoshita herself. This was a woman who would nitpick until she plucked out every hair on your head after all. Offering some shoddy support would only hold Yukinoshita back.

As if she'd figured out what my silence meant, Ms. Hiratsuka had a twinkle in her eye. "All of this was thanks to the understanding and cooperation of parents and guardians. Wouldn't you say so, Chief Organizer Yukinoshita?" She jokingly clapped a hand on Yukinoshita's back and smiled at her. Yukinoshita looked bewildered to have the discussion suddenly turned to her.

Then she figured out what the teacher meant by that additional remark after her formalities. "Y-yes. I express my gratitude as the one responsible for this plan." Yukinoshita was suddenly much more courteous than before and made a clean bow from the waist to her mother. "While I wouldn't assume the event is without its flaws, since this is a major life event for us, it's my hope that you will not look upon the prom too harshly. If any of the guests have doubts or reservations, I will respond with explanations as needed." Yukinoshita slowly straightened again to look her mother in the eye. There was a clear distance and tension in that gesture and in her expression.

"Indeed. We may be mother and child, but a little more dignity is required. You're finally acting like someone in charge... Well then, as the trustee of the parents' association, I will have the honor of evaluating this event."

"Please go right ahead."

Seeing her daughter's resolution, Mrs. Yukinoshita smiled boldly. She flicked her fan over the twisted split of her smile to hide it. "If I might cut to the chase and cover a few points? First, about the ending time and what comes after…" Her pleased tone reminded me of ringing bells.

"Yes, you mean establishing security for the venue and surrounding area? It's in the documents that I've arranged over there. Please follow me." Yukinoshita took the lead, and her mother and Ms. Hiratsuka followed.

Behind them, a few steps back, Haruno walked off. Then as she passed by, she touched my shoulder and whispered in my ear, "You did a good job sucking it up… It's best like that." Her gentle tone was sweet enough to send shivers down my spine, but I could hear the loneliness in it.

With that, Haruno Yukinoshita departed without waiting for my response.

Left there all alone, I expelled a deep, dismal sigh and turned my face up to the ceiling.

× × ×

Before, I'm sure I would have thought up something clever and butted in.

There's no need for that from now on. To be more precise, I finally understood that I couldn't do that.

The things that I *could* do and *should* do were incredibly limited. As for the current situation, there was only one thing I should do—work.

Sighing to my heart's content, once I'd had a short rest, I decided to return to the tech booth.

My feet clanged up the narrow stairs, and I opened the door.

"Thank you for your help," Isshiki called from inside, slumped back in the rolling chair and spinning around in boredom.

I pulled out the chair beside her and sat down in front of the soundboard. While I was at it, I put one of the headsets I was carrying in front of Isshiki. "Ditto. Here's your headset."

"Okaaay, thanks." Isshiki rolled her whole chair over to me and took the headset. And then, like an afterthought, she leaned in to my shoulder and lowered her voice to whisper. "Everything good? Did that old bag say something?"

"Old bag…? Come on…" That lady is super youthful for her age—although I don't know what her age is. But being the mother of those two, she's beautiful and generally comes off as intensely scary, but she's also occasionally charming, you know? Even if that's scary, too!

I considered saying this to defend her, but I got the feeling it would be pointless. Since Isshiki had gotten into that nasty dispute with her before, she wasn't going to think well of her. Ohhh, what a coincidence! Me neither, me neither!!

So I abandoned that defense and just answered the question. "Yukinoshita is handling her fine. Everything's all right."

"Huh," Isshiki answered disinterestedly, leaning her chin on her hand on the desk. Then she murmured, "It doesn't seem like you need a translator anymore."

"What?"

"You were talking normally with Yukino, weren't you? During the meeting. Just now, too," Isshiki said, jabbing the end of her chin toward the little window. It seemed she'd seen everything that had just gone on in the wings of stage left.

"…Yeah. Well, work-based discussions don't really require translation. I'm bad at small talk and chatting, but I'm actually quite good at business communications."

"Uh, why're you bragging about that…?" Isshiki was weirded out, waving a hand to stop me. But then she put that hand to her cheek, letting out a wafting sigh like she didn't know what to do with me. "But I guess some people are like that—boys who count business talk as conversation."

"Hey! Some boys just can't talk to girls without an excuse. Those poor guys. Cut them some slack." I tried to get Isshiki to knock it off, but she wasn't about to listen.

"Generally, with guys like that, once you've talked about three times, he suddenly starts to call you by your first name, and by the fifth time, he'll invite you to hang out. And then he confesses he likes you, and after that, he stops talking to you."

"Stop it, stop it, stop it. Seriously, stop. Hey, what the heck, did you go to the same middle school as me?"

"No... But it's true you've made excuses like that, too..." Isshiki shot me a blank stare. Then a thought struck her, and she scooted away from me. "Ah! Wait, I hope you didn't use this work talk to get closer to me 'cause you were gonna confess to me 'cause I don't mind going to hang out but for any more than that please make it after everything is over I'm sorry."

She finished off that garble of words with a neat bow of her head.

"Yeah, yeah, once it's all over," I told her. "So do your job. It's not gonna get done otherwise."

"He did it again... He didn't listen to me at all..."

You think I'm gonna listen to all that...?

"And anyway, it's not like I hate working, you know." Isshiki gave me a huffy look as she put on the headset. Then she made a show of spreading open the schedule and pulling out her laptop to start typing something. I watched her in my peripheral vision as I checked over the soundboard operations.

Isshiki burst into laughter out of nowhere. "...I really like these times, you know."

"Well, being backstage staff is fun in its own way." It feels weirdly fulfilling to handle equipment like a soundboard or to put on a headset and play assistant director. I immediately put on the headphones to check them, and Isshiki spun around in her chair and turned to me again.

"Why not do it next year, too?"

"Next year I'll be one of the people being sent off..." *Even if this kind of work doesn't bother me, doing it again for my own graduation is kinda...* I grimaced at the thought.

But Isshiki wasn't smiling. "...That's not what I meant. I'm talking about the Service Club," she said earnestly, putting her hands on her thighs and straightening her back. She surely meant that in a number of different ways.

But even if I did attempt to interpret those, my answer wouldn't change. "Ask the person in charge. I don't have any authority over club activities," I answered, but her eyes on me wouldn't allow any evasive answers. I broke under the pressure and looked away. "…Besides, there won't be a Service Club anymore."

This was probably the first time I'd said it aloud.

Yukinoshita, Yuigahama, and possibly Ms. Hiratsuka had sensed it, but I don't think any of them had made it explicit verbally. Even if it had popped out of their mouths casually as a joke when it had come up in conversation, I don't think it had ever been declared, or if anyone had seriously sought to confirm it, so I'd always managed to avoid seriously thinking about it.

But now that I had said it out loud, it was a clear and unavoidable fact.

"So there's no reason for me to work." Getting this far, I was finally able to look into Isshiki's eyes.

When our gazes met, hers turned gentle. She smiled, then declared quite nonchalantly, "I had the feeling that might happen. But isn't that fine?"

"What…? Why…?"

"You don't have to do this kind of stuff as a part of your club. The form it takes doesn't matter. You could do it as a member of student council… We actually have an open position," she added jokingly with a determined smile, and I smiled back.

"Then talk to Yukinoshita. I think she loves that kind of thing."

"…I do plan to. And I'll invite Yuigahama, too. We can all do it together."

"Don't go too far. There's only one extra position."

Puffing out her chest, Isshiki chuckled with a broad smirk. "Then I'll fire the vice president."

"How mean…" *He's working so hard, though…* I felt bad for him, and I broke down in wibbling tears. *Oh, but it seems like things are going well with him and the clerk, so maybe I don't have any sympathy for him. Stop screwing around and do your job.*

I got that Isshiki was joking. I also knew that dream wouldn't come true, so I didn't reject the idea. This was to remain a fun, happy chat.

Otherwise, I'd wind up thinking maybe that was a good idea.

I'd meant to put up a good smile, but I'm apparently garbage at that sort of thing.

Isshiki's gentle expression felt mature, as did the way she tucked her hair behind her ears. She looked like an adult. No—she *was* way more of an adult than I was.

"Honestly, I think that's the most realistic route," she said. "It wouldn't be so bad to go along with your cute junior's willful whims, would it? We're both used to bringing out the worst in each other, right?"

It was a terribly attractive proposal. It might have been the closest to my ideal. For an instant, my heart wavered.

Isshiki smiled enchantingly, as if she'd seen right through me, leaning forward from her chair. Her pale hair swished across my cheek. The sweet perfume of her shampoo tickled my nostrils. Setting her hand on the elbow rest of my chair, she brought her other hand to her mouth and whispered in my ear, "…I could give you an excuse, you know?"

The casters of my chair rattled when I jerked away to put some space between us. Isshiki thumped back into her own chair.

My heart was pounding, and I was gushing waterfalls of sweat. Meanwhile, she was entirely composed, as if she was certain nothing would happen.

If Isshiki had honestly and sincerely asked me to help her with the student council, either as the vice president or for general affairs, I probably would have agreed. And even if there wasn't a job for me, I wasn't opposed to helping her as needed.

This is Isshiki—she knows how to manage me just as well as my sister does. I think I understand that much. Plus, I have a reputation for being completely weak to little sisters and younger girls. If either of them sincerely asked me, I'd probably complain a lot, but I'd obviously

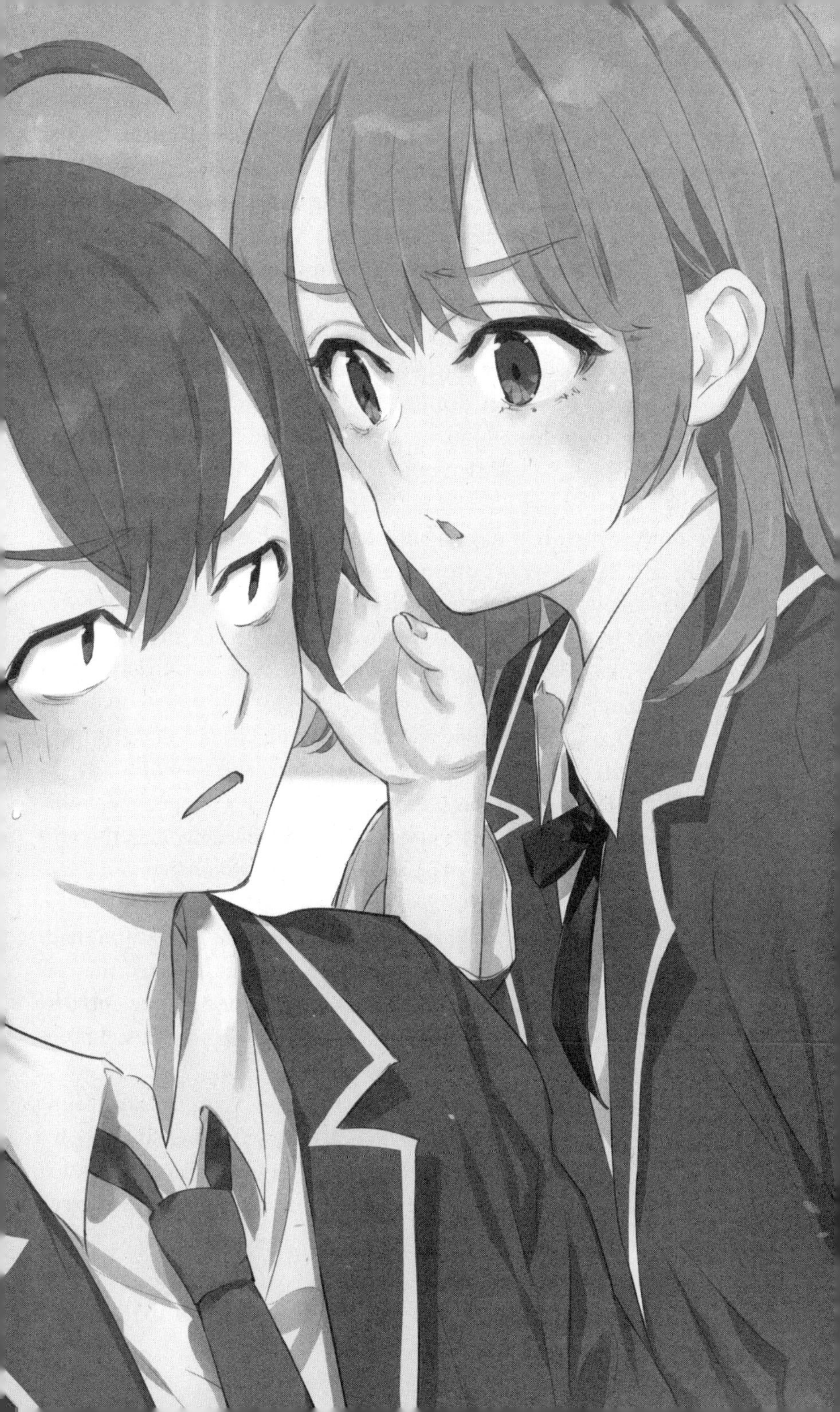

help out. That was how things had gone all this time, and Isshiki knew that.

But despite that, she'd used her coaxing and wiles just now. Even I could understand her intentions.

"You really are a good person..." A chuckle slipped out of me along with a sigh.

She gave me a sideways peace sign and a wink. "Right? I may not look like it, but I'm a pretty convenient woman." Everything about that was done in such a cute yet cunning way. She was making sure that, as my junior, she'd put her all into being there for me.

I wasn't sure if I'd call that *convenient*, but at the very least, she was definitely a good person.

That was why I had to give her a response that was in character for me, too. "I'll make every effort to look into that proposal."

"That's how you answer when you'll never do it... Well, that's very you." Isshiki let out a short, exasperated huff. But then she did a one-eighty into a nasty smirk. "I may not look the type, but I don't know when to give up."

"Nope, that is exactly how you look..."

We smiled.

Isshiki broke away to check the clock. "...It's just about time, huh?"

A crackling noise ran through the headset over my ears. Next, I heard a cool voice say, *"This is Yukinoshita. We're beginning on time, so be ready. We're letting in the guests now."*

"Roooger from Isshiki. Putting on the *bee gee eeeem*." Isshiki made eye contact with me, and I nodded back at her. Then I pressed the Play button and slowly pushed up the fader. No issues for now. My job here was just to put some appropriate music on loop during the bustle of the waiting time.

It seemed the guests had arrived, as the space was gradually filling with hubbub. If there had been a monitor, I would've been able to get a proper view of the state of the venue, but that was too much to ask for. I leaned forward through the little window of the tech booth to get a peek.

The scene below was positively resplendent. From a distance, all the multicolored dresses flitting about looked like cherry blossom petals.

They say that flowers in bloom are beautiful because they fall. Maybe this scene was beautiful because this was the end.

It was finally time for our last event.

× × ×

There had been many twists and turns to reach this point, but once the prom actually began, the program went smoothly.

There was a good turnout, and things continued to move along without any particular problems. The slideshow had been a concern, but that had gone smoothly, and after some time for friendly chitchat, it was finally time for the dance.

Isshiki pumped up the mood as the MC, and then on Yukinoshita's cue, she proceeded to put on the playlist. The audio equipment for the dance was already all hooked up, so I didn't really touch anything after that.

I leaned back and sank into my chair—I'd been stuck at the table for a long time, so my back was stiff. I gave it a good stretch. The chair creaked, and my spine made pleasant popping noises along with it.

"Pretty tired?"

Isshiki, who had been on stage until just now, had returned to the tech booth.

"Mm, oh, nice MCing."

Isshiki pulled out the chair beside me with a *Good grief, what am I going to do with you?* sort of expression. "Why don't you take a break for a bit? I can cover here." Isshiki was being weirdly considerate, maybe because she'd just heard my back popping.

I wasn't particularly tired, but, well, I did want to use the little boys' room, so I would thankfully take advantage of her offer. "Mm, then I'll pop out for a bit."

"Okaaay," she replied lazily, and I left the tech booth.

As I was rotating my stiff and tense shoulders, I also pulled the headset off my ears and tapped lightly down the stairs, my legs feeling a bit lighter. The sound of my steps mingled with the bass of the club music that shook the pit of my stomach.

When I came out to the gym floor, I found a crowd of people gathered in the center of the dance floor. The whole gym was filled with enthusiasm. As an outside onlooker, I thought it was fair to say the party was booming.

With everyone so dressed up, people in school uniforms stood out a lot. At one end of the gym, at the corner of a long table that had the catering and drinks on it, I found Yuigahama.

She noticed me as well and waved a hand. When she beckoned me over, I nodded back and walked toward the drinks.

"Hey, Hikki." Perhaps to avoid being drowned out by the booming of the speakers, Yuigahama came right up to stand beside me.

"Hey. All done with reception?"

"Yeah, by this time, there aren't many more people coming. So we're taking turns, and I'm on break."

"Things are really underway, huh?"

"Yeah. I'm super-hungry," she said, whisking across the table to start raking up snacks and such. "Want some?"

Um, I'm not that hungry... But without even waiting for a reply, she built an empire of sweets before my eyes. Seated on the throne in the center of that nation was the palace of honey toast. *I see—a very Instagram-worthy selection...*

Unlike the honey toast that students had served during the cultural festival, this was quite elegant looking, covered in fruit and whipped cream... *But it's still bread in the end, right? I mean, this really is bread. No matter how much stuff you put on it, bread is bread. They weren't gonna try harder to get rid of the bready feeling? This is undisguised bread. Totally bread.*

"Hya!" And with a cry that didn't sound at all like a sound you make when you're sharing food with someone, she took that undisguised bread and doled some out on a paper plate.

So you'll do it with bare hands… Not that there's a problem with that.

As I was standing there bewildered, Yuigahama began popping it into her mouth. "Oh man! The whipped cream is great!"

She's always so happy when she's eating… Her reaction made the honey toast more appetizing.

The kind I'd had before had been made by what you'd call an amateur. This one had been ordered from an actual specialist—I wasn't sure if it from was a delivery place or Uber Eats or what, but this was what you'd call pro honey toast. It had to be good…

And so with faith in that, I decided to give it a shot. Om-nom-nom-nom.

Mmm… Bread…

It's so dry in my mouth, just all dried up. Maybe 'cause it's been sitting out here a while. I guess I should have eaten some earlier. Well, the whipped cream and honey are as sweet and nice as you'd expect, so it's fine…

As I was smooshing it around in my mouth, Yuigahama giggled. "You're making a face just like before, Hikki."

Uh, I can't help that. I mean, this is so bready… My mouth was still occupied by a sweet, semi-hard substance somewhere between a sponge and an ink eraser that absorbed all moisture, so I just chewed and chewed and complained with my eyes.

I somehow gulped it down in the end, much to my relief. Figuring I'd have a coffee or something, I was reaching out to the table when the music playing on the dance floor and the lighting suddenly changed.

A slowly turning disco ball had been shining lights in all sorts of colors, but now white strobe lights started to flash down along with the house-sounding beat.

In my flashing field of vision, Yuigahama's smile faded. "…Have you already decided on your wish?"

My face moved closer so that I could hear her. "Well…I can't think of anything worth mentioning right now. What about you?"

"For me… Well, I've gotten just about everything I mentioned before… Like helping with the prom, and going to an after-party, and celebrating Komachi-chan… Oh, I forgot about hanging out." Yuigahama counted down on her fingers, but when she remembered, she popped one finger back up.

"Once the end-of-year exams are over, how about we go somewhere?"

"Oh, exams…" Yuigahama slumped. She must have immediately turned her thoughts to future plans after our tests, because her sunny disposition returned. "Hmm, maybe that'd help me study hard!"

She's such an open and good girl, it makes me want to offer her extra service. "If you have any more requests, just shoot. Anytime, really."

"Oh, yeah? Then, maybe I could ask one more thing," she said, her feet tapping lightly as she stepped away from me.

Then she plucked the hem of her uniform skirt, drew back her right foot, and bent a little at the knees and at the waist. "…May I have this dance?" With her bun swaying, Yuigahama gracefully curtseyed.

The sight left me stunned.

No, I was entranced.

Eventually, Yuigahama slowly lifted her head.

Even in the dark, I could tell her once dignified expression was now bright red. "J-just being silly… Ah-ha-ha…" Her fingers leaped into her bun at warp speed. She fiddled with her hair, obviously hiding her shyness.

I finally unfroze myself and cracked a slight smile of my own. "This isn't that kind of dance…"

"R-right! Oh… I'm so embarrassed…" She covered her face just before she jerked her head toward the ceiling, flapping her hands to fan herself.

I really was letting myself get carried away. How could I be dancing to her tune before we'd even hit the dance floor?

With my exasperation came a deep sigh.

Geez. I'm annoyed—at what I'm about to do.

I sighed again. This time it wasn't out of frustration but out of a need to propel myself into action.

I came a few steps away from the table with the catering on it and turned halfway back. Yuigahama tilted her head curiously.

"...Your hand, milady," I said, putting a hand to my chest and bending at the waist as I offered my right hand.

Yuigahama stared at me blankly before bursting into laughter. Covering her smile with her fingers, she looked through her lashes teasingly. "Even though it's not that kind of dance?"

"You started it..." She'd been formal with me, so I was just giving it back in the same overwrought way. *But this is so embarrassing... I shouldn't have done this...* With surging feelings of regret and self-recrimination, my proffered hand dropped.

But before I could pull away, Yuigahama grabbed me. "Let's go!"

Pulling me behind her, she weaved through the waves of people until we entered the cluster on the dance floor. The swinging spotlight and scattered lights of the mirror ball were whipping up everyone's energy. The crowds on the dance floor were swinging around just as hard.

The song playing had a crunchy, quick beat. There are too many subgenres with this kind of music, so I didn't know what to call it, but, well, it was club music at the end of the day. At the very least, it wasn't one of those romantic couple dances.

Yuigahama was swinging my hand in hers everywhere, and I went along with it, spinning around, taking a step instead of staggering. We were bathed in sound, enthusiasm, and light, jostling around in the crowd all the while. Our flailing moves were far from trendy.

But I didn't care how uncool it was.

No one here cared what you were doing so long as it was fun. They wouldn't be bothered if people around them were dancing or standing like M. Bison. Nobody was going to stare.

The only person who was paying attention to me was Yuigahama.

None of the lights were shining on any single person; they slid back and forth along with the beat, so we never got a long look at each other.

But I was able to see the smile on her face and her hand in mine.

With everyone decked out in their best, we stuck out in our school uniforms, but people who were enjoying the moment didn't seem bothered, and Yuigahama and I naturally merged with the crowd. The dance floor was overflowing with so many people it was like, *Is this a barrel of monkeys or what?* I'd sometimes put an arm around her shoulder, sometimes going with the flow, sometimes spinning away in a turn to avoid the waves of people as we kept dancing.

As sound poured down on us from the speakers, my knees kept the beat, and that made my shoulders sway with the rhythm. I thrust up a fist. *Yeahhh! Put your hands up!*

Yeah, my fake dance was a sloppy mess, but there was a big difference between watching from the sidelines and actually doing it yourself, and it was tougher exercise than I'd imagined.

This is harder than I'd thought it would be, mostly mentally...

Her hand touching me, her face coming close to me, and her breath reaching my ears.

As my energy drained, my eyes met with Yuigahama's, and she burst into laughter. "You look like you really hate this!"

"This is a really tough wish to grant..."

"Sorry, sorry! I won't bring it up again!" Her laughter mixed with the music, then faded along with it.

And then her quiet mutter melted into it. "...Next one'll be my last, okay?" She was right beside me, close enough that she was within the ring of my arms, and her forehead dropped onto my shoulder.

I think I'd managed to stammer out a reply to her whisper, but that was buried by the music, too.

Eventually, the track faded out into a different song. Dance time was almost over, as this was a fairly slow-tempo song. In terms of playlist order, the one after this was a bit of a more energetic standard number, and then there would be the finale. This was the last chill-out moment, so to speak, and it was also time for me to return to my post.

"...I've gotta head back," I said.

"Yeah, me too."

We both let go at nearly the same moment and stepped back.

And then, like a bell, the bass heralded the end of this magical time.

× × ×

My footsteps clanged up the stairs to the tech booth.

It was not glass slippers or lovely bare feet stepping upward, but my worn and slightly dirty indoor school shoes. The magical time had passed, and just like Cinderella, I was returning to my dusty room.

What awaited Cinderella at home after the spell wore off was her wicked stepmother and stepsisters, but whatever is waiting for me? I wondered as I opened the door of the tech booth.

"Welcome baaack! You're late tonight. Do you want work? Or more work? …Orrrrrr…looots of work?"

Despite this classic newlywed move pulled with a bright, sunny, and mischievous smile, what awaited me was my junior acting like a wife from hell. She was pissed.

And though she was totally going for the new-wife vibe, not a single one of these three ultimate options was domestic in nature. What happened to *A bath, dinner, or me?* Well, not like any of those were happening.

"Yes, I'm sorry. I'm here to work…" I sighed.

"I was calling you like crazy on the headset. Well, you made it in time, though, so it's fine." Isshiki puffed up her cheeks at me and hopped to her feet. "Okay, I'm gonna prepare for the final remarks, so I'll be counting on you for the rest."

"Roger. See you later."

"Byeeeee!" Isshiki energetically pattered out, leaving me alone in the tech booth with only the pounding, muffled bass.

I compared the clock and the schedule, and it seemed the times had gotten pushed around a bit, but various adjustments had led us to end on time. Next, Isshiki would make the closing remarks, and then it would be the grand finale. I put the headset I'd taken off for the break over my ears again.

Then there was a crackle of static in the headphones, followed by a cool voice. *"Isshiki, are you on standby?"*

It was the order from Yukinoshita, who was managing the event. After a few seconds' pause, there was an answer. *"Isshiki here, I'm at stage left. All okay. I'm taking off my headset."*

"Roger. Well then, stand by until I call you on."

"Okeydoke. Later!"

The headset went silent.

The chair's back creaked as I folded my hands behind my head and looked up at the ceiling. Eventually, the music shifted to the next phrase. From the cheers on the dance floor, I figured it was a fairly well-known number that was a standard at clubs. We had reached the end of the playlist.

Picking up the microphone of the headset that hung over my chest, I clicked the button. I already knew how to use it. I paused for a few seconds to make sure it picked up my voice before talking. "This is sound, last number playing now."

"Understood. I will be cuing the ending from stage right. Make sure not to miss it," Yukinoshita answered, and I peeked out the window of the tech booth.

Yukinoshita was standing there in the wings behind the drop curtain.

When I leaned my face on my hand at the window, gazing down, she looked up at me. She brought her mouth to the headset mike that was pinned to her collar. *"Can you see?"*

"Yeah, perfect."

"All right. So then where are you? In the audience?" Yukinoshita peeked out from the wings as she put on the act of looking all around.

"I'm above, above. Look up. Hey, you've been looking at me this whole time," I answered grumpily. Yukinoshita drew back behind the drop curtain and hunched over a bit, shoulders shaking. She hadn't pushed the switch on her headset, so the mike didn't pick up her voice, but I could see she was laughing.

Eventually, with the smile still on her lips, she turned to the tech booth. *"I'm not used to looking up at you, so I just missed you."*

"So you're used to looking down on me? I'm pretty used to that, so it's fine."

"*Your servile nature is the one thing about you I can respect. You're so far above me in that regard, just trying to catch a glimpse makes my neck and shoulders stiff.*"

It's not big enough to give you stiff shoulders… Not saying what "it" is, though!

As I was silently having these thoughts, Yukinoshita glowered at me. She was clenching the lonely lapel mike from the headset against her chest. "*Did you just say something? I couldn't hear. Could you repeat that?*"

"I didn't say anything…," I said—hastily at the start, so the mike might not have picked up the beginning.

Remembering how we'd had a similar silly conversation over headsets before, I couldn't help grinning. There had been other people listening then, which was embarrassing. This time, it was just the two of us.

When there was enough distance between us, communicating through a device over something trivial, conversation came naturally. It felt like we could continue talking forever.

But our time for that would run out.

The second count on the soundboard indicated the remaining play time on the music. It was just a few dozen seconds before the end would come.

Tearing my eyes from the screen, I poked my face out the window again.

Under the drop curtain in the wings at stage right, Yukinoshita tilted her head as she looked up at me to ask wordlessly, *Is something wrong?* I'd suddenly disappeared from the window after all.

"It's nothing," I muttered under my breath, hardly moving my lips at all; I wasn't using the headset, so there was no way she could have heard.

Yukinoshita continued to be curious, her head still tilted to the side.

I shook my head back at her. That must have satisfied her, more or less, because she gave a little nod.

The wings were dim, but occasionally the disco ball would shine a ray of light there to give me a good view of her elegant features, her innocent gestures, and her beautiful smile. From where she stood, the light of the tech booth was behind me, so it would be a bit hard for her to see me.

Thanks to that, it kept her from glimpsing my expression right then. I couldn't possibly show her such a stupid look on my face—my dumb grin from imagining something equally ridiculous.

It had to be our relative positions that had made me think something so absurd. Being divided by stage left and stage right, one looking up, the other looking down.

It was like a stage play I'd seen a long time ago.

The little window of the tech booth was nothing like the high windows of a balcony, the boy and girl were in totally opposite positions, and we were having a businesslike discussion through a radio, really nothing like the whispers of lovers—none of it was alike. Our ending would surely not be theirs, either.

Imagining something like that, I laughed.

We wouldn't get a sweet conclusion, yet this time of ours would still reach a finale.

Calculating backward from the ending time on the digital clock, I squeezed the headset mike. "The song's about to end." I was speaking through the headset, which had some lag.

Pressing the headphones with her fingers, Yukinoshita shifted her eyes to her feet. *"Roger."* The crackling continued in my headphones after that short answer. It sounded like she was still holding on to the headset switch.

Two seconds, three seconds passed.

Yukinoshita squeezed the mike switch along with her collar in her hand as she whispered, *"Listen, Hikigaya…"*

I waited for her to continue. I heard only the crackling noises of the mike and her quiet breathing.

"…Please make it come true."

Then the headset cut.

I couldn't see Yukinoshita's downturned expression.

There was a time delay and physical distance, a one-sided and staticky passage. We'd been focused on work when not shooting stupid jokes at each other, avoiding anything difficult.

This had to be the right distance apart.

So there was only one right answer I could say. "I know."

The song was coming to an end.

It ended with a bang, and then the echoes of the outro faded. Meanwhile, the lighting dimmed, and the guests sensed that dance time was ending, all with different expressions as they excitedly waited for the farewell celebration. The dance floor was filled with clapping, whistling, and cheers.

"...*Thank you. Let's wrap this up.*" After waiting for the noise in the gym to settle, Yukinoshita put a hand up and cued me.

"All right, then," I answered to myself without the headset.

I put on the beginning of a track that had been selected as her intro tune at low volume, and the chattering of the audience gradually quieted. With an eye on the crowd for timing, I gradually pushed up the fader. It was a very emotionally staged ending.

Pressing the switch on the headset, I waited a few seconds before starting to talk. "Okay, I put on the track."

"*Roger. After the narration, once Isshiki reaches her position, lower the fader. I'll signal you on when.*"

After a phrase or so of the music, the audience calmed down quite a bit, patiently awaiting the end.

When the moment arrived, Yukinoshita began. "To all graduates: Thank you very much for coming to the Soubu High School prom today. Once again, congratulations on your graduation. To bring this night to a close, we have some closing remarks from the organizing committee."

When Isshiki came out to a round of applause, a spotlight followed her. The path of the light eventually reached center stage.

Yukinoshita looked up at me.

With sparkling particles of dust hanging in the air between us, she quietly raised a hand from the gloom.

Her thin arm lifted only partway, as if she wasn't sure whether to raise or lower it.

With a sorrowful smile, she was signaling the end.

And then she quietly waved.

Going along with that gesture, as if drawing curtains closed, I gently lowered the fader.

Interlude...

The little window of the tech booth felt unreachable from the darkness I stood in.

This scene, extending an arm to a high window just out of reach, reminded me of Shakespeare. Our relationship, our relative positions. Everything about this situation was different, but the stage setting was the same, so I couldn't help thinking it. I couldn't help smiling at my foolishness, either.

Our relationship would not come to such a happy and easily understood ending. It would always remain undefined.

Me, him, and her.

The relationship we have has no name.

But a rose by any other name would smell as sweet.

The same goes for the relationship between the three of us. No name given to it would change it. That had to be true. It couldn't be anything else.

Despite not believing that at all, I swallowed those sweet, poisonous words and put myself to sleep.

Thanks to the backlighting, I couldn't see his face in the shadows, but I got the feeling that he was smiling. I was about to ask him through the headset if there was something wrong, when static crackled in the headphones.

And then I was informed of the coming end. There was no more time for fun chitchat.

Here was the end.

I replied with a *roger*, and after a brief remark, I brought my hand away from the lapel microphone. When I read out the announcement from the microphone on the stand behind the drop curtain in the wings, the ending ceremony began. The music swelled; then once the presenter stood onstage, it would be over.

Now all I had to do was give the signal.

I raised my hand up toward the tech booth. I knew I couldn't touch that high window, so I didn't even try.

This hand had nowhere to go now; it had nowhere left to be.

So I just quietly waved.

5

Gallantly, **Shizuka Hiratsuka** walks ahead.

We ended the prom as scheduled, and by the time we'd cleaned up the gym, it was late at night. The space was hollow and desolate now. I left that behind me as I headed to the meeting room in the main school building.

Everyone from the prom staff was gathered there, but it wasn't like it was a big crowd. There was the core staff, headed by Yukinoshita and the student council, Yuigahama and me, the lackeys from the sports clubs that had helped out, then Ms. Hiratsuka and some people from the parents' association.

It was a simple post-event celebration for the organizers, performers, and staff—what's commonly called a wrap party, and as a reward for those involved, a modest spread had been arranged. Snacks and drinks were set out on a long table, and the event staff stood in clumps around it.

At the head of the room, Isshiki was glancing around restlessly. She checked that every hand had gotten a paper cup, then jabbed at Yukinoshita with an elbow. "Yukino. Start the toast."

"M-me?" Yukinoshita was confused, and Isshiki nodded at her, exerting a wordless pressure to just do it already.

A silent tug-of-war continued for a while as the both of them stared at each other, but eventually, Yukinoshita let out a short sigh. "Well then, if I may..." With her eyebrows and mouth in reluctant upside-down Vs, she took a step forward with her paper cup in hand.

She jerked her chin up with a brisk smile. "Thanks to all of your help, we've managed to hold a successful prom. I express the sincerest gratitude to everyone who assisted, and to the core staff, thank you as always for your work. With the hope that this will become a regular event in the future at Soubu High School and that you can send us off next year...a toast."

Despite her previous attitude, that toast didn't sound reluctant at all. It was actually full of cheer and rather on the long side. Everyone chorused "Cheers!" in return.

I raised my own cup to a modest height, and Yuigahama at my side held her cup toward me. "Great work today!"

"Yeah, likewise," I replied, and though we touched cups, no conversation followed...

Since that dance, I'd felt too awkward and embarrassed to comfortably look her in the eye. She must have felt the same; when I snuck a glance, I saw she was sipping from her paper cup and on her phone, at a loss for what else to do.

After some time, she seemed to remember something and smacked my shoulder. "Oh yeah, I got a message on LINE from Orimoto. She was asking about next time."

"Huh? ...Ohhh." For a moment, I wondered what she was talking about, but I quickly figured it out. I'd roped in Kaihin High to make the dummy prom plan seem more realistic. Though we'd had a single meeting in order to make a show of it and list it as an accomplishment, with all the kerfuffle of the prom, I'd lost track of some things.

Whoa, I'd totally forgotten... Since the prom had been wrapped up successfully, now I had to clean up the dummy prom, too. Specifically, as the one who was responsible for it, I had to bow down on the floor, or get roasted and bow on the floor, or be deep-fried and bow on the floor—I just had to make a crisp and juicy apology.

"I'll talk to them. Can you ask for her e-mail or phone number? Either's fine."

"Mm, roger," Yuigahama replied, immediately contacting Orimoto. It seemed she got an answer straightaway, as her phone rang *ta-tiiing!* ♪ "Mm, sent it."

"Thanks…" When I checked my phone as well, I had indeed gotten a message from Yuigahama.

All right, so then how should I apologize? I was wondering when I noticed that the conversation with Yuigahama had trailed off again. The scene was like a microcosm of modern Japan—despite being side by side, we were both on our phones.

It really did feel overly self-conscious to be so silent when we were right next to each other, but I couldn't think of any witty or snappy conversation.

As I was groaning to myself, Isshiki shuffled into the center of the reception room. She raised her hand high to gather ears and eyes. "Excuse meee. Sorry, this is just leftovers from the catering. We didn't arrange for any other snacks, but please help yourself. Whatever's left has to be thrown out, so please eat it all!" she said cheerfully while pumping a fist.

She was being so blunt about it, and now the mood was awkward. "Nobody's gonna feel hungry after hearing that…," I grumbled.

"Ah-ha-ha… Guess I'll try some," Yuigahama said with a strained smile as she trotted up to the food. I leaned against a wall, watching her go.

Well, when the conversation peters out, it helps to occupy your mouth with something else instead as a distraction, like food or tea. You can make the excuse *My mouth is full right now! That's why I can't talk!* Cigarettes also have the same effect—the data says that 80 percent of smokers smoke in order to cover silence or not talking (personally researched).

Maybe it was because of those thoughts, but I could have sworn I could smell heavy tar.

"Nice work today. You were going at it pretty hard. It was fun to watch." Ms. Hiratsuka, apparently recently returned from a smoke, came over with a wave.

"You were just watching? This was the big event. You should've joined in," I said. This prom was for people who were leaving the school. That originally meant the graduating students, but I figured Ms. Hiratsuka deserved that, too.

She shrugged nonchalantly. "The departure ceremony is the stage for me. I'll be the star of the show then." The mild theatricality of her humor made me crack a crooked smile.

The departure ceremony was supposed to be at the beginning of April. You could indeed say it was a stage for Ms. Hiratsuka.

But being a school function, it wouldn't have the same unrestrained atmosphere. We would just be solemnly saying farewell, her as a teacher and me as a student.

It was a bit sad to think about, but there was no point in saying so. Quirking up one cheek like always, I smirked. "You obviously can't dance at the departure ceremony."

"Yeah. It's too bad. I wanted to dance with you, too," she said with a chuckle, and those words stuck with me.

Too? Wait... The moment I understood what she meant, the water in the paper cup I held rippled.

"...You were watching?" Trying to hide how upset I was, I glared at the teacher, and she gave me meaningful grin. What she'd said earlier about how I'd been working pretty hard and it was fun to watch seemed to be implying something. *Whoa. I wanna die.*

As I was hanging my head and drowning in anxiety, I caught some loud voices chattering pleasantly. I lifted my head right as Yukinoshita and Yuigahama came over together. Her head bobbing as she walked, Isshiki was right behind them.

"Thank you for a job well done," Yukinoshita called out to me, and I nodded back. When she raised her paper cup slightly as a cheers, I raised mine in the same way.

"...Same to you... It's great things went well," I replied.

"Yes, thank you..."

We just calmly exchanged those remarks without touching our paper cups. The water in my cup didn't waver, either.

Yuigahama and Isshiki were also both smiling as they said their thanks, and we spent a very peaceful time showing appreciation for one another's efforts.

Having the core staff gathered together meant that people going around to pay respects would naturally come to us. Among those people was, of course, Yukinoshita's mother.

"It was such a nice party," she said.

When Mrs. Yukinoshita came with Haruno in tow, Yukinoshita set down her paper cup on the long table, straightened her posture, and bowed her head politely. "Thank you very much for your cooperation with this event. It was your guidance that enabled us to bring it to a close without any grave errors."

"Oh, no, we are the ones in your debt for listening to our sudden requests." Mrs. Yukinoshita returned that suffocatingly formal greeting as she bowed deeply as well.

Once they had lifted their heads, they exchanged a look and giggled at each other.

"Great work taking care of the prom. You did wonderfully. Your mother was quite impressed." Mrs. Yukinoshita put her fan to her mouth with a gentle smile.

Her mother's teasing tone made Yukinoshita twist around bashfully. Acutely aware of the eyes around her, she cleared her throat quietly. Well, it's a bit embarrassing to talk with your mom in front of everyone…

As lukewarm eyes gathered on the Yukinoshita mother and daughter pair, people smiled and sighed wistfully. Some amused laughter rang out as well.

"I had fun watching, too. How nice, how nice."

They were nothing words—pleasantries—but coming from Haruno Yukinoshita, I couldn't help but find a different meaning in them. Though the air was superficially peaceful, I felt something disquieting in it and scowled, while Haruno's amusement grew.

With that smile like a Cheshire cat, she stood between mother and daughter. "This is the sort of thing you want to do, huh, Yukino-chan? This is part of your goals for your future, right?"

"What she wants to do…?" Mrs. Yukinoshita tilted her head, shooting a look at Haruno.

Haruno's smile turned cold; then she looked away. "Why don't you ask her?" she said quite indifferently, and her mother's gaze slowly slid from the elder to the younger sister.

Yukinoshita's fingers twitched; she was anxious. "About that… I'm interested in Father's work, and I'm thinking I'd like to be involved in the future."

Listening to her daughter slowly bring up this subject, Mrs. Yukinoshita put a hand to her lips. I think she had thought better of whatever she was going to say.

Yukinoshita's eyes dropped; her mother's hard gaze was too much for her. "I understand this event won't connect directly with my future and also that this guarantees nothing. Besides, I'm not talking about right now; I mean further down the line…" She wrung out one word after another, then sucked in a quiet breath. "But I just want you to know that's how I feel." Slowly lifting her face, she met her mother's eyes.

Mrs. Yukinoshita said nothing as her daughter spoke, and once she was finished listening to everything silently, she snapped her fan and narrowed her eyes. "…You're serious about this?" she said in a tone that would make even me feel a chill. Her eyes were no longer mild, and the lukewarm air was gone; now Mrs. Yukinoshita's stare was full of loathing. None of us could even breathe. As the atmosphere froze around me, my eyes drifted away and eventually landed on Haruno. She was examining her nails in boredom.

Yukinoshita momentarily flinched at the sharp light of her mother's eyes, but eventually, she nodded back.

Her mother wordlessly observed her daughter's stiff expression for a while, but then her lips broke into an unexpected smile. "I see… I understand how you feel. If that is sincerely what you wish, then I will support you. Let's take our time considering this from now on. There's no need to rush."

As if drawn by her smile, Yukinoshita nodded. Mrs. Yukinoshita straightened in her seat. "It's getting late. I should go," she said, glancing over at Haruno. Haruno just gave her a look of acknowledgment in return, her eyes telling her to go on ahead.

"Well then, pardon me." Mrs. Yukinoshita bowed deeply, and Ms. Hiratsuka came up to her side.

"I'll walk you to the entrance." "No, I don't mind saying farewell here." "No, no, please let me accompany you." "Oh, no, truly, there really are students still here after all." "I'm greatly obliged by your consideration, but then let me send you to the exit at least, please." "Oh dear, do pardon me, thank you very much. Thank you so very much for your care of my daughter."

With that torrent of pushing and conceding to one another, they slowly wore each other down and edged toward the door, where Ms. Hiratsuka sent off Mrs. Yukinoshita. I was weirdly impressed. *Ms. Hiratsuka really is doing the adult thing, huh?*

Isshiki addressed everyone else. "How about we call it a night, too? Um, student council members! Let's get to sending everyone off, locking up, and doing our final checks." With a couple of claps, Isshiki sent all the student council members shuffling out. They were thanking everyone for the help and whatnot but also definitely chasing them out.

And as for us, we were assaulted by exhaustion. We heaved great sighs.

"That was kinda really scary...," said Yuigahama.

"Right... Mamanon is scary...," I said with feeling.

"Mamanon...?" Yuigahama smiled wryly, making us all relax, and then she turned that smile to Yukinoshita. "Anyway, that was great. Right, Yukinon?"

"Y-yes... It was... Thank you." Yukinoshita's smile was still kind of hard, perhaps from the lingering anxiety of having just faced off with her mother. But she slowly said the words, and the tension in her shoulders melted away with it. "Thank you for everything, Haruno...," she murmured.

Haruno cocked her head quizzically. "For what?"

Yukinoshita blushed and started muttering. "Lots of things... Like putting in a good word for me."

Yuigahama smiled at the way she said it—brusquely with a hint of shyness.

I remembered that, before, Haruno had promised she would put in a good word with their mother. She did have more of a big-sisterly side than you'd think.

However, the one being thanked had no emotion on her face at all. Not only that, she was combing her fingers through her hair like she was annoyed. "Ohhh, that? I wasn't really trying to help you out, though." Her voice was ice-cold, as if to say she couldn't recall ever having made such a promise. It was a complete change from her earlier gentleness. Ignoring our bewilderment, she touched her index finger to her chin and tilted her head. "Hmm, well, I guess that won Mom over? I don't know about anyone else, though. Right?" She was smiling brightly, but no matter how you interpreted what she said, all I could sense there was malice.

"...What are you getting at?" Yuigahama glared at her. Yukinoshita was squeezing Yuigahama's hand, maybe reflexively. The air felt so harsh, I was bracing myself without realizing it.

Despite the hostility directed at her, Haruno Yukinoshita never wavered. "At the very least, it hasn't won me over," she replied in her usual cheery tone.

"...Huh?" The sound just popped out of me. I must have looked incredibly foolish with my mouth hanging open.

Haruno snorted scornfully. "I can't say it's acceptable."

Those words were spoken with Haruno Yukinoshita's voice—but perhaps she wasn't the only one with that sentiment.

I felt like a doubt that had always been deep in my heart, lurking and slumbering and festering, had been given form in language. I could hardly protest.

My silence spoke more eloquently than words, and however Haruno took it, she added brightly, "Oh, don't get the wrong idea. I frankly don't care about family stuff, you know? Not like I want to take over the family business."

"So…," Yukinoshita began, but Haruno's cold smile stopped her in her tracks.

Haruno's expression remained the same as she continued. "After treating you that way all this time, she's not going to suddenly be like *Oh, yes, I see*. After making all those concessions and assuming there's nothing you can do about it, this is what you get… Don't you think it's pretty unlikely that will win anybody over?"

Yukinoshita's expression of mingled confusion and sorrow made me grit my teeth. She looked down. "…Why are you saying this now?" She sounded more childish than usual.

"I'd like to ask you the same thing… Why are *you* saying something like that now, Yukino-chan?" Haruno chided her in a gentle, soothing tone. For the first time, Haruno Yukinoshita's expression twisted. Yukinoshita's voice caught in her throat.

Yukinoshita pitied her sister. Haruno narrowed her eyes; she didn't like the heartbreak she was seeing on her sister's face. "I can't acknowledge that a conclusion like this is worth as much as my twenty years of life. If you're seriously telling me to yield to you, then I want you to show me something that outweighs that." Though her words were rational enough, she couldn't contain the hostility in her tone. The corners of her lips were smiling, but her eyes were intimidating.

We were too overwhelmed to speak.

In a moment as silent as the early dawn, Haruno's antagonistic expression softened. "All right… Maybe I'll go say hi to Shizuka-chan, then go home. See you later," Haruno said, and she strolled away. Right as she closed the door, she waved at me, then left the meeting room.

The door quietly closed, and until the faint sounds of her footsteps faded out, we didn't dare move, not even to twitch. We couldn't look each other in the eye—or maybe I was the only one staring at the ground.

With nobody but the three of us there, the meeting room was far bigger and colder than before. Things were awkward, hushed, and cooling further.

Yukinoshita muttered, "Um, I apologize. For my sister saying... those strange things."

"She's always like that. I'm used to it," I said.

"Yeah, maybe." Yuigahama cracked a smile.

That relieved Yukinoshita a little. "Yes... Thank you for saying so." The mood relaxed, but Yukinoshita's expression was still dark. "...Still, I believe she was somewhat serious today. Twenty years can feel heavy."

She would feel that because they had lived together. There was no way an outsider like me could imagine it, and I couldn't possibly empathize.

This wasn't the time for blithe, joking comebacks. Even I had that much social awareness. All I could do was stay silent and nod.

But Yuigahama picked a different option. Coming just a bit closer, one step then another, she approached Yukinoshita. "This past year... Our past year was just as heavy. I don't think it's about the amount of time," she said gently, making Yukinoshita raise her head. Yuigahama's earnest expression captured my attention, too.

Yuigahama took a little breath and then puffed out her chest cheerfully. She pumped her fists at us. "The past year's been super weird, you know!"

"Weird...?" The tension in my shoulders all released at once. That response really did sound brainless, if I do say so myself. Beside me, Yukinoshita was also stunned, but after a while, she started to giggle.

That enabled me to let out a faint smile. "Well, I guess it *was* weird. I mean, it was crazy from the start—the Service Club, I mean."

Yukinoshita shot me a look. "I believe the majority of that was your fault, though."

"Yeah, yeah," Yuigahama replied. "But that made it fun... We did all that weird stuff, so when things got sad or awful or painful..." Her gaze drifted downward, and Yukinoshita and I did the same. She wasn't looking down at her feet, but at her path coming all this way. She didn't need to tell us.

We'd reflected on the past year before, too, with silly smiles to avoid ever touching the core of it. We'd tried to only reminisce about the good parts.

This time, we let ourselves relive the feelings that tightened our chests, the memories torturing our hearts, and our fleeting emotions.

We happened to chuckle quietly at the same moment.

Yuigahama lifted her head to look at us gently. "But even more than that, I spent a long time having fun and being happy, enough to fall in love with it."

"Yes," Yukinoshita agreed. "...I'm sure I can say that with pride as well."

"Mm-hmm." I dipped my head a bit in response. I didn't have to bother saying it out loud.

It had been the longest year of my life.

And that year would finally come to an end.

Yukinoshita's gaze stroked the deserted meeting room, empty but for us. "And now our final job is over," she murmured. Those words and that look were not directed at us. The catering still laid out over the long table, the paper cups with nobody to drink from them, the darkness outside the windows, the feeble light of the streetlamps in the courtyard, the special-use building lost in the night, the wall clock that ticked on without ever stopping—those were the things she was speaking to.

Eventually, her eyes slowly returned to us. "...I believe that if we can bring it to a close, then now is best. This really is a good punctuation mark, regardless of what my sister said."

"...I think it'd be nice if we could keep going, but...if you're okay with this, Yukinon, then I am, too."

Two pairs of once-clear eyes were now tearing up. They were waiting on me.

They didn't even have to ask for my reply; there was no way I would oppose it.

This had only happened because Ms. Hiratsuka had forced me to join the Service Club. Plus, Ms. Hiratsuka would be leaving at the end of the school year. The competition she'd set up had also ended with my loss.

So I wasn't opposed.

"…I—"

This was fine. This was correct. There was no mistake in ending it. Everything made sense. As the both of them said, this was the way we wanted it to happen, the right way for it to be. A conclusion.

But not a single word came out of me.

The air stuck there, hard enough to hurt the back of my throat. I swallowed my wet breath to ease the dryness, and the words returned to my lungs. I put my hand to the base of my throat to hopefully wring them out. But all I got was a sigh.

The two girls were waiting for me the whole time. More heavy sighs rang out for the umpteenth time in the quiet room, and I clenched my teeth.

And then a hasty pattering joined those sounds. The door opened with a *clack*, and we all looked toward it.

"Thanks for the help, guyyys… Huh, did something happen?" Isshiki had returned with the student council and shrank in on herself as soon as she saw us. Maybe she'd picked up on the weird moment.

I casually shook my head. "No, it's nothing. Already done?"

"Yep. This is the last room. Anyway, thanks for today, guys."

"Oh… Likewise. Then see you," I said.

"Huh? Oh, we still haven't cleaned up here…"

Ignoring Isshiki's response, I hurried out of the meeting room.

But before I'd gotten even a few steps down the hall, my feet faltered. It kept getting worse.

It was already dark outside, and the glow of the old fluorescent bulbs in the hall was feeble. With everything so dim in front of me, I started to lumber along, dragging my heavy legs.

Then faint footsteps came up behind me.

"Hikigaya, wait." Suddenly, a frantic voice called me to a stop, and I felt a weak catch on my sleeve.

I really didn't want to turn around, but I couldn't ignore the tug or turn back.

The fingers caught in my cuff to keep me from getting away were the one thing tying me to this place, like a lifeline.

I couldn't move. My voice had nowhere to go, and I found myself looking up at the ceiling with a sigh. Once I'd finished blowing out all the air in my lungs and finally pulled myself together, I slowly turned to look over my shoulder.

Yukino Yukinoshita was standing there behind me. Her beautiful hair, blacker than the darkness of night, was slightly mussed, and she combed it with her hand to fix it. It seemed she'd rushed to catch up to me, and she was panting a bit.

She squeezed the breast of her uniform as if she was catching her breath, then slowly put the words together. "Um…I thought I would tell you properly."

Her eyes wandered around as if she were searching for the words, and eventually, she looked at the window of the hallway. I couldn't look straight at her delicate, fair face, either, and my eyes slipped over to the dark glass.

Under the hallway lighting, our faces reflected back at us. I stared at the girl in the glass.

"Thank you for helping today," Yukinoshita said to me. "…Not only today, but all this time. I'm sorry for causing you trouble."

"It's nothing to apologize for. If we're talking about causing trouble, I've done way more of it. I figure we can call it even." I smiled back at her reflection with one raised cheek.

When our eyes met in the glass, Yukinoshita smiled. "Indeed. It really was quite the struggle. Well then, I suppose we're even." She said it teasingly, but there was something fragile about her expression. Or maybe it was just the light. "Thank you, honestly. You helped me with so many things. But I'm…all right now. I'll do my best to do better on my own going forward." The grip on my cuff tightened just slightly, and I automatically turned back to her.

For an instant, the high beams of a passing car lit the dark hallway. As I narrowed my eyes in the glare, I could see she was on the verge of tears.

"So…" As the engine roar and pale lights grew distant, Yukinoshita's voice faded out along with them. I never got to hear the rest of what she had to say, but I could more or less figure it out.

It had been a constant refrain in my heart ever since just a few days ago, when she had locked the door of the clubroom and then released its cold handle.

We had repeated time and time again that we'd had enough, that we would end it.

"…Yeah, I understand. It's all right," I said.

The truth was, I didn't understand anything. I was just… I was just saying that to end the conversation.

"See you."

I meant that to be good-bye, but her delicate fingers remained caught in my sleeve and showed no sign of releasing me.

It wasn't like she was holding on particularly tightly. One gentle tug of my sleeve would instantly shake her off, but her slim fingers looked so fragile. I couldn't be rough with them.

So I touched them slowly, doing my best not to break anything, and gently, gently pulled them away with my own boorish fingers.

But my fingers hesitated to touch her, and maybe that was what caused them to tremble for just an instant. Or maybe she was the one trembling, startled at the touch.

But before I could be sure, our fingers were apart.

"Bye…" Remembering how cold my fingers were, I stuck them in my pockets and turned around. Then I left without looking back.

With every pace forward, I only ever heard my footsteps ringing in the hall.

× × ×

The lights were already out on the second floor of the main school building, which was where the guest reception had been. They were still on in the office to the left coming in from the entrance, but only a little of that light reached the entrance area itself.

The rest of the light came from the little window to the reception room; thanks to that, I was able to see the woman leaning against the glass. I didn't have to see her face to know who it was. It was Haruno Yukinoshita.

She seemed to be killing time, her eyes on her phone. Its backlight shone over her beautiful and well-proportioned features. But her expression was the picture of boredom, and she came off colder than usual.

She must have heard my footsteps, because she glanced up at me. Her head was tilted down and the streetlight outside was shining behind her, so I couldn't really see her expression, but it seemed like she giggled.

When she took a step away from the glass, I could finally see her face clearly. With an icy gaze and a small, dark smile, she said teasingly, "…I knew you'd run away out here."

My eyebrows twitched in reaction, and I just about clicked my tongue. Haruno smiled as if my scowl amused her.

I really couldn't stand this woman. She saw right through me, to my intentions and everything in my heart. So I put up some minimal resistance by saying spitefully back at her, "You're the one who said that stuff to make me come here."

Haruno didn't deny or demur. She just shrugged. As she'd left the meeting room, she'd told me where she was going while giving me a meaningful look. Any moron would have picked up on what she wanted.

I could have pretended not to notice and just gone straight home, but if I'd done that, I would have gotten either a phone call or some form of contact through Hayama or Komachi. Haruno had, in fact, gotten a hold of me like that before. It was less of a hassle to go to her.

In the end, I couldn't ignore her.

The way she talked like she saw through me, her terrifying voice that seemed to stab into my throat, the glint in her eyes like an ice-cold knife, the beautiful profile that so much resembled her sister's, her mask that played the adult and acted cheerful, the innocence she would unexpectedly reveal, and her tragically gentle smiles all bothered me way too much.

She could probably tell I was thinking that, too.

I knew she was leading me around by the nose, and yet I had to ask. "Why do you say stuff like that? What are you trying to do, ultimately?" I was irritated. I'd been holding on to this question all this time in my gut.

What Haruno Yukinoshita said and did had always caused ripples in my heart—in *our* hearts, actually. Even now, when we were trying to end things peacefully, she was tossing in rocks in an attempt to spread more ripples.

I couldn't let her stir things up any further.

My questions came out sharper than I'd thought they would.

Haruno remained cool as ever. "I told you. Whatever's fine with me. I don't care either way. I don't care about this family stuff. It's all the same, whether I do it or Yukino-chan does it." She'd said basically the same thing as before. I let out a heavy, weary breath.

Haruno must have found fault with that, her gaze shifting out the glass door. "...I just want her to persuade me. The results don't matter," she added at a murmur, almost a repetition of earlier. The words themselves were mostly meaningless, but her voice was lonely, almost plaintive.

Every time... Every time I think I understand Haruno Yukinoshita, she throws me for a loop.

She'll wrap up good intentions in malice, not even balking at being hated or loathed sometimes. She has the propensity to make herself the villain—but then she'll occasionally speak with terrible gentleness and even dare to reveal her sorrow. If that contrast was acting, then I had no choice but to throw up my hands. I would be dancing in her palm no matter where I went.

"You mean like *show me your sincerity*? You sound like you're from the yakuza..." *She is really and truly incomprehensible*, I thought with a big sigh and an exasperated smile.

Haruno giggled. She must have liked that. "I won't deny it...but I think our mother isn't convinced, either."

"She sure seemed to be," I said, thinking back on her mild smile.

Haruno burst into laughter, giving me a look of utter contempt that said, *What the hell is this idiot talking about?* "Of course that would never be enough to convince her. That's why she gave an answer that was neither a yes nor a no. A null. It looks like Yukino-chan figured that out, though."

That way of speaking—asserting that she had indicated her understanding while putting it off a yes or no—was diplomatic language. Yukinoshita must have picked up on what that meant as well. Now after the fact, I understood that was what her hard smile and stiff shoulders had meant.

"...You really are family." You have to build up a life together on a daily basis to get an accurate grasp of the subtleties of others' feelings. Komachi and I were a good example of that.

Since it had been less than a year since I'd come to know Yukinoshita, I wouldn't know anything that deep. And that went double for her mother and sister—it would be impossible for me to read their true intentions from trivial changes in their expressions and gestures. I didn't know the deeper meanings behind their words.

I was beginning to think I would never learn to pick up on these things, but then Haruno laughed. "You don't have to be her sister or mother. Anyone with eyes could tell... Even people who are just her friends like you two can reach that conclusion, can't you?"

"I'm not sure we're close enough to be friends, so I couldn't say."

"Oh, what an answer. After all that... You really don't know when to give up." Though Haruno did smile at me, her eyes remained cold. Now that her amusement had worn off, she sighed and opened the glass door. "...That nonsense won't convince anyone."

With that comment, she stepped outside. I followed after her, taking a step down into the lowered entrance area.

But my indoor shoes were still on my feet. Glaring at them, I clicked my tongue. It was too much trouble to go change my shoes now. I went outside with them still on and hurried down the steps.

Catching up to Haruno right before she got all the way down, I called out to her. "Um, why not?"

Haruno came to a stop. She slowly turned back to me.

Her big black eyes were a little wet, reflecting the streetlights, and her expression was serious. I got the sense she was mourning something. "...I mean, this 'wish' of hers is just compensatory behavior."

That one term made it feel like the ground shuddered under my feet, and I staggered.

Compensatory behavior—a term to describe when you can no longer accomplish a certain goal due to some obstacle, changing it to a different goal, and then accomplishing that in order to fulfill the original desire. Basically, it's deceiving yourself with a fake one.

Supposing, as Haruno Yukinoshita said, that her wish was nothing more than an excuse for the sake of covering up something else, would I be able to accept that?

When my voice caught, Haruno went one step up the stairs, locking eyes with mine as she whispered gently, "Yukino-chan, you, and Gahama-chan all did your best to feel convinced, huh? You played around with words on the surface so that you didn't have to look underneath..."

Stop it. Don't say anything more. I know that myself.

But no matter how I wished that, Haruno went on with a pitying gaze and a soothing tone. "You made good excuses, you rationalized... You avoided the issue and hoped you could trick yourselves." Her comments were entirely unsolicited, but I listened anyway. It all seeped into the depths of my heart like eroding water.

In the back of my throat, there was a moan that I couldn't even identify as an inhale or an exhale. I couldn't get any sound out.

I'd known—while blustering on about a man's pride—that what I was doing was ultimately no different from what I'd been doing all this time.

No. It was even worse than before. Now I was forcing the two of them to swallow a great big lie, too.

I was clenching my teeth so hard it felt like they would break. Haruno stroked my tense cheek. Her long, slim fingers moved gently, as if handling a breakable item. "Didn't I tell you?" With a faint smile, her fingertip slid down to poke me in the chest. "You won't be able to get drunk."

"…Looks that way," I rasped.

A smile that truly befitted Haruno rose on her face, and then her features crinkled in sadness. That ephemeral, near-tearful expression sent pain through my chest.

I'd seen that fragile smile back in the stage wings before the lights had gone out. It had vanished into the dark with a little wave.

The ache I had felt then still tortured me.

"You have to settle things properly, or it'll smolder in you forever. It will never end. I've been avoiding things to get by for twenty years, so I understand it well… That's the sort of phony life I've led." Haruno's soliloquy of regret was brittle and ephemeral. Her teary eyes focused on something in the distance. I couldn't sense even a hint of her usual adult composure and bewitching sense of danger. She seemed almost younger than me in this moment.

I felt like, for the first time, I'd gotten a bewildering glimpse of who Haruno Yukinoshita really was.

She backed up a step and turned away from me. "Hey, Hikigaya, is there such a thing as something real…?" There was the faintest ring of loneliness in her words, lost in the night wind.

Haruno combed through her mussed hair with her hands, and then, as if following where the wind had gone, she started off. She continued down the steps, and when she approached the school gate, she turned halfway back to me and gave me a little wave with a delicate smile.

Stunned, all I could do was watch her stride away in that beautiful, squared-shoulders fashion of hers. I couldn't even manage a wave back at her.

Once she was completely out of sight, my legs went slack. I sank straight down onto the steps.

I'd thought I just wanted Yukino Yukinoshita's choice from the heart, her decision from the heart, her words from the heart. However, if her wish was just compensatory behavior, a decision she'd made in defeat, then that was the wrong answer after all.

I was sure none of what Yukinoshita had said had been a lie—it was just that the premise before arriving at that answer in the first place had been twisted.

Rather—I, Hachiman Hikigaya, had twisted it.

I'd known only one answer would be allowed, but I'd continued to avoid that choice, layering on excuses, putting it off, twisting words to mean what I wanted them to mean and creating a lie. I was leaning on her kindness and taking advantage of her sincerity, pretending to be drunk on a momentary dream. I'd insisted that it was the right answer.

This was no mere mistake anymore.

It was a hopeless fake that would depreciate every moment it existed.

× × ×

As the school building sank into the darkness of night, I was still sitting on the steps, heedless of the cold wind blowing while I stared blankly ahead.

Some cars went by, but I paid no attention to anything else around. It was already well past time to go home. I hadn't seen anyone in a good while.

As I sat there, unable to summon the energy to stand, the glass door behind me opened. The sound of brisk footsteps made me automatically turn around.

Then I felt a slight impact on top of my head.

"Hey, don't go outside in your indoor shoes." Ms. Hiratsuka was waving a karate-chop hand. She'd just clonked me.

As I rubbed my head with the out-of-place thought that *it's been a long time since she's smacked me like this*, Ms. Hiratsuka breathed a short sigh.

Then she offered her raised hand to me. "I was just about to lock up. Hurry and change your shoes."

I really couldn't stay like this forever. I hadn't been looking at the clock, but quite some time must have passed. With her prodding me, I finally got up, patting off the sand stuck to my coat.

I started going up the stairs two at a time, and the teacher folded her arms with a sigh. She was watching to make sure I was actually going home. Coming to the top of the steps, I bobbed a bow at her, then went into the school building.

There were still lights on in the office and the teachers' room, but most of the hallway lights were off. The outside light coming in through the windows and the emergency lights meant I didn't struggle to walk around, but my legs were heavy anyway.

Night had fallen, so it had gotten quite cold, and I found myself hunching over.

"Hikigaya," a voice called out.

I turned around to see Ms. Hiratsuka coming after me with soundless steps. She was still in her socks and hadn't put on her indoor shoes or slippers. While getting ready to go, she'd picked up her heels to carry them.

With her winter coat flapping instead of her white lab coat, she came up to stand next to me, then gave me a light clap on the back as if she was correcting my hunched posture. "...It's late, so I'll see you off," she said with a smile.

"No, it's fine. I came on my bicycle."

"Come on. Why not? Leave your bike behind."

What the heck was this woman, the *oitekebori youkai*?

Ms. Hiratsuka did not engage with my protests, pushing my back to hurry me on. In the end, she accompanied me to the front entrance and practically dragged me to the parking lot.

There was nobody around and only a few cars left. One of them, an expensive foreign car that seemed a bit out of place at the school, blinked its lights. Ms. Hiratsuka had a smart key.

Approaching her baby, she gave a cautious scan around before beckoning me. "Get in already; hurry up."

"Uhh-huhh." Doing as she instructed, I went to the passenger seat and did up the seatbelt while Ms. Hiratsuka slid straight into the driver's seat. When she turned the key in the ignition, it rumbled low in my gut.

As she slowly stepped on the gas, I leaned back and relaxed.

It had been a while since she'd last given me a ride. The leather seats were well maintained and comfortable. The aluminum finish on the seatbelt was brightly polished. I could really tell that she took good care of the vehicle.

Her desk in the teachers' room is such a mess, though, I thought with a wry smile tugging at my lips for a second, but thinking about how I wouldn't see those piles of papers, figures, and empty noodle cups anymore, I suddenly felt kind of lonely. I turned my head to the window.

On the way from the school to my house, orange streetlights came and went. Ms. Hiratsuka seemed to know the way, humming as she handled the wheel.

Then her humming came to an abrupt halt. "Guess your work's done for now, huh?"

"Yeah. Well, though I didn't really do anything."

"That's not true. You worked hard. Let's go out for drinks to reward you, since the job's over…is what I'd like to say, but I'm driving, so…"

"I can't even drink in the first place…"

Ms. Hiratsuka didn't turn to look at me, still facing forward as she smiled wryly. "True. I'll look forward to that in three years."

That made my words catch in my throat.

I should have responded with some trivial noise to show her I was still listening, but I just foolishly left my mouth hanging open. The mellow tune playing on the car stereo filled that silence.

"What's wrong? Stop ignoring me, come on. I have feelings, too, you know," Ms. Hiratsuka said sulkily, snapping me to attention. When I looked over at the driver's seat, she was pouting.

"Oh, sorry, well, it's like, I can't quite imagine it…" I grinned sheepishly.

Ms. Hiratsuka inclined her head with a sidelong look at me. "What can't you imagine? You becoming an adult? Or still associating with me three years in the future?"

I knew if time continued to pass without incident, eventually I would become an adult. But the words *becoming an adult* didn't quite click with me.

If I wanted to get a job or have a family—to engage in society—I figured I could manage to do it with effort or the right connections. If just a fantasy of it was enough, then a decent vision would come to mind. Still, I wasn't sure you could call someone an adult based on that. There are good-for-nothings out there who will waste their years and abuse their own children, so age, social position, or having a family can't be the basis on which you determine adulthood.

But, well, I could probably live my life without breaking any laws or harming others. If you considered the long term, like ten or twenty years, then somewhere along the line, there would be moments to correct my trajectory.

But asking about three years in the future felt too real, so I couldn't even imagine anything fantastical.

"Well, both… If anything, the latter, I suppose," I answered honestly, making Ms. Hiratsuka sigh in exasperation. Considering my temperament, it was doubtful our association would continue in the future.

We got stuck at a light, and the car came to a gentle halt. In the brief time the car was at the stop, Ms. Hiratsuka cracked open the power windows, dexterously pulled out a cigarette with just one hand, and put it to her lips. There was the flick of the flint, making sparks fly in the dark vehicle. A tiny flame illuminated her soft profile for just a moment.

Eventually, the traffic light turned green. She blew a puff of smoke out the open window, and cold night wind and warm words filled the car instead. "You don't get it. Associations don't end that easily. Even if you don't meet every day, you'll see each other about once every three months over stuff like birthday parties or when everyone goes out to drink."

"Is that how it is?"

Ms. Hiratsuka nodded, still facing the windshield, and went on. "That eventually turns to once every six months, then once a year, and you see them less frequently, and then finally you'll only see them at weddings, funerals, and alumni events. Then eventually, you stop remembering them."

"I see... Hmm? Huh? Those endings seem pretty easy to me." Her tone had been so relaxed and measured, even I was almost convinced. But that was totally the end of things, no matter how you interpreted it. She was making it sound like relationships ended with little effort.

"I'm saying that's what will happen if you don't do anything." Crushing her cigarette in the ashtray, she smiled pleasantly. "Let's take a little detour."

"As you wish." She was the one giving me a ride home, so I couldn't complain.

Instead of giving a reply, Ms. Hiratsuka flicked on her blinker and turned the wheel.

I stared through the windows, wondering where we were going. Eventually, the car went onto the national highway, headed in the opposite direction from my house.

Humming along cheerily with the song from the car stereo, Ms. Hiratsuka stepped firmly on the gas, and the engine growled. The streetlights, the headlights of the cars in the opposing lane, and the taillights of the cars in the lane beside us all flowed behind us.

Eventually, large trucks and trailers became more prominent on the road, and when the nighttime view of a steel mill came into view, Ms. Hiratsuka gently slowed her baby down and flicked the turn signal. The car continued on to a facility on the left-hand side.

She rolled through a particularly spacious parking lot and slowly came to a stop near what looked like the building entrance. Then she put the stick into park with practiced motions, pulled the emergency brake, and stopped the engine. It seemed this was her destination.

"We're here," she said, getting out of the car.

But where is here, though...? I followed her.

Getting a good look at the building, I figured it was a big games arcade. A massive green net was set up over a section of the roof, and occasional pleasant cracking sounds rang out. There was an adjoining batting center.

When I stood there, zoning out, Ms. Hiratsuka beckoned me. She walked with the confidence of a regular here, and I followed behind.

The building was your classic arcade. There were more than just what you'd call arcade cabinets—there was a wide range of games, including darts, table tennis, free-throw basketball, simulation golf, and stuff like that. There was plenty to play here.

But without so much as glancing at those games, Ms. Hiratsuka went up the stairs in the center, straight to the batting area.

"Oooh, we made it in time for metal bat hours," she said.

When I looked at the info board, I saw that it stated they changed the bats in the evening to avoid excessive noise pollution.

Ms. Hiratsuka gleefully bought some tokens, whipped off her coat, and tossed it over to me. "Hold that for me," she said as she rolled up the sleeves of her shirt and passed under the net to head for the batter's box.

After inserting a token, she went into the right batter's box, picked up the bat, and swung it lightly. Her form was clean, properly maintaining her center of balance. Then she held the end of the bat straight out ahead of her and tugged up her sleeves before readying herself.

Wow, she looks pretty legit…

The pitcher displayed on the LCD monitor ahead did a big windup, then there he went, first pitch!

"Hatsuhiba!" Ms. Hiratsuka called out as she followed through with her hit, and a pleasant sound rang out. The ball soared in a high arc to fly behind the machine.

Ms. Hiratsuka smirked at my applause. She got into position again for the second pitch.

"Hori! Saburou! Satozaki! Fukuura!" She struck the balls that shot out one after another while, for some reason, yelling the names of famous baseball players from the Chiba Lotte Marines each time. After that, she followed up with Ootsuka, Kuroki, and Julio Franco. The batting order was a mess, but it was a tasteful lineup, very nice choices.

Her shouts were good for building energy, but her form was the same for every name, so I kind of didn't get if there was much point. And hey, Fukuura is a left-handed batter… And Kuroki in particular is

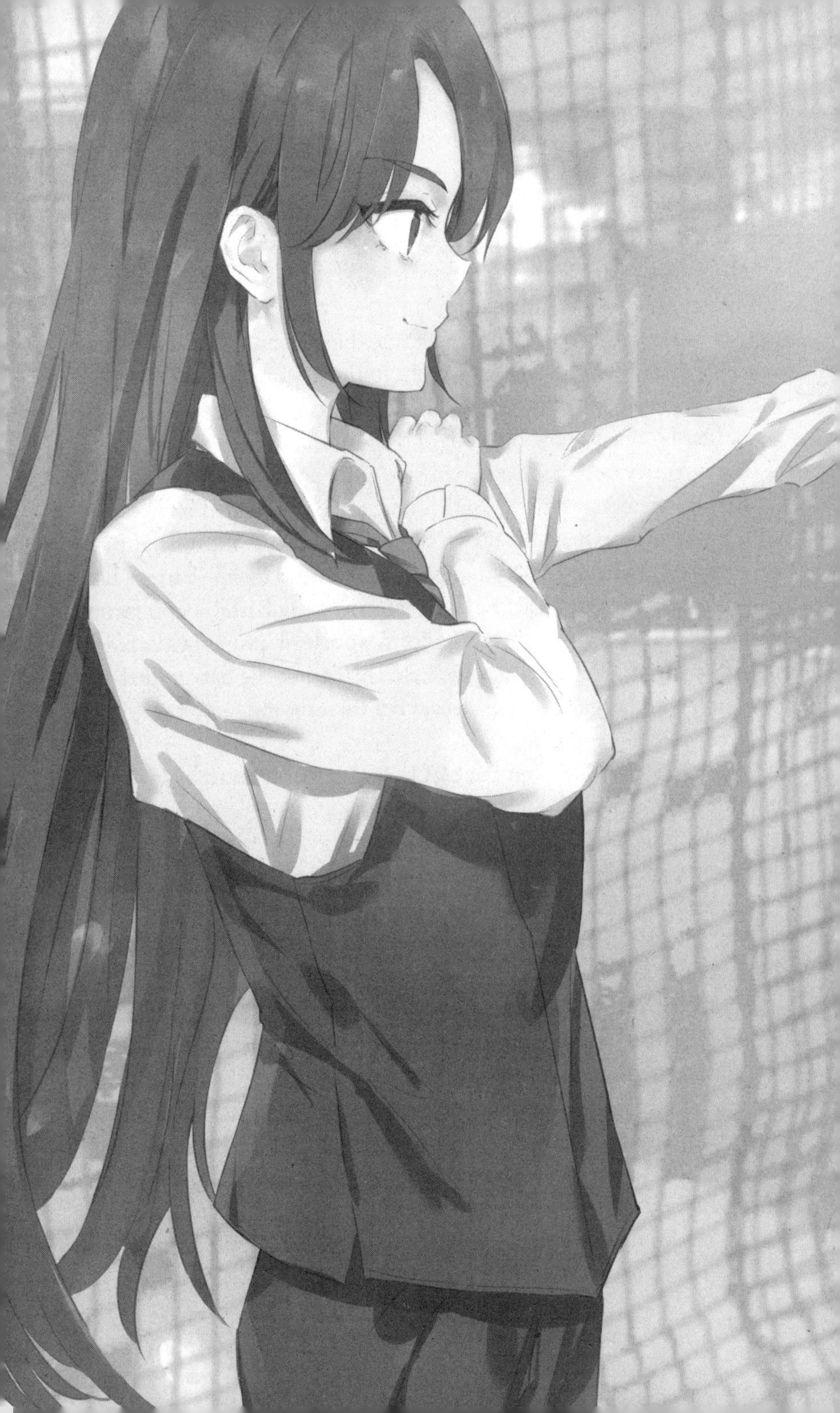

a pitcher... But most of all, since none of them were currently playing professionally, pour one out for Ms. Hiratsuka's age!

Her light swings made it look easy, but the reading on the ball speed indicator was over 130 km/h. *She's kinda intense. Go for pro, man. Lotte'll let anyone on the team anyway.*

Ms. Hiratsuka practiced hitting for a full twenty pitches, and after working up a sweat, she flapped the collar of her shirt as she went under the net to return to me.

When you do stuff like that, it makes me not know where to put my eyes. Spare me, please...

"Wanna try, Hikigaya?"

"No, I..."

Despite my refusal, when she flicked a token over at me, I had no choice but to accept. *Now that I've taken it, I have to do it...*

Still, having no experience, there was no way I could hit 130 km/h, so I obediently went over to the 100 km/h booth. When I tried copying what she'd done, lightly swinging the bat, Ms. Hiratsuka folded her arms behind me and nodded to herself with a know-it-all look.

You're making it harder for me...

Actually standing in the batting box, when the first ball shot at me, I thought, *Whoa! This is faster than I thought.* I struck out hard. *I'm not hitting it at all...*

When I was wondering what to do, I got a call of encouragement from behind. "Look at the ball more. Hold higher up on the grip. Your side is open. Don't try to swing wide to get your first shot. Work your way up to it to figure out the timing."

She's annoying...

Nevertheless, I tapped the end of the bat on the home base and went into position again. Following the teacher's advice, I did a compact swing, and this time it rang out with a pleasant sound: *swoo-woosh-CRACK!* Feeling a tingling numbness in my hands, I whipped back to see Ms. Hiratsuka nodding clearly with a little thumbs-up, with an added wink. ☆ Now I was all pleased and shy, so I couldn't help but laugh, too.

All right, I get the idea... I went into position for a third time, and I focused on hitting the balls that came flying at me. While I occasionally struck out and had a lot of bad strikes, I got a really nice crack every so often. Once I was done, I let out a big *phew.*

When I exited the batting booth, Ms. Hiratsuka was having a smoke at the bench behind the back net. She was holding a drink she must have bought at some point and a giant *takoyaki.* "Mm."

"Ah, thanks." Graciously accepting the can of coffee she wordlessly held out to me, I took a seat beside her.

"Feel a bit better?" she asked me.

"If exercise made you feel better, athletes wouldn't do drugs." Despite the kindness she'd shown me, the nasty quip rolled out of me.

Ms. Hiratsuka turned that aside with a knowing grin. "You're not very cute."

"...But I am honestly grateful for your consideration... Sorry, I've kinda been causing you trouble right up to the end," I said.

She gave me a puzzled look. Then with a big *agh,* she pushed back her long hair before putting that same hand on my head. "You can occasionally be cute. That's what really makes it so infuriating," she said, rubbing my head hard enough to hurt. I had a lot of objections to this—it was embarrassing and I was shy—but firstly and mostly, it just hurt. I escaped and inched about one fist's worth away, and Ms. Hiratsuka finally drew her hand back.

Her lips were slightly parted and quirked into a hint of a smile, which she stuck a cigarette into. With a flick of her lighter, she blew out a thin line of smoke and asked, "So then what were you doing out there?"

"...Ahhh, well, you know." Her remark was so sudden. I tried to avoid it.

But she saw through that, and her grin didn't falter. "Did Haruno say something to you?"

"...Well, she said lots of stuff," I answered, feeling desperate, but Ms. Hiratsuka's eyes focused on me, as she waited for me to continue. I could tell that any attempts at evasion weren't going to work now, so I let my still-unformed thoughts trickle out. "She said I can't get drunk, just like her."

"Well, that's true for her… You're not talking about alcohol, are you?" the teacher asked with slight unease.

I nodded back with a wry smile. "…I guess it means, like, on the atmosphere or on relationships. She says our relationship is codependent. It pissed me off to think she was right, so I tried fighting back a little, but…well, it's pretty hard."

With anyone else, I wouldn't have said that. I wouldn't have been able to handle exposing weakness. Not out of cowardly conceit, but out of arrogant shame.

So no matter how hard someone pressed me for answers, I would always fool around and shoot back jokes to avoid things and throw out distractions.

But I had one person I didn't feel the need to put up a front with. Ms. Hiratsuka was the only person I didn't have to try to act cool for. She was there as someone clearly more adult than me, and she always drew a line in the sand for me.

She didn't ask any unnecessary questions now, either, just puffed her cigarette as she considered what I meant.

"Codependency, huh? That choice of language is very like Haruno, but she uses it as a metaphor. She understands that about herself but says it anyway… She really likes you."

"Ha-ha, that doesn't really make me happy…"

"It's easy to take what Haruno says too harshly if you read too much into it… Ahhh, you two are both good at reading too deep into things," she added lightheartedly, and I forced some more laughter.

A smile cracked on Ms. Hiratsuka's face, and she crushed a cigarette on the edge of her ashtray before she turned her body toward me. "But I don't think that's what's happening in your case. The relationship between you, Yukinoshita, and Yuigahama isn't like that."

The thin line of white, wavering smoke vanished, replaced by a burst of a heavy tar smell. That odor was deeply familiar to me now.

There was nobody else in my life who smoked these cigarettes, so it would eventually become a nostalgic memory.

"Don't tie it all off with a simplistic term like *codependency*." Her fingers, still carrying that unforgettable smell, reached out to wrap an arm around my shoulders. "Maybe that logic will convince you. But don't twist someone's feelings with borrowed words like that... Don't write off those emotions with easy-to-understand symbols." Gazing into my eyes, Ms. Hiratsuka gently asked me, "Can your feelings be written off with just one word?"

"...No way. I couldn't stand that. You can't really communicate it with just one word in the first place."

Even now, I hadn't properly expressed my thoughts, my feelings, my emotions, or anything. If there was no meaning in them, then it was no different from barking. It was just howling, *Don't slot it into a single emotion*, baring your fangs to say, *They'll never get it*, while you're tucking your tail between your legs, thinking, *They don't have to get it.*

I was so frustrated. I'd been unconsciously digging my fingers into my coffee can.

Ms. Hiratsuka released my shoulders and nodded with satisfaction. "The answer is inside you. You just don't know how to get it out. That's why you're trying to convince yourself with words that are easily understandable. You're trying to fit a complex peg into a simple hole you can use to get it over with."

Maybe that was it. I had been clinging to the word *codependency*, figuring it would express my feelings in the most succinct way, to include everything, good and bad, love and hate. Because that word meant I didn't have to think about anything else. It was thought-stopping. It let me escape reality.

"But there isn't one right way to do things. Even with a single word, there are infinite ways to express it." Ms. Hiratsuka drew a pen from her breast pocket and swung it smugly. It was like a magician's wand.

Then she started to jot down something on a paper napkin. "For example, there are lots of things I feel for you. Like you're a hassle, a loser; you make things too complicated; your future is a concern…," she said as she scrawled out those words on the paper napkin.

"Geez… You're really digging into me there…"

"This isn't even the half of it. I've got lots, lots more to say. So much that it'd be a pain to bother saying it all," Ms. Hiratsuka said, and then she stopped writing down any more characters. She turned it into a scribble.

Her pen scrawled around the paper napkin, burying it in ink. Gradually, she blacked it all out from the edges, but the center part alone remained white. Eventually, ink encroached on the center as well, until the blank space formed a single phrase.

"But if you put all that stuff together…"

Before I could figure out what shape the blank space would take, Ms. Hiratsuka shoved the paper in my face. "I care about you."

"…Huh? Ah, uh, whaaat?" I looked at the paper she shoved at me, and inside the all-black canvas was that phrase cut out in white. I was so startled, confused, pleased, embarrassed, shy, and all sorts of other feelings. I couldn't react properly.

"Don't be shy, don't be shy. You're my favorite student. In that sense, I really do think well of you." Ms. Hiratsuka smirked like a naughty kid who'd succeeded in some mischief, and then she mussed my hair again.

Whoa there! Ohhh, that's what you meant? That was real close there. I just about took that pretty seriously, I mean I even thought, I totally love you and stuff, too. My hair's all sweaty now.

I twisted around, and once I'd wiggled my noggin out of her grasp, I breathed a sigh of relief.

Ms. Hiratsuka delighted in my nervousness as she lit a new cigarette. "If one word won't do it, then use up as many words as it takes. And if you can't trust words, then just combine them with action." She blew out a breath of smoke and followed its path with her eyes. I watched it go with her profile in the foreground.

"You can express yourself with all kinds of words or actions. Just gather up each one like dots to put together your own answer. Maybe if you fill in the whole canvas, the white space that remains will take the shape of what you mean."

The smoke that had been lazily lingering eventually vanished.

When my field of vision cleared once more, Ms. Hiratsuka was looking right at me. "So show me. While I can still be your teacher, show me your ideas, your feelings, everything. Hit me with all of it. Shove it at me so hard that you can't make excuses."

"Everything?" I asked.

She clenched a fist in front of her chest and nodded emphatically. "Yeah. A large serving with the works."

"Is this ramen…?" I said, slumping, and Ms. Hiratsuka beamed at me. That undid my tension, and I was able to put on a loose grin. "Well, I'll try. I don't know if anyone would understand, though."

"If understanding came so easily, there'd be no suffering. But if it's you… If it's you kids, you'll be all right." She clapped me lightly on the head.

And then, as if to say this conversation was over, she stretched wide. "All right, then let's have some ramen and go home. How about we go to Naritake? Naritake!"

"Ohhh, good idea."

"Right?" Ms. Hiratsuka cracked a cool smile and crushed her cigarette out before rising to her feet. Following suit, I got up, too.

Even as we walked and chatted about things, Ms. Hiratsuka always went a few steps ahead of me.

My feet suddenly came to a stop as I saw her back in front of me. She was standing so tall, so cool. She felt totally unreachable to me.

I wanted this teacher, the only one I could say was a teacher I respected, to watch. I wanted her to be assured of my action.

No matter how awkward, creepy, and pathetic it was, no matter how awful and low and hopelessly pathetic, I had to show her Hachiman Hikigaya's answer.

I was certain that bringing things to an end wasn't a mistake in and of itself; the way we were ending things was wrong.

Clinging to borrowed words, pandering to the pretense of a

compromise—this relationship had gotten so twisted up. There was no undoing it, and it probably wasn't what we had sought. It had become a hopeless sham.

So I would at least damage this imitation enough to break it, for just one single something real.

With my own hands, I would put an end to my youth gone wrong.

6

Just like that time before, **Yui Yuigahama** implores.

My second year in high school was coming to an end.

After the graduation ceremony and the prom, there were only a few more school days left for those of us not graduating. Most of those were allocated to the final exam, and the rest were for handing back the exam papers and attending the year-end ceremony. Once final exams were over, suddenly a spring break mood was taking over the school.

The clubs that had been off during the exam period started up again that day, and energetic shouts and the pleasant crack of metal bats resounded from outdoors. The sports clubs that used the gym were the exception. Normally, the volleyball or badminton clubs would be putting up poles and nets, but right now, temporary dressing booths and folding chairs were set up there. The club members were nowhere to be seen. Instead, there were the new first-years who would be coming in the spring, as well as some of their parents.

One pair among this crowd was me and my sister, Komachi.

That day, there was an event called the "information session for new students" at Soubu High School, and they were also taking measurements for uniforms there. In other words, it was the first unveiling of Komachi in her school uniform. Our parents were very busy, so in their place, I'd rushed over to witness the event.

Before us were temporary dressing booths divided off by partitions and curtains. I watched Komachi go in and fidgeted in my uncomfortable folding chair.

As I was waiting for Komachi to finish trying on the uniform, I happened to think back on what the classroom had looked like.

It had been bubbling with the post-exam feeling of release. As I'd been quickly getting all my stuff together to go, loud chatter had been flying back and forth. Some kids had just marched jauntily home, while others remained in the classroom to chat about the exam, like "I sooo blew it—awww, I'm definitely gonna have to retest!"

Some people? This is Sagami... As expected of original Sagami. Her choice of conversational topic was very not shocking.

Meanwhile, the sports club types like Totsuka, then Hayama and the guys, were happily heading to their clubs after having spent some time away. At the usual seats by the rear window of the classroom, Miura, Yuigahama, and Ebina were chatting about where they would hang out later. Before, I'd talked with Yuigahama about where we'd meet up after exams, but that was happening either tomorrow or the day after that.

What should I talk about, then? I considered while I crossed my legs the other direction.

In front of the folding chair was the dressing booth. On the other side of the curtain, it sounded like Komachi and the staff member there were talking about something.

"How does it fit?"

"Hmm, it seems okay... Oh, the skirt length..."

"Yes, about that..."

Their whispering and murmuring snapped me out of my thoughts and back to reality. *The term* skirt length *is kind of anxiety inducing...* Inclining my ears to Komachi's voice as I glared at the curtain, bouncing one knee, I waited for her impatiently.

Eventually, there was a *fshht* as the curtains were drawn. "Ta-daaa!" Komachi said, coming out of the dressing booth wearing a Soubu High School uniform.

"…Ohhh." I unfolded my arms to clap.

That seemed to bolster her cheer, as she puffed out her chest a little, put her hands on her waist, and did a fancy pose. "So? What do you think? Cute? Komachi's cute, right?"

"Yeah, yeah, the cutest in the world."

"Whoa, there it is—he doesn't even care!"

I actually do think she's not only the cutest in the world, but cute enough to beat all of recorded history, afterlife included. However, more importantly, I had many points of concern about this outfit, which drained the attention from my compliment.

Unable to let these concerns slide, I frowned and tilted my head. "But, like, isn't that skirt too short? It makes Big Bro worried."

"Whoa, someone's obnoxious." Komachi had looked pleased until now, but now her face momentarily twisted in disgust.

But she could make as many faces at me as she wanted—my fashion check wasn't over. "Well, skirt length can be adjusted, so that's fine. But the blazer…," I said.

That must have bothered Komachi, too. She stretched her arms out front to check the blazer cuffs. The sleeves were rather long, covering about half her palms.

Komachi dangled the sleeves, flapping her wrists like a waving cat statue. "Ahhh, these?"

"Yeah, those. Cute."

I *hmm*'d to myself as if to say, *Oooh, they're doing nice work.*

Komachi looked disgusted. "Whoa, creepy… But if it's cute, then okay." She fluttered her sleeves, satisfied.

The staff standing beside her awkwardly commented, "It may look a little large, but everyone goes with this much extra hem in their order."

"Oh, this is totally fine! I'll take it, please," Komachi said hastily, and the staff smiled and nodded.

"Well then, this way…" And so, the fitting was coming to an end.

But there was still something I had to do. "Oh, can I take some photos? I want to let our parents know, just in case," I said.

The staff checked around the area. "It doesn't seem there's anyone else waiting now... So go ahead; take your time. Please let me know when you're done."

There had to be a lot of people who took photos, as the staff smiled like they were used to it and withdrew behind the fitting booth.

I pulled out my phone and pointed the lens at Komachi. "Then let me get some shots," I said, activating camera mode and snapping the shutter a few times. *Niiice, niiice, let's go for something bold.*

"Okay, new pose, let's try spinning around. Right, then pose again right there."

Komachi put on a cool look as told, switching up the way she stood, and then at the end she spun around and grinned brightly with that sideways peace sign. ☆

"Mm, guess that does it. Right, okay." Once I finished playing photographer, I sat down on the folding chair where I'd been before to check the images. *Hmm, a perfect ratio of usable shots.* With a few taps, I attached the top picks to an e-mail and sent it to our parents.

Ignoring me, Komachi sighed and went slack. She must have been a little tired, as she ambled over to sit down on the folding chair next to me. She happily stroked her uniform as her gaze swept over the gym. "It's not long before Komachi's gonna be going to this school."

"Is it sinking in?"

"Yeah. Komachi's looking forward to it!" As if expressing endless excitement, eyes sparkling like, *I wanna do that, I wanna do this, I wanna do more and more* in a dreamy state of mind, she started to speak in a dreamy-cute way. "There's so much stuff Komachi wants to do in high school! Like studying...is, well, that's pretty whatever, but like a part-time job or going to hang out with friends after school! And Komachi wants to try events like the prom."

I was listening, nodding along to mean *Studying isn't "whatever." I'd like you to try a little.*

Suddenly, Komachi's gaze dropped. "...And club activities and stuff," she added at the end, giving me an examining look. I knew what she meant by that remark, and my words caught in my throat for an instant.

I couldn't leave her in the dark. I had to tell her about the day of the graduation ceremony and the prom, Hachiman Hikigaya's longest day.

I'd already found my own answer that day, through the education from the teacher I respected most. Though I wasn't yet sure about the method or how I would prove my intentions, I had acquired a solution.

"About clubs… There won't be a Service Club anymore," I told her.

Instead of answering, Komachi nodded with a sad smile. She'd been leaning forward, but now she slowly settled into the back of her chair, her small shoulders weakly falling. Her eyes were focused on the skirt of her brand-new uniform. "Oh. It's disbanding, huh…?" she muttered like she was talking to herself, hanging her head.

"…Yeah. Because I'm gonna make it go away." I clapped a hand on Komachi's slouching back. Then I stuck up a thumb, jabbed it at my own face, and put on the coolest smile I could.

This was the conclusion I'd been unable to offer as an answer back then. I wouldn't leave it to anyone else—I would make this choice of my own will. Even if I was blustering right now.

Komachi looked at me blankly. But a moment later, she burst into laughter. "You don't have to try to look so cool about it…," she said with a faint *Good grief* sort of sigh.

"Sorry if it gets kinda awkward, I guess?" I joked, lighthearted.

"Oh, that's okay. Komachi will have fun on her own. Since Yukino and Yui are Komachi's friends, even without you and the Service Club!" Komachi tapped her chest and put on a cheery smile. Then she leaned her head to rest on my shoulder and whispered softly, "So you can do what you want."

"Thanks," I answered, and Komachi smiled and hopped to her feet.

"Then I guess I'll get changed."

"Yeah… Then let's get home."

When I stood up along with her, she nonchalantly rejected that. "Oh, Komachi's going out to eat with the other new first-years now."

"Huh? The heck?"

"I told you. High school students these days are connected on social media before school even starts. And then we go out for dinner together to deepen future friendships." Chuckling in amusement, Komachi headed for the fitting booth.

Watching her go, I sat back down on the folding chair as I turned my thoughts to the new students I still had yet to see.

A social gathering before starting school…

Doesn't that mean the people who couldn't go to that are guaranteed to be loners before school even begins?

In the era of social media, modern high schoolers are on hard mode…

× × ×

Since Komachi was headed to her meetup, I parted ways with her at the gym and set off for the main school building.

Between the school uniform fitting to the try-on to shooting photos and whatnot, quite some time had passed. The sunlight slanting through the window was quite low in the sky, and it was beginning to faintly color the halls red.

From the distant courtyard could be heard the calls of the sports clubs and the tones of wind instruments, but in the hallway, there was only the rhythm of my footsteps and one single shadow drawn out long.

It was the ordinary, commonplace sights and sounds of after school. If it had been just one year ago, I don't think I would have thought anything of them. But now they brought me loneliness and nostalgia.

Basking in the crisp air and chilly sentimentality, I headed for the entrance, where I discovered someone.

She was sitting at the umbrella stand, holding a large bag in front of her chest as she vacantly stared outside. The door had been left open, letting wind blow in from the entrance, and it made her pinkish bun occasionally sway in the glow of the sunset.

It could be no one else but Yui Yuigahama.

In the dust that sparkled in the westering sun, her profile was filled with an ephemerality between sorrow and loneliness. It was a far more mature expression than usual, and it was terribly beautiful.

I hesitated to speak to her—I started to call out but then swallowed it. Instead, I took off my indoor shoes and stuck them in my shoe cubby before dropping my loafers on the ground.

The sound made her turn toward me. "Oh, Hikki."

By the time she called my name, she had her usual bright smile on. It relieved me, and after changing my shoes, I walked over to her. "Hey, what's up?"

"I was waiting."

"Huh, why…? …Huh, hold on, did we have plans?"

As I was getting anxious thinking maybe I'd shirked out of something, Yuigahama waved her hands. "Oh, no. It's not really anything… It's just that when I looked at the shoe cubbies, I thought, *Oh, he hasn't gone home yet…* So then I just kinda…" The hands she was waving in front of her chest gradually slowed, eventually coming to a stop. One idle hand reached across her eyes to tuck her hair behind her ear. She turned away a little shyly.

"…I was waiting." The tip of her ear and her soft-looking cheeks were as red as if they'd copied the sunset.

Now I was getting shy, too, and I wound up mumbling, "O-oh… Okay…"

Yuigahama chuckled at my flustered comment, covering the awkward moment as she combed at her bun. "We talked about going somewhere once exams are over, and I was just thinking we hadn't been able to talk during the exam period. So I thought maybe I'd try waiting a bit for you."

"Sorry, I should've messaged you."

"It's totally fine!" she said brightly, shaking her head to ease my worries, but then her smile turned fragile in a heartbeat. "…'Cause I kinda…wanted to try waiting." She seemed to be gazing out the window, beyond the glow of the sunset in the distance, and when I saw her profile, my voice caught.

Maybe there wasn't much of a reason, like she said, or maybe she was avoiding putting it into words.

I didn't know the truth, but now that I thought about it…

...she had always been waiting.

For me, or for us.

It had taken long enough for me to realize. "...Oh, thanks," I said.

Yuigahama nodded, then got herself some energy with a *hup* and stood. She kept that momentum going to shove the big bag she'd been holding against her chest at me. "Help me take these things back." Her hands now free, she brushed at the hem of her skirt and adjusted her backpack like it was heavy. She'd always been using that pack, and it must have had lots of end-of-year stuff in it. It looked somewhat bulky.

Figuring if I was going to be carrying her stuff anyway, then I'd take that, too, I reached out. "Mm."

"Mm?" She looked at my hand and tilted her head curiously, but then she clapped her hand over mine.

When she did that, now I was the one tilting my head. *Why does she do such cute things?* "I don't mean shake a paw. Your stuff—I'll carry it."

"Ohhh... T-tell me that sooner!" Blushing, Yuigahama smacked my hand and shoved her backpack at me. Then she quietly murmured "Thanks" and briskly strode ahead.

"Owww," I muttered, shaking the hand she'd smacked, even though it didn't hurt. I had to say something stupid like that, or something else would pop out of my mouth...

× × ×

The afterglow of the sunset was seeping across the western sky, pouring over the trees lining the way to the station as I pushed my bicycle through the pale light leaking between their leaves and branches. Yuigahama was walking along beside me.

She brought up lots of things to me on the way, but then she interrupted herself. "Oh, right! Did you go somewhere?"

"Komachi's entrance info session. She was getting fitted for her uniform, so I went with her."

"Ohhh, I'd have liked to see, too."

"You can see her anytime once May comes," I said, but my tone was a little hollow.

May was supposedly just around the corner, but I couldn't really imagine it. That probably showed on my face, as Yuigahama's expression darkened for a moment, too. "Ah, yeah…" She must have been aware she sounded glum, as she clapped her hands and made a cheery show of saying, "Oh, then maybe I'll look for a present to go with her uniform. Something she could use on a regular basis."

I made an effort to stay on the light side of things, too. "That sounds good. I think she'd really love that."

Yuigahama took a tiny step ahead to stick her hands into the basket of the bicycle I was pushing. The large bag she'd handed me was in there, plus her usual backpack. She took her phone out of her backpack and started to make a note. *It's dangerous to walk while being on your phone! Good children, don't do this!* But instead of telling her off, I came to a stop. She must have understood my intention, as she stopped there to use her phone.

Once she was done typing, she put her phone back in her pack and nodded at me to say, *Now we're good.*

I nodded back, and as I started pushing my bike again, I looked at the large bag she'd put inside my basket. "So what's up with this bag?"

"Oh, this? School's almost over, so I figured I'd take my stuff home. Once I got everything together, it wound up being a lot."

"Wow… Well, that's common at the end of the semester." You see that a lot before long holidays like summer and spring vacation. It's particularly remarkable with elementary schoolers. With all their paints, drawing boards, and calligraphy tools held in both arms and on their back, it makes you think, Is this the Freedom with the METEOR Unit or what? You never know when they're gonna fall over and go into Full Burst Mode. I'm starting to think I used to dump out everything in my bag a lot…

As I was taking a trip down memory lane, Yuigahama glanced at my bicycle basket. "You don't have much stuff, Hikki?"

"I didn't really have much to begin with."

As we chatted, we approached Yuigahama's home, stopping in front of the convenience store by the front yard of the apartment complex.

She looked up at the apartment building, then turned back to me to ask a little shyly, "Um...do you wanna come over?"

I smiled sardonically at the way she said it. "Nah, I'll skip it. I feel like I'd wind up getting dinner again."

"Oh. Yeah. Ah-ha-ha... Oh, I know. Wait a minute," she replied with a shy little smile. An idea must have struck her, because she ran into the convenience store alone.

I figured if she was just going into the convenience store, then I'd go in, too, but she'd told me to wait. I may not look it, but I've got a higher IQ than the Gahama family dog, Sablé. Yep, it's your same old Hachiman, hi, that's me.

After parking my bicycle, I sat down on a bumper in front of the convenience store.

I glanced behind me to check on how Yuigahama was doing inside in time to see her buying the coffee they sold at the register. She was filling the cup at the dispenser.

I waited for a while, and she came back, carrying a cup of coffee in each hand. "Here, this is my thanks."

"Ohhh, you don't mind? Thanks." *Is this for carrying her stuff? Then I won't say no.*

But I'd come on my bike that day, so it would be a bad idea to drink while riding. *Whatever shall I do...?*

I was puzzling out how to rectify this, but Yuigahama headed straight from the convenience store to the nearby park. It had a gazebo and benches and stuff, and around this time of day, the warm sunshine of the afternoon was cooling down, so it would be a comfortable spot. It was perfect for a coffee break.

The park was full of neighborhood kids running around, falling, crying, then getting up again, playing a game of tag with rules I didn't understand. Yuigahama and I sat down on a nearby bench while we watched them from a distance.

The wind felt good. The evening was peaceful.

Yuigahama put her lips to the straw to sip the sweet café au lait, then let out a content exhalation. Then she looked into the distance beyond the wide park. "This feels kinda relaxing…"

"Yeah… We've been running around a lot lately," I answered as I drank my coffee.

Yuigahama turned in her seat to face me. "Uh-huh. It's fun to hang out with Yumiko and everyone, but we go all over to do stuff, and, like, we've gotta be focused on the clock at karaoke, and things move so fast. It's still fun, though."

"Well, it's always gonna be like that for places where you pay for time. Like at manga cafés or saunas and stuff, you go in for two hours, but then before you know it, the time's all gone, and you really panic at the end," I said, and Yuigahama immediately smacked my shoulder.

"I totally get that!" Then she screeched to a halt. "…Though I don't know about saunas."

"Huh? You don't know about saunas? What country are you from?"

"Why're you asking me that? Where do saunas come from, anyway…?"

"Saunas are from Finland………according to some."

"What's with that whisper at the end?!"

"Well, it's difficult to explain… You can find steam baths all over the world, Japan included. If you limit yourself to the narrow definition of a Finnish sauna, though, you can say the origin is Finland, but our Japanese linguistic ambiguity, saunas and steam baths are seen as equivalent. So in that broader sense, if you're asking when and where did something sauna-*like* originate, I'm forced to say there are a variety of theories." I was rambling ultra-fast and ultra-quiet as Yuigahama *hmm*'d at me and stared vacantly.

Then she cringed away a little. "You're kinda really cree…know a lot. It's kinda creepy…"

"You tried to reword yourself at first—where did that go?" I shot back wearily. *I would've rather you didn't correct yourself. Sometimes consideration can hurt people unnecessarily, you know!*

Yuigahama giggled before putting her lips to the straw again. And this time, she let out a big sigh of satisfaction and stretched wide. "…It's kinda nice to spend time like this." Lowering her raised arms, she added, "Right?" and looked at me.

I gave her a lazy nod. "If it's sometimes… If you did this every day, you'd need more to do."

"Ahhh. Stuff to do… I do have a lot of time on my hands when I'm not going to club. Though, like, I didn't think that at all before."

"Yeah. I've just kind of been going almost every day ever since the second year started. I can't even remember what I was doing last year."

"That's so true… I wonder how we'll spend our third year." Yuigahama put her hands down on the bench, legs stuck out in front of her to swing them as she gazed far, far ahead into the sky.

I, on the other hand, was rolling a stone at my feet. "Soon enough, you won't be able to talk like that 'cause of entrance exams."

"Yeah, maybe." She pulled a wry smile, and I did the same.

Both our expressions faded around the same moment. Maybe it was because despite talking about the future, we couldn't see any of the important things. Just the most practical elements.

No, that probably wasn't it.

It was because we'd skipped talking about the present at all. I don't know about Yuigahama, but I, at least, realized that I'd been intentionally avoiding bringing it up.

A cold air was beginning to mingle in the twilight winds; "Yuuyake Koyake" played from the park speakers. When they heard the tune, the playing children started trickling home.

The western sky burned with the glow of the sunset, while the east was colored indigo as if washed in thin ink, and the space between was a mix of the two. Eventually, the skies would turn to the hues of the blue hour.

As we gazed up at the sky silently, Yuigahama said softly, "…Hey, Hikki."

"Hmm?" Hearing her speak, I looked beside me. Though she'd called my name, she was staring at her feet, her lips firmly pressed together. She kept breathing shallowly as if worrying whether to say anything.

But eventually, full of determination, she lifted her chin and looked me straight in the eye. "Do you really think this is okay?" she asked.

I thought I understood what she meant. "It's not a question of whether I'm okay with it…" But before I could say, *It's just not my decision*, she shook her head and cut me off.

"Think about it properly before you answer. If it really is okay, if this really is the end. Then I'll tell you my wish… A really important wish."

When she stared directly at me, the words that had been about to fall out of my mouth dried up. My teeth caught my lip unconsciously. I looked down.

When she was this troubled, I wasn't allowed to give her a poorly considered answer. No careless evasion, lies, or self-aggrandizing pretense. If I joked in reply and created a distraction, I knew she'd smile and forgive me for running away, but I couldn't take advantage of that.

I couldn't betray her. This was the one person in the world I didn't want to hate me.

"…I'm not okay with it."

I struggled to say it, and Yuigahama smiled faintly, nodding. With that encouragement, I finally got out more.

"I think the club was always going to end. We'd have to retire it at some point next year, just like any other club, because we'd be graduating. Besides, our club advisor, Ms. Hiratsuka, is leaving. So ending it isn't wrong in itself, because it has to end eventually anyway." Yuigahama kept nodding, so I continued. "The club going away is unavoidable. I know Yukinoshita doesn't want to keep it up, either. All the reasons for ending it make sense… I think it's okay to let it die."

I was finally able to voice how I felt to their faces.

Now I could say good-bye to my immaturity: I'd been aware of the ending all this time but unable to acknowledge it.

Having gotten that weight off my chest, I let out a sigh from deep in my soul.

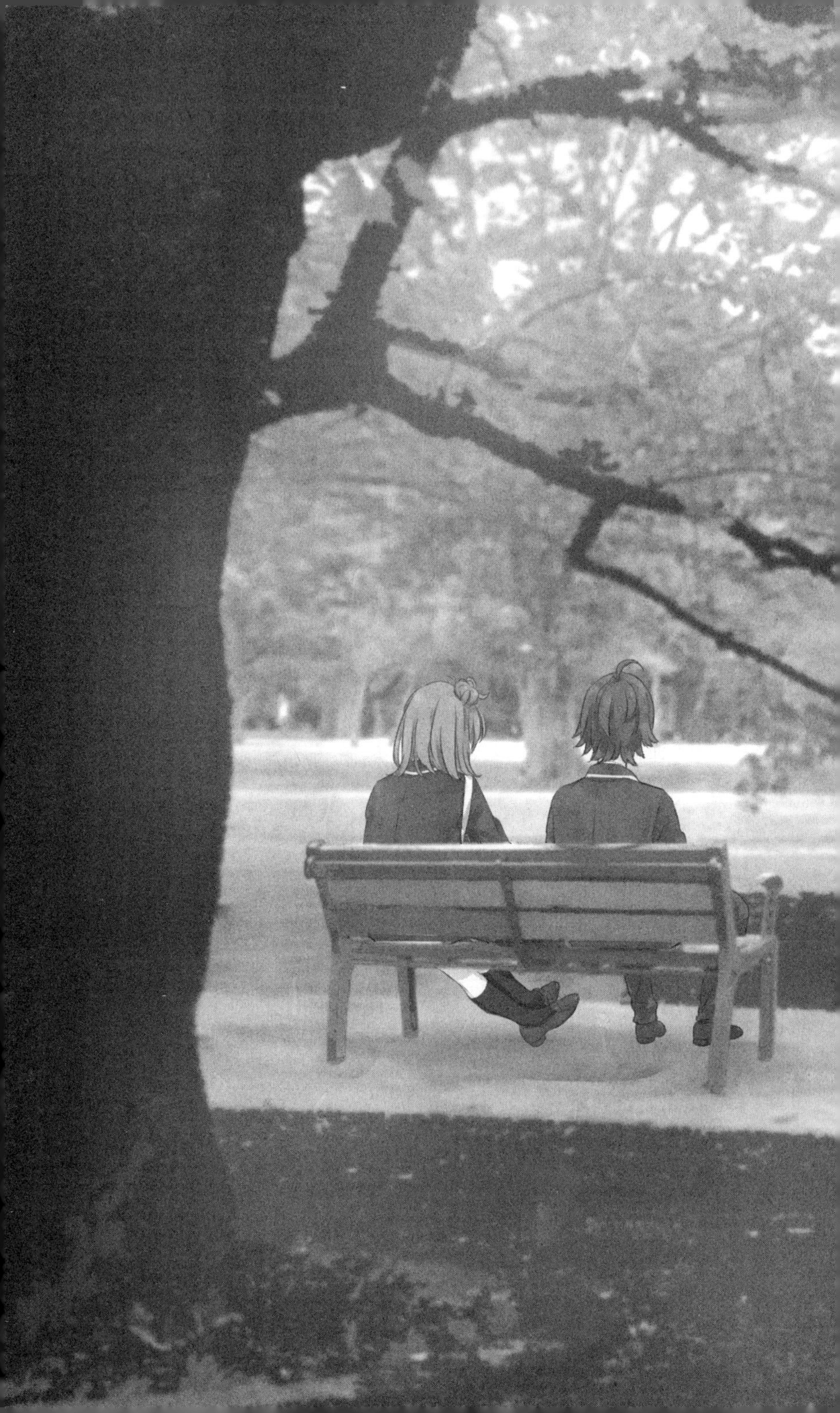

Yuigahama set the cup she'd been holding to the side, straightened her back, put her knees together, and faced toward me. "Oh…then…" She opened her mouth hesitantly, cautiously choosing her words. Her hands fidgeted on her lap, but eventually gaining her resolve, she squeezed her pleated skirt. "So then—"

I didn't deserve to hear what came next—because I still had something else I should be saying.

"But there's just one thing I can't accept…," I said, cutting her off.

She froze. There was surprise and confusion in her eyes, but she didn't protest, quietly nodding to show she was listening. That gesture prompted me to continue.

"If she's just compensating for what she really wants, if this is because she's given in and she made this choice to hide it, I can't accept that. If I'm the one who twisted things up, then that responsibility…," I started to say, then gave up.

I knew it was wrong even as I said it. Once again, I'd just about tried to escape with stupid word games. How could I still be trying to gloss things over with roundabout logic?

There was something else I needed to say.

When I suddenly went silent, Yuigahama grew concerned, uneasy, even suspicious.

I sucked in a big breath, then smacked my cheeks with both hands, and Yuigahama jumped in her seat. Putting a hand to her chest to calm her heart, she said timidly, "Th-that startled me… Where's this coming from…?"

"Sorry. Forget that part. I was kinda trying too hard to look cool."

Her eyes widened, and she blinked two, three times. Then she burst into laughter. "Whaaat?" Catching her by surprise must have weirdly hit her funny bone. She was giggling. Even I thought I was being ridiculous, and I came to find it amusing, too.

It really was a bad habit of mine. I just couldn't get rid of those pointless self-conscious impulses, and without even realizing it, I wound up putting on an act in front of her.

With a sip of bitter coffee, I washed down all the pretentious fancy words stuck in there, and this time I didn't try to be careful with my words. "This is gonna sound weird, but it's just, well…I don't want our relationship to die, so I can't accept how this is ending."

Now that I'd said it aloud, it sounded so stupid to me. It was an extremely brain-dead statement. It was such an inept thing to say. A self-deprecating grimace quirked in the corners of my lips.

It seemed to startle Yuigahama, too, but she never laughed. She softly closed her eyes. "…I don't think you'd cut off contact."

"Well, not normally. You'll occasionally run into each other for one reason or another and have small talk, and keep in touch and go to get-togethers and stuff. People tend to keep in touch to a certain degree." I repeated this common opinion, the one from my conversation with Ms. Hiratsuka in her car.

That said, a common opinion wasn't necessarily universal.

"…But I'm not like that. I can't stand those sorts of relationships, like fake friends who only talk when they need something."

Once I'd gotten it out in the open, it finally clicked with me. When the words took form, for the first time, it made sense to me.

It was nothing at all. It was just that I hated growing distant from people like that.

I'd kneaded the logic to death and lined up everything from reasons to excuses to environments to situations, and all I had to show for it was this hopeless conclusion. I even thought to myself, *Just how childish and pathetic can you get?*

So while I was being pathetic, I put on a self-mocking expression one more time. "Even if I try for a while, I'm sure we'll definitely grow apart. I'm an expert at cutting off relationships."

"Don't act proud about it…" Yuigahama smiled awkwardly, but she didn't deny it was true. Having associated with each other for nearly a year, we both knew that much.

And there was one other person who had been around me for that long. "While I'm talking about this, Yukinoshita is probably like that, too," I added.

"…Well, yeah."

"Right? So if we stop spending time together now, it'll probably stay like that… I can't quite accept that." I was so useless, I couldn't think of any way to talk around it, fancy or simple. All I could do was force myself to put on a fake-happy face.

Yuigahama kept looking at that pathetic expression of mine without a word, but eventually, she sighed in exasperation. "No one's ever gonna get that if you don't say so."

"Even if I do, it's not like you're definitely gonna understand… It doesn't make any sense, and it's not a reason, either. It's nonsense."

My expression was twisting as I tripped over my thoughts. Despite the selfish equivocation, I couldn't understand it myself. Right from the start, I'd resigned myself to never being able to amend my feelings into existing language.

Yuigahama nodded nonetheless. "Yeah, I honestly don't get it at all. I don't get what you mean. It's just creepy."

"Yeah. I totally think so, too… But aren't you hammering that in a bit hard there?" After that one-two-three punch, even I would get a little depressed.

But Yuigahama's eyes were filled with fondness. "…But, like, I kinda get it. That stuff is so you."

"Is it?"

Yuigahama put about a fist's worth of distance between us and sat back down again, pointing her knees at me. "Yeah… That's why I think you've got to tell her that."

"Even though she won't get it?"

I instantly took one of her light punches. Yuigahama frowned in a huff. "She doesn't have to understand! Or, like, Hikki, the issue is you don't try to let people understand you."

"That's painfully true."

It really was. I'd always given up on them ever seeing where I was coming from. That was why I'd never been able to say what was important.

She'd voiced the problem so completely.

"I think it's true that words aren't enough to express your ideas…

But then I'll just spend that much more effort trying to understand, so it's fine. Yukinon probably will, too." Yuigahama chided me in a gentle tone with earnest passion. She narrowed her eyes in the sunset's glare.

Ohhh, is that all? I understood everything about Yuigahama now.

It was true that, right now, I was trying to understand what she'd put into words. Although, it wasn't rational at all. It wasn't the sort of thing you could explain with logic, and there was plenty of subjectivity and intuition mixed into it.

By doing that, we would take turns filling in the blanks.

"Listen, I already decided a long time ago what my wish would be." Yuigahama hopped to her feet and spun away from me, then looked up at the setting sun. The sunset I saw beyond her reminded me of another.

I thought back to that snowy sunset over the gently rolling ocean.

"…I want everything," she said.

There was no scent of the ocean or sparkling snow falling down, but the words were there, just like that time. Eventually, Yuigahama breathed a quiet but great sigh and turned back to me again. "I want Yukinon to be here for ordinary times after school like this. I want to be there with you and Yukinon, too."

With the sunset at her back, in the warm light and cold wind, her tone shifted into desperation. "…So you have to tell her."

The sunlight was dazzlingly bright, but I never turned away, even when my eyes watered. I wouldn't ever forget the image of her strong gaze and fragile but beautiful smile.

"It'll be okay. I'll tell her." I said that to myself as well as to her with as much sincerity as I could.

She cracked a smile. Sitting down on the bench again, she examined my face. "Really?" She was teasing me.

"Yeah. Well, I'll need plenty of prep, and it won't be easy, but I'll manage somehow."

At my dubious answer, Yuigahama's smile turned suspicious. "Prep?"

"Lots of stuff… I mean, we've both laid out plenty of defensive lines, excuses, pretexts, simple titles, and escape routes… So first, I'll eliminate all of those," I said.

Yuigahama's expression then was complicated—unease, anger, a lot of mixed-up feelings. Anxiously, she closed her mouth, then opened it again to say coolly, "I don't think this is that sort of thing."

"I know… I just feel like I have to do all of that first, or I won't be able to say it. I have to draw both of us out to a place where we can't run away." My reply was pretty pathetic, what with her quiet anger bearing down on me.

I was actually quite exasperated with my own cowardice, if I do say so myself. But when you've been Hachiman Hikigaya-ing for sixteen years, you've got to beat down all the equivocation you can think of and chase yourself into a corner first, or it won't work at all.

When I let out a smothered sigh, Yuigahama got a kind but pained expression. "You just have to say one thing."

"How's just one thing gonna get it across?"

That would be enough for most people, but I could never be satisfied with some kind of verbal template. I felt like it needed more, but it also felt like too much. I really wasn't sure if I could come up with the right way to express myself that wasn't too much or too little. Most of all, I wouldn't be able to stand boiling my feelings down to something simplistic.

Even right this moment, it didn't feel like a simple answer would get anything across. Yuigahama was staring at me. *I guess that really wasn't enough of an answer.* I tried to explain more carefully at length.

"It's what happens when you look smart, but you're just as stupid as anyone and a total hassle of a human being to boot, and you're really stubborn with a tendency to make things worse, and even if you do talk, you deliberately misinterpret things and run around trying to get away from people, which pisses them off, and then you don't believe in words themselves…," I grumbled along.

Yuigahama was still staring at me. Eventually, she let out a little sigh and cocked her head. "Who are you talking about?"

"I mean me," I said, and she gave me an exasperated *You're hopeless* sort of smile.

I agreed with the sentiment. I was always making other people deal with my troubles, and they forgave me every time. I've always taken advantage of her kindness. It was so comfortable. I'd been letting myself fall asleep, putting a lid on it, pretending not to see it, and she kept on helping me. Those days were so important to me, so irreplaceable and legitimately fun, and so seemingly happy, it made me entertain such completely convenient fantasies.

"…Sorry for being a pain," I said suddenly.

"Huh?" Yuigahama cocked her head.

"I'll be able to do better someday. I think eventually, I'll probably be able to communicate things properly, even without playing with words and logic so that I can get things across how I mean to." Slowly, cautiously, I said the words that hadn't quite come together yet. Eventually, once I became a slightly better adult, maybe I would be able to say this stuff without hesitation. Maybe I'd be able to say something else, be able to communicate some different feelings properly.

"…But you don't have to wait for that," I finished, somehow wringing it all out, and Yuigahama listened silently, anxiously.

I must have been rambling too much. She had a twinkle in her eye. "What? I'm not gonna wait."

"Yeah. That was kind of a creepy thing to say."

"For real."

I smiled lightly to cover my shame over my own lack of wisdom.

Yuigahama chuckled, then hopped up from the bench. "All right… let's go."

I stood up as well and pushed the bike I'd parked beside me to follow after her.

Not long after leaving the park, we reached the apartment building where Yuigahama lived.

"Thanks for carrying my stuff," she said in front of the entrance, taking her things from my bicycle basket. "See you at school later."

"Yeah, see you."

Once Yuigahama waved me off, I pushed my bicycle along.

The only sounds were my tires clicking and my loafers crunching on gravel for a while, but then that suddenly stopped. Though there were people going back and forth and moving all around in the sunset crowds, I was the one person stopped in place.

I decided to start running.

Tensing my legs, I jumped off the ground, and right as I threw one leg over the seat, just for an instant—just one fleeting moment—I looked behind me.

She was still waving, and when she saw me look back, she gave an extra big wave.

I raised one hand casually back at her, and with my attention focused on what was ahead of me, I pedaled frantically, panting hard.

Interlude...

I wasn't able to cry. I'd already shed so many tears.

So while I was waving and watching him go, I had a really good view of his back. I had plenty of time to burn that image into my mind.

Finally, he was out of sight, and I dropped my hand.

The plastic bag wasn't all that heavy, just bulky, but it did feel like a lot of weight on me out of nowhere.

As I shuffled into the elevator, the bag in my arms was rustling and too loud. His words echoed over and over, deep in my ears. I did my best to ignore it and opened the front door to find Sablé yipping and rushing up to me.

"I'm hooome!" Squatting down at the door, I petted him. He licked my hand, and I couldn't help but smile at the ticklish feeling.

A single drop of water plopped down onto my hand.

Even though I was smiling, the tears fell one after another, and Sablé looked up at me in confusion.

It's nothing. I'm okay. I'm fine, I told myself, squeezing Sablé in my arms.

Then I realized words weren't coming out at all. It was just wet air running from my tight chest to the back of my throat and out my mouth over and over again. When I tried to wipe my eyes to do something about my blurry vision, there was a squeeze on my hand.

There was Mom. "You'll make your eyes puffy, so just leave it, okay?"

She smiled kindly, and when her warm arms wrapped around me, my voice finally came out. I didn't have to hold back my tears anymore.

But the words still wouldn't come.

The stupid words won't come.

I can't even say I love you.

That wasn't the point; the issue was more than that—it was out of the question with these feelings.

I—we—really fell in love for the first time.

Interlude...

The prom was over, and the final exams were done, too. All we had left were the answer sheets coming back that day and the next, then it was a holiday, and then a year-end ceremony. And then a loooong break was waiting.

Meguri's graduation meant the student council room was now entirely my castle, in name and reality, and that was where I was. I was messing around on my phone wondering what I should do for spring break as I finished up some work with the vice prez and the clerk.

There were so many things left to do—putting together some documents for Yukino to handle, making the vice prez work until he died, and having the clerk bring him back to life—but it was more or less fulfilling.

This was how my first year of high school was supposed to have come to an end.

Until Ms. Hiratsuka suddenly came into the student council room. "Pardon me."

...*She never knocks, does she?* Well, she was just like that, so whatever.

"Did you need something?" I got up and trotted over, although internally I was hoping this wouldn't be trouble.

Then she shoved her phone right in front of my face. "Were you aware of this?"

I leaned in to get a good look at it like, *Oooh, lemme see.*

On the screen was some kind of blog.

I was just reading along like whatever, thinking, *Yup, there's some stuff happening* when I saw something that made no sense and that I hadn't heard about at all. In particular, my eye was drawn to some big text reading, *Soubu High School / Kaihin Makuhari High School Regional Joint Prom, This Spring!*

"...Huh?" My mouth just wouldn't stop hanging open. *What the heck is this?*

With trembling fingers, I pointed at Ms. Hiratsuka's phone. Incidentally, my voice was also shaking, and my lips were quivering and glossy like a pudding.

"Wh-wh-what the heck is this? I haven't heard about anything like this..."

Ms. Hiratsuka folded and unfolded her arms in excitement. "Ah. You don't know, huh...? Hikigaya strikes again, then."

Why does she seem so pleased...?

I was feeling kinda freaked out, but Ms. Hiratsuka was humming cheerily, about to stride right out the door again. "I'll ask him about it. Sorry for bothering you." She waved coolly back at us, but I immediately snatched her hand and tugged on it.

"Hey, hey, hey! What the heck is this? Is he up to something?! Come on, we really can't have this! This is gonna be a disaster!"

"You really had no idea?" she said, like it was nothing at all, and then she explained.

Apparently, when the prom we'd originally been planning had gotten complaints and had almost gotten canceled, he'd come up with an even worse plan so that our comparatively more reasonable prom would be allowed. In other words, it was like a fake or a setup or something like that.

"...I don't get it," I said. I couldn't even pretend otherwise.

"Right?" Ms. Hiratsuka said with a smirk.

Seriously, why does she seem so happy...?

"Huhhh. But that's all over, right?" I said. "I mean, we did have the prom..."

"That's what I was thinking, too…but for whatever reason, this website was suddenly updated today or yesterday."

"For whatever reason…?" I glared at her.

Ms. Hiratsuka scratched her cheek. "Oh, I heard about it from some parents just now."

Ahhh, gotcha. Things happened just like the other time, which meant that maybe Yukino's family had shown up at the school. I got the general situation now.

The only thing I didn't get was him. "But why would he do something like this now…?"

"…He must have ideas of his own," Ms. Hiratsuka said like a nice big sister, and she really did still sound pleased.

I couldn't figure this out.

Was he stupid? Would you normally go that far? Or, like, would he actually do something like that without telling me? It's not like I don't not not *not* get that he was doing it for us last time, though. Not that it was for me.

Yep, I didn't get it.

I had no clue when I had started pouting, and seeing that, Ms. Hiratsuka tap-tapped on my shoulders. "Well, if you want the details, ask the culprit himself. Then let's compare notes," she said with a kind smile, then left the student council room with a cheerful stride as if she were going out on a date.

I was at a loss.

But there was no point in me standing here and doing nothing. Whatever was up with this joint prom, I had to respond as the student council president. I'd be annoyed to be left out now anyway.

First, I had to gather intel.

I immediately Googled that blog, and once I got a good look at it, I could sense a feminine touch in the design sense… Besides, there's only one other person in his life who would help him with something like this.

So then I copy-pasted the page I'd searched and dumped it into LINE. While I was at it, I wrote *Do you know about this???* and sent it off, and I got a quick reply.

!??@!???

That was definitely a text of confusion. She sent an image of a doggy wailing "I dunno!" So she hadn't heard.

I continued with a follow-up strike, asking, *Do you know who made this site??* And this time, I got a proper text back.

The snowflake. And the two first-year guys who play games! They seem good with computers! They all have glasses! Then there was a barrage of glasses emojis.

Aha. Wait. What part of this is a proper text?

Well, since his list of associates was comically short, just saying *glasses* alone should have been able to narrow it down quite a lot.

Since the ringleader would be getting investigated by Ms. Hiratsuka soon, I'd go string up the accomplices to get information.

I spun around in my chair and called out to the vice president, who was practically in tears in a corner of the student council room as he dealt with the remaining business.

"Vice Prez, do you know who 'Snowflake' is? Someone with glasses? Apparently, he hangs out with a couple of first-year boys who seem like they'd be good with games and computers."

His hands paused in his task, and he started to think. *But please keep working, all right?*

"Snowflake…? Oh, maybe it's that guy. He's kind of an odd one…," he said vaguely, finding a nicer way of saying it. It seemed he had an idea.

"Could you bring him here? And those two first-years while you're at it."

"Huh…? But I don't really know those two…"

What? Searching for them is part of your job, though… Of course I couldn't say that, so I just smiled like, *Yeah, of course, I don't know what to do, either.*

Then the clerk beside us timidly raised a hand. "Um…"

"Yes, Clerk?" I jabbed a finger at her, and she answered in an ultra-quiet murmur.

"I think the two first-years might be Hatano and Sagami from the UG Club."

"UG Club? Hatano? Sagami?" I cocked my head at the unfamiliar names.

The clerk gave a strained smile, clearly uncomfortable. "They're in your class, though, Iroha-chan…"

"Oh…" *Whoa. The clerk has fear in her eyes now.* But I thought we'd been getting along lately! I didn't have many female friends, so the clerk was important!

I cleared my throat and clapped my hands. "Oh, yeah, yeah, right. Vice Prez, please go grab Hatagaya and Sagano while you're at it, please!" I ordered the vice president, sticking my tongue out with a sideways peace sign. ☆ I added in a wink as an extra.

The vice president stood up with surprising eagerness. Maybe he was just glad to get away from work. "All right. I'll go look."

"I'll go with you, too," the clerk offered. "Makito, you don't know what they look like, right?"

"Thanks, that'll help."

The two of them left the student council room together.

Wait, didn't the clerk just speak casually to the vice president? Didn't she just use his given name? Are they dating? Don't give me that junk. Uhhh, do your job?

× × ×

Some time passed, resulting in the vice president and the clerk managing to drag in the accomplices.

As per my intel, it was a glasses trio.

I sat the three of them down at a long table, and to keep them from getting away, I firmly stationed the vice prez and the clerk at each side. The trial (judge: me, prosecutor: me, defense: me, sentence: death) began in the specially arranged courtroom of the student council room.

"Could you explain to me the meaning of this?" I asked kindly as I pointed to the screen of my phone, which was Evidence Exhibit A.

The trio was freaked out for some reason, cringing away and exchanging looks to see what the others would do.

Zero signs here that this conversation will go smoothly...

Calm down, Iroha. That guy's such a hassle, but you deal with him all the time. You should be able to manage others decently, too. Do your best, Iroha; you're so great, Iroha.

Blowing out a deep sigh, I put on a bright Irohasu smile and tried to adopt an *it's not like I'm really mad, you know?* sort of vibe. "Why is it that there's a joint prom operation that the student council isn't aware of, hmm? Hmm?" I gently asked.

I added a cuuutesy ☆ smile for emphasis, and this time it seemed to work. All three twitched in their seats. For some reason the vice president twitched, too, and the clerk quietly muttered, "Yeek..." *Good, good, let's keep the questioning going just like this. Wait, huh? Yeek? That's like a "Yeek, she's so cute," right?*

The one in glasses on the right-hand side muttered, practically gasping, "Th-the right to remain silent..."

"Denied. ♪"

This is the student council room, and I am the student council president—meaning I am the only law, and I don't really acknowledge the right to remain silent.

Next, the glasses on the left-hand side raised his hand slightly. "The presence of a lawyer..."

"Denied. ♪"

Because I'm the lawyer around here. If you have any complaints, then I'll listen, okay? Though listening is all I'll do.

This pressure must have been apparent, as the large glasses guy in the coat sitting in the middle raised both hands. I'd seen him before. I had a feeling he was probably the "snowflake."

"I have a deadline for my manuscript, so..." He immediately rose to his feet and tried to escape, but the vice prez caught him firmly. Putting a hand on his shoulder, he forced him to sit back down.

You'd better talk while I've still got a smile on my face… I started smacking the desk. "Explain. Your. *Self!*"

"…Yes'm." Snowflake wilted, nodding reluctantly.

My glare communicated, *So your explanation?*

The ones to his right and left exchanged a glance, then started mumbling together.

"W-well…we suddenly got orders yesterday, and we were forced…"

"Y-yeah! H-he asked us to do it, so we had no choice!"

"A-ask Hachiman for the details! We were ultimately naught more than well-meaning third parties!" Snowflake yelled like some kind of stage actor. The guys on either side nodded along in agreement.

"There are plenty of things I'd like to get straight from the horse's mouth… But right now he's in a very exciting and exclusive interview…," I said as I pressed my hand to my throbbing temple. I turned to the window. "Why would he deliberately pull something that would cause this much trouble…? I don't get it," I grumbled under my breath and then sighed, glaring at the phone on my desk.

The trio must have heard me, as they all lowered their voices and started talking secretively. "For sure, I really don't get what the point of this is. We told him it'd never happen."

"He was like, 'We've got it as long as we publicly post the info…' He really has to be crazy…"

"He even declared that failure would pose no issue. *'I don't geeet it.'*"

The snowflake must have assumed I wasn't listening; he was doing some kind of impression of me, and the other two were snickering at it like an in-group joke.

I can hear you, okay? When I clicked my tongue and glared at them, the guys on either side went silent. Only Snowflake in the middle didn't take a hint and started muttering with all sincerity in a really full and fancy-sounding voice, "…'Tis human nature to want to help when asked with such desperation."

Something about that seemed off.

…He asked them so desperately to help make the joint prom happen, but it's okay for it to fail?

That meant his goal wasn't to make the joint prom a success.

But the process for putting on the joint prom *was* necessary… That was why they only had to publicize the information.

Hmm…wait, wait, I kinda feel like I'm getting somewhere. I hummed as I gathered my thoughts. All the while, the three stooges were excitedly whispering something.

"Indeed… He was so intent on his request. Bowing on the floor and everything. That was the first time I'd ever seen someone do that IRL."

"Same here. If he's going that far, then who are we to refuse, you know? Like, it's a 'no words needed in a promise between men' kind of thing?"

"Herm. Although, when Hachiman prostrates himself, it's a mere pose. For him, it is naught but a type of yoga."

"The hell's with that? That's awful."

"His sense of ethics really is dead, isn't it…?"

Ahhh, I get that… He'll do anything to achieve a goal…

As I found myself smiling at Snowflake's remarks, it suddenly struck me.

"Well, and then he kept strolling back in demanding more do-overs, so he really is out of his mind."

"Telling us to come up with another three variations for the design—I thought he was gonna kill us."

"Aye, I understand not why he would do such a thing. It makes me wonder if he has a human heart. Ogre, demon, editor!"

I had a light-bulb moment, and my head jerked up right as the trio was pushing up their glasses in their enthusiastic backbiting session.

"I'm thinking. You're annoying. Be quiet," I told them off flatly, and the three glasses finally fell silent. *Good grief, if you're having a backbiting party for him, please do it another time. I'd absolutely win.*

Yes, that senior of mine really was the worst, really an incredibly, totally rotten brute. Although his eyes were super rotten, his personality was even worse.

So he'll do anything for his goal.

Even though the joint prom was a big event that would involve everyone and everything, he just thought of it as a simple means to an end.

So then that goal is…

As I hit on the answer, the words slipped out of me with a smile.

"…I really don't get it."

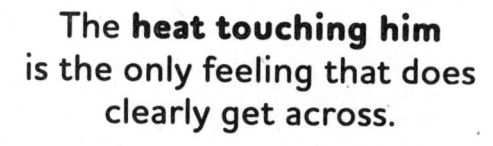

7   The **heat touching him** is the only feeling that does clearly get across.

I've never once managed a clean resolution before, and I never will. All I've ever done is force feelings that leave a bad aftertaste on the people around me.

If I'm going to be honest, deep in my heart, I'd kinda known there might be another way. It wasn't like I couldn't see a simpler, more straightforward resolution, a way that wouldn't cause trouble down the line and make everyone feel bad, too.

I just couldn't find any worth in something that could be changed with a word or a single action.

I couldn't help but feel that if one little action—so small and easy to erase—could resolve everything so whimsically, it would diminish all the suffering, pain, and anguish that lead up to it.

To the one dealing with it, pain and worry are not at all as petty as others may say, and it's always a choice between the two options of life and death. It would be too insincere to settle it all with just one remark.

If a single declaration would change things, then it would obviously be able to overturn and betray that change, too—but then you wouldn't even be able to take it back.

That's why I always wound up using questionable methods. I flail around and hurt people way too much, while praying that I'll be able to rely on others.

What I could do didn't amount to much. Even if I gave it all my effort, it was all out of my reach anyway.

So...I decided to do the most I could.

It was arrogant to hope for something unbreakable and real, so I had to use everything in my power to twist it, smash it, hurt it—test it, or I wouldn't be able to believe it really existed.

But there aren't many things someone like me could do. Even if I threw away everything I had, it wasn't like I could influence much. I had no decent options, pieces, or cards, and I was basically always doing nothing and planning nothing.

Right now, the most I could do was send one e-mail, get down on the floor and bow, and make one phone call. By doing these things, I was finally able to get a grip on a single handhold. Even if it was just one method, even if it wasn't a wise way of doing things, it would be better than nothing.

Monday, the beginning of the week. We'd spent the day getting back answer sheets, and in the classroom after school, I was staring at the phone in my hands. Displayed on the screen was the joint prom event website for the two schools, labeled *Soubu High School / Kaihin Makuhari High School Regional Joint Prom, This Spring!*

The dummy prom plan lived on, unbeknownst to the world.

Rather, I had revived it myself.

The day before, I'd sent a big whopper of an e-mail to Kaihin, telling them we'd gotten the go-ahead, and then I'd marched into the UG Club and used a prostration attack to get them to update the dummy prom site.

Of course, there was no such plan. It was nothing but a massive lie, a bluff, papier-mâché. Nothing at all had changed since the time it had been the fake to prop up the original prom plan.

Consequently, I'd gone through all the same procedures—including the part where I'd called Haruno Yukinoshita to have her leak the info about the joint prom.

Haruno and I hadn't talked all that much, but her loud laughter over the phone still lingered in my ears. "What's the point in doing something like this?" she had asked me.

There was no point. There was no point at all in the event itself.

So I'd answered with a half laugh and the words, "I'll show you a real prom… I'll show you something real."

Thinking about it now, it really had been a ridiculous point to make.

That had to be why Haruno Yukinoshita had tittered scornfully. "You're an idiot! We've got an idiot here." Her snickering had rapidly turned into full laughter loud enough to make my ears hurt, and she'd hung up on me without even telling me if she was going to help.

I'd tried calling her again, but she'd never answered, I never learned if she would carry out my request, and now here we were.

I had jabbed my stick into the bushes without knowing what snakes or *oni* I would be disturbing. Nothing good would come of it either way, so now there was only to wait. The dice had been thrown, or maybe the towel had been thrown in, and now all there was to do was cross the Rubicon.

In the end, the result came quickly.

At the end of a half day with kids scattered about getting ready to go, she came to me in the classroom.

"Hikigaya." Ms. Hiratsuka called out to me from by the door. She looked a little concerned as she beckoned me with a hand.

My first bet had panned out, for now.

× × ×

Ms. Hiratsuka took me to the same reception room I'd visited the other day. Immediately after opening the door, I met eyes with Yukinoshita's mother, who was sitting in the seat of honor. A broad smile filled her face.

Up to this point, it had been just the same as the other day. The difference now was the presence of another person.

Haruno was sitting beside Mrs. Yukinoshita. She looked at me, then gave a little wave and a wink. She'd laughed scornfully at me over the phone, but she'd successfully set the stage here. I had to admit I was thankful.

And then, on the sofa near the entrance, I saw Yukinoshita, too.

"Hikigaya..." She must have been told about the situation beforehand, as she clearly looked uneasy. I didn't say anything to her worried eyes, just nodded back.

Then I looked around the reception room, scratched my cheek, and laughed sheepishly. "Um, why was I called here...?" The question was completely unnecessary, since I knew the answer better than anyone, but I put every effort into playing dumb. This was Hachiman Hikigaya's once-in-a-lifetime performance.

But I guess I'm a really bad actor. Mrs. Yukinoshita was wearing a thin smile that said she saw right through it. In the unbearable silence, Haruno failed to hold back a snicker.

"...Just sit down." With a deep sigh, Ms. Hiratsuka bopped me on the shoulder. Judging from her expression, it seemed she'd seen through my act. Whatever, that was fine...

As prompted, I sat down beside Yukinoshita, and Ms. Hiratsuka sat down on her other side.

Once we'd taken our seats, Mrs. Yukinoshita drew a phone from her coin purse. Her mild smile never faltered. "...I thought we might as well speak with you," she began and showed me the phone screen on which the dummy prom website was displayed. Only one thing there was different from before.

Written across the simple website in louder primary colors was the line *Soubu High School / Kaihin Makuhari High School Regional Joint Prom, This Spring!*

"Oh, what...?" I feigned confusion and trailed off meekly.

"We've seen this plan before... Could you talk with us about it a little?" Rubbing her temple with her fingertips, Mrs. Yukinoshita let out a tired sigh. "We had managed to gain the understanding of most of the parents and guardians with the earlier prom. But now this. I thought it would be best to hear an explanation from the one responsible. How exactly did this happen?" Confusion was clear in her gentle tone.

From where she stood, this joint prom plan should have been just a fake used to get the real prom plan through. She'd instantly seen through that ploy herself, then chosen to play along with my clumsy negotiation and concede. She had also gone to the trouble to win over and quiet down those parents who had complained.

At that point, the dummy plan's role had been complete.

But then, unbeknownst to her, the decision had been made to hold the event. That news had to be a shock to her—even a betrayal.

Mrs. Yukinoshita was looking almost disappointed. All I could do was choose my words carefully and humbly offer a sincere, wholehearted explanation. "It seems there's been a misunderstanding… Perhaps it was poor communication." I poured everything I had into this performance.

Mrs. Yukinoshita giggled. "I see. We can see take this as a simple error. Well then, if you could quickly remove this website and arrange for a cancellation—"

"Oh, I'm not sure that can be done. Since it's been publicized now, announcing that it's canceled would cause trouble," I said, practically cutting her off.

Mrs. Yukinoshita's eyebrows twitched. "So then what would you do?"

I responded to her question with an arrogant chuckle. "At this point, we have no choice but to just go through with it, do we?"

Before the woman opposite me could counter, Yukinoshita jumped in. "What are you talking about? Don't be ridiculous." Then she turned to face her mother and took over the discussion, speaking in a formal manner. "Listen. The prom was held under our discretion. Resolution of any incidental issues is also our responsibility," she said, and her mother nodded, prompting her to continue. "That plan was originally devised to make our prom succeed. We should be the ones dealing with this, on principle. So…"

Yukinoshita cut off there again, hesitating as her gaze slid away.

"...He has nothing to do with this."

Her mother listened to everything, nodding slowly, absorbing the information. "I see... How would you deal with it, specifically?" Her eyes weren't on me anymore, but Yukinoshita. The sharp glint of her eye seemed to be looking not at her dear daughter, but at a leader taking responsibility for the situation.

"We discuss it with Kaihin Makuhari High School immediately, then arrange to announce its cancellation and release an apology. I'm also willing to mediate when explaining circumstances to related parties if necessary," Yukinoshita said. The proposal was coming not from Mrs. Yukinoshita's daughter, but from the individual in charge of the prom.

"...Well, that sounds about right." Mrs. Yukinoshita nodded, seemingly convinced. "I doubt there's anything more that can be done." Ms. Hiratsuka was nodding, too, apparently with no objections.

That relaxed Yukinoshita somewhat. "Yes, it's best to act quickly when putting out a fire."

The moment it felt like the situation was resolved and the air had relaxed, the corners of my mouth ticked up in a leer. "Wellll, I wonder if that will convince people."

"Huh?"

Everyone there was giving me *what are you talking about* looks, but I laughed it down. I couldn't bear to let it end here!

"Saying we won't work with Kaihin after we were able to have a prom for just our school doesn't make sense, does it?" I said, keeping my tone casual.

"We simply need to explain to them." Yukinoshita became indignant, instantly striking down my idea.

But I struck right back the other way. "Do you think Tamanawa and the rest of them will be satisfied with that? If we tell them it was a no-go without even trying, they're the types to say, *Let's think of a way to do it together.*"

That threw Yukinoshita for a loop. "Well...you may be right."

If she thought back on what had happened during Christmas when we'd done a joint event, she would know firsthand just how difficult it was to convince the Kaihin crowd, Tamanawa being the chief example. Tamanawa really is such an incredibly convincing guy. I was borrowing his abilities right now for this rhetorical bombardment.

"And besides, if the information has been publicized, that means the plan has already gone through and been approved by the school, parents included." I managed to lay it all out as if it were already an established fact.

Of course, it was a lie. I was pulling it all out of my ass. I hadn't checked that with Tamanawa at all. I doubted he was that on the ball with his planning. Actually, he obviously hadn't gotten everything together.

I refused to let that show on my face, so I grinned at them instead. "If we were to object to that decision now and start a quarrel with them, wouldn't that cause trouble?"

Judging from everything that had happened so far, Mrs. Yukinoshita had a clear tendency to avoid any trouble or conflict with her husband's constituency. Hayato Hayama had once mentioned that Mr. Legislator would not want to deal with needless conflict with other schools because the school faculty and parents were all voters. If I implied that the interests at stake here were beyond just those at our school, they wouldn't try to kill the plan for the convenience of some parents without consulting the other side.

Mrs. Yukinoshita touched her fan to her lips, then paused thoughtfully for a few moments. All the while, she carefully evaluated me with her eyes alone.

Eventually, she snapped her fan shut, then tapped her shoulder with it and opened her mouth with a tired expression. "That would indeed be unreasonable… But if, hypothetically speaking, their side has approved of this plan, the issues on our end have not been resolved. Have you forgotten the reason the prom was rejected in the first place?" Her manner indicated she saw through my lies, and she had also pointed out the fundamental issue at hand, refusing to let me shift the point of contention. It really was a bad idea to challenge this woman in a negotiation or verbal dispute.

"Your endgame is lacking," she said flatly to finish me off, and I winced. I had nothing.

Then Yukinoshita's lips came to my ear as she whispered quietly, "That's not enough to convince my mother."

"...Yeah," I muttered as meekly as a mosquito buzz. Frankly speaking, I hadn't thought this would be enough to argue her down.

I knew full well that she was beyond me. That merely meant I had to reconfigure the discussion. Standing tall, I began. "As to the concerns of certain parents and guardians, I believe we can win them over this time." I felt eyes gather on me and my superficially confident attitude. I gave them all a thin smile. "Once the students see the attempt end in failure, they'll give up on the idea. Then no one will be talking about having a prom. Isn't that exactly what those parents want to happen? If you allow us the opportunity, you are welcome to witness the failure for yourselves."

My well-worded BS was met with pure exasperation.

"Why would you want the plan to fail...?" Yukinoshita put a hand to her temple as if restraining a headache, and Ms. Hiratsuka let out a deep sigh.

"Hikigaya..."

Haruno was sputtering, somehow managing to keep herself from bursting into laughter. "I thought you were a little brighter than that..."

Mrs. Yukinoshita sighed, her eyes disappointed. "That's not sufficient for negotiation. You haven't presented us enough return for us to approve of the risks."

"Indeed, since it's not like I'm negotiating with the parents' association to begin with. I'm only offering you an earnest explanation of our intent to carry out this event," I said civilly with a crooked smile.

Mrs. Yukinoshita's eyebrows twitched. "...I see. So you intend to see this plan through, no matter what." Her gaze stabbed through me, her icy tone sending a chill down my spine. I had no choice but to nod back. I had to communicate this to her with my attitude—that it wasn't a negotiation, that I was simply informing her of the situation and declaring my determination. This was just a distraction. Both parties were aware there was no point in this exchange.

There was no point in negotiating with this woman.

I had no more cards.

I had already played my strongest card, the one that would be most effective on Yukinoshita's mother; there were no means by which I could negotiate with her advantageously.

But if I had no trump cards, then I just had to make one. This was a con.

In our talk the other day, Mrs. Yukinoshita must have seen Hachiman Hikigaya as a fraudster. She probably only thought of me as entertainment in the game of negotiation and dispute. While this was just a hopeful observation of how I wanted it to be, right now, I would bet on that possibility.

Even if Mrs. Yukinoshita had come to see me as someone who couldn't be ignored, she would certainly wonder why Hachiman Hikigaya would blatantly feign ignorance in an attempt to force through this joint prom, when it had such a low hope of success.

"I don't really understand why you're doing something like this." Mrs. Yukinoshita pressed her fan against her lips and rubbed her temple area. Rather inappropriately for the situation, I found it charming.

I could sense how alike mother and child were from every minute detail of their gestures and use of words.

As I was appreciating this, I got an elbow jab from the side. Looking out of the corner of my eye, I saw Yukinoshita biting her lips slightly, a wrinkle between her eyes. "…What are you trying to do?"

"What?" I played ignorant, and Yukinoshita gave me an intense glare.

When I looked away from her angry expression, there was Mrs. Yukinoshita in front of me, a smile on her beautiful and delicate face. She looked as innocent as a child solving a puzzle. "You planned all of this, didn't you?"

"Hardly. It was simple human error, an unintentional misstep," I answered with a shrug.

Haruno chuckled. "You mean intentional misstep," she quipped icily, and everyone there quietly nodded.

At this point, continuing to play dumb would work against me. Everything thus far had been for the sake of bringing one person to the negotiation table. In other words, the real game started now.

"However we got here, I think it's worth it for our school to hold the joint prom…since there were apparently certain parties who were not satisfied by the previous one… Right?" I directed an ironic smile at Haruno Yukinoshita.

My question made Haruno blink, but her lips soon quirked into a smile. But she offered no answers.

Leaving aside her reasons why, Haruno Yukinoshita was the only one who had expressed clear dissatisfaction with our school's prom. Therefore, she was the only exit from this situation.

You've been toying with me this whole time. Play along with me, just this one last time.

When I blatantly gave Haruno a look, Mrs. Yukinoshita stared at her, too. "…Were you dissatisfied in some way?" she asked.

"Not reaaally?" Haruno said with a lighthearted little shrug. "I have no complaints. It seems Yukino-chan was satisfied with it, and you're okay with it, too, right? So it's not my place to butt in."

Her challenging manner of speaking left Mrs. Yukinoshita with a blank expression, and Yukinoshita sighed quietly.

Mrs. Yukinoshita just put on a mild smile. But if she wasn't denying it, that was basically her answer.

That didn't particularly shock Yukinoshita, and she took it well. Even without hearing her mother's response in words, she understood.

The unexpected silence hung heavy like tar.

And that was why my voice sounded out loud and clear. "I'm not satisfied, either," I said, and immediately all eyes gathered on me.

Mrs. Yukinoshita narrowed her eyes in deep interest, Haruno smirked as if to say, *Makes sense*, and Ms. Hiratsuka nodded, watching.

But Yukino Yukinoshita was looking down. Mrs. Yukinoshita shot her a look of concern before turning to me. "Might I ask the reason?"

"I mean, the plan I came up with was clearly better, right? Isn't it natural to wonder how things could have gone if we'd made it happen?" I said blithely, like a joke.

Multiple thin sighs came at the same time, followed by a silence dead enough to hurt my ears.

This was beyond just an angel passing. It was so quiet, you'd think it was a whole crowd of angels on the level of Professor Zaizen doing his rounds.

I was hit with wordless protests: From the right, Ms. Hiratsuka was poking me, while from the left, I was getting a firm pinch in the thigh. As I was twisting around in low-key pain, I saw Haruno turned away in her seat, shoulders shaking.

Meanwhile, Mrs. Yukinoshita seemed to me mulling this over with a *hmm*. "…You mean to say this is your selfish whim?"

"I guess that's what it is," I answered with a wry smile.

But Mrs. Yukinoshita was tilting her head like she wasn't satisfied. Her eyes seemed to be examining me for my true intentions. "But given the current situation, it's unlikely it will be realized. I assume you would understand that much…" Confusion was apparent in her tone. From where she stood, that was the obvious question.

But to me—or to her—this was a self-evident truth. "…Even if it doesn't go well, we should come up with a proper answer. We have to settle this right, or it will be this vague thing forever," I said with a pathetic, sheepish smile.

Haruno burst into laughter. "What an idiot! We have an idiot here… You're going to all this trouble to stage a prom just for something like that? You've got to be an idiot."

I didn't need her to say it. I truly did think I was stupid, if I did say so myself. Even I'd laugh about it.

"As you have pointed out, it's incredibly personal rationale, so I won't seek to gain your understanding or support," I said.

But this was the only answer I had.

This was the only answer I had for Haruno Yukinoshita.

Haruno dropped her smile, put a finger to her glossy lips, then slowly stroked them. Her eyes seemed inhuman. I could sense no warmth in them at all. It felt like ice water pouring over all my nerves, and all the hairs on my body stood on end.

I pushed that feeling down and opened my mouth. "Fortunately, it's not associated with the student council, so if it's purely a volunteer activity—"

"That's not happening." Haruno cut me off. Tapping her fingers on the table, she continued with a scornful smile. "We were the ones who took down this fake plan and silenced those parents who've protested, you know? If you go through with this, we'll get complaints," Haruno said, and her mother made a little noise of agreement.

It was a fact that the joint prom posed risk to the Yukinoshita family while functionally having no return. Mrs. Yukinoshita had come out here before, ostensibly to negotiate, back when there had been opposition to the original prom, but she'd actually just been a representative for the parents who had complained. In fact, it was fair to say she had been more of a mediator between us and them. The joint prom plan went against the wishes of the Yukinoshita family and would damage their reputation.

Haruno continued in a critical tone. "And this is already our problem, too. Yukino-chan made her own decisions about the prom and worked hard on it, and Mom acknowledged that, too..." Haruno examined Yukinoshita with a glance, then settled her dark eyes on my face. "Are you going to deny that, Hikigaya? Do you understand what it means to meddle in our family's concerns?"

"That has—," Yukinoshita began. I'm sure she meant to continue with *nothing to do with it.*

But I wasn't going to let her say the rest. I cut her off with a sigh, then nodded a few times. "I understand."

I knew I sounded ridiculous. I'd known that long ago. I'd been asked countless times already. I understood what it meant so well I couldn't stand it.

That was precisely why every time I had been asked for an answer, I'd run away, or evaded, or even covered it up. Haruno wouldn't allow any vagueness, and she had continued to pursue, denounce, and accuse.

After all, this was Haruno Yukinoshita. I'd known that even now, after everything, she would demand this.

I'd been waiting for that question this whole time.

Geez. Saying something like this right here, in front of these people, was really the worst. It was so humiliating, I wanted to pull at my hair and curl in on myself.

But this was the only card I could come up with.

"…I do intend to…well, take responsibility for that, too. If it's possible," I muttered, quiet enough that even I thought it was pathetic, for how hard I'd jumped on that chance. I turned my face down, unable to stand being seen.

Then I heard an almost-chuckle of a sigh. "Wow. You really are an idiot." That tone was surprisingly kind, and it drew my attention. Haruno had a terribly lonely expression in her eyes but a soft little smile on her lips. "…If you're gonna say it, you might as well say it with your whole chest."

Mrs. Yukinoshita swished open her fan and hid her mouth. But even if I couldn't see her lips, I could tell from her eyes that she was smiling—but it wasn't a warm one at all. Hers was a look of amusement and curiosity. Like a cat presented with a mouse toy.

When I twisted around in an attempt to escape from that gaze, Ms. Hiratsuka cut in for me. "If it's as a volunteer activity, then it's difficult for the school to be involved. Of course, we will prompt caution, but we will not engage in any direct guidance."

"Yes, that does make sense." Mrs. Yukinoshita nodded coolly. Her eyes shifted right to me. "However, even if it is an independent event, I cannot agree to a plan we all know is bound to fail… Do you truly believe you can do it?"

"You don't know anything until you try," I replied with a shrug.

Mrs. Yukinoshita refused to look away. It didn't seem she would release me until I gave her a clear answer.

I understood best of all that this event was far from being realized. I couldn't talk my way out of this. I opened my mouth, but right at that moment, I heard a faint sigh beside me.

"…You don't even need to try. We've used up just about all our budget, and since it was never a student council event, we can't expect any supplemental funds from them. Most of all, there is far too little time. And since the scale is larger, you won't be able to maintain disciplinary control over possible disruptions, which was a concern even before. It's impossible," Yukinoshita said, covering just about everything I'd concluded. She stared coolly ahead, and I knew she had given up entirely on this idea.

It seemed that answer was enough to convince her mother as well. With a nod, she offered her challenge. "So she says?"

"Well, it would be impossible for me," I answered honestly, and Mrs. Yukinoshita nodded *Of course* like she was not that surprised. That response was a little aggravating in its own way, but, well, it was the truth, so what you can do. She silenced me with her look of amusement, and her eyes seemed to be asking me wordlessly, *Well then, what will you do?*

As she smiled like she was looking forward to checking my answers in a pop quiz, I gave her a nasty smirk back. "…But fortunately, I do have someone in mind, someone who's experienced in running a prom. I mean your daughter."

"Wha— Huh? Hey…" Surprised, Yukinoshita stood slightly out of her seat to grab my shoulder.

Restraining her gently with a hand, I fixed my eyes forward. "Or perhaps you doubt her capabilities? Did you still have some ongoing concerns regarding the previous prom?" I challenged her with an almost sarcastic level of politeness.

Mrs. Yukinoshita smiled wryly. "It doesn't seem your conclusion will change, no matter how I answer."

A fine observation.

If she answered that she had no concerns, then I would interpret that as a go-ahead, and if she did have concerns, then I just had to smugly say, *Well then, let us have her prove her abilities for you to witness.*

From the beginning, nothing about my conclusion had changed. I had no intention at all to negotiate with Mrs. Yukinoshita or Haruno

Yukinoshita. All I had done here was bring the discussion to this point in order to create this situation.

Mrs. Yukinoshita must have picked up on that, as she snapped her fan shut and sneered. "We've heard your explanation. If this is to be an independent event that will not touch the student council budget, then as the parents' association, we cannot challenge it."

Haruno joined in with a titter. "As a representative from the parents' association. What about as a mother?"

"Honestly, Haruno…" Mrs. Yukinoshita put a hand to her cheek, at a loss for words, then sighed heavily. "If Yukino truly wishes to study her father's work in earnest, I believe she should choose a more appropriate environment and gain experience in a more practical scenario. Saying anything is experience may sound good, but there's nothing to be gained by her involvement in something we all know will fail."

As she coldly laid out the facts, Yukinoshita's shoulders descended bit by bit. Everything Mrs. Yukinoshita said was reasonable, with no room for argument.

"As her mother, I'm against it," she finished off with a truly concise remark. Unable to say deny any of it, Yukinoshita closed her eyes and looked down.

And then, striking her while she was down, Mrs. Yukinoshita continued. "So, Yukino, you decide… You're the one in charge, aren't you?" she demanded, sounding accusatory.

Yukinoshita's chin jerked upward, and she was met with a testing gaze. She was bewildered, and her voice caught. But she immediately shook her head, finding her strength. "…I don't even have to consider it. I already know my answer."

That was right. Yukino Yukinoshita had already decided on an answer—in her mind, everything was over.

I'd known she would answer that way, no matter what anyone asked her.

So there was just one thing I could do about it. I had only one play left at my disposal.

All along, there'd been just one person I had to negotiate with: Yukino Yukinoshita.

"...Yukinoshita," I said. She jumped a little in her seat.

I'd been thinking of so many different words to say to her, so sure none of them were right. It was all wrong.

Standing at this precipice, I knowingly chose the words I thought were the most wrong.

"Honestly, I'm not confident it could work out. We don't have enough time or money or anything, while at the same time, we have more and more things to worry about. Bluntly speaking, there are way more issues here. Serious problems could well crop up. There are no guarantees. This is ultimately just me being selfish, my personal rationale. There's no reason to make yourself do this. I think these conditions are pretty difficult. You don't have to force yourself."

There was a snicker. "A little late for that now."

I mean, I agreed. A tense and bitter smile slipped out of me.

But this was how an exchange between Hachiman Hikigaya and Yukino Yukinoshita should be.

Yukinoshita was completely at a loss, and her eyebrows scrunched up as if she were about to cry. "...That's a cheap attempt to provoke me." Her voice was trembling and so weak it seemed it would fade away, and it also sounded like she was sulking, and angry.

Well, either was fine. I was here to hear her voice. "Yeah. Sorry, but indulge me. I know it's impossible, but I'm asking anyway—save me." Shoulders trembling, I let out a humid breath.

Yukinoshita sighed deeply, then lifted her chin. "All right, I will. I'm not the type to admit defeat after all," she said in a dignified tone, beaming while she wiped the corners of her eyes. I had a feeling she was telling me, *You're hopeless*, and it felt like it had been quite a long time since I'd last seen her this way.

Once she'd tucked away that smile, she turned back to her mother and sister. "...As the one responsible for this situation, I will bring matters under control," she said firmly.

"I see…" Her mother nodded with that mild expression of hers. However, she then quietly closed her eyes.

By the time her eyelids slowly opened again, her expression and tone had completely transformed. There was a spirit in her icy gaze that would make whoever she faced shrink away. I flinched, but neither Yukinoshita nor Haruno was rattled.

"Yukino…I've said what I should say, as your mother. But if you would still go through with it, then make sure to follow through."

"…You don't have to tell me that." Sweeping the hair off her shoulders, Yukinoshita smirked boldly, indomitably. Seeing her like that, I realized she looked just like Haruno when she was being scary.

× × ×

A while had passed since the discussion in the reception room.

By the time we'd finished a basic meeting about the plans from here on out, the sun had fully set. As I left the school building to head to the bicycle parking, my legs were wobbling unsteadily from extreme anxiety and exhaustion.

Even so, I somehow managed to push my bike up to the school gates and was about to leave when it happened—I caught sight of Yukinoshita trudging along just ahead.

With heavy steps, she was going back toward the school, then turning around to go back to the gate, fiddling with her coat and scarf and hesitating as she inched her way along. It was nothing like her usual gallant manner. With her walking like that, I would eventually catch up to her, even pushing my bike slowly like I was.

I'd feel bad to just go on past her, but I also felt kind of awkward about giving her a good-bye and then leaving. I couldn't quite figure out what would be appropriate, and most of all, I didn't feel like just one remark was enough to cut it.

So in the end, I was still racking my brain on what to say when I decided to just go for it.

Slowly pushing my bicycle, I came up beside Yukinoshita as she puttered along.

She looked over at me with momentary surprise, but her eyes immediately flicked down again. And then, still without saying anything, she started walking faster. I sped up, too, to keep pace.

Though there was a bit of push and pull between the rattling wheels of my bike and the slapping of her loafers, in the end, we maintained similar speeds.

We continued walking in silence at that pace for a pretty long time. Since we'd come this far for this long without saying anything, we were probably both just getting stubborn about it: *I'm not gonna be the first one to talk.* Plus, it was just kind of extremely awkward.

There were a number of bus stops and intersections on the way, but I didn't look at any of them or at the person walking by my side, focusing only on going straight down the road.

Well, I'd been the one to dump all this trouble in her lap, so it would be reasonable for me to be the one to start a conversation. I made up my mind to say something when we went under the Keiyo Line railway overpass and waited for my moment.

I took one step forward, then another, and then finally, when the train ran right above us over the bridge, just for an instant, I felt like the bustling noise of the city all dropped away.

I blew out a deep sigh and called out to Yukinoshita, a half step ahead of me. "…Sorry for dragging you into this," I managed to say. Simple, inoffensive.

"…I had to do it," Yukinoshita answered curtly in a lower tone, without turning back to me. "I couldn't possibly refuse in that situation. Just what is going on with you? I really don't understand the point of this." As she complained, her words and her steps both gradually sped up. "You were like a missionary for some new religion or a door-to-door salesman."

"Hey, it wasn't that bad. It's true I mixed a lot of truth and lies to get things going, but it wasn't like I suggested any specific resolution. I was actually just asking you to save me."

"If you're not even offering something helpful or salvation, that's less than a con artist… You don't think you're far worse?"

Inducing anxiety with nonexistent risks and then bringing up the solution is indeed a perfect example of fraud. The big difference here was that I had presented no solution. On that point, I was even worse than a fraudster. She was right.

Yukinoshita heaved a sigh. "It was frightening, seeing my own family be taken in."

"I wasn't really taking them in… And, like, if that were enough to trick them, I wouldn't have had to make up such a big lie in the first place. How they gave in was actually scarier…" A deep sigh emerged from the bottom of my heart.

I doubted either Mrs. Yukinoshita or Haruno had believed my ridiculous and reckless nonsense. The joint prom plan itself had been completely shot down during that reception room discussion. I think they were amused by my clumsy negotiation, but still, the Yukinoshita family had always seen the plan as a risk to be avoided.

Yukinoshita also understood that, obviously. Still walking a half step ahead, she adjusted her school bag over her shoulder before muttering, "True… Neither my mother nor my sister is the type to back down over that."

"Right? And they were damn scary at the end. The heck was that? What are they thinking?"

"Who knows? I have no way of finding out." She jerked her face away sulkily and strode on ahead.

The long path that came all the way from the beach eventually reached the national highway. Turn left here, and you would hit the way to my house. But while we'd been walking and talking, I'd completely missed my opportunity to part ways.

…No, that's not it. There had been opportunities for me to do so all this time, but I'd completely ignored them. When we approached the pedestrian overpass that went over the national highway, I pushed my bicycle with sure footsteps, no hesitation.

Yukinoshita didn't turn back to me as she went up the stairs, and I followed. But since I was pushing my bicycle up the ramp, I inevitably fell behind a bit. Gradually, she pulled one step, two steps ahead, and she came to the top first.

I hurried to catch up to her, pushing my rattling, creaking bike up to the top of the ramp. Yukinoshita, standing at the top, looked back at me. She was waiting for me. When I thanked her with a look of *Sorry*, she shook her head like, *It's fine*. But our eyes only met for an instant. Then she turned away again and started striding off.

I hustled after her to keep from falling behind, then finally came up beside her. The distance between us—always half a step ahead, widening to two steps on the stairway—was gone now.

When our footfalls finally matched, Yukinoshita was the one to continue. "The way my mother looked at me, it was the way she looks at my sister…"

"…Does that mean she's acknowledged you?"

"Or abandoned me, perhaps." With a mildly self-deprecating smile, she shrugged. "It didn't seem like she thought much of me over the other prom to begin with. Taking on something with even greater risks in spite of that would exasperate anyone."

It sounded like she was talking about her own feeling just then. I hesitated, wondering what to reply, and my steps slowed for a moment. Yukinoshita took that opportunity to get another few steps ahead.

Carefully choosing my words, I upped my pace. "…Sorry. I know an outsider shouldn't be butting in on family issues or talking about your future and stuff. In the end, I meddled and caused you trouble… I will take proper responsibility for that."

"I don't need that. There's no reason for you to take responsibility for my choices. There are other things you should be doing." Her words reached me just before I caught up to her, and her pace slowed a little.

After a faint, hesitant sigh, she murmured, "…Why would you say something so reckless?" Her face was angled downward, so I couldn't really tell what her expression was, but there was a sad tone to her near-silent voice.

What should I answer?

It was just the briefest moment—just enough time for two cars to pass under us on the national highway and for Yukinoshita to take just three steps forward. My feet weren't moving.

It wasn't time for thinking. It was time to take the plunge.

"...It was the only way to stay involved with you."

"Huh?" Yukinoshita's feet came to a stop, and she spun back to me. Her expression was filled with surprise, and I expected her to ask *what do you mean* at any moment.

"I mean, there won't be any way for us to interact once the club is gone. I couldn't think of any other excuses to drag you out."

"Why would you do such a thing...?" As Yukinoshita was standing there around the center of the pedestrian overpass, stunned, the light of a vehicle coming from a distance lit up her face. I could clearly see her gently biting her lip in the pale light. "...What about that promise? I told you to grant her wish." Her voice was trembling with accusation, her eyes lowered regretfully.

This was just the reaction I expected.

And yet, because of my own selfishness, I decided not to consider how I was causing trouble for anyone else, and I continued. "Well, this technically is a part of that."

Yukinoshita looked at me, uncomprehending, asking me with a tilt of her head instead of words. The orange lights of the pedestrian overpass stung just like the sunset of that day, and I narrowed my eyes.

"...She told me that she wanted you there on ordinary days after school." I told her what Yui had said.

Yukinoshita's voice caught. Then she turned away, maybe to hide tears in her eyes. "...If that's all, you could do that without going to all this trouble."

"No way. I could call you lots of things, an acquaintance or associate or friend or classmate, but I'm not sure I can maintain that kind of relationship very well."

"Maybe that's true for you...but I will. I'm sure I'll get better at it... So it'll be all right," she said as if ending the conversation there, as if shaking off the past as she moved onward.

That show of courage was so charming. I couldn't help the sarcastic grin tugging at my face. "It might sound bad to say this, but not only do you and I have fairly poor communication skills, we really tend to complicate things. And while I'm at it, I'll say we're really garbage at getting along with people. I can't really get clever about it now. Once we drift apart, we're not just going to stay like that. I'm sure it'll be worse, and we'll drift even further. So…"

One step behind, I walked after Yukinoshita.

Watching her draw further away, I started to reach out my hand, but I wound up hesitating.

I knew if I was going to continue talking, then I should call to her to stop. And I mean, even if we kept walking, it wouldn't be hard to converse. It was out of the question to touch her hand when there was no reason for it in the first place.

But there was a reason.

A single reason that I couldn't back down from.

"…Once I let go, I'll never be able to get a hold again." It was a warning to myself. I reached out my hand.

The gesture was awkward, since I was still pushing my bike, and my hand was sweaty. I didn't know how hard I should try to hold it, either.

Even so, I grabbed Yukinoshita's cuff.

Her startlingly slim wrist fit right in the palm of my hand.

"…" Yukinoshita's back twitched, and she stopped walking. She looked between her hand and my face with surprise.

I immediately kicked my bike stand down, parking it dexterously with just one hand. She might run away like a shy kitten if I released her for even a moment.

"It's so embarrassing to say this… It makes me wanna drop dead on the spot, but…," I began, but what came out next was a big sigh.

Yukinoshita twisted around uncomfortably, and it felt like mild resistance. She might pull away from me. She was just like a cat that didn't like water touching its toes. I wanted to let go, but I also wanted to keep her there until we were done talking.

"It wasn't enough to say I'd take responsibility. I'm not just trying to be reliable. I'd like to take responsibility, or, like, I mean, I want you to let me take it..." As I spoke, the waves of self-loathing washing over me weakened my grip. It felt so gross of me to say something like this. My hand on her wrist slid off and fell limply downward.

Yukinoshita didn't run away. She stayed right there. She rubbed her wrist as if adjusting her cuff, squeezing the spot I'd taken. Though she didn't meet my eyes, it seemed she meant to listen, at least.

That was a relief. I slowly opened my mouth. "Maybe that's not what you want... But I want to continue...being involved with you. It's not an obligation—it's about purpose... So let me skew your life a little." My mouth started closing many times along the way, but I forced myself to inhale every time regardless, expelling shallow breaths over and over so I would absolutely make no mistakes, and after taking a long time, I finally finished saying each and every word.

Yukinoshita didn't interrupt once that whole time, her eyes patiently down on the cuff in her grasp.

All I could hear were the chilly wind and the cars passing by. We went so long without words, I started wishing we had no sound at all.

"...Skew what? What do you mean by that?" she abruptly replied.

Then, as if to fill the silence until that moment, the words broke through the dam to overflow. "Because I don't have enough influence to actually change your life. We'll both probably go on normally to university and get jobs even if we don't want to and live pretty decent lives. When you get involved, though, it means lots of stuff, right? Like detours and stalemates... So it'll skew your life a bit." My words wouldn't quite come together, but finally, Yukinoshita smiled. It looked a bit lonely.

"...If that's what you mean, it's already quite skewed."

"I think so, too. Meeting each other, talking, coming to know each other, and coming apart...I feel like it's twisted each time."

"You were twisted to begin with... I suppose I was, too," she said with self-deprecating humor, and the both of us smiled a little.

To anyone else looking, we would make a skewed figure—I was too twisted and bitter, she too upright and pure. We were so different, you'd think we wouldn't mesh, but those distortions made us the same. And then, on the occasions when we did make contact, whenever we collided, we changed form bit by bit. I think we'd already changed enough that there was no undoing it.

"I'll skew it even more, from now on," I said. "But I do plan to offer compensation."

I knew mere words were worth nothing.

"…Well, my assets are about zero, so anything I can offer you is insubstantial, like my time, feelings, future, or life."

I knew a promise like this meant nothing.

Still, I kept on. "I'm not living that much of a life, and there's not many prospects down the road for me, either… But since I'm getting involved in someone's life, I've got to put mine on the line, too, or it's not fair."

Nevertheless, wielding words like a chisel, I dug out what it was I had to say. I knew my meaning would never reach her, but I still had to give it voice.

"I'll give you absolutely everything, so let me be involved in your life."

Yukinoshita's mouth opened slightly, and for an instant, she started to say something, but she immediately swallowed that with some air.

Then she fixed me with a sharp look and spoke with a shaky, hoarse voice. "That's not a balanced offer. My future, my career, isn't…worth that much… You have…more…" I'm sure that's not what she was originally going to say. Her wet eyes pointed down, and then, the moment her words trailed off—

As haughtily and arrogantly as I could, with my usual weak, ironic smirk, I said, "Then that's a worry off my back. My life is hardly worth anything at all right now. Being an unpopular brand, I can't depreciate anymore, so this is practically rock-bottom pricing. In a way, this actually guarantees your principle investment. Right now is the best time to buy."

"Isn't that a standard line for fraud? Your sales pitch is the worst."

As we faced each other, laughing with tears in our eyes, Yukinoshita took one step closer to bop me over my lapels. With tears beading in the corners of her upturned eyes, she glared at me. "…Why do you always keep going on and on with your stupid nonsense? There are other things you should be saying, aren't there?"

"I can't say that… No way could this be put into words." My face crinkled up with a laugh that even I thought was pathetic.

It wasn't enough.

Even if I used up every honest feeling and every pretense, every joke or standard line, I didn't feel like I could communicate it all.

It wasn't such a simple feeling. Yes, a feeling I could communicate with one word was a part of it, but forcing it into that framework would make it a lie.

Piling words upon so many words, playing a ridiculous number of logic games with myself, arranging the rationale, environment, and situation, eliminating every excuse, filling the moat, and blocking all escape routes had finally brought me here.

There was no way she'd know what I meant from this. She didn't have to understand. I was fine if she didn't.

I just needed to say it.

Yukinoshita patiently watched my pathetic, bitter smile, but eventually, she opened her mouth hesitantly. "I think I'm probably quite a hassle to deal with."

"I know."

"I've just been causing you trouble this whole time."

"Old news."

"I'm stubborn and not very nice."

"Well, yeah."

"I wanted you to deny that, though."

"Don't ask the unreasonable."

"I have a feeling I've been entirely reliant on you, and it will get worse."

"Then I just have to get even worse. If everyone's useless, then nobody's useless."

"…And—" When Yukinoshita still tried to search for more to say, I cut her off.

"It's fine. I don't care how much of a hassle you are. It's fine if you're trouble. Actually, that's a good thing."

"…What? I'm not exactly glad to hear that." Yukinoshita's head was hanging as she whacked my chest again.

"Ow…" It didn't hurt at all, but I said that to be polite.

She pouted. "There are other options."

"You make things too complicated, and sometimes I seriously don't know what you mean, and sometimes you do make me mad. But for me, that's all like, *Eh, what can you do?* I'm pretty similar anyway… So I can probably go along with most of it, even if I do complain," I said, and this time, she smacked me without a word.

I resigned myself to it, and I gently took that delicate hand.

I really wish there had been something else. But this was all I had.

I wish there had been words that would get it across more simply.

I wish it had been a simpler kind of feeling.

If it had been ordinary love or yearning, then I'm sure I wouldn't have felt so intensely. I wouldn't feel like this only happened once in a lifetime.

"I'm sure it's not enough to make up for messing with your life, but, well, I'll give you everything. If you don't need it, then throw it away. If it's a hassle, then you can forget it. I'll just be doing what I want, so you don't have to offer me any kind of reply."

Yukinoshita sniffled, then nodded. "I will give you one." And then she gently touched her forehead to my shoulder. "Please give me your life."

"…Whoa, that's pretty heavy!" A huff came out the side of my mouth.

Yukinoshita's forehead clunked into me again, like a protest. "I don't know any other way to say it…" Shoving her forehead at me like a cat would, she grabbed at my lapels was like a kitten play biting.

Her heat touching me was clearly communicating a feeling that could never truly be put into words.

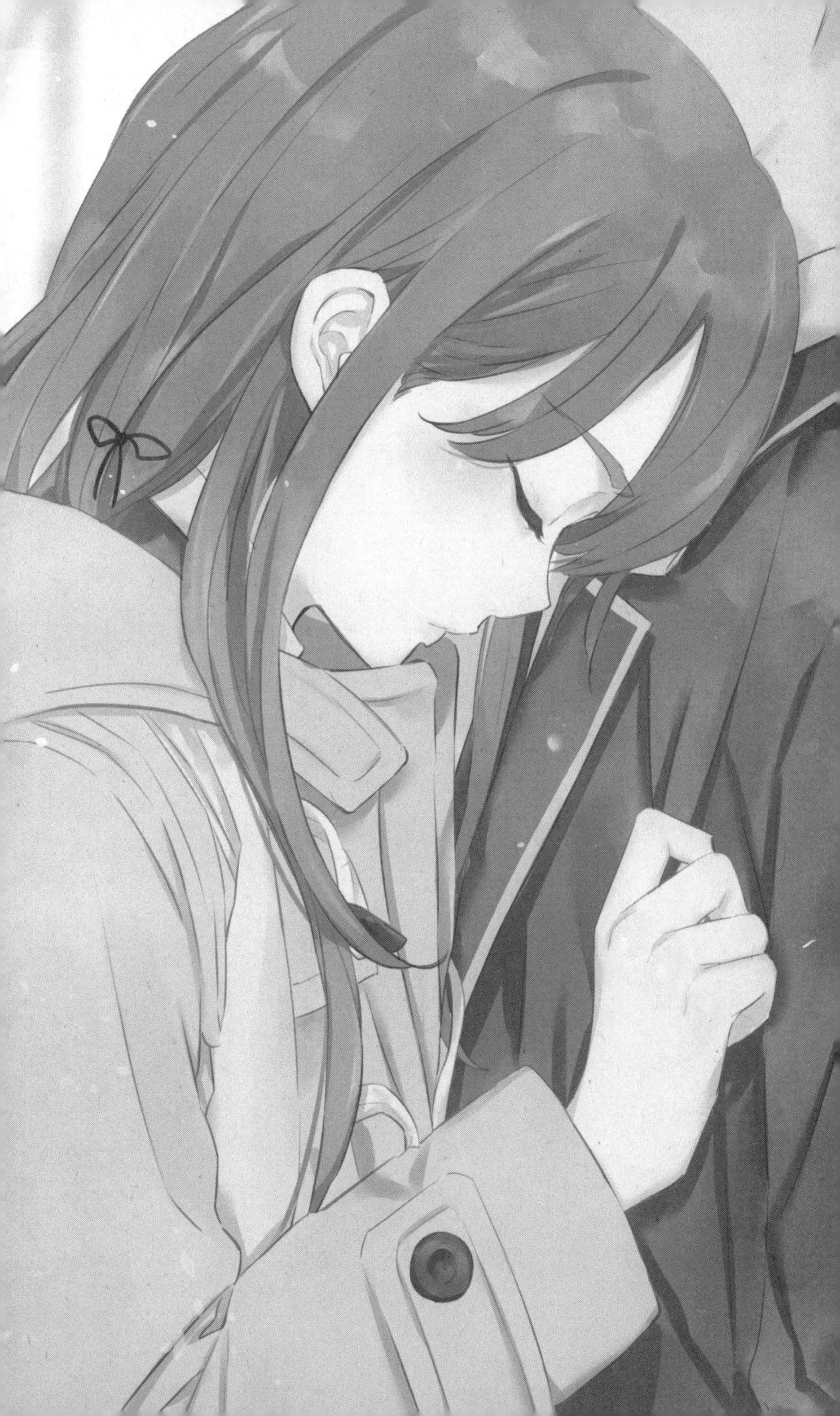

8

That door is opened once more.

I think if they ever invented a time machine, I'd go back to the previous day and kill myself.

Just remembering it was mortifying; I felt so pathetic and gutless. I was endlessly interrogating myself, wondering if there had been another way to voice my feelings, a smarter or cooler way of doing it.

But no matter how many times I thought back on it, that really was the limit of what I was capable of. The one thing I could say proudly was that even if that hadn't been the best answer, it definitely hadn't been a mistake. In fact, considering my prior behavior, I even kind of wanted to give myself a pat on the back for conquering my excessive self-consciousness.

But that was that. This was this. What is not to be must not be.

The night before in the shower, I'd screamed my heart out while the sound of the water could drown out the noise, dived straight into bed, covered my head with a futon, and wound up tossing and turning.

I would have liked to take all my vacation time over the next three years in one stretch, but…

See you tomorrow…

What she'd said wouldn't leave my brain.

Since it had been long past dusk, we'd both just kind of started walking home, hardly even looking at each other, making nothing but superficial conversation, and then right when we'd parted ways at the station, I'd waved my hand awkwardly like a lucky cat statuette. That was when she'd quietly said that good-bye to me, so I had to go to school.

To be quite frank, there was an exceedingly long list of reasons why it was hard to go to school and into that classroom. However, since I'd already steeled myself once, now my self-consciousness was going the other way and wouldn't let me try to escape. It was ridiculously pathetic, but I had a bad habit of protecting my worthless pride with a stupid "cool" facade.

In the end, I conceded to my self-consciousness and compromised by sliding into the classroom just barely on time, kept myself facedown on my desk for most of class, and then desperately spent the rest of the time in the bathroom.

Fortunately, if I got through the day, tomorrow was a public holiday, meaning no school. Then the day after that was the year-end ceremony, resulting in no classes and a half day, so I could go straight home. And then spring break! This restless anxiety would only go on a few more days.

There were no more real classes, and in the flurry of typical end-of-year happenings, such as the selling of textbooks and taking personal photos, the time passed in a blink. Before you knew it, the half day went by and school was over, and the classroom was bubbling with the anticipation of release.

Some people were talking about going to eat lunch, some were talking about how they would spend the holiday, and others were rushing to their clubs. Everyone was going off to spend their time how they pleased.

I rose to my feet without a sound, intending to lose myself in the flow of people going into the hall, and made my departure.

I went into the courtyard and stood in front of the vending machine. The spring sunlight and southern breeze were comfortable, and my fingers moved on their own to press the button labeled COOOLD.

Lightly shaking the Max can, I lazily strolled down the hallway to the special-use building. This weird anxiety was making me thirsty. I tried sipping some coffee, but its thick sweetness just made me thirstier.

I'd meant to walk slowly while pondering how to face her, yet I wound up in front of the clubroom door.

I'd thought for sure it had only been a short time that I hadn't been coming here, but it truly felt like forever since I'd last seen this closed door. It even felt like a year, by my internal clock.

Standing there, I heaved a sigh and tried to energize myself. My hand went from rock to paper to rock back to paper again as I reached out to the handle and grasped it several times.

My fingers had felt totally cold ever since that day, but as I hovered my hand by the handle, I could feel warmth circulating through them.

I gave the door a firm pull.

It rattled loudly. It refused to open. I tried again and got the same result. I yanked and wrenched, but the door wouldn't budge.

"Locked…" With a little click of my tongue, I leaned against the door and sat down.

As I was pouring the rest of my Max can down my throat, I caught sight of a figure down the hall.

"My, you're early." Yukinoshita saw me but didn't rush my way. She kept her pace easy. She was usually in the clubroom before me, so this was rare. Maybe the weird awkwardness and embarrassment had slowed her feet down.

"I'm sorry, were you waiting?" she asked.

"…I just got here." Even though I thought it was a stupid conversation to have, I gave the standard response.

The corners of Yukinoshita's lips turned upward, but her expression betrayed her anxiety. "Could you open the door for me?" She tossed the key at me.

I caught it perfectly, safe and certain.

It was the first time I'd ever touched this key, but now that I actually held it, it was a tiny, light, and ordinary piece of metal.

She must have been holding it in her hands on the way here, because there was still warmth lingering in the tiny key in my palm.

× × ×

It was the first time in a long while that I'd stepped into this classroom, and it felt kind of deserted.

Yukinoshita and I sat down in our usual spots, two desks at opposite ends.

I had thought I'd gotten pretty used to this distance, but now it felt colossally far.

My eyes wandered, and then they met with Yukinoshita's. Not sure what to do with this awkwardness, I failed to say anything. She jerked her gaze away.

Then after a while, she flicked me an examining look.

…*This is bad. As for how bad… Like, really bad.* Specifically speaking, I had all the symptoms: elevated heart rate, sweating, fever, palpitations, and shortness of breath. Bad status effect such as a cold—detected.

What should you do when you catch a cold?

The answer is simple: work! Not being able to take time off even when it's tough is the way of the Japanese corporate slave!

And so, I would talk about work.

"…How about we have a meeting, to start?" I suggested.

"Of course."

I pulled out the proposal papers I'd printed out and slid them over to Yukinoshita. Seeing the papers stop halfway across the desk, she sighed. She stood, picked them up, pulled her chair to a closer position, and sat down there. "…Since it's hard to discuss," she muttered with her eyes focused on the sheets.

"Y-yeah. Well, true." I moved my chair beside hers.

The distance between us felt delicate; we were side by side with one chair's worth of space between us, and it made me even more nervous than before. My breaths became shallower as a soapy scent tickled my nostrils with every inhale. It really did smell so good.

In an attempt to fan it away, I flipped through the papers of the proposal. "This is the proposal I showed Kaihin. I'm thinking it'll basically be something like this, more or less."

We just had to focus on our job. When it was about work, we wouldn't struggle with conversation. It would also reduce the awkwardness and embarrassment.

Yukinoshita nodded as well, scanning the proposal. With every nod, her long, glossy black hair swished down, and she combed it through her fingers to fix it, then tucked it behind her ear. As she was reading along, her red earlobes also gradually cooled. "Well, you've written quite a sloppy proposal here."

"Well, yeah. I had no time back then, and I was desperate."

"Yes, you truly were," Yukinoshita muttered in amusement, humming as she began red-penning the proposal.

I'm delighted to see you in such a good mood, but I'd rather you leave some of the paper untouched...

Once she'd finished an overall check, she smooshed the red pen on her soft lips. "Since the proposal was made as a throwaway plan to begin with, it seems it would be quite difficult to actualize. We are severely lacking in budget and personnel."

"The budget depends on Kaihin. For personnel, well, there's always using our students within an inch of their lives."

"Yes, someone who would be glad to take this on...," Yukinoshita said, her gaze turning to the chair between ours.

That was the chair where Yuigahama used to sit, all this time.

"...Well, I couldn't bear to cause her trouble every single time," I said. "I'll try someone else—"

"No, I'll speak with her." Yukinoshita cut me off, then brought her hands to her chest and fiddled with her uniform ribbon. Then she dropped her gaze to the empty seat and continued slowly, as if she were trying to convince herself. "It will be all right. Leave it to me. It will be difficult to explain it well, but I want to be the one to tell her... If not, I think she'll be angry and ask why we didn't invite her." I caught a shade of misgiving in Yukinoshita's voice, but she put on a lighthearted, tough smile.

"…All right. Then on my end, I'll go hit up the people I can think of."

"Yes, please do."

Relieved that her bright tone and small smile had returned, I nodded back, and my hands continued to flip through the pages of the proposal. There were the items Yukinoshita had just pointed out, noted clearly. "Assuming that'll be enough for help, next, we've got the budget. The budget… Well, we use Kaihin's money and…location? Huh? Location?"

"Since this is an independent effort, I doubt we can use the school," she said. "Besides, since more than one school is involved, it would be best not to make the location a specific school facility."

"Ahhh…true."

"Regarding budget and personnel, since that could vary widely depending on the location and plan, I would like to decide on location first, if possible."

"Yeah. Even if we decide the date and everything, we won't get anywhere if we can't book it."

"Yes, so we should come up with options for dates, then select a venue available during that time."

"A venue, huh…? The place in this plan was the one I had already discussed with Kaihin. That's what the initial website was based on."

I made sure Yukinoshita knew I was listening while I flipped through the proposal paper. It was true that I'd been wondering about location back when I'd come up with this dummy prom plan before, too.

Back then, I hadn't had the slightest intention of actually holding the event, so I'd just come up with some nonsense about waterfronts and sunset beaches. "This thing says *beach event…*"

"You're the one who wrote it."

You sound pretty unhappy with that…

A deep sigh left my lungs. I had no clue what to do. Who came up with this idea? I'll kill the guy. Think about the people who actually have to make it happen…

I jerked my chin up. "If the info we released already mentions the ocean, can't we use the beach?"

Yukinoshita immediately pulled out the clubroom laptop, cheerily put on her glasses, and started looking something up. Her slim, graceful fingers clattered all over the keyboard. "It seems there are places actually holding events…" But then her hands froze. "But it seems you need permission from the city…and even more importantly, a sponsor or funding to give it a chance of happening. You can't have a fire, and permission for use is on a case-by-case basis," she said, rotating the laptop over to me.

Turning my head, I got a peek at the screen. "There was a barbecue spot at the seaside park…so if we can get permission for use of the park, then there's a chance they'll allow a fire," I said as I reached a finger out to tap on the keyboard. "Ah, here, here." I displayed the park map on the website for the seaside park next to the school.

Yukinoshita cocked her head and peered at the screen. "It's a municipal facility, so it doesn't cost much… There's also a lot of greenery, and if we're using the park, we might be able to make it seem like a garden party…maybe." Her eyes shone animatedly. Light-bulb moment! The look on her face was so overwhelming, and she was so close and all, it made me bend slightly backward.

Yukinoshita also noticed how close we were, so she scooted back. Removing her glasses, she added in a mutter, "…Well, we won't know unless we actually go see."

"Y-yeah…" I nodded, contemplative.

Well, she was right. We had to come up with candidates for where to hold the event and then also check if we could actually use them, or we wouldn't know. So that meant we had to survey the area directly. Yukinoshita didn't know all the details of the proposal, and I couldn't make judgments about specific numbers or about how realistic my ideas were; it would be most efficient to go together. Since it was for work, of course we should prioritize efficiency.

Okay, my logical armor was perfect.

"…Th-then…let's go look… It's close, and there's no school tomorrow," I said, but I wound up weirdly stuttering, and once I actually put said perfect logic into words, it immediately crumbled to pieces.

"Y-yes... Tomorrow...," Yukinoshita stuttered back, nodding. I couldn't figure out if that meant yes or no, or if it was a simple indication she was listening. I nodded back at her, and the whole moment was very weird.

× × ×

The seaside park on that holiday was blessed with sunny skies, so there was quite a crowd.

The sports field had a proper green, so there was an endless stream of people coming and going for clubs like soccer or futsal, and there was something like a dog show going on by the parking lot, so that meant heavy traffic. When we finally got into the park, there were families and joggers all over like they owned the place.

It was like they were all thinking, *Every citizen has got to make use of public services paid for by their stupidly high municipal taxes, or you're losing out!* as they celebrated the world in spring. I suppose the taxes really were high...

Up even higher than those taxes flew the strings of kites. On second thought, nah, taxes were higher.

I watched the kites soaring in the clear blue sky, sitting on a bench in the shade with a Max can... It was a moment of sheer bliss.

On the other hand, that refreshing breeze blowing through the swaying treetops was giving Yukinoshita a moment of hell.

That day, she was in a girly blue cardigan and a white dress with a basket bag and a beret—at a glance, I could tell it was a rich-girl look. However, with her slumped shoulders and hunched back, you could probably add "frail and sickly" to her character background.

"I got another Max can. You want it?" I offered.

"Thank you..." She extended a wobbly hand to me. She squeezed the can in both hands and took a sip. Maybe it was the hydration, or maybe it was the sugar, but she finally looked awake. "So the park is this busy during the holidays... Honestly, I underestimated it. It's also big. So big."

"You're so tired, your vocabulary died…"

Yukinoshita sighed, took off her beret, and started undoing one of her pigtails. Holding the hair elastic in her mouth, she carefully combed her hair in her hands and retied it. The way she checked herself in a hand mirror at the end struck me with nostalgia.

I'd been thinking about her wearing a hat and her hair being different, but now I remembered these pigtails were just like that time she'd gone out with Komachi.

"It's been a while since you've had your hair like that," I said.

"Has it? …Well, I don't do it at school." Instead of putting her hat back on, Yukinoshita lowered it and stroked her hair with a thoughtful *hmm*.

"Huh… So it's just on weekends? Well, I guess it takes time." I had never done it, so I had no idea, but it seemed hard to make pigtails even.

When you get to my level, it's nothing but tracksuits on weekends; as long as Komachi didn't see, I'd easily dress myself in just a T-shirt and boxers, so I was genuinely impressed by someone being conscientious enough to change her look to do something new every day.

As I was examining her closely, Yukinoshita touched her hat to her mouth. "…I don't wear this style much on weekends, either, though."

Huh? What the heck…?

You were actually so cute just now, it startled me. Huh, wait. Cute. Aw man, what the heck?! This girl is really cute. She's a hassle, but that's cute in its own way… Wait, or is that actually the cute thing? Well, it's cute, so whatever (brain at capacity).

"It's comfortable to see the usual, but something fresh is nice in its own way, yeah. It's nice…" All my vocabulary was disappearing along with any thoughts. As I earnestly muttered, "Nice…" just like a philosophical *otaku*, Yukinoshita put the beret on and pulled it deep over her eyes as if she didn't like it and turned away. *Yeah, that's good, too…*

"Based on what we've seen looking around, we can't do anything that would damage the grass, so we probably wouldn't be able to set up an aluminum truss stage." Yukinoshita was looking ahead to the sports green that people could request to use.

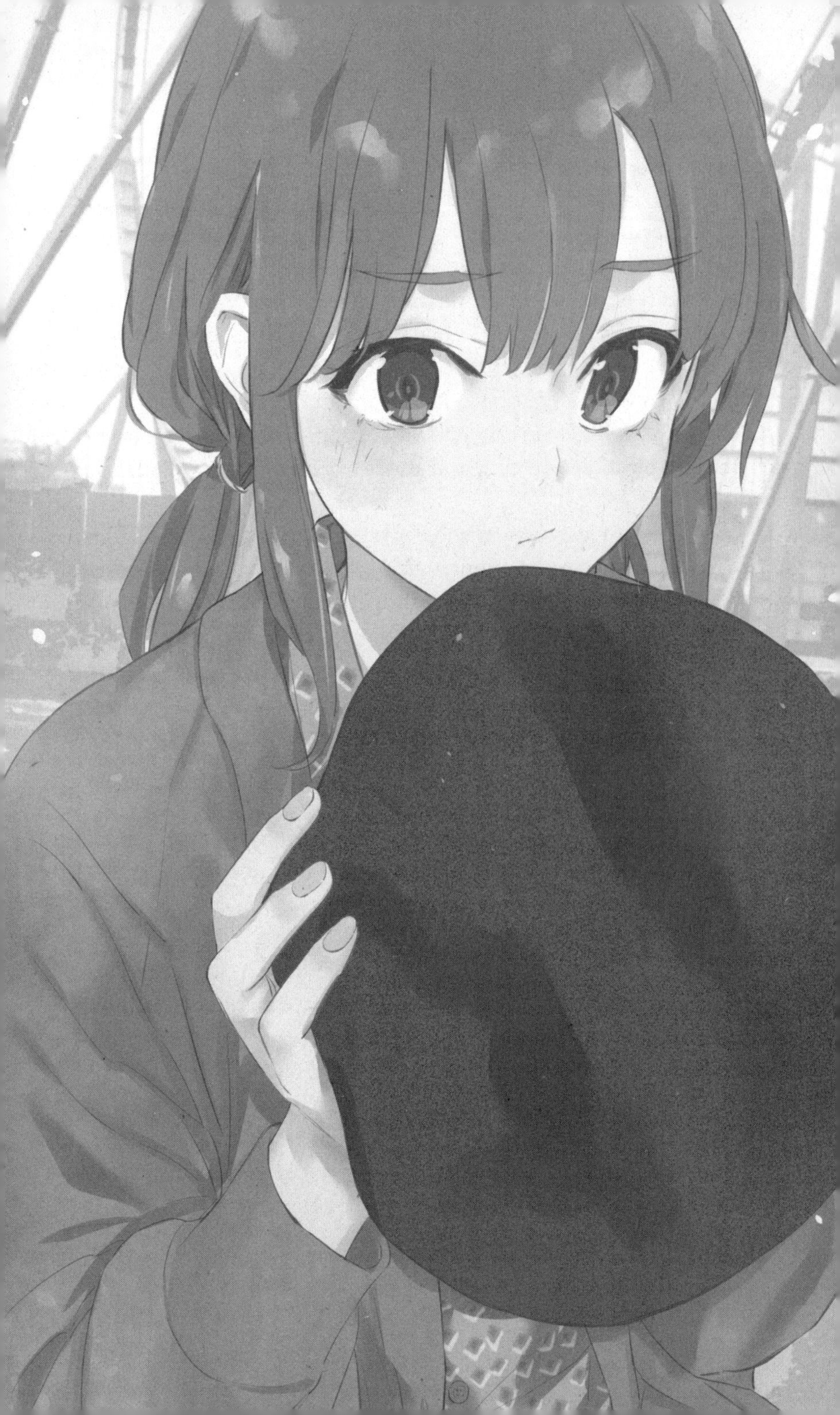

I examined that area as well, which propelled my brain power and vocab to come back in seconds. "There's the issue of sound equipment and a power source, too," I said. "It'd be good if we could get electricity from somewhere. Well, I guess we've gotta just lease a generator… And there's the weather to consider." It'd be nice if we had an absolutely 100 percent sunshine girl, but you don't find such children of the weather so easily.

"We could put up tents, but that would affect the turnout, and it really would be impossible to walk all this way in a dress if the ground gets muddy." She swayed her legs, flapping the thick-soled sandals on her feet.

My gaze was subconsciously drawn to her white calves, but I managed to only glance out the corner of my eyes as I nodded with a knowing expression. "Yeah… Seems like it'd be hard to secure lines of movement, too."

In conclusion, using the park as a venue was unrealistic.

We've got to come up with another way, I thought as I got up from the bench. Patting off the sand stuck to my butt, I focused on the dirt and grit. "Might as well look at the beach, too."

"Yes, might as well." Yukinoshita stood up after me, and we strolled over the green grass through the park.

A single pathway separated us from the sprawl of the beach. The beach obviously wasn't open yet, so we didn't see anyone swimming, but there were some people splashing around at the water's edge. The blue of the clear sky made the long white beach sparkle all the brighter. The blowing sea breeze still felt quite chilly, but the air was refreshing thanks to the slowly rising temperatures lately.

It wasn't a bad time of year to be walking by the water. There was a gazebo here, too, and the location itself looked pretty good for an event. Based off what I saw from the usage contract signboard, we couldn't really use it as a location for the joint prom, but it'd be a nice place to stop by after the event.

Gazing at the horizon in the distance, I stretched wide. "Chiba's ocean is the best…"

"This is Tokyo Bay, though...," Yukinoshita retorted as she walked beside me. She suddenly came to a stop. Holding down her hat to keep it from being blown in the wind, she turned back to me. "You really do love Chiba, don't you? ...Will you stay here?"

"So long as I don't get kicked out. I do plan to go to a university in commuting range."

"Any place you would take the entrance exams for would generally have campuses in the city."

"How do you know which places I'm taking the exams for? Scary..." My honest impression slipped right out. I hadn't even decided exactly which exams I'd be taking yet, so how did she say it so nonchalantly like it was so obvious...?

Yukinoshita answered huffily, "If your grades are similar to mine, that automatically narrows it down."

"Well, I guess we'd have similar educational routes."

"Yes... So then we might go to the same university."

"That is possible." It's common enough to go from the same high school to the same university. I've gone over the list of universities kids from our school got into, and you could see plenty of such examples.

"But we wouldn't necessarily be in the same department," I continued. "And besides, after that, we'd have different careers no matter what."

It was a completely meaningless hypothetical, but even if Yukinoshita and I did go to the same school, we probably wouldn't be living in the same spheres. I've heard if you're on different tracks, then you won't see each other at all. And on top of that, I really didn't think I'd be able to actually go to all my classes. I'd probably choose independent study whenever it rains, then drop the credits for all first-period lectures. Actually, it wouldn't even be strange for me to wind up getting nothing but credits from Mah-jongg University or Pork University instead of credits from the school I should actually have been attending.

Of course, Yukinoshita understood that, and she nodded back. "And then after that?"

"I haven't decided yet, but that depends on how my job hunt goes," I said.

Yukinoshita's eyes widened. "So you do intend to get a job. I thought for sure you would still be spouting your nonsense."

"Though it is my sincerest regret, it does seem I have a decent aptitude for corporate slavery... I think I will probably actually get a job, whether I want one or not." I sighed deeply with all my heart.

Yukinoshita grinned. "I can just see you being shoved into the east-west line every morning, rotten-eyed."

"Uh, I'd obviously rather move to Tokyo than ride that."

That was one of Japan's most packed commuter lines at rush hour, priding itself on a crowding rate close to 200 percent. I'm sure in the future, business efforts and such will somewhat mitigate that, but the way things were now, I didn't have the courage to choose riding that every morning and then actually working on top of that.

Besides, if I got a real job, that would mean leaving my parents' house. Or maybe while I was in university, I might start living on my own because commuting to school every morning would become a hassle—in order to get some sense of independence, not only for the sake of convenience.

Way down the coastline, there was the hazy view of the clusters of skyscrapers on the opposite shore. Gazing at the place I would one day go, I came to a stop.

The sound of her feet crunching on sand came to a halt there, too. Looking over, my eyes met hers. "But I think I'll come back here someday," I said. "'Cause it turns out I do like this place. I feel like this is where I belong."

"...I see. Then that's good." She smiled and then crunched along the sand again. Her steps were lighter and closer together than before as she walked a little ways ahead, then spun back to me. "You really do love Chiba, don't you?"

"...Well, yeah."

Did she understand what was behind those words or not? She smiled teasingly, as if to keep me from finding out, and I found myself grinning back in my twisted way.

Our footsteps crunched along, side by side.

It seemed we'd walked far enough to reach the next train station. As we made our way along the beach, a very fancy building came into view.

It had balcony seating where you could enjoy an ocean view, and the second floor was glass-walled with bare concrete, a very designer sort of restaurant. On the first floor, in the part that corresponded to the courtyard, was terrace seating. According to the sign, it seemed like this was a different business from the restaurant, and it had written there BAKERY CAFÉ in English. There was a substantial space with fluffy sofas placed under the blue sky.

Yukinoshita wordlessly pointed over there, cocking her head a tick as she said, "Want to go over?"

I nodded, and she smiled in satisfaction. Halfway to the counter, she whirled back around to me. "Can you grab seats for us?"

"Sure."

I sat down on the sofa seating closest to the ocean, where there was a pleasant wind blowing through. As I waited for Yukinoshita, I zoned out and looked around the café space.

It was a fairly hipster sort of place, so the menu was pretty fancy-schmancy. Not only were there subspecies of bubble tea, with the standard milk tea with pearls at the top of the list, they really had all the works, like caffeine-free rooibos tea or superfruit-and-vegetable smoothie and that sort of stuff.

Come on, this is Chiba. Do you think it's okay to be doing something this fancy...? Dude, this is too much. At this rate, Chiba is gonna be on the cutting edge of trendy.

As I was bemoaning the hipsterization of Chiba, Yukinoshita ambled over with a tray in hand and sat herself down beside me. "Here. To repay you for earlier," she said, handing me a bubble tea. It seemed this was supposed to offset the cost of the Max can.

"Uh, this costs way more, though... Are you bad at math?"

"Better than you are. Just pay me back with something else later," she said cheerily before sipping her own bubble tea.

So she actually does drink the stuff you'd normally expect girls to like,

I thought for a second, but then I realized she does like normal cute things like cats and Grue-bear... Although I don't quite know if bubble tea is cute or not.

Anyway, I generally didn't drink this stuff, so I figured I'd take a picture to remember it by and snapped a photo with my phone camera like you do when the ramen arrives. *Is this the sort of thing they like on Instagram?*

"Ah!" Yukinoshita exclaimed. I turned to her, wondering if something was wrong, when I saw her staring vacantly at the bubble tea she'd already started drinking. Her dejected expression was saying, *I should have taken a picture, too...*

"Uh, I haven't had any of mine yet, so you can take a picture. Go ahead..." I kinda felt bad for her. When I held out the cup, she pulled out her phone.

"R-really? Thank you...," she said as she fussed with her bangs, rose from her seat, and slid over the sofa. She sat down again right next to me and, with some reservation, wound her hand around the arm I held out the cup with. Then she snapped the shutter of the front-facing camera a couple of times.

As I was frozen by this total surprise attack, Yukinoshita checked the image, smiling bashfully, and said in an ultra-quiet voice, "See, here..." as she let me get a look at her phone.

The photo was completely unedited and unaltered, and awkwardness oozed from it. Even though our arms were linked, we were sitting weirdly far apart. Looking at the picture, I sighed deeply. *Is she for real...? She's far beyond what I imagined; it's bad for my heart...*

"Uh, that one's no good...," I said, covering my blushing face with both hands.

Yukinoshita panicked, backpedaling immediately in a fluster. "I-I'm sorry, um..."

"Let's do it over. My eyes are way too dead," I said as I raised my own phone.

Yukinoshita gave me a blank look, but then she hastily fixed and adjusted her bangs and checked her posture. She inched her way closer and then, bracing herself, spread her arms open. "G-go ahead..."

Uh, you don't have to spread your arms; it'll make me nervous, too—cut it out, I thought. But I extended my arm just like before, getting just a few inches closer. "Here we go."

"O-okay…" Yukinoshita sounded worn-out, but her back was ramrod straight. I could feel her tension through the shoulder touching me. Her arm linked in mine even felt like it was trembling a little.

Oh, well, I'm shaking even more than her.

Believing in the power of image stabilization, I snapped a shot, then immediately showed her the phone. Yukinoshita timidly peered at it, and then she suddenly burst into laughter. "Your eyes look exactly the same. They're nice and rotten."

"It's okay—it'll work out somehow with editing. The power of science is almighty."

I instantly downloaded a photo-editing app and swiped around to tweak things, as Yukinoshita watched with deep interest. Well, her face needed no corrections…

Killing time fooling around like this, we finished off the bubble tea. Before I knew it, the sea and sky had turned red, and the sun, the color of a smelting furnace, was on its decline.

It might have been the first time I'd ever seen a sunset up so close.

Yukinoshita and I were both silent, watching it together.

Eventually, the wind carried the sound of chapel bells to us. As I turned in that direction, I noticed they were closer than I'd thought.

"Want to go see?" Yukinoshita rose to her feet. We followed the source of the ringing to the end of the path that went along the ocean.

There was a group there dressed in bright formal wear. They were taking photos with a couple in a white tux and wedding dress in the center, with the magic hour of sunset and the beach in the background.

Observing from a distance, I figured it was a wedding.

Beside the building with the restaurant was a chapel. Then one down from that, in a separate building, was some kind of event hall for receptions and such. The pamphlet we snatched from the rack at the building entrance said the latter was called the "banquet hall," and on the second floor, they had two different event spaces with different aesthetics. There was also a lounge with a woody interior on the first floor, beyond which was a wide-open terrace facing the ocean.

When we took a casual peek at the terrace, there was a fire lit in the center, its warm flames gently illuminating the area.

Wow… Places like this exist? Weddings and stuff really aren't my world, so I didn't know about this kind of thing. I still have yet to master Chiba.

I was thinking with the pamphlet in hand, reflecting on my ways, when I felt a tug on my opposite hand.

"What?"

"I like this place. Let's do it here." Yukinoshita was pulling at my sleeve with sparkling eyes. She seemed really worked up about this, even emotional—either way, she had so much energy about her that I didn't feel like I could ask what she meant we should do.

I have the feeling if I ask, I really will be in checkmate…

I mean, this was a wedding hall.

"…Isn't that, uh, moving a little fast?" I said gently, choosing my words as carefully as possible.

Yukinoshita looked puzzled, titling her head. But eventually, she gasped with realization, jerking away from my sleeve. Then she put a hand to her temple and heaved an exasperated sigh.

"You're already lacking in social skills and personal development. If you get slow on the uptake, what will you have left? Look closely," she said as she pointed to various spots on the pamphlet in turn. "There's the beach, an open-air fire, and an event hall with proper facilities."

"…Oh yeah. The prom." *Oh no, silly me, I'm so embarrassed! Dummy, dummy! Stupid Hachiman! You worm!* I had meant to be calm, but I'd gotten pretty carried away. Guess I'll die. Would it be best to die soon?

With my head rapidly cooling, as if I'd been splashed by cold water, finally the capacity for actual thought returned to me. From what I saw of this facility overview, if we were going to make my ridiculous bluff proposal a reality, this was the ideal place to do it.

"You're right. If we're gonna do it, it should be here," I said.

"Yes, this place will probably fit the conditions best," Yukinoshita said with a confident, triumphant smile.

It wasn't so bad to see a new side to her, but this expression, the one I was used to, was even less bad.

× × ×

It was the day after we'd landed on a good place to hold the joint prom.

Right after the year-end ceremony, Yukinoshita and I headed for the Service Club room.

We immediately requested copies of their facility information documents and inquired into the availability and cost of the facility. However, you couldn't get a same-day response for requests like these, so we expected it would take a few days before we received a reply.

There was still lots of work to do in the meantime. Setting aside location and schedule, there were still the issues of budget and personnel.

In order to deal with the latter issue, Yukinoshita and I had invited people to explain to them the gist of the joint prom.

And so our honored guests had arrived. Standing in front of a lineup of three pairs of glasses, a total of six lenses, I cleared my throat. "Ummm, following up on last time, we'd like to ask you to put up with this," I said sharply with a posed look.

Sagami's little brother, Hatano, and Zaimokuza all pushed up their glasses with sighs of dissatisfaction. "Agh…"

"Huh?"

"Ngh…"

Mm-hmm, they've got energy. Wonderful.

"And so, these are our promising new assets." *Take a look to the right, if you would*, I indicated with a glance.

Then Yukinoshita rose to her feet. "Good to meet you. I'm Yukinoshita. I apologize for the trouble Hikigaya has caused you. Thank you. We'll be counting on you again." A pure, delicate smile accompanied her polite statement and courteous bow. She came off so much softer now, you wouldn't even imagine the person she'd been just a short while ago.

That had to be a shock to the UG Club pair, who only knew her from the time she'd been pointed like a knife sharp enough to hurt anyone who touched it.

Sagami and Hatano were actually both trembling.

"She doesn't—"

"—remember—"

"—us!!" And then even Zaimokuza was shuddering in his shoes.

At the trio's questionable responses, Yukinoshita raised a dubious eyebrow. There was just a flicker of her earlier thorns in that ice-cold expression.

"Whoa, she's scary!"

"She really is…"

The three of them all huddled together and whispered to each other until Zaimokuza came to tug at my sleeve. "Come on… Hachiman, do something."

"Don't worry—you can get into it, too, when you appreciate it for what it is. I'm frankly addicted. Once you're hooked, the contrast is so intense."

I'd thought I'd said it quietly, but Yukinoshita shot me a glare. "…Something you'd like to share?"

I shrugged, making eye contact with the glasses instead. *See?*

They expressed great admiration, like "For sure," "I get that," and "Could it even be anything else?" I had expected no less from this trio. I high-fived my comrades, who had yet again touched upon a new door of truth. We were just about ready to toast each other. *To our friendship, wishing you happiness.*

However, that energy evaporated within a moment.

There was a reserved knocking, after which the door opened with a rattle. The knocker hadn't waited for a reply. "Hey, guyyyys."

Who would drop in on us so casually but Iroha Isshiki? The executives of the student council were following behind her.

"Thank you, Isshiki." A gentle smile crossed Yukinoshita's face.

"No, no, this is us returning the favor for helping us out." Isshiki chuckled indomitably. Behind her, the vice president, the clerk, and everyone else, were looking glum. They were not here by choice, methinks.

The glasses trio were no lesser in their dark sentiments.

"Iroha…"

"Isshiki…"

"Irohasuuu…"

Isshiki smiled brightly at the UG Club plus Zaimokuza, popped off an inoffensive bow, then smoothly and immediately ignored them. It was like she could see them but also couldn't, which was even meaner than ignoring them from the start. It was like something out of Natsuhiko Kyogoku's mystery *The Summer of the Ubume*.

As expected, the trio all pushed up their glasses, saying, "I could get into this," "I feel like I'm getting it now…," and "'Tis inevitable," with new portents of change. *Sagami's tastes are a little warped, aren't they? Is he okay? Is it because of his sister?*

As I was getting concerned, there was yet another knock on a new door of truth. After that modest sound, the door opened a crack. This newcomer seemed more inquisitive than anything.

"Come in," Yukinoshita called out, and the little crack slowly opened up. An angel in a tracksuit popped his head in.

"Pardon me… Ah, Hachiman, I'm here." Totsuka beamed, waving as he stepped on over. Then he looked around the room curiously. "What's the occasion?"

"I invited all the people I don't feel bad about bothering."

"O-oh…" Looking half weirded out and half sympathetic, Totsuka examined each person there. Then it seemed to suddenly hit him, and he pointed at himself, cocking his head.

I smiled wryly at him and nodded back. "Sorry, you'll be a big help. Frankly, this is gonna be a huge hassle, but lend me the whole tennis club, you included." I bowed my head, and Totsuka smiled helplessly.

But then he clapped himself on the chest for me. "The whole club...? Yeah, okay."

So what's the trio think...? I wondered, but before I could see their reaction, the door was flung open.

"'Suuup!" An obnoxiously thick voice came in with the cheer of a shift lead trying for a promotion. The way Irohasu gave him a *Shut uuup* sort of look and just clicked her tongue at him is what makes her the best.

But after that, she immediately switched over to a cutesy attitude. "Ah, Hayama."

Hayama, following after Tobe, casually chatted with Isshiki as he lightly raised a hand in greeting at me. *The hell are these guys here...?* I wondered, eyeing the two of them, while Hayama noticed the UG Club and Zaimokuza, who were with me. He waved at them.

And then, at this, the glasses trio were like, "Omigod, I can't even," "Wow, I can't, I'm weak," "OMG, we stan," and started yammering away at one another the most they had all day. *Don't you guys think you like Hayama too much?*

But their excitement dropped when they saw Miura, spinning her hair as she stayed glued to Hayama's side, intimidating everyone around with a single displeased glare.

That glare made certain people react with twitches, especially Yukinoshita. She looked over at me, then scooted up beside me and whispered in my ear, "Did you invite her here?"

"...No. Huh, you weren't the one to call her?" I replied, and Yukinoshita gave a little shake of her head, looking mildly confused.

So then it must have been... I put my hand to my chin to puzzle this over when a figure appeared at the door that Tobe had left open.

"Hello, hellooo!" With that cheery greeting and her glasses flashing spookily, Ebina came in, with Kawasaki following, practically hiding behind her. Kawasaki took in the whole room, incredibly awkward expression on her face.

"Thank you for coming, Kawasaki," Yukinoshita said to her.

"Huh? Oh, well, if it's just hearing you out..." Twisting around like she was uncomfortable, Kawasaki closed the door behind her before moving to the corner, but Ebina caught her firmly once more. Kawasaki stopped fighting it, letting herself be pulled along by the hand to the center of the room.

With more people now, the clubroom was alive with chatter.

But there was still one missing, if it were to be as lively as it had once been.

Yukinoshita glanced at the clock. It was already past time. She still wasn't here.

People who had their own club activities were one thing, but the year-end ceremony was over, and we were in spring break now. If she was going to help us from now on, then of course that would mean taking up her spring break. Frankly speaking, it was a pretty high bar, and I figured it was an unreasonable request.

She had any number of good reasons to say no. I wouldn't have minded. I wouldn't be able to stand dragging her into my selfishness any more than I already had. Those were the kinds of excuses I made to myself.

I looked at the clock one last time.

"...Should we get this meeting started?" I prompted quietly, and Yukinoshita nodded. But even after she opened her mouth, no noise came out; her warm gaze alone argued me down.

That gentle gaze of hers slid to the door.

There was a shine like certainty in her eyes as she patiently waited for that time.

Ten seconds passed, twenty seconds passed, and eventually, the sound of hurried footsteps joined the ticking of the clock hands.

Even through the door, I could envision the sight of her hair bouncing in a bun, her big backpack swaying side to side, and the restless pattering of her indoor shoes.

I could tell right away. *Oh, it's her.*

And then with a loud rattling, the clubroom door opened.

"Yahallooo!"

Panting a bit with her hand raised high, Yuigahama showed off a smile even brighter than her old ones.

× × ×

Once we started spring break, the preparation for the joint prom began in earnest.

And Yukinoshita also got serious. She had become Miss Yukinoserious.

Beginning with the arrangements for the venue, estimates, schedule adjustments, and personnel allotments, she aggressively flew through work, ticking off tasks with a frightening speed. The only pending item was the budget, but we were planning to work that out during the meeting with Kaihin that day. In attendance on our side were Yukinoshita and myself, plus Isshiki, the student council president.

And as for the meeting with Kaihin, that's where the good old community center came in again.

It was now spring break, and we couldn't use the school because this was an independent activity, so we would be counting on the community center for the next while. Yukinoshita had managed to secure the community center meeting room every day until the joint prom—a glimpse of Yukinoserious in practice.

Right then in the meeting room, Zaimokuza, the UG Club, and others were making production items like handheld signs for guiding guests, while Yuigahama, Miura, and the rest of the advertising group were busy with their own tasks.

Obviously, not everyone could come every day, so we'd accommodated everyone's schedules to put together shifts. We'd borrowed underlings from the tennis and soccer clubs (mainly Tobe), plus the student council as well (mainly the vice president), so we weren't so pressed for manpower. Thanks to Totsuka's natural virtues, Hayama's leadership, and Isshiki's iron fist, we had a wonderful labor environment, making free use of fundamentally zero charges and exploiting their passion all we wanted. I have nothing but gratitude for our students!

So now the parts that didn't involve a budget were no problem.

Our issue was the guy who sat before us right now, who was tapping on the venue pamphlet with his fingers in an awfully cheery mood: Tamanawa.

"I like this. This is a great venue. It goes with everything you've got on your proposal. It's spot-on." Tamanawa praised the choice, properly rhyming *got on* with *spot-on*.

He immediately slid the pamphlet to the seat beside him, and Orimoto, who was sitting with him, also agreed. "Yeah, looks good!"

Isshiki and I nodded at him, too. The response from Kaihin was great so far.

To continue our advance, Yukinoshita said, "But the only available day will be in the first week of April… That's exactly the day of the departure ceremony. Will it be all right to book it then?"

"Of course. We have our departure ceremony at that time as well, so I'm sure plenty of the graduating students will be available then, which will make it comparatively easy to get people to come."

"I like that! It'd be tough if we can't get anyone together after all." Orimoto enthusiastically gave us a thumbs-up.

Well then, guess we'll get to the main issue…

Clearing my throat, I said nonchalantly, "So for the issue of cost, can we count on your student council budget?"

"Yes," Tamanawa agreed. "We should be prepared for a little spending, even if we're splitting it, so I think we can shoulder a certain amount."

"…Uh, about that… Our wallet is on the slim side."

"Hmm?" Tamanawa responded in an extremely placid manner, as if to suggest he hadn't heard me.

Touching her index fingers together in a cutely manipulative gesture, Isshiki started chuckling evasively. "Um, we can't exactly use the student council budget…"

But it didn't work on Tamanawa. He just replied in the exact same tone as before, "Hmm?"

Yukinoshita was suspicious about this exchange, cocking her head quizzically. "Have you not heard from Hikigaya? This isn't being sponsored by our student council. It's a volunteer activity."

"Hmm… Hmm? So then you mean we can't use your student council budget?" Tamanawa said, and all three of us nodded. There wasn't much choice. When you've got nothing, you've got nothing.

A blatantly forced smile spread on Tamanawa's face. "…I—I really don't think we can manage the full sum, ha…ha-ha-ha."

"I see. So those matters had yet to be discussed," Yukinoshita grumbled quietly, then pinched my thigh sharply under the table.

Ow, ow, ow!

When I twisted around silently, Isshiki gave me a look that seemed to say, *What're you getting all worked up about all alone over there?* A second later, it shifted into *Then again, you're always all alone.*

After nodding to herself, she slid her gaze over to Tamanawa. "So then I guess it's got to be pay-your-own-way, huh?"

"I'm not sure that will work… Some people might not like the idea of paying to go." Tamanawa folded his fingers with a grim expression.

Well, I could get what he was trying to say. Pay-your-own-way basically meant cash on the spot. I could understand the feeling of *Why do I have to cough up the green, huh?!* when they were the ones being celebrated, but we had to squeeze them for some dough, or it would be really hard to make this joint prom happen.

We would have to do something about that. "Then we go with crowdfunding. We invite those who've pledged money," I suggested.

Tamanawa abruptly lifted his face from the pile of papers. "…I see. If we do that, it may be possible."

Orimoto half-heartedly agreed. "Yeah, that's it! Though I dunno."

But Isshiki's eyebrows came together skeptically. "…Is it? They're still paying in the end, so how is that any different from pay-your-own-way?"

"No, it's a different sense," I said.

"Uh-huh…sense…and dollars?" Isshiki stared at me, and I imagined she wanted to say, *What the heck is this moron talking about…?* Then her eyes flipped to Yukinoshita, and she actually did say out loud, "What is he talking about?"

"What Hikigaya is trying to describe is the psychological hurdle, the feeling that you're getting a good deal… Something of that sort, right?"

"Well, you could put it like that, I guess," I replied. "To put it in an easy-to-understand way, it's like the difference between paying with an iTunes card or using a credit card."

"That makes it even more difficult to understand...," Isshiki grumbled.

"It's about the feeling of actually paying money. Some people may feel resistance about handing over cash but will readily pay online or with a card," Yukinoshita supplemented, and Isshiki made a "Huhhh..." sort of reply. It was anyone's guess whether she understood.

Then Tamanawa started spinning around his hands; this was his moment. "That's not the only advantage to crowdfunding. The element of investment, or support, is also powerful. So those who contribute could be called collaborators rather than merely customers. In other words, some collaborators may pay more than they would in a regular pay-your-way system."

"Hmmm," Isshiki drawled. She didn't even try to hide her lack of interest.

"Then the issue is providing a return on their expenditure... Assuming we keep the invitations to the prom at a minimum, we need to add something to the higher investment tier...," Yukinoshita put a hand to her chin, pondering over suggestions.

At that, Orimoto immediately raised a hand. "Oooh, oooh! How about, like, a limo escort?! Something photo-worthy! Isn't that a great idea?"

"Oh, I like that! That's like *The Bachelor*." Isshiki immediately jumped on that, too.

But Yukinoshita smiled wryly. "Even if we could arrange that, it would ultimately cost money, so it's dubious if that would add to our income."

But such opinions from the girls were valuable. Even if I thought it was stupid, there would be enough female guests at an event like this that it shouldn't be rejected out of hand. "Limousines and *The Bachelor*, huh...?" I muttered as I flipped through the venue documents. Eventually, a place that tied together those two words leaped to my eye.

"…The parking lot," I said. "Let's turn the right to use it into profit. The guests will have just graduated from high school. Lots of them will want to come in cars."

"Oh yeah… Some of them might have, like, their boyfriends picking them up in their cars," Isshiki said.

"I'm sure there will be a demand for that. Either way, we can't secure parking spaces for all the visitors. So let's sell them off at the highest prices we can."

Chiba is the largest big-city metropolis after Tokyo (personally researched) and also a great car society. Even in the Reiwa era, around the Kisarazu area, there are still bright and sparkly cars running around so studded with spoilers and aerodynamic parts, they look like squid-fishing boats. I hear that even if you're going the speed limit down the highway, they'll often casually tailgate you. It's not a good car society at all, huh?

Well, put another way, it meant they were just that attached to their cars. Their vehicles functioned as status symbols. Of course people who had nice cars would want to show them off. They'd want to take them to their special day.

Bringing up things like limos and *The Bachelor* was about the special feeling of a glamorous celebrity, a *unique experience just for me!* that female guests want, something that can make great Instagram shots to use for social dominance.

And then to make themselves attractive to such women, men gathered in an attempt to capture that special feeling. Geez, was this a scene from hell?

But anyway, once you understood the demand, what you needed to provide naturally becomes clear.

"Then I figure we can just set aside one of the waiting rooms as a VIP room to make a profit on that, too," I said. "Then we can generate additional value with zero funds at hand."

"You'd be amazing if you ever got into fraud…," Yukinoshita said.

"No way. I'm bad at math… I could never do all the calculations on income and expenditure." I honestly couldn't tell if what I'd just proposed would bring us any return. Frankly, when it actually came to practical business, I'd tossed it all off on Yukinoshita for many of our previous events. I bobbed my head in a bow to let them know I was counting on them for the rest.

That made Yukinoshita smile a bit. "I'll handle that part, so it's all right. For now, let's consider luxury features such as limousines an optional extra," she said as she jotted down some notes.

With a glance at what she wrote, Isshiki cleared her throat. "Anyway, is this about it?"

"...I like this. I'm getting the feeling this could work." With a smug grin, Tamanawa blew his bangs up. His face was brimming with motivation and confidence.

How reliable—we can always count on him... And since he's so reliable, maybe I'll dump a bunch of stuff on him!

"Okay, so then I guess we can leave everything to you. I think we'll probably need other plans to generate returns as well, so we're counting on you for that, too. And we're honestly lacking in know-how about crowdfunding... You guys seem like you're used to it." I made several requests rapid-fire.

Tamanawa blinked in high speed but eventually put on a vague smile. "...O-of course." And then, as if to say *Bring it on*, he smacked his chest.

He's covered in cold sweat, though, so can we really...? But right now we had no choice but to believe in Tamanawa. *If it's Tamanawa...I know he can do it!*

I actually had no idea how he would pull it off, but, well, he was saying he could do it, so we'd leave it to him. I heard that you didn't even need a credit card these days for making payments, you could just use your phone, so that would be plenty to work with for students. Personally speaking, getting Tamanawa motivated and then dropping all the work on him was enough for me. At this point, I wouldn't question his methods or process.

"In that case, I'll send you the estimates and trial balance sheet, so could you contact me once you have the general framework mostly nailed down?" Yukinoshita tapped the edge of her stack of documents on the table.

Once that was settled, Orimoto energetically replied, "Roooger!" and Tamanawa nodded as well.

"We'll make sure we can participate within a few days as well," he said.

"Yeah, thanks," I replied. "The main thing is the financial management, so you don't have to force yourself so much with personnel. Oh, just get us people for the day of the event."

"Okay, I'll hit up some people." Orimoto wrapped that up casually, and so the first joint prom budget committee meeting came to an end.

Watching Orimoto and Tamanawa go, I let myself thud back into my chair. A sigh whooshed out of me. "So we have some tentative prospects for the budget."

"If the crowdfunding goes well… What do we do if we come up short?" Yukinoshita asked.

With a deathly grim expression, Isshiki said, "Well, if it's a reeeeeally small amount, then it's not like the student council doesn't have absolutely nothing…"

"Now that doesn't sound reliable at all… Well, it depends on the amount, but up to a certain value, I can pay out of pocket as a worst-case scenario," I said, also making a very, very grim expression.

Yukinoshita's eyes widened in surprise. "Even though you don't have savings?"

"I don't, but my parents do. I'll borrow it on no interest and then shirk the bill. I'm at least that dependable."

"Can you call that being dependable…?" Yukinoshita smiled in exasperation, and I shrugged at her.

I actually didn't mind if we wound up a bit in the red. I had the feeling that imprudently producing profit could lead to a different set of problems. This was basically an event held by high schoolers, so we wanted to maintain the not-for-profit pretense. If this was weirdly profitable, the tax office would come…

As I was indulging in some optimistic fantasies, Yukinoshita had begun tapping away on a calculator. "I don't want to cause someone so young to take on debt, so I will consider cost cuts on my end as well."

"Make my pay the one thing you don't cut, okay?" I shot back.

"Don't worry. It was zero to begin with, so there's nothing to cut."

"What a wonderful workplace..." *There was never money to pay personnel, so I knew that already. It's all good...*

It was the first time in a long while that this exchange had felt normal. Meanwhile, Isshiki, sitting beside us, let out a sigh.

"You guys are all friendly now..." She examined the surroundings with a quick glance and cleared her throat with an *ahem* before lowering her voice to a whisper. "...Just curious, but...what's your relationship?" she asked.

Yukinoshita and I froze on the spot.

Ah, well. I thought someone would ask that eventually.

Isshiki had personally witnessed us fighting until just the other day, so she would naturally be confused after we suddenly said we were doing an event together.

When we struggled to reply, Isshiki shot us a low-temperature glare.

I've got to say something..., I thought, giving Yukinoshita a look out of the corner of my eye to see her doing the same to me. We were both embarrassed.

"Hmm, yeah, good question...," I muttered meaninglessly just for the sake of filling the silence, and Isshiki's gaze sharpened. When she turned away with a *yikes* kind of look, Yukinoshita's mouth opened and closed in an attempt to say something.

"Th-these sorts of things are difficult to explain...," she prefaced with flushed cheeks, her face turned down, then muttered the rest under her breath, "Like a p-partner...or something? Perhaps..."

"That's it!" I leaped on that with all my might. "Oh yeah, now you actually say that, I don't really get it, but yeah, it's probably something along those lines."

Yukinoshita rapidly nodded back. "Y-yes, I don't know, but it's probably something in that realm."

Isshiki was just staaaaaaaaaring at us without saying anything, but eventually, she expelled a tired breath. "Uh-huh. Gotcha. Well, if you guys are okay with that, then okay." Then she smirked. "Though I think you should be clear with each other." She smiled meaningfully, then hopped out of her chair. Humming, she made to leave the meeting table.

But her feet froze on the spot.

Right ahead of her was Miura, walking toward us, clearly displeased as she spun her loose waves of fluffy golden hair in her fingers.

Miura came up to us and sighed dramatically. "Can we go eat?"

"S-sure." Yukinoshita answered the sudden question with some discomfiture.

Even after getting permission, Miura focused on me and Yukinoshita for a while before whisking her gaze toward Isshiki instead. "You coming, too?"

"Huh? Uh, ahhh… Um, I dunno…" The sudden invitation must have startled her, as she couldn't quite manage to refuse. I feel like she'd normally be like, *Huh? No.* But this time it seemed her confusion overwhelmed her dislike of Miura.

Yeah, huh, these girls don't get along… Suddenly seeing some YumiIro interaction, I'm feeling flustered, too…

As we were all totally at a loss, Miura didn't say anything, just glanced at me. Her gaze immediately went back to Isshiki as she tilted her head, waiting for a decision.

Seeing that gesture, Isshiki let out a short *phew*. "…Well, I'm getting hungry, so I wouldn't mind going."

"Mm." With a nod, Miura spun around. Her back was saying, *Follow me.*

"Well, see you later." Isshiki took her leave and strolled on after her.

There was more than enough there to infer the reason for Yumiko Miura's attitude. She didn't say anything or ask anything, but she was probably trying to be considerate. Not to me, but to the three of us. *She really is a good person…*

With Isshiki in tow, Miura headed to the entrance of the meeting room.

By the door were Yuigahama, Ebina, and Kawasaki, who must have been waiting for Miura, as well as Zaimokuza and the UG Club guys, who were in conference like, "What do we do? What do we do?" She'd apparently invited the glasses as well. Miura really was a good person...

As they all left the meeting room, I found myself watching them.

Since the preparation for this joint prom had begun, I'd often seen Yukinoshita and Yuigahama talking about various things, but I'd had too much on my plate to join in. To be blunt, I was using work to put off lots of things.

But I thought that would eventually work out—somehow.

I believed somewhere in my heart that once we'd brought it all to a close, and our time after school went back to normal, things would work out one way or another.

As I was leaning my face on my hand toward the door, someone tapped on my upper arm. The gentle poke really tickled, and it made me jump in my seat.

When I looked over out of the corner of my eye, there was Yukinoshita, smiling with a hint of redness in her cheeks. "...How about we get some food as well?"

"...Yeah," I answered, and we got up, too.

× × ×

It was just a few days until the joint prom, and the work was reaching a climax, too.

After dumping almost the whole budget on Tamanawa's crew, we were expecting it to be slightly in the red, but we did have some decent prospects. Plus, we had safely booked the venue, so now we just had to work our asses off.

But we would only be able to make use of the venue the day before and the day of to set up. For any other day, we had to book a separate place to work, and so we ultimately continued to meet day after day at the community center.

It was mostly for lots of meetings, decorations, and other various items, but thanks to having people from both Soubu High School and Kaihin, we got the sense that we'd somehow barely…maybe…make it.

Unfortunately, things had recently stopped going smoothly. For the past few days, there had been a tendency for working hands to grind to a halt.

The biggest contributor was the distinctly springlike weather. The temperature was rising up and up, just like the staff's building excitement. This meant that if you were doing desk work, the pleasantly warm sunlight would make you sleepy, but then if you did physical labor, you'd work up a sweat. Essentially no matter what kind of work you did, you'd generally feel irritated about it.

Furthermore, the evil of humanity that is deadlines was torturing our spirits twenty-four hours a day.

Once I had finished a task, I flapped the top of my shirt, which was stuck to my chest with sweat. "It's so hot… I'll leave it at this for today and go home."

Yukinoshita, who was sitting opposite me with an energy drink in hand, cocked her head questioningly. Her hair was tied up that day, which left her neck cool. "You went home yesterday and the day before as well, didn't you? Do you intend to return today as well?"

"Why is it bad for me to go home every day? I still have a place I can go home to. There's no greater happiness." *Sorry… You understand, don't you? I can work anytime, so…*, I narrated in my heart.

With a faint sigh, Yukinoshita said, "…Well, it seems you're taking work home, so I'm not going to complain."

What, you found me out? Wait, so are you a Newtype? "But, like, hey, you take your work home, too. Give me some of the stuff you're handling before you hit your limit," I said a bit aggressively, and Yukinoshita's hands paused in their task.

Then she hung her head somewhat regretfully, and she nodded surprisingly readily. "Yeah…"

"Uh, yeah…?" *She's actually real exhausted, huh…? Her vocabulary is starting to die.* "Are you okay? Is it kinda bad?"

"It is. I really don't feel like we'll make it. It's bad. I could kind of die." Yukinoshita was already completely exhausted. Man, this was bad, whoa.

She started staring at the documents in front of her again, hitting the keyboard of her computer and clicking on her calculator. Her slightly askew blue-light-cutting glasses and the cooling sheet stuck on her forehead were heartbreaking to look at. The front of her desk was piled high with chocolates and rice crackers and stuff, perhaps for emergency calorie intake, or perhaps they were gifts from people.

She didn't just look on her way to the grave—she had one foot inside it. Someone else had noticed her exhaustion as well.

"Yukinon, I'm taking this, 'kay?"

"Oh, then I'll take thiiis one."

Yuigahama and Isshiki showed consideration to Yukinoshita in various ways, retrieving some papers and the calculator along with some snacks every time they passed by. They clearly had something to show for having worked through so many events together. It seemed everyone was on the same page with their concerns.

As for what I could do, it was just to initiate her into wonderful life hacks like *Pouring grape juice over caffeine pills is faster than having energy drinks!*

The only other option was to steal her work against her will and press her to take a break...

So when I was pondering like, *All right, so how to take the work away from her and make her rest?* a black shadow popped up to loom behind us.

Wearing a twist headband on his head and holding three nails in his mouth was Zaimokuza. There was a mysterious style to the way he was knocking against his shoulder with a hammer as he rubbed his chin. "Hachiman, we are lacking in materials."

"That means shopping at Mr. Max. I'll go, so come along to carry stuff."

"Aye. While we're at it, can we stop by Bikkuri Donkey? Come, just for drinks," Zaimokuza said, making a gesture of tossing something back.

"Whoa... Sure, I guess. So it's not just curry? Salisbury steaks are drinks for you, too?" I gave Zaimokuza a pitying look. *Is this guy okay...?*

For some reason, Zaimokuza looked all smug. "Lately, *tonkatsu* are drinks, too..."

What the heck? Freaky...

As I was trembling in fear, Isshiki, who had apparently been listening near us, sneaked over. "I like that idea. It's about time to eat after all. Right? Right?" she said as she snapped one eye shut in an eye signal at me.

What is that, a wink? Maybe she's a lonely tropical fish.

She bopped me in the side to get me to handle food plans.

Ow... I was muttering under my breath when Isshiki gestured toward Yukinoshita. I looked to see Yukinoshita in exhaustion mode, zoning out with her eyes on the clock. *I see—so now is the time to snatch her work away...*

Yukinoshita was rubbing her temples as she breathed a tired sigh. "...So it's already this late. How about we eat? Could you buy something for me while you're out shopping?"

"Ahhh," I said. "...Um, well, I can't buy you anything. We'll be out a long time."

"Why?" Yukinoshita cocked her head with a puzzled look.

With a very serious expression, I said slowly, "...Because we're going to a sauna."

"What?" That one syllable was enough to tell me Yukinoshita was close to losing it. Her implication was *What the heck are you talking about?*

But even if I launched into some explanation to try to convince Yukinoshita to rest, she would obviously say something like *I'm still fine.* So then there was nothing for it but to put up a different reason to convince her.

Fortunately, right by the Mr. Max where we were about to go shopping was a super *sento* called Yukemuri Yokocho. A saunist could not go someplace near a sauna and then not go into the sauna.

As Yukinoshita's partner, and also as a saunist, I would argue her down thoroughly and thoughtfully.

"Listen up, okay? This is also important for work. By going to a sauna, you get your autonomic nerves all sorted out, and relaxing increases the efficiency of your following work, so this is what's most necessary for us right now. So in a sense, you could actually call a trip to the sauna an employee benefit. It should even be covered as a necessary expense. I'll get receipts, so just tell me who to charge it to." Partway through, it turned into just about 100 percent my opinion as a saunist.

Upon receiving my enthusiastic, passionate speech, Yukinoshita recoiled. "...I—I see."

Then my passion turned to murmuring, transmitting all around.

"...Is that a part of a sauna?"

"I wanna get sorted out."

"I wanna be steamed..."

"Ah yes, the *rouryu*. Though sometimes it's also called *aufguss*."

The guys, chiefly Zaimokuza and the UG Club pair, all indicated their agreement. Tamanawa was already making hand gestures like a master heat waver mixing up the air. The Kaihin boys also all raised all their hands in agreement, as if asking for another gust of the hot wind swept up by that *aufguss*.

"Cold-water baths are the gateway drug to saunas."

"True. The cold-water bath is what brings out the high cultural standard, so it's important."

"Speaking of cold-water baths, I'd like to try going to Shikiji sometime."

That's a sauna that even young people these days like. It's wildly popular among modern youths sensitive to trends, and I suspect the Kaihin students would have highly sensitive antennae. They had to have their eyes on it.

This is why I keep saying that a sauna anime is going to be a big hit one of these days! You've got to go study to be a sauna-spa health advisor right now to get your qualifications sorted out ('cause it's a sauna). I've already gotten my sauna-spa professional qualifications, you know?

Watching the boys all rising to their feet along with me, Yukinoshita pressed her temple and sighed. "...Let's break for now. Could you tell me where that is, just in case?" she said, closing her notebook computer with a *tmp*.

× × ×

The water of the outdoor bath sparkled under the slanting rays of the sun.

After leaving the community center, we'd gathered everyone who'd been doing physical labor outside, like the tennis and soccer clubs, and here at Yukemuri Yokocho, we were going out for this major break before our final charge.

As everyone was relaxing in their various ways, I was alone, peacefully getting steamed.

There was a TV installed in the sauna room, but it wasn't too loud. In fact, this moderate background noise was nice. The hot air had opened my pores nicely, and now the voices on the TV were slowly oozing into me to merge with the beating of my heart. The heat and sound made for a soothing combination.

With the high-temperature air on my naked skin, the exchange of heat started to warm my blood in my veins. It melted everything in the dark the corners of my mind, washing it all away into *emptiness*.

After being exposed to the heated winds for a while, your ideas, concepts, and notions all disappear... You gain an absolute enlightenment here that can only be expressed as simply, *Hot... It's so hot...* Though I'm sure I was thinking about many things at first, it all became so unimportant, and all I could think was *So hot...*

In a sense, this could be called the ultimate form of concentration and, simultaneously, the greatest form of relaxation. *Hot.*

However, the true pleasure of a sauna is not complete within the sauna room. After sufficient steaming, if you wash away the sweat with hot water, then soak in the cold water for a little bit, the clarity of mind is unparalleled. Not only of the mind—it awakens every single cell in your body. And then the water that has been warmed by your body heat envelops you just like the delicate robe of an angel, granting an overwhelming sense of ease. And then, when he shatters that robe with his own hands, man knows courage. That determination, just like leaving your warm house to head out into the cold winds whipping across the wastelands, is most worthy of the name *courage*. But anyway, man, it was warm...

To go even further, I might say the bit after this cold-water section is the best part of a sauna. In other words: the open-air bath. Having been steamed and then chilled, the moment he relaxes his body under the open air is when man will, for the first time, know the feeling of being sorted out...

After being warmed in the sauna room, the chilling of the body constricts the blood vessels. However, relaxing in an open-air bath causes the body to once again begin to produce heat, and the heart pumps, and the blood vessels widen and begin to circulate a large volume of oxygen. Repetition of this process will put everyone in order.

It's just like the history of the world.

Beginning in the age when molten rock spewed from the mantle, then going to the Ice Age that froze everything, you arrive in our era of inhaling oxygen to your heart's content. After alternating between bathing in hot and cold, you come to feel the meaning of the aphorism *Humanity lives between cool composure and hot passion* in your very bones. Bodies that are steamed in a sauna produce clear heat from the inside, and then when chilled in the cold water, they squeeze tight so as to keep that heat from escaping. Then when they are exposed to the open air, they release everything. There lies true freedom, release from every form of oppression. *Waaarm*.

About when I was getting pretty nice and zoned out from the heat, I glanced over to the clock in the sauna room. Five minutes had passed.

Generally, my routine was to do seven minutes in the sauna, two minutes in the cold bath, and three minutes in the outside air bath, totaling twelve minutes in one set, and I would do three sets. This made perfect use of the twelve-minute clock inside the sauna room. However, this was ultimately my own private ideal; in fact, the time spent would change depending on the temperature of the sauna room (above ninety-eight degrees Celsius is preferable), the temperature of the cold water (below sixteen degrees Celsius is preferable), and whether they had a space to put yourself in order (preferably, a deck chair where you can recline). A good saunist took into consideration how crowded it was that day, as well as how they were feeling, to make the most of the experience.

The bath is outdoors, and it's nice and sunny, so I'm sure an open-air bath will feel nice…, I thought. On days like this one, I wasn't opposed to extending the time of the open-air bath.

Ahhh, I want to get into the cold water already, and then I want to get sorted out… It's so hot, it's hot, it really is hot.

Eventually, all my thoughts evaporated, flowing away with my sweat.

Mmm…

"Whoa! This is, like, boiling! No way, no way, no way! This hot as hell!" a rough voice cried.

In such comfort of the heat, even that could vanish like steam. *So hot…*

"Whoa, whoa, whoa, Hayato, this is too much, man! Dude, dude! Up at the top is hot as hell! And, like, how can you be okay sitting there, Hikitani? Ah, man!"

…Tobe is so obnoxious.

He was so loud. He was completely breaking my concentration.

I slowly lifted my eyelids right as Hayama, Totsuka, and Zaimokuza all came in together after Tobe.

"Hachimaaan! Let's sit together!" Of course, the one plopping down next to me was him.

Yoshiteru Zaimokuza.

I kind of get why Totsuka has a bath towel properly wrapped around his waist, but why is it that Zaimokuza's got full defenses up, too?

Completely ignoring Zaimokuza, I turned my whole body and face away from him to find an angel sitting on my opposite side.

"It's so hot, huh…? I feel the blood's gonna rush to my head." Totsuka fanned his face with his hands, and with every wave, sweat drops like pearly orbs streaked down his smooth, porcelain skin. The brief moment they caught in the indent of his collarbone, they shone like jewels. Totsuka shyly drew up the towel that was wrapped around him, averting his eyes.

For an instant my consciousness just about left me.

I mean, it probably was in space by now.

"So, like, isn't a sauna boring?" someone babbled in a thick voice, bringing me back to reality. My memory of a few seconds earlier was gone. "There's nothing to do, man. Wanna compete to see who can stand it longest?"

"That's not what a sauna is for. Shut up," I grumbled. *I'm desperately trying to fill in the gaps of my lost memories, okay? Let me concentrate.*

And a sauna isn't a place you have to withstand in the first place. It's like—you have to be saved by the freedom. However, anyone who tries to pull a no-splash (not washing off their sweat before they go into the cold-water bath) or sweat *rouryu* (wringing the towel they wiped their sweat with over the sauna stones) are inarguably guilty. If I see you doing that, I'll murder you with an arm lock. ☆

Though of course I didn't go that far, I immediately cut down Tobe's reckless remark.

However, it seemed Tobe was also the type to forget things after a few seconds. "How about whoever's the last to stay wins?" he spouted off willfully.

Hayama stopped him with an aggrieved expression. "We all came in at different times, so it's not fair."

"True! So then whoever says *hot* loses. Any words that sound similar like *hawt* or whatever are also out. This way, it won't be a contest."

"Fine, fine. Okay, start." Hayama said that quickly while clapping his hands, blatantly annoyed with Tobe.

After he gave the signal, a moment of silence passed.

But a few more seconds after that, Tobe started mussing his hair impatiently. "Whoa…this is boring. You don't need to go all quiet, man. Shouldn't we talk about something?"

"Then you start a conversation, Tobe," Hayama told him.

"Huh? Talking about what? Ah..." Tobe considered for a while. Then with a thought, he snapped his fingers. "Oh, so, like, Hikitani. Are you, liiike, y'know...dating Yukinoshita?"

The sauna room burst into murmurs.

Hayama and Totsuka looked at each other and breathed aggrieved sighs. Zaimokuza muttered, "Ohhhh, no, no... You're not, right? Right? Say it's not so. You can be honest. It's all right—I won't be angry. Okay?" He was like a mosquito in my ear, whispering at length.

"......"

When I maintained my silence, Tobe inched toward me, turning his torso my way to press for an answer.

Hayama jabbed Tobe lightly in the head. "Don't..."

"Yeah. Didn't we all decide we wouldn't mention anything because he'd just say no to any questions?" Though Totsuka was also keeping his voice quiet, he was earnestly lecturing Tobe.

What...the heck...? Everyone kinda sorta picked up on it but said nothing out of consideration...? That's just kinda, I mean, whoa...

Wiping off sweat, I jerked my face up to look at the ceiling.

Wow, I want to die...

I really, really did. I blew out a hot, deep sigh.

"Uhhh, Tobe said the no-word, so...he's out," I announced with complete apathy. Maybe that would help me forget what just happened.

Zaimokuza went along with it. "Out!"

"Huh, wait, why?! I didn't say *hot*!"

He's so obnoxious. Excuses like that won't work in the face of my power of Taboo. It was generally accepted that if you said the *ha* and *t* sounds all in a row, then you were out. Since words similar to *hot* were also banned, it also caught Tobe saying, "Huh? Talking..."

When I made a *Shoo, shoo* gesture with my hand to wave him away, Tobe reluctantly got up.

Watching, Zaimokuza slapped his thigh and stood up next. "Hmm, I have also been heated to my limits!" And then he went out, practically pushing Tobe ahead of him.

"Me too...," said Totsuka as he swayed off after them.

With fewer people now, the inside of the sauna was suddenly quiet.

It was just me and Hayama, who went silent and still as if he were meditating.

Neither of us exchanged any words—the only sound between us was moist breathing.

We both stoically steamed ourselves, and you might even think we really were competing. Finally, Hayama broke the silence. "So what is the deal with you two, actually?" he said smoothly. There was a kind of pressure in his words that gradually sizzled my skin. The muscles of his back were telling me that he wasn't going to move until I answered.

"It's not like that... Or, like, it's just not the time," I said with a sigh, and Hayama twitched.

Then he burst out laughing, holding his stomach.

He laughed for a while, and then once it had settled, he let out a deep sigh and stood up. Looking over his shoulder at me, he smirked. Despite his breezy, charming persona, there was an ironic nastiness behind the expression.

"...It's hot here," he said coolly, and then he left the sauna with a leisurely stride.

× × ×

After taking my sweet time getting sorted out, I was feeling quite a bit lighter in body and mind.

Refreshed, I headed to the shoe cubbies while tapping away on my phone, sending Komachi the message *I won't need dinner*. I immediately got back the reply *Roger! Do your best with prep! 'Cause Komachi's going to the prom, too!*

You don't have to come..., I thought with a wry smile as I changed my shoes and went outside.

When I pushed up the split curtains at the entrance of Yukemuri Yokocho, the setting sun was low in the sky, making the distant seas burn in a vivid red.

While walking, I touched the chilled Max can I'd just bought to my forehead and neck. The spring wind felt pleasant on my steam-warmed skin as I narrowed my eyes in the stinging brightness of the setting sun.

"Hikki."

Turning toward the call, I saw Yuigahama sitting on a bench as she waved. Yukinoshita was next to her, her hair completely down after having it up for work, her cheeks faintly reddened from the sauna as she sighed in satisfaction.

Isshiki was beside her, peeking out past her shoulder to give me a critical glare. "You took foreeever."

"Or maybe you just got out too fast," I retorted as I approached the bench, fully aware I'd come out last. "Where are the others?" I asked as I looked around, but there was no one else nearby.

"They went ahead to get dinner," Yukinoshita replied briefly.

"Oh," I answered, and there was no more conversation after that. But there was no sign that the girls were heading off to Bikkuri Donkey, where everyone would be eating.

Yukinoshita, Yuigahama, and Isshiki all remained seated on the bench. I stayed there, too, giving the Max can in my hand a light shake before I opened the tab with a *pshht*.

I leaned back against the wall by the bench, and as I sipped my canned coffee, nobody said anything. The time passed in peace.

We were silent, the four of us zoning out and gazing at the sunset in the evening post-bath cool.

Being all in the same place with no conversation should be uncomfortable. You should feel like you're at loose ends. It's normal to go on your phone to distract yourself.

Yet there we were, all mysteriously calm, immersing ourselves in that serenity.

It reminded me of the mood that had hung in clubroom that one day after school.

Even if nobody was really saying anything, I felt like I could stay here forever without getting bored.

Isshiki was humming the standard prom dance number while swinging her legs, letting her skirt flutter dangerously. Her humming occasionally stopped and started. Maybe it was because of the sunset, but it had a nostalgic ring to it, like a lullaby.

It seemed to be putting Yukinoshita to sleep. The comfortable post-sauna feeling probably helped her along, as she let out a little yawn before letting her head clunk onto Yuigahama's shoulder. Yukinoshita leaned right in, as if to keep that warmth from escaping.

Suddenly, a chilly and unseasonal night wind whooshed through, making me draw my shoulders inward. I looked down at the bench out of the corner of my eye, wondering if they might start shivering after coming out from the hot sauna, but it seemed they hadn't been in the path of the wind.

They were still in a warm patch of sun, so much like that comfortable sunlit room. Like that place where we had watched that sun set into the sparkling room.

Surely, I—

Or perhaps we…

We knew this twilight would eventually be over; we knew that a moment like this would never come again. Maybe we were thinking about lingering here forever.

But the time to leave came.

It would be a lie to say I wasn't reluctant to part ways. Of course that attachment lingered, and I felt an invisible pull coming from behind.

I had cared deeply enough about that place to feel it.

By now, I was finally forced to acknowledge that I did love that time, that place. I had to acknowledge it before I left it.

It was so bright and dazzling to the eye, so burning hot, it would leave a mark. It would hurt me and become a fault in me, so I wouldn't forget it. Seeing that scar, I would one day think, *Yeah, that did happen* and regret it enough to die.

Before the lingering light went away, I took one step forward to leave that warm place.

"…Let's get going, then," I called, turning halfway back.

Yukinoshita, who'd been nodding off, opened her eyes with a blink. "Yes..." With that short answer, she straightened in her seat again. With a quiet thanks to Yuigahama, she adjusted her twisted collar.

Isshiki didn't wait for her, lining up her swinging legs and hopping to her feet. Her loafers crunched on the sand as she spun around on the axis of her heel. "Yep! ...Let's go." A gentle smile came to her face as she called over her shoulder to Yuigahama.

Yuigahama was looking up at us, squinting at the glow of the sunset behind our backs. She lowered her eyelids, then nodded a few times. "Yeah," she said quietly. "We should go now..." After that momentary hesitation, she rose to her feet, and without a hitch in her stride, she walked off and didn't turn back. She quickly caught up to Isshiki, and then, shoulder to shoulder, they left.

On the bench was Yukinoshita, done fixing her clothes.

When I said *How about we go, too?* with my gaze, she nodded in reply, about to stand up.

And then without a word, I offered my hand.

She cocked her head a tick to the side before cracking a small, crooked smile. "I can stand on my own..."

"I know." I was aware she could stand on her own, and that she would say as much.

But I'd offer my hand anyway. I'd probably keep doing so.

The dying sun shone even brighter, and the shadows stretched out sharply. Our shadows overlapped, and you couldn't tell whose was whose.

My face, her cheeks, and everything else was dyed red, and she smiled in exasperation and gently took my hand.

Interlude...

The joint prom was starting soon. We had mostly finished our preparations for the venue, so now we just had to wait for the guests to arrive. I was working reception, so I didn't have any real preparation left. I waited near the entrance and let my mind wander.

Just like that, I was gazing at the place where I had been.

At the back of the lounge, the two of them were having some kind of meeting, and a little earlier, I'd been there, too.

But that was over now. I would be somewhere else.

Just like before, I was just watching a place I couldn't enter, from a distance.

"What's wrong, Yui?"

I turned around to see Iroha-chan.

"Ah, no, it's nothing..." I smiled evasively on instinct, although I knew my answer wasn't convincing. Iroha-chan accepted it with a grin, not pushing me further. I didn't know what to say, so I squished my bun again. It was definitely my nervous habit.

"Yuiiii!" The familiar voice made my eyes jerk in that direction. It was Komachi-chan in our school uniform, running with big flaps of her arm as a wave.

Seeing her in that outfit kind of startled me, and I grabbed her without thinking. "Komachi-chan! Your uniform! It's cute! I love it!"

"Ngh!" Komachi-chan made a strange sound in my arms.

Iroha-chan watched us with a *Who's that?* look on her face.

Oh yeah, maybe they've never met. "Ummm, this is Hikki's little sister, Komachi-chan," I explained, pulling away.

Iroha-chan narrowed her eyes and stared before nodding in understanding. "His little sister... Oh, the rice girl." It was a dubious thing to say, and Komachi-chan gave her an equally dubious expression in return.

"Hmm... Well, probably yes," Komachi-chan replied.

Iroha-chan bobbed downward in a little bow. "I'm your brother's junior, Iroha Isshiki. Good to meetcha."

"Ah, hi-hi, you're Iroha? Thank you for always handling my brother. I'm Hachiman's little sister, Komachi. Komachi's arrived to wipe his b... Komachi's helping out!" After amending her statement, Komachi-chan did a cute salute. And then she looked all around. "Where is he anyway...?"

I glanced over to the place I'd been watching. "Over there... They're having a meeting, so maybe it'd be best to wait a bit. It seems like it'd be bad to get in their way."

"Oh..." Komachi-chan looked kinda lonely, and it made me think she maybe had an idea about how things went. Maybe he did tell her.

Aw, it kinda looks like I forced her to be considerate of my feelings..., I thought with a quiet sigh.

I meant to keep that exchange really, really quiet. I heard Iroha-chan loudly yawn next to me.

"Why *not* just get in the way?" she said so nonchalantly. To her, it was obvious. I tilted my head, and she grinned like a little devil. "There's no way those two will last, right? Doesn't matter if you interfere or not."

"Do you think...?"

"Definitely. Those two make everything complicated. Don't you think they'll be over the instant something happens?"

"Huhhh? Um, speaking as his sister, I dunno if you should say that…" Komachi-chan was frowning. I felt just as iffy about this whole conversation.

"Y-yeah…"

Nonetheless, Iroha-chan beamed at us. "Come on, now—in another three years, you'll be able to drink, right? Then just pretend you're drunk and go for it! Just do it! Make it a done deal, and then you win. That guy's obsessed with taking responsibility."

"I-I'm not so sure about that tactic… And besides, I don't know anything about three years from now…" A fountain of ideas burst up and flooded my mind, and I think my face was red enough that even I could tell.

As I tried to find a way to end this thread of conversation, Komachi-chan tilted her head with a curious look. "Isn't it in two years that Yui can drink alcohol? Three years is Iroha, isn't it?"

"Shut up, Okome-chan, shut up."

"Okome-chan? Rice girl?! It's Komachi! Komachi's name is Komachi!"

"It's a cute nickname, isn't it? ☆ When you meet another girl for the first time, you have to establish a pecking order like this, or you'll fight later."

"Whoa, what's up with you? You're kinda mean!"

"Ha-ha! I don't wanna hear that from you!"

Oh no. Maybe Iroha-chan and Komachi-chan aren't very compatible… It'd be easier and more fun if they got along… Can I mediate somehow? "Come on, guys…," I tried with a forced smile as I made *calm down* gestures with both hands.

Komachi-chan put her hands on her waist with a big sigh. "Aghhh. You might be younger than him, but you don't understand the perspective of a little sister. Listen, okay? Komachi's brother is an ascetic monk, so that stuff won't get you anywhere. Before he seriously gets drunk, he'll pretend to fall asleep to get out of the situation. That's the Hachiman mentality." Komachi-chan wagged a finger. Iroha-chan and I both nodded along.

That really is true. Absolutely, I get that.

And it seemed Iroha-chan was of the same opinion. "Ahhh, the tofu mentality."

"No, it's the Hoshino Coffee soufflé pancake mentality," said Komachi-chan.

"Oooh, those are great; I love them," Iroha-chan said, and this time Komachi-chan nodded, too.

...Maybe they do get along? I really don't get these two.

Then Komachi-chan gave Iroha-chan a disparaging smile.

On second thought, maybe they really don't.

"If that's all you've got," Komachi-chan said, "Komachi can't really call you Big Sis."

"What? Uh, that's totally fine. I really don't need that... Hey, what is up with this girl?" Iroha-chan stiffly grimaced as she turned to me.

"Ummm, Komachi-chan really has a brother complex," I said with a wry smile.

"Of course." Komachi-chan thumped her chest with pride. "Just who do you think has been loving my loveless brother for the past fifteen years? When he was little, oh, he was so cute..." Then she gleefully pulled out her phone. Probably to show us old photos.

"Oh, I wanna see, I wanna see." I popped in for a peek.

"Whoa... I don't actually care, but I do wanna see a couple," Iroha-chan grumbled, following after.

While she searched for the photos, Komachi-chan asked, "Which do you want, before his eyes died, or after they died? Then there's also after his eyes rotted."

"Wellll, just when he was cute is fine. Or, like, was he *actually* cute?" Iroha-chan asked in disbelief.

"You just called him cute there...," I said weakly.

Komachi-chan mentioned something like that before when the two of us went out together. The memory pricked at my heart, and the smile I was forcing faded slightly.

Iroha-chan blew out a sigh. "Yuuup, there are guys like that. They'll brag about how they were cute when they were little or how they're popular in Ni-chome. They're small-time garbage who just try to score points by moving the goalposts."

"That's pretty harsh!" I refuted. "U-um, but I feel like that's not really true... Oh, look, Komachi-chan is legitimately cute!" I squeezed her shoulder and shoved her forward.

That made Komachi-chan get all fidgety and blushy, and she gave Iroha-chan a coy glance. The she tapped her index fingers together. "...Ummm..."

"What is it?" Iroha-chan looked at her sharply.

Komachi-chan fixed her puppy-dog eyes on Iroha-chan. "Could Komachi call you Big Sis? Starting with *provisional* in front of it for now?"

"What?! No!"

"Eh-heh-heh, Komachi kinda just figured you're on the same wavelength as him."

"Huh?"

"Komachi has always thought that to deal with the big brother issue, you have to pull him from above or push him up from below... but yeahhh, hmm. I forgot you could both be trash."

"Huh? The heck is she talking about...? Um, I'm really not that bad, though. His looks are what they are and his brain is what it is, and his personality is garbage, so."

"And he's trash, too! He'll barely take care of himself and his own feelings, never mind other people's!" Komachi-chan giggled gleefully.

"Why do you seem glad about that, Okome-chan...?" Iroha-chan jerked away in horror. She looked at me for help.

All I could do was sheepishly say, "Ummm, Komachi-chan *really* has a brother complex..."

But Komachi-chan smiled bashfully and did a clean little bow. "He's just that bad a brother, so please stick with him just a little longer until he gets his act together."

"Well, we'll be around each other whether we like it or not for another year. It's all good...," Iroha-chan said reluctantly. She was taken aback, but she also made it clear that she wasn't happy about this…and then she turned to me. "What about you, Yui? What will you do?"

"I…" I didn't know what to say after all.

"Well, I really like that about you, though." Iroha-chan sighed as if to say, *What can you do*, then came a couple of steps up to my side and whispered into my ear, "Is there a law that says you can't like someone who has a girlfriend?"

"Huh… I don't think so…"

"Right?" Iroha-chan popped away from my side again with a bold chuckle and a hint of grown maturity.

That smile was too cute, the kind that maybe I'd had before, too—the smile of a girl happily in love.

"…Is that true for you, too, Iroha-chan?" I asked her.

"What? Uh no not at all I'm thinking more or less that I should take my shot at Hayama. And then it's like worst case, if I win on a discard, then that's fine for what it is but I'm not gonna bother trying to wait for a different tile or abandon going for a winning hand when I'm just one tile short." Iroha-chan was flapping her hands around, totally disgusted.

"Huh, then why did you say that…?"

"Isn't it obvious?" With an exasperated exhale, she swished her hair aside with a hand, then moved that hand right to her cheek. "Not giving up is a girl's prerogative!" She flashed a peace sign by her face. She smiled more smugly, boldly, and cunningly adorable than anyone. Though I was sure she was putting on that girlish act to butter me up, that grin was the absolute coolest.

I was entranced, and all I could say was "Oh…"

It wasn't a sigh. It wasn't a word that meant anything, but it was a sound from my heart.

The two of them beamed. It was so perfectly timed together, totally unlike their earlier prickly exchange. It was kinda heartwarming.

I kept nodding to myself, reflecting on all that had happened, digesting everything they'd said.

Iroha-chan and Komachi-chan exchanged a glance and smiled.

Then they both inched just a bit closer to each other and started whispering.

"But, like, are you okay with that, Okome-chan?"

"Heh, Komachi has her own thoughts about things."

"Huh."

"Hmph! Why're you acting like you're not interested"

"'Cause I'm not. Like, at all…"

"No, no, Komachi may just have a good offer for you, too. If I could borrow your ear a moment…" She whispered to Iroha-chan, who wrinkled her nose.

"Whaaa…? Whose side are you on, Okome-chan?"

"My brother's, of course. Oh, and that was worth a lot of Komachi points."

"Whoa, what's wrong with you? Gross."

"What did you say?! Rude! Komachi'll never take *your* side!"

"I didn't ask for it anyway!"

The two of them probably wouldn't get along, but they also probably wouldn't be enemies. I couldn't help but smile as I watched them together. Maybe this was their way of encouraging me.

I felt so glad, I went to give the both of them hugs, and Komachi-chan wrapped her arms around me tightly while Iroha-chan turned her face away and acted like she wasn't into it.

I hadn't sorted out my feelings.

I didn't think that was okay.

I knew this sort of thing was a mistake.

All the same, maybe it was okay for me to bask in this just a little longer—in that warm, dazzling spot of sun.

"Okay! Now I'm feeling better! Let's go!" I wrapped my arms around their shoulders and pushed their backs as hard as I could in return for pushing mine.

I took my next steps forward, and I raced out toward where I wanted to be.

9

Even if it's faded by the passing months, that green remains green.

Once the formal departure ceremony was over and done with, we were finally ready for our own sort of farewell.

No remarks on a stage, no presentation of bouquets, no tearful good-byes. This was an environment for people to party, have fun, and enjoy themselves in while we, the organizers, would be so exhausted we wouldn't have the energy for sentimentality. You know the kind.

Though there had been many twists, turns, trials, and tribulations, we had brought the joint prom to fruition.

With the help of many people, setting up the venue proceeded without issue, with balloon art and flowers dressing up each floor and the background music already put on low. We were all set up. Maybe it was just excitement from being dressed up, but the staff who'd come in ahead of the general guests were all buzzing with energy, too.

I continued to sense the building expectations as Yukinoshita and I had our final meeting in a corner of the lounge.

"Well then, Hikigaya," she began, "you'll be supervising the floor for the Soubu High School side and managing all staff."

"Right."

"And check with Hayama and Totsuka as necessary regarding

outdoor guidance and security, since we've had the tennis and soccer clubs handle that."

"Roger."

"And keep an eye on the catering as well. The lounge is open for people to relax and cool down in, so make sure to work with Zai... Zai......with those three."

"She gave up..."

"Kaihin is managing stamping for reentrance, but you're supervising the indoor staff, so keep an eye on the mats and swap them out when appropriate. People will be heading out onto the beach, so make sure no sand gets into the hall."

"Rog... Wait, isn't that a lot of work for me? This isn't management and supervision, this is all odd jobs, isn't it?" I said.

Yukinoshita stared at me blankly. "You and I are the only ones with an overall grasp of the event, so there's no way around it, is there? Since I'll be directing the event and won't be able to leave my post... Or can my partner not manage something as simple as this?" Then she swished the hair off her shoulders with the back of her hand and a challenging smile. In the face of her indomitable spirit, my responses were limited.

"I can do it..." If she was going to call me her partner, that was the only answer I could give. Even if I was mumbling it under my breath.

I wasn't sure whether she heard me, but she cracked a smile.

The venue went quiet as soon as our meeting came to a close. I could have sworn there had been a distant buzzing, just like insects during the long nights of fall, but it stopped all of a sudden.

When I turned around, wondering what it was, there was Yukinoshita's mother; her sister, Haruno Yukinoshita; and one other coming over, sucking the air out of the room. The women in question must not have intended it, but they were beautiful. One had age-appropriate charm while wearing expensive traditional clothing, and the other was stylishly attired in a fancy dress with open shoulders and back, showing off her collarbones. The fabric of her dress fell downward in a mermaid line from her waist. And then behind them was a lady in a pants suit wielding all the punch of her long-legged figure, a woman so cool you might take her for a belle in men's clothes—it was Ms. Hiratsuka. There was no way the three of them wouldn't gather attention.

The trio cut through the waves of people to come toward us. Yukinoshita looked over at them and flashed a confident grin. "My, you came."

Mrs. Yukinoshita responded to her daughter's rude treatment with cheer. "Yes… I thought we should arrive in the proper fashion." There was an almost-hostile force at the end of her remark.

Oh no, she's scary as ever…, I was thinking, sneaking back to hide in Yukinoshita's shadow, when Haruno came to poke fun without any concern for my anxiety.

"Oh, I just came for the free drinks."

"We're not serving alcohol," Yukinoshita said, exasperated.

Haruno took Ms. Hiratsuka's hand and tugged her into linking arms. "It's fine, it's fine. When I want drinks, I'll just go with Shizuka-chan in the restaurant across the way."

"I drove here, though…," Ms. Hiratsuka grumbled, but she didn't try to shake off Haruno's hand. Still looking like she was on a grown-up date, the teacher looked at me and Yukinoshita in turn and smiled. "I'm going to have a good time tonight, too."

"Do your best, Yukino-chan. You too, Hikigaya…" Haruno paused before sidling up a step and whispering the rest in my ear. "…Prepare yourself, okay?"

"Wha…?" The pathetic noise just popped out of me. She was terrifying in both words and tone, and it sent something cold running up my back.

However Haruno took that, she smirked, then leaned even further in to murmur, "Well, if you have any problems, then tell Big Sis. I'll help you."

"Frankly, you're my biggest problem…" I took the opportunity to answer sarcastically, since she'd so graciously made the offer.

Haruno's face went blank for just an instant. Then her eyes went wide, only to narrow immediately like a beast with its prey before it. "You really are cute, Hikigaya… From now on, I'll dote on you just as much as I do Yukino-chan."

She was talking like she'd been holding back all this time. *You've got to be kidding—it gets worse...?*

But now that I thought of it, this was Haruno Yukinoshita. There was no way that would be enough to satisfy her. She would continue to test me in the future, too.

And then, as if to prove my point, Haruno chuckled seductively in my ear. It made me squirm—her bare skin brushed against me, her sweet breath tickled my earlobe, and a floral fragrance tickled my nose as a shiver ran down my spine. *Oh no, she really is scary...*

While I was trembling, Yukinoshita cut between us, smacked Haruno's hand away, and used her thumb to jab outside. "The building with the restaurant is that way."

"Oh my, I made her mad. See you," Haruno joked, then waved, and with Ms. Hiratsuka as her escort, she strolled off. Yukinoshita watched them go with a smile, then turned to her mother.

This face-off between mother and daughter was nothing like the one between sisters. The air froze around them. Mrs. Yukinoshita touched the fan in her hand to her jaw. "...Yukino, whenever you begin something new, there will always be resistance. No matter what sort of rationale you might come up with, it will never win over everyone. That's even more true for this event, which has no clear backing... After this is over, there will most certainly be complaints coming to the school, and to us."

"I'm sure," Yukinoshita replied.

"After having warned you once, I won't be on your side...no matter what sort of outlandish scheme you've decided to go with." And that icy gaze of hers turned on me. Maybe it was her way of implicitly referring to what had happened.

But Yukinoshita intervened; coming just a half step in front of me, she put on her own icy smile, resembling her mother. "That won't be an issue. The job of the person in charge is to take responsibility. We've always taken this into account."

"I see. Well then, let us see what you have to show us," Mrs. Yukinoshita threatened with an unyielding, amused smile.

This mix of aggression and almost playfulness made me think of wild animals raising their young. The mother's attacks were likely fiercest when it was time to make her children leave the nest.

I remembered what Haruno had once said—nothing makes someone grow like the presence of an enemy.

I'd only kind of sensed that before, but now, I could finally be certain of it.

To this mother and child, or to these sisters, opposition was communication, and hostility was education.

The heck, is this a family of rakshasas? So then is the whole clan a hassle to deal with? I have to avoid involvement with them as much as possible! I thought with a careful half step back.

I assumed Mrs. Yukinoshita sensed my fear, because she smiled brightly back at me. "We'll be causing trouble for you, Hikigaya, but we're counting on you." Her expression pinned me there.

I couldn't say *Uh, no way*, so the only answer I could give was a strained, vague, and cloudy smile. "Huh? Ah, well, yes. Since it's work…"

That response must have been enough to satisfy Mrs. Yukinoshita, as she smirked behind her fan and walked off. Even with her petite little kimono steps, I could tell she was in a fine mood.

Watching her go, Yukinoshita heaved a great sigh. "They finally left… Let's continue our meeting."

"There's more…?" I asked wearily.

She pressed her temple. "Yes. It's frustrating to admit, but they pointed out that I haven't been entirely thorough."

"Huh?" *When in the where who did what in the how?*

I wanted to ask all of the 5W1H, but before I could, Yukinoshita explained, "Alcohol was my blind spot. Though we're not providing it, it's not as if there won't be people bringing it in. When patrolling, pay attention to that. Just in case."

"More work… But, well, roger. What else?" I asked.

Yukinoshita put a hand to her chin. "Hmm…" She spent some time like that in thought, and then her gaze roamed around as if she might find the words on a wall somewhere, but eventually, she muttered, "This should be somewhat satisfactory for now…I think."

"Understood. Then let's get started."

"Yes." She confidently raised her head. We both exchanged short nods and, just about simultaneously, walked out toward the backstage.

And then the curtain rose on the final party.

× × ×

I didn't think I'd gotten a decent break since the joint prom had begun.

The amount of work I had to manage was massive, and the time passed in the blink of an eye.

Everything about the scene before me was brilliant, the sight of dresses of every color moving around like falling cherry blossoms swept away in the spring winds. Nothing could be more perfect for a parting occasion.

Club music was playing everywhere as familiar faces bustled around in the halls. Every single time I ran into someone I knew, they called me over to shower me with complaints, insults, and nastiness.

It was all because of the garbage title of "supervising floor manager." It sounded great, but it really meant you were the complaint box. And so I acted as a liaison for every section, dealing with every problem that cropped up.

I was racing my legs off yet again for some other minor problem when a call came from behind to bring me to a stop.

"Hikki."

There was only one person who would call me by that name. I spun around and saw her.

Yuigahama.

"Ohhh, hey. How's it going?"

"We're good. It feels like it's settled down a lot. But Iroha-chan's dead in the back room. What about you?"

"Busting my butt. It's bad. I'll go check on Isshiki later. Actually, there isn't enough catering. Do we have any snacks in the back?"

"There was some light stuff. Should we serve that?"

"Yeah, thanks. Right now, Zaimokuza and the guys are dashing out to buy more, but I'm at full power pretending we have more than we do until they come back," I said.

"Oh. Heh-heh," Yuigahama chuckled.

"Was that supposed to be funny?" I asked.

She tried to hide her smile for a moment. "Yeah… It's just that this sort of thing is so us." But her heartwarming smile refused to go away, and soon it took over her face again.

It tortured me in just the slightest part of my heart, but I combed back my hair and forced myself to grin back. "Sorry for roping you in to help in the end."

"Oh, no." She gave a little shake of her head to say it was nothing, then swept her gentle gaze around the area—at the guests dancing around in dresses and laughing boisterously, at Yukinoshita running around busily, at the heaps of bodies of the totally exhausted staff.

Yuigahama smiled. "Because I think this is what I wanted to see."

"…Oh." That was when I found myself honestly smiling.

She was right—I think this was a lot like what we'd always been seeing. We'd never managed a nice neat ending. We'd quarrel and make things worse. We'd struggle until we were up against the wall, and in the end, we'd let momentum take us into a last-minute patch job, desperately trying to make it all work.

Maybe that excitement was what had made those times so fun.

It was the same right now. I was so busy, I wanted to murder the culprit who'd come up with this crazy plan, and yet I somehow liked this lifestyle.

"…Hey," she whispered to me, so I took off the headphones still on my ears for the moment.

"Hmm?"

But then she ducked out, shaking her head. "It's nothing. Next time."

"O-okay…"

"Hey, don't forget about work! Hurry, hurry!" She rushed me along.

"O-okay…" And so I pattered off at a run again while I heard a tiny call of "Do your best" from behind me. I had to give it my all now.

After all, if someone tells me to work, I'll complain about it, and I won't really do what I should be doing properly—but I'll finish up about 60 percent, enough to excuse myself. That's my creed.

Most of my problems were far from resolution, but if it was just dissolution, then I would somehow make use of various bluffs, lies, and nonsense. That was how I both put out fires and put things off.

At some point soon, that would backfire on me. I would be forced to pay the full tab, up to and including my shirt, and all the responsibility would fall on me.

I probably wanted that, though.

I'd get all worn out, running around like a headless chicken, complaining about it but still doing it anyway. Just like now.

I want to use myself up and wallow in regrets until the bitter end. In my old age, I'd complain on my veranda to Komachi's grandchild, Grandkomachild, that my youth was full of mistakes and nothing good.

Going on and on and on with the tedious ramblings of an old man, I'd deal with all the work.

While I was busy with all that, the sun set on the horizon, and Tokyo Bay out the windows began to turn red. Some people headed out to the beach, while others relaxed in the lounge, and others chatted around the open-air fire. Everyone spent the time as they pleased, until eventually, they all gathered on the dance floor.

The time for dancing had begun.

The sound and the lighting were all even fancier than the earlier prom, and the excitement was a couple notches higher, too. It was actually really tough to do my work while avoiding the waves of people.

A standard number at dance parties was playing from the massive speakers. The spotlight jumped around, and the light of the disco ball rained down. The torrent of lights was kind of like a revolving lantern, and each switch of the music to a new track forced me to realize again that the end was drawing near.

I removed myself from the frenzied whirlpool to watch it from the outside.

When I leaned against the wall, a sigh of exhaustion and satisfaction spilled out of me.

Nothing about this was my thing—the popular EDM, dancing along with the rhythm, the strobe lights that hurt my eyes—but I didn't mind spending a little time in a dark corner in the sound.

But I was only able to zone out like that for a short time.

The headset summoned me, and giving me a neverending stream of instructions and a few insults, too. "Roger," was all I said; without the time to catch my breath, I rushed out once more.

× × ×

Although the joint prom had held major problems from its inception—plus there were minor incidents and accidents on the day of—nothing happened that could be called a fatal error. It was fair to say things came to a fairly smooth conclusion.

From what I could tell, people actually did enjoy themselves. The graduates from both schools as well as some other students, plus a very small number of staff mixed among them, sang, danced, and had a blast.

So once it was over, the place felt gloomy.

The party was finished; the guests had all left the venue. The only one left was me, the one in charge of the dance floor, the supervising floor manager.

I was solemnly picking up garbage and checking for lost items as I gazed out over the completely empty dance floor. It had only just been overflowing with spotlights, music, and loud voices, but now it was filled with only painfully deep silence.

As I was slowly making my way through every corner of the hall while looking around, I heard the sound of heels clicking on the linoleum.

I turned around, and there was Ms. Hiratsuka.

"You're still here?" I said.

"Yeah… Well, I forgot something," she said, her clicking steps approaching the center of the dance floor. Despite what she'd just said, there was no hesitation in her steps, like she knew where she was going.

But I'd just been scanning the hall myself for lost items. "I basically checked all around…" I turned my head back and forth, wondering if I'd overlooked something.

"This is the thing I forgot." Ms. Hiratsuka stopped right in front of me, holding her hand out.

But her palm was empty; she was just holding it out to me. Considering the way her palm was facing, it didn't look like she was looking for a handshake. I had no idea what she wanted, so I just said, "Uhhh…"

Then that hand stretched out a little further to me. "I completely forgot to dance with you."

Just like a prince, Ms. Hiratsuka reverently took my hand, then smiled very handsomely.

It was so sudden, I couldn't come up with a reply in actual words. "Huh?" I stared at her with my mouth hanging open.

Unsurprisingly, this must have made her feel a little shy, as her smile turned bashful. Despite how handsome she'd just looked, now she was like a young girl. The contrast was dizzying.

She tugged on my hand, compelling me to reply.

That snapped me out of my stupor, and I just said the first thing that came to mind. "…Ah, well, I've never done any real dancing before."

But Ms. Hiratsuka didn't care about that at all and just smiled. "Me neither."

And then with my hand still in hers, she swung her arm wide.

That was my only warning before Ms. Hiratsuka went straight into a willful, whimsical, and wild dance step.

There was no music and no hyperactive spotlight. There were no laser lights or smoke. There was just Ms. Hiratsuka's careless humming.

But the rhythm ticked out by her heels and her cheery song echoing through the hall felt like enough.

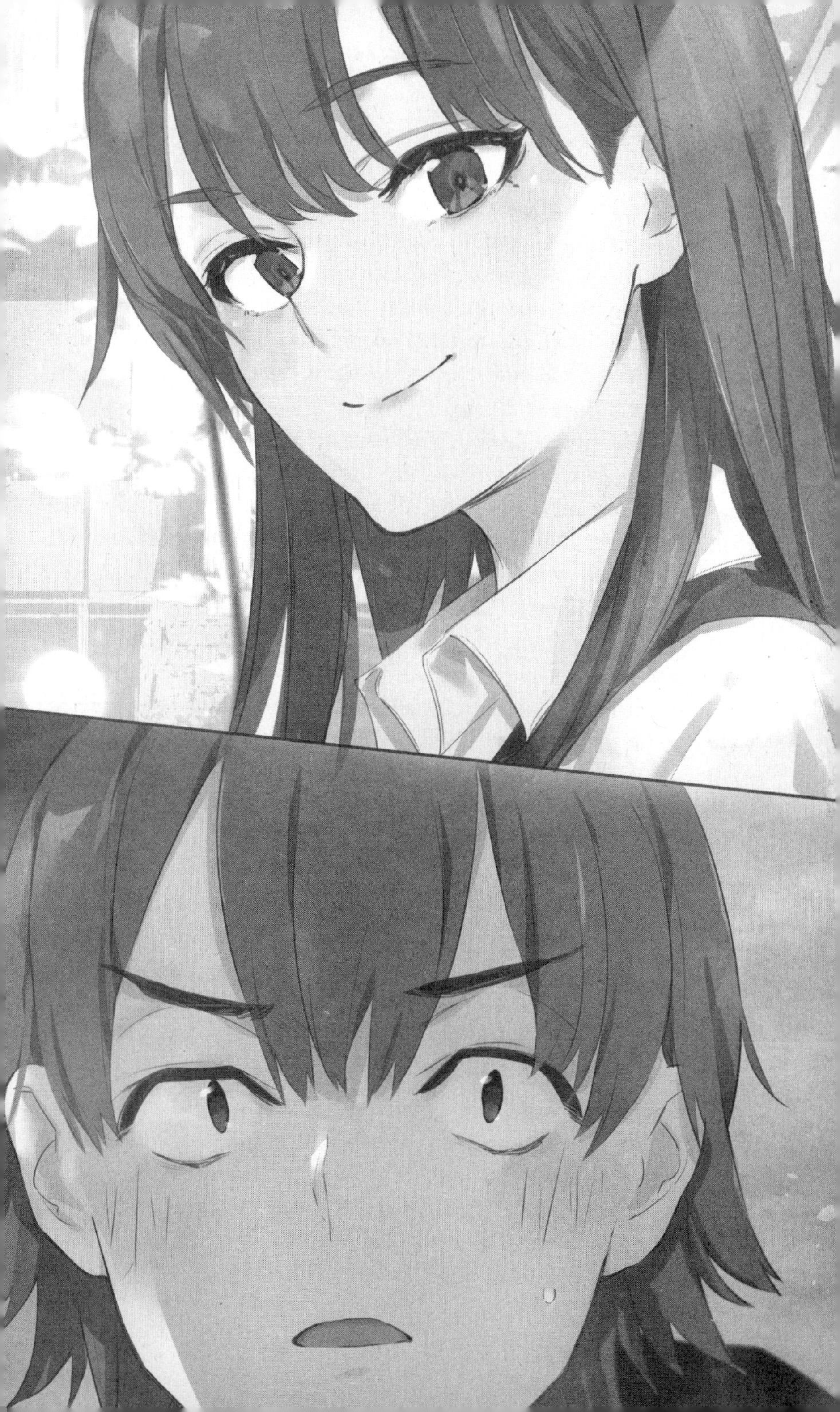

Neither of us knew how to dance anyway. So we'd toss in vaguely remembered bits of choreography and imitate steps we couldn't pull off; we jokingly posed with our suit jackets and whistled along.

It was ridiculous…and ridiculously fun.

When our bodies unexpectedly touched, Ms. Hiratsuka thrust me away, releasing my hand, and spun in a beautiful turn. It was too sudden, so I lost balance and tottered on my feet. Before I could fall, she grabbed my hand and pulled again, swinging me around.

Eventually, as we were singing out *laa-la-la* with glee—

—Ms. Hiratsuka's heel stepped hard on my foot.

"Ow…"

The jolt of pain knocked me off balance, and Ms. Hiratsuka and I went splat on the floor, one on top of the other. I hit my back, and Ms. Hiratsuka landed on top.

She was far lighter than I'd imagined, but her soft spots still felt weighty. A quiet "Ouch…" tickled my ear, and when she stirred, her long, smooth hair touched my neck and face. I couldn't breathe.

The teacher slowly raised herself up from where she'd been pressed right against me, then sat herself down on the ground, swept back her mussed hair with one hand, and grinned with the composure of an adult. "You got lucky there."

"…Your heel stomped on me, though?" I sat up from the floor as well, rubbing the throbbing top of my foot. *Seriously, please don't say stuff like that. Do you see how ridiculously insensitive this is? Do you understand how easy it is to hurt a pubescent boy? My foot and heart both hurt like hell from getting stepped on.* But there was no harm done on my end, so it was all good.

"Ahhh, I'm tired. That was fun." Ms. Hiratsuka folded her previously flung-out legs and leaned against my back.

She exhaled a deep breath, perhaps from all that wild dancing, and I could tell she was actually pretty exhausted. So I was forced to commit to being a backrest and listen to her voice from behind me.

"After all that, it was a good event in the end, wasn't it? Things did get really tense, though, and you worried me when you started lying...," she said, sounding displeased about that. She was probably referring to the earlier scene in the reception room. With Mrs. Yukinoshita, Haruno, and Yukinoshita present, I'd kept feigning ignorance about deciding to hold the joint prom. But, well, I wouldn't go so far as to say I'd lied. I'd just played dumb.

And now once again I shrugged and did the same. "I haven't really lied, though. Just pretended not to know some things."

"You're terrible," Ms. Hiratsuka said with a tired sigh, and then she leaned her head backward, clonking it against me like she was scolding me. It didn't hurt, but her swishing long hair tickled. That, along with the nice smell, made me squirm.

Then, she chuckled pleasantly. "...Well, maybe you can call that you spending your youth."

"Pardon?" That strange turn of phrase bothered me, and I craned my head around with a questioning look.

Ms. Hiratsuka glanced back at me over her shoulder, with a mischievous smile. "You haven't heard? Youth is lies; youth is evil..." She stuck up a finger and began to sonorously recite something.

I wasn't sure what she was getting at initially, but once I remembered where that was from, I did a double-take back at the teacher. "Whoa, now that I'm hearing it, that's super embarrassing... Agh, please don't remind me." My hands covered my face. There's nothing more embarrassing than being confronted with something you wrote a long time ago. It really does make you want to die.

My former teacher laughed for a while, but eventually, her smile settled. "How was this past year? Did something change?"

That reminded me of report I'd written back then. The binding of it had once been green and raw, but the sun had faded it over the years. It wasn't as striking as it once was, but you would still have no difficulty calling it green.

This past year had been so incredibly short and yet impossibly long. After some reflection, I answered. "...Nope."

That didn't satisfy Ms. Hiratsuka, and she clocked me with the back of her head again. "I shouldn't have asked like that… Did you find your something real?"

This time, I didn't need a long time to reply, because this was something she had taught me.

Thinking and struggling and suffering, floundering and worrying… My answer was clear. So I clunked her head back and chuckled out the side of my mouth. "I dunno. I think it's too complicated to find that easy."

"She'll get mad at you if she hears that. Or cry silently off somewhere out of earshot."

"Ugh… Don't say that; I don't want to imagine it… And, like, who do you mean? It's not like that, okay?"

"I see. Maybe it's not like that." Ms. Hiratsuka's shoulders shook in laughter, and she scooted over to sit at my side. "If you've been feeling sympathy, collusion, curiosity, pity, respect, jealousy, and more for one girl, then surely it's not enough to say you 'like' her." Leaning her chin on her hand, elbow on the knees of her folded legs, she counted down on her fingers as she listed out all those feelings, then gave me a hard look. "You can't separate or leave each other; you're drawn to one another, even if you're apart, even with the passage of time… Maybe you can call that something real."

"I'm not sure about that. And I'll admit it." I shrugged with a hint of irony in my voice.

I'm sure I'll never know whether we made the right choice or not. Even now I was still thinking, *What if I'm wrong about this?*

But even if someone did drop the singular correct answer in my lap, I doubt I would ever accept it. "I'll always doubt it. Most likely, neither of us can believe in it that easily."

"That's a long way from a right answer, but it's a one hundred percent score from me. You really aren't cute… That's exactly why you're my best student." Ms. Hiratsuka reached out and roughly ruffled my hair.

As my head was getting rolled in circles, there was a crackle of noise through the headphones on my ears. After a few seconds' pause came Yukinoshita's voice. *"Hikigaya, can you come to the wood terrace now?"*

I didn't reply immediately and instead turned to Ms. Hiratsuka. "Sorry, I still have work, so I've got to get going."

"I see. Then I'll be off, too." She hopped to her feet, then offered me a hand. She had to mean to pull me up.

I smiled at that and shook my head, then stood on my own.

Ms. Hiratsuka smiled like she was just a little lonely. She started to drop her hand, but before she could, I squeezed it.

And then I bowed.

"Thank you for everything."

Ms. Hiratsuka was struck silent, bewildered, and then when she realized it was a handshake, she chuckled. "Yeah, you really took on a lot of work." She smacked my hand, then released it. And then, as she leaned on one leg with her hand in her pocket, an austere, mature smile rose on her face. "…Good-bye."

"Good-bye, Ms. Hiratsuka." I twisted the corners of my mouth slightly as well in a very faint adult-like smile.

Ms. Hiratsuka nodded in satisfaction, then slowly started walking to the exit. She steadily continued, and once I had burned that image, growing distant, into my retinas, I spun away from her again.

Squeezing the headset mike, I said rapidly, "Sorry, I was busy. I'm on my way."

Then with hardly a pause, the response came: *"Please do."*

Rushing a bit, I headed for the opposite exit as Ms. Hiratsuka. I could hear the sound of heels clicking on the floor, and I heard when they halted.

"Hikigaya," came the call, and when I turned back, Ms. Hiratsuka was looking at me over her shoulder. She cupped both her hands around her mouth and yelled, "Normies can go die in a fire!"

"That's so old. It's a ten-year-old meme," I shot back.

But before I'd gone even a few steps more, I wound up turning around. Ms. Hiratsuka's coat was fluttering as she faced the other way.

With dignified steps and the bright sound of her clicking heels, her stride was crisp and sure.

There was no way she could have known I was watching, yet without a word, she raised a hand.

I bowed in return and then turned away as well.

And then I ran to the person waiting for me.

× × ×

Leaving the hall that had served as the dance floor, I headed for the wood terrace.

Darkness had already fully enveloped the outside world. The ocean view we'd taken pains to secure was now just some dots of light that seemed to be from boats on the distant horizon.

But in exchange for being unable to see across the ocean, if you traced the coastline over to the right, there was the Tokyo seaside area. If you looked to the left, it was the nightscape of the Keiyo industrial region. Being able to see both of them was rather beautiful, in its own way.

All right, so where is Yukinoshita...? I wondered, looking around. I found her by the fireplace lit in the center of the wood terrace, sorting documents. Even with a chilly breeze starting to blow, that one spot looked warm.

Inside the fireplace, a fire in an open tentlike enclosure burned softly. The wavering of the flame lit up Yukinoshita's narrow white face, giving her an even more fantastical aura than usual.

I was struck with the urge to keep watching her like this forever, but then the logs crackled and popped, and the sound made Yukinoshita's face jerk up. When she noticed my presence, a smile rose on her cheeks, faintly flushed. "Oh, Hikigaya. Thank you for today."

"Likewise. Sorry to keep you waiting," I replied, moving toward her.

But then she raised a hand. "Wait. First, look at the ground."

"Huh? The ground..." The only thing on the ground at my feet was a sand-covered mat. I couldn't see anything else remarkable… *Huh, what is this, a riddle?*

When I cocked my head quizzically, Yukinoshita sighed. After tapping the edge of her documents on the table to even the stack and then tucking them under an arm, she strode up to me.

She pressed down the back of her skirt to squat down and slide one finger over the floor, then showed that slender, graceful fingertip to me. "Look how sandy it is."

"Oh…" Why show me this…? All I thought was *Yeah, of course. So what? Is she playing the nagging in-law?*

Yukinoshita cleaned her finger off with a wet wipe, then touched her hand to her temple. "Didn't I tell you to make sure to change the mats when appropriate so that sand doesn't get into the hall?"

"Ahhh…" She had told me, yes. Of course, I'd been too busy, there hadn't been time for that. But I couldn't say that, so I just replied with a *whoops* kind of face.

Wait, was I called here just for a lecture?

The fantastical air had now dispersed like mist, replaced by cold, hard reality. Yukinoshita, who had even seemed ephemeral, now looked quite vigorous, and she was going beyond mommy energy into mommy-in-law energy. Setting her hands on her hips, she scolded me with complete calm. "Well then, before we leave for the night, make sure to clean up."

"Yes, ma'am…" I hung my head.

I was heading back into the building, wondering where the broom was, when Yukinoshita said, "Oh, also…"

I turned around, waiting for the rest of what was to come. Yukinoshita put a hand to her chin and continued further. "While you're at it, could I ask you to check the waiting room? I think you, me, and the boxes and such are all that's left, but just in case. I'll handle the payment for additional orders and return the keys."

"O-okay… Even more work now… Well, I guess not really. Off I go."

If I could complete those tasks, then I'd officially have finished the job, and we would be able to put the venue behind us. The joint prom had been so short yet felt so long. It had finally come to an end. The night air stroking my cheeks and the hazy, distant scenery came together to really tug at my heart.

But right as I was thinking that, Yukinoshita stroked her lips and said one more thing. "...Also, after we're done here, can we meet at the front entrance? It would help if you could keep an eye on the parking lot while you wait, just in case. If you see anyone still hanging around, please ask them to leave."

"...Okeydoke," I replied, but I was starting to get a bad feeling about this. This wasn't some miserable technique to continue increasing my workload as I listened, was it?

It filled me with trepidation. As I expected the jobs to pile on, Yukinoshita voiced a tiny *ah* as if she'd thought up something else. "Also..."

"There's more? Isn't that enough already? Isn't this fine?" I said, fed up.

In response, Yukinoshita meekly slid one step closer. "No, I have to say just one last thing." She turned away and quietly cleared her throat.

After all those eloquent demands, now she pressed her lips tight. I thought she might be about to smile, but she took a deep breath in and out, squeezing the stack of papers she was holding against her chest even tighter.

Her beautiful eyes slowly rose from her feet all the way up to my face, and then she said with whispered certainty:

"I love you, Hikigaya."

The surprise attack froze me in place, and she smiled bashfully. Hiding her pink cheeks with her stack of papers, she briefly glanced at my face, searching for a reaction, but then she inched away. The silence must have been unbearable.

And then, without waiting for me to say anything, she rushed off.

Come on, for real? She really is such a hassle.

I can't do anything if she says that and runs. What the hell? Doesn't that mean I'll have to say something again, some other time? That stuff is so damn hard, though. Seriously, what a hassle.

But I don't mind if it's a ridiculous hassle. That was ridiculously cute.

10 That's why **Hachiman Hikigaya** said...

The final spring of my time in high school had begun.

The cherry blossoms were not yet in full bloom, but the petals were still unfurling in a brilliant show below the window in my new classroom.

Whether the starting dash of spring was to be the stone world or an ordinary life, it was still a very important thing. In that sense, you could say I'd gotten off to the worst start.

To be concise: It was the worst class division.

I didn't care if there was nobody I knew or if I had no friends in the class. I was used to killing time and getting shoved in with the extras when we split up for groups on field trips.

The hardest thing is people you *kind of* know.

Of the many, many acquaintances I had, I'd pulled just about the worst personal result in the class division gacha: Hayato Hayama and Hina Ebina, totally bombing my pulls. Even Tobe would have been better...

Every time Hayama or Ebina ran into me, they'd make brief and inoffensive conversation with me for no particular reason. The two of them tended to gather attention, so it was low-key agonizing to be exposed to curious stares whenever they talked to me. And I was already bad at small talk. The stress of it was shaving years off my life. To make my time in the classroom as close to zero as possible, I raced out of the class at the after-school bell. As I hurried through the aerial hallway on the way to the special-use building, even the flowers in the beds of the courtyard below were telling me of the visiting springtime.

However, whether the seasons changed or my year changed, that did not erase the debts of the past. The tab racked up from the reckless joint prom was still on my account.

Yukinoshita and I were still spending time in the clubroom even though it should have already concluded its business.

Basically, we were dealing with leftover affairs from the event.

Thanks to Ms. Hiratsuka's help as a parting gift, plus with permission from the student council, we were provisionally allowed to use the room we'd originally used as the Service Club. The room was too big for just the two of us, but overflowing work filled the empty space.

Finishing up stacks of invoices for that aforementioned joint prom, pushing our way through a mountain of receipts, and being buried in a valley of reports, we dealt with it all one step at a time, with as much care as possible.

Normally, Yukinoshita would have instantly cleaned up such a trivial amount, but even she was distracted.

Maybe she wanted to linger on the memories even just a little longer, just like me.

"How about we take a short break?" she said.

"Sure."

When my hands stopped their task, she tapped at her shoulders, then started to quietly pour out vividly colored black tea into the cups that had been left there—my traditional one and her fancy Western teacup.

The mug had also been left there, untouched. No dust had built on it, and it had been washed clean, but there was no steam wafting from it.

"Here."

"Thanks." I accepted the cup and took a sip.

Yukinoshita took a drink as well, then sighed contentedly. "At this rate, it seems like we'll finish tomorrow."

"Yeah, probably."

"And then we have to deal with this." Yukinoshita swept a look over the personal belongings. There wasn't much, but the tea set items would be bulky.

"I'll help you carry it. I hardly have any stuff after all."

"Oh? Then perhaps I'll have you do it." She smiled, and then with hardly a pause, her smile never faltering, she followed with a statement I couldn't ignore. "While we're at it, why not come over to dinner tomorrow? My mother has invited you… She likes you quite a lot."

"…I can't refuse?"

"Do you think *I* can refuse?"

"…Oh, I've got stuff tomorrow," I said like, *I re…membered!* and Yukinoshita cocked her head quizzically.

"If you mean Komachi, she says she'll be at school late, choosing a club. And Totsuka has tennis school, and Zai…Zaitsu? He won't mind this time, will he?" Yukinoshita said all that like it was nothing, but her casual grasp on the schedules of people in my life was terrifying. She'd eliminated just about all the excuses I could think of.

I choked back half-baked reasons. Yukinoshita laid her elbows on the desk and peered at my face. "So then who's left? Hayama?"

"Nope, no way. Never. No way in hell." Why would I have to spend time with him? All else aside, I'd argue to hell and back against *that*.

Yukinoshita adopted a victorious smirk. "So then you have no plans? Great."

I could offer no further rebuttal.

I could manage a physical escape of those plans the next day, but there would be no point. A similar offer would simply be forced on me another day.

It wasn't like I couldn't give her something like *The possibility is not entirely unlikely that I am not fully unwilling to go have lunch or something with Yukino Yukinoshita as an individual. In fact I'd love it—let's go to*

Naritake? But dealing with Yukinoshita's family in particular meant this was a different story.

I had made it across the outer moat to the castle, but the inner moat was still hale and hearty.

What do I do...? With building panic, I looked for an escape. My eyes darted to the door.

And then someone knocked.

"Come in," I answered immediately, seeing this as my lucky out, and the door was flung open with a rattle.

"Hello! I came to join the club!" announced a girl in a brand-new uniform—my little sister, Komachi Hikigaya.

"Welcome, Komachi," said Yukinoshita. "That uniform really does suit you."

"Yukino! Thank you!" Komachi glomped her. Though it seemed to frazzle Yukinoshita, she remained at Komachi's mercy.

I had to find a good moment to stop my little sister. "Komachi," I said, "the club is gone now. We aren't recruiting members, and there's no club time."

"...That's right. We've just come up with some appropriate rationale to have working control over this room."

"Whoa, that's a way to put it. But no worries, because..." Komachi turned back to the entrance.

Isshiki was leaning against the door frame, panting hard. "How can you be so fast, Okome-chan...? I don't get it..."

"Uh, 'Okome-chan'...?" I said. "What's that supposed to be, a nickname? It's true that Komachi could be called the heart of the Japanese people at this point..." *In essence, following Little Sister of the World, my little sister also earned the title of Heart of the Japanese People, functionally achieving a double crown, hasn't she?*

So I was starting to think, but these two coming over here was posing a far more pressing question. As I was vaguely wondering if these two had ever even met before, Yukinoshita asked something similar. "Isshiki, too... Did you need something?" Still in Komachi's embrace, Yukinoshita suddenly seemed dubious.

Heaving a great *agh*, Isshiki rattled the door shut.

And then she came up to us and showed us a piece of paper.

Written on it was *Application for Creation of a Club*. The words *Service Club* jumped out at me. And furthermore, written in the *Club Captain* column was *Komachi Hikigaya*, with Yukinoshita's and my name listed below.

It seemed all the necessary items had been filled out, and it had been stamped with the permissions of the student council.

"And so from this day forward, this will be the location for Service Club activities," Isshiki said nonchalantly.

"Huh?" Yukinoshita and I were both confused.

Komachi grinned. "Now there's no problem! Let's get started!"

"This is nothing but problems…"

Is this not actual forgery of private documents? Is that not a crime? How are they innocent?

"Get started…? There's nothing for us to do, though…" Yukinoshita sounded utterly bewildered, and Komachi and Isshiki stared at each other.

Isshiki shrugged, blowing a sigh of exasperation. "It won't be long now."

"What are you talking about?" I blurted out, but neither Isshiki nor Komachi replied. They both snickered nastily.

You two are all friendly, huh…? A little sister and junior combined to make a formidable foe.

As a big brother and senior, I was delighted to see those two getting along. It did make me happy, but…unfortunately, those two were rather tricky people, so you couldn't let your guard down.

Komachi wasn't too bad, but she was a schemer, and Isshiki was cunning and scummy. Now the pair had gotten together to try to pull something… *This is bad; I have only bad feelings about this. What are these two after…?*

The answer to that question came suddenly, along with the weak knocking of a visitor.

"…Come in," Yukinoshita answered somewhat suspiciously.

We heard a squeaky "P-pardon me" from the other side of the door. She must have been nervous.

The door was pushed open just a crack, which she slid through. Apparently, she didn't want anyone seeing.

Her uniform was on the loose side and worn casually, and her hair was pinkish brown. When she entered the clubroom, her bun swayed along with her step.

"Y-yahallo…" Offering her usual greeting with an awkward, embarrassed smile, Yui Yuigahama raised her hand slightly.

When Yukinoshita saw her, she jumped out of her chair, ready to burst into tears. Before long, she let out a sob. "Yuigahama…you…came…"

"Eh-heh-heh… I'm here…" Yuigahama shyly brought one hand to her head to comb at her bun.

With her presence, the piece that had been missing in this room clicked into place. I was glad from the bottom of my heart.

I wondered what to say to her as I tossed back my tea.

As I did, I saw something dastardly—Komachi's *meh-heh* of a smirk and Isshiki's nasty little grin.

And then Yuigahama shot me a glance.

Putting the three together, I was unsettled indeed. No—more accurately, this was just ominous.

My gut feeling at times like these was generally trustworthy.

"Um…it's a request, or like a consultation, I guess?" Yuigahama began, and Yukinoshita nodded with a smile. Her eyes were full of life, promising to help her with anything.

Meanwhile, I was feeling quite viscerally that my eyes were starting to die, die, die.

Eventually, Yuigahama sucked in a little breath and put a hand to her chest. "The guy I like has someone who's kinda like a girlfriend, and she's my best friend……but I want to stay close with them forever. What should I do?"

She looked at me meaningfully, and I averted my eyes. They met with Yukinoshita's, and they were cold enough to make me shiver. Searching for a place to look, I focused on the cup in my hands.

But of course that place was no escape, and the tea in my cup just sloshed around.

"...Let's hear what you have to say." Yukinoshita smiled brightly, then pulled out the chair beside her. It was the chair that had always remained between mine and hers. "Please sit. Since it seems like it will take a long time."

"...Yeah, it might take a long time. I don't think it'll get done today, or tomorrow, or the day after... It'll keep going forever, eh-heh-heh." Yuigahama looked directly at Yukinoshita with a smile that hid nothing at all.

Yukinoshita was blank-faced for a moment but soon smiled. "Yes... I'm sure it will go on forever."

She filled that lonely mug with amber-colored tea.

Warm steam and the scent of black tea filled the room. The sun, which had begun to descend over the horizon, slanted in through the windows.

It created a peaceful spot, a sunny spring afternoon. The warmth made my spine turn cold and my face turn pale.

I see—so this is a green spring. A new season had once again come.

Ahhh, it's as I expected...

I have to say, this is just as I expected.

My youth romantic comedy is wrong, as I expected.

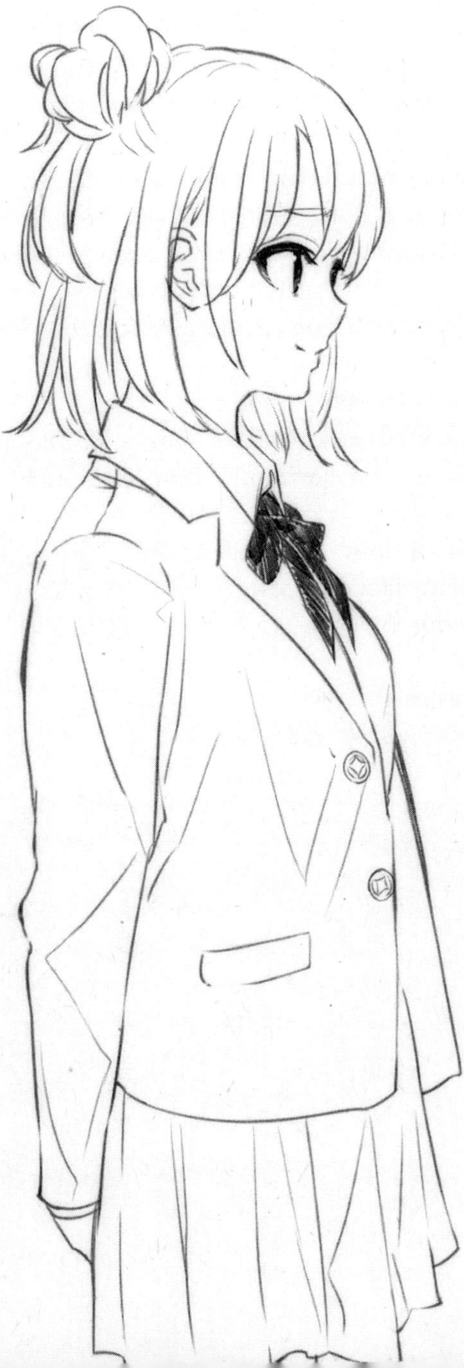

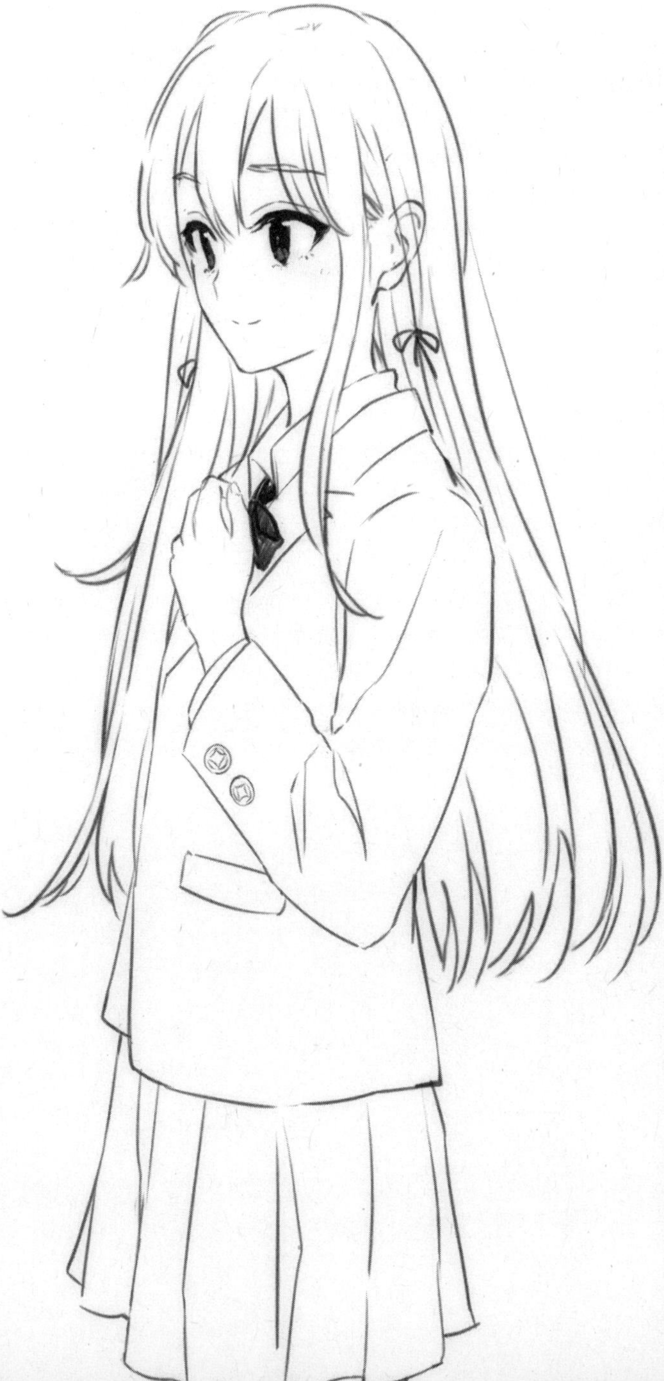

Afterword

Hello, this is Wataru Watari.

Since it's been a very long time since I've written an afterword, I'd completely forgotten what I usually wrote about here.

To go back and look at the older volumes to write this afterword, rereading what I wrote myself rather takes a lot of courage. Even glancing at the book makes me go "Aaagh!" before I slam it shut.

I'm sure some of you can cheerily reread your old work with the famous wild positivity of the party types, like *Wooow, I was soooo young back then!* ♪ *We had such fun times!* For you instinctively upbeat "Whoo!" people, your lucky item of the day is a Galfy sweater.

I could write something like that, but I'm starting to worry a bit about how many people would get the joke. Would *Shironeko-chan sandals* make more sense to readers?

To offer a very rough note for those who have no idea at all, to the Chibanese of our generation, the kind of person who would wear a Galfy sweater and Shironeko-chan sandals and hang out in front of the Don Quijote was always some kind of delinquent. Generally, their friends were rough-looking types. This is super-biased, though. Galfy is a very nice brand.

But you can go to Don Quijote even if you're not a delinquent, and little girls will wear Shironeko-chan sandals, so I don't think you can completely express something with one single term. However, everyone who wears Galfy sweaters is, without exception, a delinquent.

On the other hand, you have both delinquents who are antisocial and halfway into gangs and the mild former naughties who will go with their families on Saturdays to the Aeon food court, and both will still wear Galfy. It's a very difficult stereotype to reconcile.

This is what makes words so hard…

There are feelings that you can communicate simply and feelings that no words can truly convey. That's precisely why you use every method you can in an attempt to give those emotions form.

For example, isn't a novel the greatest example of that?

There are things that come across precisely because they are unspoken, and things that you can't get across even after talking to death.

I have no choice but to entrust just about all interpretation to the readers, but if things go well, even a little more of these feelings may get across—it's with the hope that I spend my days writing.

Perhaps he and she will continue to do so as well. And further, him and her. I believe they will keep finding words to connect their hearts, day after day.

And so, this has been Volumes 12 through 14 of *My Youth Romantic Comedy Is Wrong, As I Expected*.

I was supposed to have put an afterword in every book, but because those volumes wound up being in a three-part format, dividing what I'd call the final volume into beginning, middle, and end, putting an afterword in the middle seemed crass to me. It seemed best not to have them at all until the arc was finished, so I'll aggregate them all here.

Since this is the final volume, I did wonder if maybe I should write something covering the whole series, but then I might go on forever. Maybe some other time it would be nice if I could write whole book like *My Youth Romantic Comedy Is Wrong, As I Expected: The Afterword*. So while I extend my apologies for this being a bit short, I will offer my thanks and remarks.

Volume 1 was published in March 2011, and it's been about nine years since then.

Though I was able to have long holidays along the way, I've managed to arrive at the series conclusion for now. I believe I have packed everything I should and everything I wanted to communicate into this story.

This series, this book, this chapter, this paragraph, this sentence, this word.

I think I have been writing all this time in order to get these feelings across.

It was a long time ago that I was in my second year of high school, but now I finally feel like that year has come to an end. It has been the longest year of my life.

To those who spent their youths with Hachiman, to those who became adults one step ahead of him, and to those who are about to become high school second-years now:

I hope all of you were able to enjoy it. Thank you very much.

With this, *My Youth Romantic Comedy Is Wrong, As I Expected* is complete.

Or so I would like to say, but it will continue just a little longer.

So let's talk about that.

As for the future—first, I'm planning to release a short story collection. The date isn't scheduled yet, but I've been thinking, *It'd be nice if I could write a bunch of different things. I'd really like to work on those, yeah.* So I am currently in diligent preparation for that.

Next, a *My Youth Romantic Comedy* anthology book is going to be published! Oh, man… Authors I love so much are going to be contributing… I'm overjoyed… It's such an extravagant team of writers, I'm gonna pee myself. I also plan to write some. Oh dear, there are so many things to write.

Also, the third season of the TV anime is scheduled to begin airing on TBS and others in the spring of 2020. This one is also a really perfect, amazingly cool, and fun anime. Please look forward to it.

Also…

I do plan to think about the future once things have settled down again, but I think it would be nice if I could occasionally write some more about their world, just for a while, just for a little longer, as I watch over the growth of Hachiman and the others.

But still, the plan is that there are no plans. Nothing has been decided, but I'll be happy if I can offer you all some notice in the future.

Below, the acknowledgments.

Holy Ponkan☆. You truly have been holy. If anyone asks me, *Do you believe in God?* I think I'll answer, *Huh? We work together.* It's thanks to your godlike character designs that I was able to write this story. Thank you for the greatest illustrations in every book. Thank you for a job well done for close to nine years. I will continue to cause trouble for you, and I'm looking forward to working with you in the future as well.

To my editor, Hoshino. Oh, I'm totally fine for the last book, ga-ha-ha! So I said once. That time feels so nostalgic… Ten years ago, back when I'd only just debuted, I frankly didn't think we would know each other this long. I thought for sure Gagaga Bunko would be gone right away. I say this every time, but I'm deeply obliged for all the trouble I've caused you, as usual. Thank you very much. I'll be counting on you again text time! Ga-ha-ha!

To Director Oikawa and the rest of the anime staff, as well as all the people involved with the media franchise:

These novels had to be so hard to adapt into anime and manga, with a lot of monologues and my wordiness, so thank you dearly for always coming up with such wonderful results. It's thanks to all of you that the world of *My Youth Romantic Comedy* or *Oregairu* has expanded. As the anime is starting a third season, I am once again sincerely in your care.

And to all the readers who have stuck with this until the end:

It's been about nine years. When you actually put it into numbers, that's shockingly long. Truly, thank you very much for following along with this story all this time. When we meet at events like book signings, thank you very much for saying things like "I love this scene!" It encourages me a lot. And I was really glad to read your letters, where you told me your thoughts on the series as well as about your lives. I read back on them with care, and while I think each time that I would like to reply one day, I totally can't. I'm sorry. At the very least, it has lent me strength to bring you books. Even if I don't put it into words, or say it out loud, or write it down, it's because of all your support that this book exists. It's because you read it that this story continues. *Oregairu* is *orega-you*!

Truly, thank you very much. I hope you will continue to stick with me in the future.

Next time, let us meet in *My Youth Romantic Comedy Is Wrong, As I Expected. Stars!*

On a certain day in October, with a MAX Coffee in hand, while roaring like in *The Shawshank Redemption*,

Wataru Watari

Translation Notes

Prelude 1

P. 4 "The tune of 'Tooryanse' coming from the pedestrian walk signal" is referencing the name of an old folk song from the Edo period that's also used as a go sound for walk signals. It's an archaic way of saying, "Go across."

Chapter 1 ··· Nevertheless, **Hachiman Hikigaya**'s life goes on.

P. 10 "Look, I show her attitude because I'm shy! You can't have gratitude without attitude!" The original pun here is on *shy* (he uses the English word) and *shai* (gratitude).

P. 10 "My eyes flared wide for her, flashing like I was about to fire off a Starburst Stream—hm, maybe I wouldn't call that flared eyes. Sharp eyes. Sharp nail eyes." The original pun here is on *kiritto*, meaning crisp or sharp-looking, sounding like Kirito, the protagonist of *Sword Art Online*. Starburst Stream and Sharp Nail are both skills he uses.

P. 13 "Deadlines dooo exist!" This drawn-out *arimaaasu!* is from a quote from the researcher Haruko Obokata, "*STAP saibou wa arimaaasu!*" (STAP cells dooo exist!), made during a 2014 press conference.

354 Translation Notes

P. 18 "Concept Sketch of the Future II" is the name of a 2009 pop song by Dreams Come True, which describes going to school in the spring.

P. 19 *"Is this the secretive moonlight lighting up the night sky? He's too star twinkle..."* "Light up the night sky! With the secretive moonlight!" is Cure Selene's catchphrase in *Star ☆ Twinkle Pretty Cure*.

P. 22 *"Might, might, you might only hear all that might from* My Hero Academia *fans."* The original pun here is on *kamo*, which means "maybe." Hachiman says, "You might only hear that much *kamo kamo* in an ad for Kamogawa Sea World..."

Chapter 2 ⋯ Eventually, he'll **become used to this relationship**, too.

P. 37 "Bright was the noon sun shining its halcyon rays over my lunch break during my time for munching, in the same spot as always." This is based on poem 33 from the *Hyakunin Isshu*: "On a spring day when the light of the sun is shining so peacefully, why are the cherry blossoms falling so restlessly?" Being a tanka, the syllable pattern is 5-7-5-7-7.

P. 41 "Yuigahama pumped her fists in front of her chest like, *You can do it!*" *Ganbaru zoi*, with the cutesy meaningless sentence-ending *zoi*, is from the protagonist of the manga *New Game!*

P. 42 "Twincool! ☆" is the catchphrase of Hoshina Hikaru from *Star ☆ Twinkle Pretty Cure*.

P. 46 "Hatano adjusted his glasses from where they'd slid down and down to wind up like Kawabata from Chemistry." Chemistry is a pop duo, and Kawabata has been witnessed wearing his sunglasses hanging off his ears to sit under his chin.

P. 47 ***"Man, I wish I could shrink away...like a northern white-faced owl in front of its natural enemy..."*** This was originally a play on *katami ga semai*, which literally means "narrow shoulders" but idiomatically means "ashamed." The northern white-faced owl gets very narrow when threatened.

P. 47 ***"So then we ought to have some light provisions."*** The original misunderstanding here is on the term *hikarimono*, which literally means "shining things" but also refers to certain kinds of sushi—specifically fish that have bluish-white flesh that shines, such as *kohada* (gizzard shad), *saba* (mackerel), and *aji* (Japanese horse mackerel).

P. 51 ***"But what does that all meeeean?"*** This line from *Naruto* was originally just Naruto saying, "What do you mean?" but then it turned into a meme on Futaba Channel. There were a number of nonsensical memes only understood by insiders ("It's Izanami"; "It's become a sacrifice"), prompting people who weren't in on the joke to respond with this line, which then became a meme in its own right.

Chapter 3 ⋯ Surely, he will **remember that season** every time he smells that scent.

P. 60 ***"I don't think this is what they mean by 'getting down.'"*** The original joke here was "Did you eat Gekiochi-kun or something?" Gekiochi-kun can be translated as "Super-Scrub-Off Lad," and it's a brand of bathroom cleaner. The pun here is on the term *ochiru*, which means both to get off a stain or dirt and also when a mood becomes depressing.

P. 64 **"Game Market"** is a seasonal event for non-electronic games.

P. 66 **"He was putting up an absolutely garbage act. But this time, I'd be willing to give him an Oscar that's not from the trash bin."**

Originally, Hachiman says *boushibai*, which means "monotone acting," while *bou* also literally means "stick." Then he says, "Just this once, I want to praise him and say, *Nice Stick!*" Nice Stick is a brand of snack. It looks like a long piece of bread.

P. 67 **"I suppose this was the moment when you'd say the festivities were at their Hakonesia Peak."** The Japanese line here was "The festivities were Takanawa Prince Hotel," which is a fancy hotel in Tokyo. *Takanawa* sounds like *takenawa*, which means "the peak of festivities." Hakonesia Peak is a location in the Japanese role-playing game *Tales of Symphonia*.

P. 71 **"Everyone was swinging and bouncing the glow sticks that Hatano and Sagami must have supplied. They were whooping and yelling their names and doing fan chants and all kinds of stuff…"** Hachiman actually uses some very specific idol *otaku* lingo here: *call*, *mix*, and *ietora*. *Call* is a broad term for everything yelled in a show, as well as specifically referring to calling out the idol's name or "*Kawaii!*" *Mix* is primarily yelled at the beginning of a song, stuff like "Tiger!" or "Let's go!" *Ietora* is wordplay for the mix "Yeah, tiger!" which is yelled at the beginning of a song.

P. 71 **"…Tobe was swinging around a wet mini-towel."** This is a normal thing to do at concerts in Japan. Commonly during summer and outdoor events, mini-towels are sometimes merch that are part of the ticket price, and the crowd will swing them around.

P. 84 **"Well, there is the Peach Festival, so maybe that influences people's impressions."** The Peach Festival, otherwise known as the Doll Festival, is on March 3 and is a celebration for young girls. It got its name from the peach trees being in bloom during the season, not when the fruit is in season.

P. 84 **"This is where a certain manga scenario writer I know of would be saying, *But Japanese food manufacturers are at fault, too.*"**

Hachiman is referring to Tetsu Kariya, the writer of *Oishinbo*, who is famous for his anti-Japan sentiment and the line "Japanese are at fault, too."

P. 85 *The Great Star Palace Strawberry Festival* is the name of the *Aikatsu!* movie.

P. 86 **"Hey, you're not thinking you should have the Chibanese eat peanuts, are you?"** Hachiman is riffing off a quote from the comedy movie *Fly Me to the Saitama*, the original being "You should just have the people of Saitama eat some of the grass over there!"

P. 86 **"Hey, did you know? Peanuts aren't fruit or nuts or donuts. They're legumes."** "Hey, did you know?" is the catchphrase of Mameshiba, a character who rattles off fun facts. In the original, Hachiman says, "They're not fruit or *kinomi* [nuts] or Nana Kinomi." Nana Kinomi is a singer/actress.

P. 89 **"...*Are you sure that's enough armor?*"** is a quote from the initial trailer for the game *El Shaddai: Ascension of the Metatron*. The line became a bit of a meme in Japan.

P. 89 **"...seeing someone wearing a kitschy and cute (i.e. kitchen-cute) apron..."** The original pun here is on *kicchinto* (properly) and *kicchin* (kitchen).

P. 89 The **"careful home lifestyle"** (*teinei na kurashi*) was a trend around the late 2010s that focused on the concept on putting care and effort into daily tasks. It received a lot of criticism for just being a repackaged "cook and clean properly" message toward women who work out of the home.

P. 94 **"...The flavor balance had been mangled like the Treasure Island murder case..."** is a reference to a case from the mystery manga *The Kindaichi Case Files*.

P. 95 *"A man will not act unless you show and tell him…"* Hachiman is garbling a quote from Isoroku Yamamoto: "A person will not act unless you show them, tell them, have them do it, and then praise them."

P. 96 *"I forgot if it was called nappage or Banagher or what…"* Banagher Links is the protagonist of *Gundam Unicorn*. His name is pronounced similar to *nappage*, which is an apricot glazing technique for pastries.

P. 101 *"…which made me feel like I can do it! and ask for more."* Dekiraaa! (a slurred way to say, "I can do it!") is a quote from the protagonist of the 1980s cooking manga *Super Kuishinbo* in response to a cook saying he can't serve a better-quality steak for the same price.

P. 101 *"Stamina Yarou"* is a special dish served at the small chain restaurant Kitchen Otoko no Bangohan. It's a large serving of a whole bunch of different meats on rice. Needless to say, it's a lot of food to eat.

P. 101 *"I looove Stamina Yarou! ♡ I love it so much, I would even crush some magnifying glasses under my butt."* This is a reference to an ad campaign for Hazuki magnifying glasses, which always include the slogan "I looove Hazuki" and people sitting on the magnifying glasses without them getting broken.

Chapter 4 ··· And then **Yukino Yukinoshita** quietly waves.

P. 112 *"Whether they'd been bad kids…they were leaving in these chairs and desks."* This is another reference to the song "Giza Giza Heart no Komori-uta" (Lullaby for a Jagged Heart) by the 1980s boy band Checkers: *I was a bad kid when I was young / At 25, they called me a delinquent / I was sharp like a knife / and hurt everyone who touched me…my passionate feelings tied down / dreams carved into my desk / They call it a graduation ceremony / but what am I graduating from?*

P. 120 **Masayoshi Yamazaki** is a singer-songwriter, associated mostly with singing with soulful acoustic guitar.

P. 121 "**Unfortunately, we *otaku* have the power of the emo-emo fruit...**" This references the devil fruit from *One Piece*, which grant people special powers upon eating them. They're usually called things like *gomu-gomu* fruit or *mera-mera* fruit.

P. 126 The "**maiden circuit**" is what gives the marionettes lifelike personalities in *Saber Marionette J*.

P. 127 **Bushiroad** is a company that makes collectible card games like *Cardfight!! Vanguard* and *Weiss Schwarz*. In 2012, they acquired New Japan Pro-Wrestling, which seemed comically out of left field at the time.

P. 129 "**It's a habit of mine to live without being noticed**" is similar to a line from Killua in *Hunter X Hunter*: "It's a habit of mine to walk without making a sound."

P. 137 "**...the kind of danceable EDM that would make someone like Tobe say *This party's gettin' crazy!***" While this is a *Devil May Cry* meme, the original line here was *ponponpooon!* which is a sound effect that the *manzai* duo EXIT came up with to use as a greeting and whenever they're excited. EXIT are known as "neo-party-types" and this sort of "Let's get pumped" slang is part of their schtick.

P. 142 "**Isshiki grinned and also made a big O with her arms like Hakutsuru Maru...**" Hakutsuru Maru is a brand of sake with a logo of a circle (*maru*). The ads often feature people making big circles with their arms.

Chapter 5 ··· Gallantly, **Shizuka Hiratsuka** walks ahead.

P. 189 "**What the heck was this woman, the *oitekebori youkai*?**" *Oitekebori*, meaning "drop it and get out of here," is from an old story about a mysterious apparition over a bridge that haunted fishermen, telling them to drop their fish and leave.

P. 195 "...**this time it rang out with a pleasant sound:** ***swoo-woosh-CRACK!***" The unique SFX here, *guwara gowara gakiiin*, is from the 1970s baseball manga *Dokaben*.

Chapter 6 ⋯ Just like that time before, **Yui Yuigahama** implores.

P. 206 "*I wanna do that, I wanna do this, I wanna do more and more*" is from the 1993 song "Dream" by the rock band Blue Hearts.

P. 211 "**...Is this the Freedom with the METEOR Unit or what? You never know when they're gonna fall over and go into Full Burst Mode.**" Hachiman is referring to the Freedom Gundam from *Gundam SEED*, which has a lot of details on it.

P. 214 "**...'Yuuyake Koyake' played from the park speakers.**" "Yuuyake Koyake" is a children's song from the 1920s—*yuuyake* means "sunset," while *koyake* is just there for the way it sounds, but its Chinese characters mean "a small glow." The tune is played in a lot of cities in Japan in the evening as a notification that the day is over.

P. 232 "*Yeek? That's like a 'Yeek, she's so cute,' right?*" Originally, she says "Scary...," and Iroha thinks, *Huh? Scary? Don't you mean cute?* "Scary" (*kowai*) sounds like "cute" (*kawaii*).

Chapter 7 ⋯ The **heat touching him** is the only feeling that does clearly get across.

P. 247 "**...you'd think it was a whole crowd of angels on the level of Professor Zaizen doing his rounds.**" Professor Zaizen is a character (a professor at a university hospital) from the popular 1965 novel *The White Tower* by Toyoko Yamasaki, which has been adapted multiple times into television series. There are many scenes of the doctor walking through the halls surrounded by a crowd of students.

Chapter 8 ··· **That door** is opened once more.

P. 265 "**What is not to be must not be**" is the final line of the code of Juu, which was an organization that educated the sons of feudal retainers in Aizu Domain in ancient Japan. The line has appeared in some historical dramas.

P. 275 "**It'd be nice if we had an absolutely 100 percent sunshine girl, but you don't find such children of the weather so easily.**" This is a reference to the Makoto Shinkai movie *Weathering With You* (the Japanese title is *Child of the Weather*). It features an orphan girl who can control the weather.

P. 276 "**…nothing but credits from Mah-jongg University or Pork University…**" Mah-jongg University is a mah-jongg blog, and Pork University is a restaurant.

P. 283 "**We were just about ready to toast each other. *To our friendship, wishing you happiness.***" This is from the lyrics to the 1988 single "Kanpai" (Cheers) by Tsuyoshi Nagabuchi.

P. 284 "**It was like she could see them but also couldn't, which was even meaner than ignoring them from the start. It was like something out of Natsuhiko Kyogoku's mystery *The Summer of the Ubume*.**" An *ubume* is generally the spirit of a woman who has died in childbirth, and the novel Hachiman refers to has some supernatural elements.

P. 289 "'**No, it's a different sense,' I said. 'Uh-huh…sense…and dollars?'**" In Japanese, Hachiman says *kibun ga kawaru* (it changes how it feels) and Iroha replies, "*Haa…kibun…hanpen?*" Kibun is a foodstuffs manufacturer, and they're known for making *hanpen*, which is a kind of plain-tasting fish paste. Iroha is making fun of him by deliberately misinterpreting his words.

P. 294 **"As I was indulging in some optimistic fantasies…"** The original Japanese here was *toratanu*, which can be short for an idiom meaning "counting your chickens before they're hatched" but is also probably a low-key reference to a small crowdfunded card game called *ToraTanu*.

P. 297 **"Wait, so are you a Newtype?"** Newtypes are the natural evolution of humanity in the Gundam franchise.

P. 299 **"What is that, a wink? Maybe she's a lonely tropical fish."** "Lonely Tropical Fish" is the name of a song by the 1980s pop duo Wink.

P. 299 **A super *sento*** is a public bath facility with added features, such as having a variety of different bath types with different themes, or things like massage chairs and general relaxation facilities. It's not the same thing as an *onsen* (a hot spring), since the water is artificially heated.

P. 300 **"…making hand gestures like a master heat waver mixing up the air."** *Seppashi* are sauna staff who add water to make steam in a sauna and fan it around the sauna, but it's become a fad recently with competitions to see who can knock down the most empty bottles with the flap of a towel.

P. 305 **"Excuses like that won't work in the face of my power of Taboo."** This is a reference to the character Yu Kaito in *Yu Yu Hakusho*. His power is to make rules within his own Territory to enforce various physical restrictions, and his preference is for making his rules language-based.

P. 313 **"Okome-chan? Rice girl?!"** Akita Komachi (Akita beauty) is a brand of rice, but Iroha might also just be going off how *kome* (rice) sounds a bit like *Komachi*. The *O* at the beginning is for politeness.

P. 314 **"...brag about...how they're popular in Ni-chome."** Ni-chome is a neighborhood in Tokyo with lots of gay bars and clubs.

Chapter 10 ⋯ That's why **Hachiman Hikigaya** said⋯

P. 337 **"Whether the starting dash of spring was to be the stone world or an ordinary life..."** Hachiman is referring to the beginning of the manga *Dr. Stone*, in which all the people of the world turn to stone at the start of a new school term.

P. 339 *"I re...membered!"* is a quote from the protagonist of the light novel series *Seiken Tsukai no World Break* when he remembers his past life.

HAVE YOU BEEN TURNED ON TO LIGHT NOVELS YET?

IN STORES NOW!

SWORD ART ONLINE, VOL. 1-24
SWORD ART ONLINE PROGRESSIVE 1-8

The chart-topping light novel series that spawned the explosively popular anime and manga adaptations!

MANGA ADAPTATION AVAILABLE NOW!

SWORD ART ONLINE © Reki Kawahara ILLUSTRATION: abec
KADOKAWA CORPORATION ASCII MEDIA WORKS

ACCEL WORLD, VOL. 1-25

Prepare to accelerate with an action-packed cyber-thriller from the bestselling author of *Sword Art Online*.

MANGA ADAPTATION AVAILABLE NOW!

ACCEL WORLD © Reki Kawahara ILLUSTRATION: HIMA
KADOKAWA CORPORATION ASCII MEDIA WORKS

SPICE AND WOLF, VOL. 1-22

A disgruntled goddess joins a traveling merchant in this light novel series that inspired the *New York Times* bestselling manga.

MANGA ADAPTATION AVAILABLE NOW!

SPICE AND WOLF © Isuna Hasekura ILLUSTRATION: Jyuu Ayakura
KADOKAWA CORPORATION ASCII MEDIA WORKS

IS IT WRONG TO TRY TO PICK UP GIRLS IN A DUNGEON?, VOL. 1-16

A would-be hero turns damsel in distress in this hilarious send-up of sword-and-sorcery tropes.

MANGA ADAPTATION AVAILABLE NOW!

Is It Wrong to Try to Pick Up Girls in a Dungeon? © Fujino Omori / SB Creative Corp.

ANOTHER

The spine-chilling horror novel that took Japan by storm is now available in print for the first time in English—in a gorgeous hardcover edition.

MANGA ADAPTATION AVAILABLE NOW!

Another © Yukito Ayatsuji 2009/ KADOKAWA CORPORATION, Tokyo

A CERTAIN MAGICAL INDEX, VOL. 1-22

Science and magic collide as Japan's most popular light novel franchise makes its English-language debut.

MANGA ADAPTATION AVAILABLE NOW!

A CERTAIN MAGICAL INDEX © Kazuma Kamachi
ILLUSTRATION: Kiyotaka Haimura
KADOKAWA CORPORATION ASCII MEDIA WORKS

VISIT YENPRESS.COM TO CHECK OUT ALL THE TITLES IN OUR NEW LIGHT NOVEL INITIATIVE AND...

GET YOUR YEN ON!

www.YenPress.com